"The novel bubbles with life and the enjoyment of it. . . . I recommend it as superlative entertainment."—*Chicago Tribune*

Davey Burnie is a fourteen-year-old whom nobody could call an angel, and some might call an imp of Satan. He and his uncle Jim, a full-grown devil of a fellow, are in flight for their lives from the Ku Kluxers they have offended.

Their hilarious and hair-raising odyssey takes them across a post-Civil War Southland filled with carpetbaggers, fast-talking medicine men and cold-hearted belles. They meet reformed pirates and Indians, both friendly and treacherous. And after near disaster and miraculous escape, they at last find a treasure in silver!

"Those who read the author's prize-winning *The Travels of Jaimie McPheeters* . . . will anticipate with pleasure the fast-paced action, the wild escapades, the frontier horrors and humor, and the stock characters who, strangely enough, come to life through the vivid descriptions crammed with details of regional history and folklore."—*Library Journal*

TREASURE OF MATECUMBE
was originally published by McGraw-Hill Book Company.

Treasure of Matecumbe

(Original title: *A Journey to Matecumbe*)

BY
ROBERT LEWIS TAYLOR

PUBLISHED BY POCKET BOOKS NEW YORK

TREASURE OF MATECUMBE

McGraw-Hill edition published 1961

POCKET BOOK edition published July, 1976

This POCKET BOOK edition includes every word contained in
the original, higher-priced edition. It is printed from brand-
new plates made from completely reset, clear, easy-to-read type.
POCKET BOOK editions are published by
POCKET BOOKS,
a division of Simon & Schuster, Inc.,
A GULF+WESTERN COMPANY
630 Fifth Avenue,
New York, N.Y. 10020.
Trademarks registered in the United States
and other countries.

ISBN: 0-671-80609-2.
Library of Congress Catalog Card Number: 61-9774.
This POCKET BOOK edition is published by arrangement with
McGraw-Hill Book Company. Copyright, ©, 1961, by Robert Lewis
Taylor. *Treasure of Matecumbe* was originally published under the
title *A Journey to Matecumbe*. All rights reserved. This book, or
portions thereof, may not be reproduced by any means without
permission of the original publisher: McGraw-Hill Book Company,
1221 Avenue of the Americas, New York, New York 10020.
Cover illustrations © Walt Disney Productions.
Worldwide rights reserved.

Printed in the U.S.A.

MATECUMBE *is the only place name in south Florida which dates from the sixteenth century and is still used to designate the same approximate location.*

1

I WENT OUT in the woods to a fallen-down sycamore I knew and reached in a hollow place and pulled out Uncle Jim's costume for the Ku Klux Klan. It didn't amount to much for such a secret and desperate society; even a boy could see that.

Last time they'd been on a raid—only they called it "riding out"—it didn't have a thing on earth to do with uppity darkies, or the Loyal League, but was aimed at a farmer named Burr who they said his wife complained he wasn't sleeping with her regular and who birched her when she got sassy, and occasionally when she didn't, to keep himself limbered up for emergencies. As far as I could see, it was his own business when he slept, and where. Anyway, some people don't need much sleep, as most fools know, and besides they mightn't have had a bed big enough for two, or maybe a few slats were out—some of those farmers get pretty shiftless.

The only reason I bring it up is, my Uncle Jim came home disgusted. I woke up when he tiptoed in, carrying his shoes, long after midnight, and when he saw I was awake, he sat down and got it off his chest. To tell you the truth, he knew perfectly well that Commercial Appeal and I spied on a meeting once, because he caught me creeping in later than him, with one of those sewed-on "K's" that they wore along the horses' skirts. It had dropped off during some of the silly shenanigans they pulled. I thought he might be sore—he was mighty easy-going, my Uncle Jim, but when he *did* flash out, he had a temper like a cottonmouth—instead he only grinned and said, "Thinking of joining up, son?"

But the time he came in after raiding the farmer, Burr,

that had the irregular sleeping habits, he threw a shoe clear across the room against the wall, where it knocked down a picture of General Jackson daring the British to come on at Barataria, and said, "This just about tears it, as far as I'm concerned. Enough's enough, and snaking a man because he married a female shrew's somewhat *more* than enough. If I had the choice of bedding down with that woman and a vixen fox, I wouldn't hang up—I'd dive in bed with the fox, and not hesitate about it, either. Why—"

"Excuse the interruption," I said meekly, hoping to get him soothered down a little, "but I don't think those Burrs own a bed big enough for both a person *and* a fox —" but he shut me up sharp.

"Never mind what you *think*. You listen, and you'll be more apt to get an education—God knows you haven't grabbed as much as a toe-hold on one yet, with the possible exception of how to catch channel cat and torment your aunts.

"They hauled that poor fellow out at two in the morning and stripped him down and tied him to a tree and welted his back so he'll wear those scars to his grave. AND—" my Uncle Jim was stamping around in his sock feet now, and he kind of stumbled over a chamber-pot, which he called several names of a nature that would have been foreign to me if I'd waited to learn them in school, and then he scooped it up and heaved it through our second story window; then he resumed: "AND, I ask you, what do you suppose that female shrew was doing in the meantime? She was standing there jouncing up and down in the moonlight, clad in her shift, no wrap, no slippers, the moonlight shining right between her, and *laughing!* Why, yes, she enjoyed it, you see. This was a spite job, pure and simple, and moreover, on top of it, I happen to know that one of *us*, one of the *new* bunch, that is, has been meeting this slut in the woods. They cooked this up together. Now *that's* what the noble Invisible Empire has come to—"

Suddenly he stopped and said to me, not ugly or threatening, only looking at me in that level cold blue-eyed way he had that made you want to find a hole somewheres, "You're not to repeat any of this, do you understand?"

Sitting there on the edge of the bed, I looked back at him just as steady and said, "I wasn't going to anyhow."

He rumpled my hair up and sat down beside me.

"I'll ask your pardon for that. I know you weren't. You aren't a bad boy, only a little balky. To be candid, you remind me of myself at your age. Except I was prettier."

My Uncle Jim was thirty-six. He'd run off to the Mexican War at sixteen, and in the War of Succession he'd been decorated for bravery on the field eleven times, which they said was some kind of record. He had several rows of medals pinned to a purple cloth with a gold fringe, but he made fun of them, and in an interview with the newspaper one time on the Fourth of July (which was a Southern holiday they celebrated, with fireworks, a picnic, speeches on the Courthouse steps that told how the South won the war, and topped off, generally, by burning up somebody's barn with a paper balloon assumption) he said he'd got them for stealing equipment from his superior officers. He said he got one for pulling a general out of a latrine ditch after it got hit by a bomb. He rambled on like that to the reporter, who was a bonehead, new on the job, and built up a story so outrageous it made a lot of people mad. They said it was demeaning to the glorious Confederate Army.

My Uncle Jim had been a captain during the war, and in between years he'd gone to Center College, in Danville. My aunts said he had a very good classical education and could quote from a number of deceased nuisances like Horace and Socrates and Pluto.

"There's trouble coming, boy," he said, pulling his shirt over his head. "Tomorrow night—tonight, you might say—that greedy toad, Givens, wants a darky squelched, to get his land. He's got a claim about as valid as a cure for old age. I stood against it, and when we ride out I'm apt to lay my ears back if matters get out of hand.

"Now listen to this—I want you to remember it, because I don't know what's going to happen tonight, and in the years to come, I doubt if anybody'll mention the Loyal League or the Freedmen's Bureau. Not if the Northern scribblers can help it, they won't."

Then he talked on about the Ku Klux Klan, till dawn nearly, and said I must write about it someday, to put things straight if he wasn't "in a position to." Well, I didn't mind that; I knew I could write a book easy enough—anybody could—but I was scared. This was the most awful trouble I could remember, but as it turned out, what I'm doing is writing our entire adventures, from that time when we escaped down the river and into the Florida swamps, and about all the things we've done since, and it's developed into more of a back-breaker than I anticipated. If you really want to know, I wouldn't tackle it again for a clear title to Kentucky.

2

I SEE WHERE I've straggled away from when I went out in the woods and hooked Uncle Jim's costume. But I'm coming back to that. One of the bad parts about writing a book is the pesky order of the thing. Just when you think you've got it nailed down, it wiggles out from under. According to Uncle Jim, the Klan, or Invisible Empire as they began to call it, was started as a lark by some young captains he knew, right after the war, in Pulaski, Tennessee, which wasn't so very far from us. We lived on what was known as the "Madrid Bend" of the Mississippi, in the town of Hanksville, Kentucky. It was a perfectly decent, sensible town, county seat, too, except they had a law where you had to go to school till you were fifteen. I heard a man loafing in front of Clark's Dry Goods Store come out flat-footed and say it was against the Constitution, but my Uncle Jim said this fellow was an ignoramus who was only interested in keeping his boys aged six and eight weeding tobacco. For my part, I thought he had a wonderful point and made a note to discuss it with Mr. Claypool, a very good lawyer there, when he was sober, if I ever got hold of fifty cents, which is what somebody said he charged for such cases (where it might have to go to the Supreme Court, you know).

Uncle Jim stated that the Klan first got off as a kind of social club, organized in a judge's office named Jones. The war was over, and these captains were bored. They were all of them educated, so they hauled out a lot of biggity foreign names and words to dress up the rules and regulations with, the way I've noticed people do in books when they haven't got much to say on their own. The head man was to be the Grand Cyclops, and they

11

had several Grand Magi, that lounged around to give it tone, and a Grand Turk, whatever that was, and a Grand Scribe, who acted as secretary, but he wasn't by any means crushed down with work, because everything was secret, you see, and he didn't have any records to keep. It was ridiculous. The messengers were "Night Hawks," and they had some guards called "Lictors," which Uncle Jim said was Latin, a language that nobody used any more except as a punishment. The ordinary members were supposed to be known as "Ghouls," but they had a quarrelsome time pinning anybody down that low, because everybody naturally wanted a title.

The name of the society itself was borrowed from some Greeks that formerly were civilized but weren't any longer, Uncle Jim said. At first it was only one word, "Kuklos," which meant circle, and then later it was broken in two to be Ku Klux. There was a Greek gentleman, very hairy and pock-marked about the face, that ran a restaurant in Hanksville, a Mr. Populous, or sounds to that effect, and I hung around there for a long time hoping to hear him use some of the Klan words, but he never did, and frankly, Uncle Jim may have been joking. You never could tell. He did say, and I believe him, that most people finally concluded that the name Ku Klux Klan came from the clicks of a rifle cocking. Anyhow, these captains were all Scotch by descent, and that's why they tacked on the "Klan."

But my Uncle Jim said there was another notion about the name, rising out of the Mexican War. He wrote it down for me. Down there they've got what they call a God of Light, along with several more working in other lines, and this chap was known to the Mexicans as "Cukulcan." The reason some folks later believed the idea is that many members referred to themselves as "Sons of Light."

You can take your choice. Uncle Jim held to the Greek words, because he was friends of the Pulaski captains. As for me, I'm not sure the rifle cocking story wasn't the best after all; it's more romantical.

Well, when they got going (and I'll tell you why in a minute), they organized all the southern states and even southern Illinois, which was more south than north, with parts of Missouri and Kentucky sticking way up above it, and had what they called Provinces, but a local or town bunch was known as a Den. After this, *didn't* they think up some titles! Geniis, and Hydras of the Realm, Grand Titans, Wizards, Furies, Grand Dragons, Grand Monks, Ensigns, and others just as gaudy. And, yes sir, they made it official: "the body politic to be known as Ghouls."

There was considerable grumbling. It rasped on a man of this status to know that his next-door neighbor might be a Grand Mogul, or a Lord High Sepulchre, with not an ounce more ability than what he had, or even a better costume. My Uncle Jim said he knew personally of a fellow that got sore and quit. He was one of the few; it wasn't safe. He told the Den, at a meeting on Dr. Carter's hill, that in two years he hadn't risen up any higher than Ghoul, and he didn't care to be affiliated with an organization where there was so little room for advancement. They offered to give him a special title of Grand Ghoul, but he went ahead and turned in his sheet. It doesn't sound likely, somehow; and there again, it might have been one of Uncle Jim's lies.

Those captains, in the beginning, only skylarked around and had fun, entertaining people with outlandish dress and idiotic notices sent to the newspapers, generally by means of a brickbat through the handiest window at night. It seems odd now, when you consider what the Klan came to, but the main requirements for membership were for a man to have "good character and not be addicted to intoxicants." But before it was over, they wrote in a rule that "there shall be no cursing during the administration of beatings." This was the one that appeared to give Uncle Jim the itch worse than anything. "By Godfrey, can you *imagine* it?" he cried, stomping around that night. "Truss a man up like a pig, remove his hide with a whip, and be careful—oh, yes, mighty genteel and upright and polite—not to offend his ears with profanity."

Uncle Jim went to the big Klanvocation in Missouri, and also to the chief one in Nashville, Room 10 of the Maxwell House, where they adopted a "Prescript." He wrote me out a copy: "This is an institution of chivalry, humanity, mercy and patriotism, embodying in its genius and its principles all that is chivalrous in conduct, noble in sentiment, generous in manhood and patriotic in purpose."

Well, it sounded good. But here's how things went wrong. There rose up after the war an organization of bad darkies run by worse whites—carpetbags, poor white trash, roughs, criminals, even—called the Loyal League, called by some the Union League. In reverse, it was exactly what the Klan turned into: that is, it was meant to badger and pester and override and threaten and abuse all the white people that had amounted to a hill of beans before the war. These League bands rode through the streets—drunk mostly—yelling and flashing knives and guns, knocking people out of the way, and driving them into the doorways of stores. But if anybody cared to raise a grievance, he could take it to the Freedmen's Bureaus, that were set up by the Occupation, and how would he fare? Why, the Freedmen's Bureaus were run by the very worst kind of Yankee riffraff and preached one gospel, as Uncle Jim said, and one only: that the darkies owned all of their former masters' property. So there you were.

Right off, when things got bad, the Klan members saw that their superstitiousness and humbug worked like a physic on the darkies, and on the white trash that pushed them. So after that the Invisible Empire got going with a whoop. But for a long time—several years—scaring and threatening were the worst they ever did. Nobody got hurt. "We leaned over backwards to be decorous," Uncle Jim said. "It was nothing but mumbo-jumbo to try and protect the people who after all built this area by hard work and superior mental equipment."

To give you an example, the Klan once rode up to some troublemakers gathered on a shanty porch, and a man got down off his horse. They were all costumed up with stars and crescents and K's, of course, and a high headdress, with masks. Well, he stepped to the well there in the littered-over yard and drew a bucket of water. Then, right in front of the darkies, he *drank it all down,* every drop. He had a tube and a funnel fixed up, you see.

"There," he said, when he finished, "that's the first drink I've had since I was killed at Shiloh, and you get mighty thirsty down in Hell."

Another time, a Klansman with a gourd placed on like a head—a very good likeness in the dark, they said—rode up to Willie Ringer, who'd never been anything but ornery in his whole life, dismounted, took off the gourd, handed it over to Willie, then said, "Here, hold my head a minute, will you? I'm tired." Uncle Jim said that Willie, on foot, passed the Orleans boat ploughing downstream on his way out of town; both the captain and the first mate saw him; Uncle Jim said he pulled the smoke forward instead of backward as he passed. Well, *I* didn't see it, and doubt it.

But to wind this part up, because descripty passages *can* get tedious, a whole new element began to filter into the Klan—outsiders, newcomers, and low-grade people that nobody would have associated with before. Later on, many of them split off and even had Dens of their own. They were called "Shams," and in the end, that's what gave the Klan its bad name. Right now we had a lot of them around Hanksville, Uncle Jim told me, and on all sides near us—across the river in Missouri, down in Tennessee just below; all around.

"They're planning to squelch Ben Woods," he said before he went to sleep. "It's on the cards for tonight, and do you know something, boy? That's one good nigger." I'd never heard him use the word before. Nobody said nigger in our house; a person could get licked for it. But Uncle Jim had been away a lot, and I guess it slipped. "I'll be on hand, and they may just hear from me—you never can tell." I pulled the covers up high over my chin. As I said before, I was scared. They didn't give Uncle Jim all those medals for nothing, and once he'd made his mind up, you could change it as quick as you could persuade a mule to be baptised.

3

I WENT TO sleep again, but I was up early, before eight, and sneaked out, so as not to wake anybody. It was one of those clear summer mornings—still, cool, kind of hushed, the trees all greeneried around, the birds going it, the grass a little wet yet, a very pleasant smell of dead fish and mud blowing up from the river, and that nice feeling of a hot summer day coming on, when you don't have to go to school, nor wear shoes, or any of that foolishness.

I went in the kitchen, found Clarissa there churning butter, and said, "Where's Commercial Appeal?"

This Clarissa was a tolerable fat darky, with pigtails though pretty, what they said was one of the best cooks in Kentucky, but so naggy it kind of soured your disposition. She must have taken lessons from my aunts.

"He cutting weeds, what you supposed to do an hour ago, add some."

"I was going to," I said, "but Uncle Jim had a toothache, and I got him some hot water."

"Where at?"

There wasn't any use going on, because the only place you could do it was here, so I said, "Shucks" and tried to slide out, but she blocked the door. My uncle Jim once stated, and he told the truth, that if Abraham Lincoln had met Clarissa early in life it might have changed the whole course of American history.

"Goin somewheres?"

"I had an appointment with a gentleman downtown," I said; "a Mr. Claypool, to see about closing up the schools."

"You see 'at door?" She pointed to the hallway that led

16

into the main part of the house, where my aunts didn't have much to do except look out for "flaws in my character," as they called it. Right now they were roiled up because Commercial Appeal and I had an accident whilst experimenting with sulphur matches, and kind of scorched one wing of the house.

"Now that's funny," I said, staring down behind her.

"Don't you try any—"

"I thought that cat got them all—he started off as a perfectly good mouser, but no, sir. *Watch it, Clarissa! He's about to run up your leg!*"

She let out a shriek and grabbed her skirts and I shot outside like a bolt of lightning. I never saw a darky so afraid of mice; even my aunts admitted it. There was something sickly about it; a rat must have taken and bit her when she was in the crib.

I went down by Uncle Abnego's shanty, where they gave me a plate of cold pork and greens and corn bread, which makes a very nice breakfast, not undigestible like some; then sidled back around the front of the house, taking care to keep the lilacs between me and the windows, and found Commercial Appeal, sickling weeds along the white board fence. He was just my age—thirteen going on fourteen.

I said, "Come on—let's cut for it. We've got to save Uncle Jim."

"Mistuh Jim save hisself. Mammy say I listen you again, she take an whup me."

For some reason, they couldn't seem to get over that little smoking the house had. It bothered them; they couldn't throw it off.

"Look here, Commercial Appeal," I said, "did I ever tell you an outright lie?"

"Yes indeedy. Plenty un em. I don't recollect you told any other kind."

"The Ku Klux Klan's going to get Uncle Jim. They may hang him. He's in deep and we've got to pull him out."

I could see him studying it, but I knew what he'd say. He and I had been friends from the day we were born, almost. Some people said Commercial Appeal wasn't over-bright, but I happened to know he had a lot more sense than most of the high and mighty smart-alecks in town, including the mayor and the principal of the school, and the real reason was, it was his name. Uncle Jim once explained that a good many darky children in the South were named by "whimsical physicians," as he said, and he said Commercial Appeal was named in connection with a roustabout that brought the Memphis newspapers off the boat and struck up a friendship with Clarissa, in a weed patch, when she was in town shopping. The same doctor figured out the name for Mr. Buckley's Consto, which was short for Constipation, because his mother was troubled in that way, you know, and spent all her money on remedies for it.

Commercial Appeal quit sickling and said, "Mistuh Jim never harmed nobody—white, black, or yaller."

"Oh, well, it may be too much trouble," I said, picking up the sickle and starting to work. "It *is* too much, now I think it over. Go get the scythe."

"Mistuh Jim freed darky folks before they fit about it. He free Mammy."

"I've made up my mind," I said. "You're right—let him help himself. Besides, I wouldn't care to get mixed up with the Ku Klux Klan."

"I ain't scared of the Kru Krux Klam," said Commercial Appeal, but he didn't look it, and neither did I.

"If you're bound to have your way, come on, but don't forget you talked me into it. Now scrunch down till we get through the gate."

We crept along the whitewashed boards clear of the yard, and then we lit out for Dillinger's Cut-off, which was a sizable stretch of wild woods, with me in front. We didn't hardly stop to rest, except once at a creek bend which made a good wading place, and it wasn't over two hours before we came to the hill-top clearing, with runty pines growing here and there, that I'd followed Uncle Jim to last spring.

"It's too silency," said Commercial Appeal. "I don't like it. Where's the Kru Krux Klam?"

"They aren't here, but Uncle Jim's costume is, and

we've got to steal it and hide it, so's he can't go to the meeting tonight."

I went to the fallen-down sycamore and pulled the costume out, and we looked it over. Most of the members' favorite hiding places were in smokehouses, and corn cribs, and hollow logs, and box tombs of cemeteries, and such like. We hauled it on out, and it was so comical and absurd I wondered how Uncle Jim could put it on; he was always making fun of foolery like that.

There was a whopping piece of black calico with three K's on each side for his horse, along with a monster white plume. But the rider's garments were the worst, being made of red calico, with white Christmassy trimmings, a high headdress of red flannel, and a white mask that had three stars in an up-and-down position. The headdress had a long tin nose, like Halloween, with a yellow moon, and the robe had stripes on the sleeves, stars on the shoulders, and tin buttons sewed on just any old place. I never saw anything so ornamented up.

"You better put em goods back," said Commercial Appeal, his voice down to whispering. "They ain't ourn, they belong to the Kru Krux Klam."

"They're Uncle Jim's costume. We've got to steal it to keep him from the meeting."

"It's ghostish—they's devil signs all over."

"It's interesting," I said, laying out the robe and picking up the headdress. "Slip it on, down over your head; see what it looks like."

"No, *suh*. I put it on, Kru Krux Klam come along and take it off, an head along with it."

"I promised Uncle Jim I wouldn't tell, but we haven't got any secrets, and you ought to know about this bunch," I said, "because they've gone bad and it may save your life some day."

"You keep Kru Krux Klam one side of town, me on the other. At's all I know an all I want to know."

"Well, at least you ought to learn the grip, which is the forefinger placed on the muscle of the arm or wrist, and the little fingers interlaced."

He didn't seem to care for it, and only kept finding

fault. Commercial Appeal got like that once in a while; there wasn't any way to argue around him.

"Time you get at grip laid on, man be over in next state on he way to Jericho. What de Kru Krux Klam need is a *simple* grip, one you could use without gettin tangled up."

"But if you're in Alabama," I said, "the recognition signal is for the party to draw his right hand across his chin, the other responding, if he's a member, by taking hold of the left lapel of his coat and shaking it."

"I ain't *in* Alabama, I in Kintucky, and fixing to stay here, if they go through such fol-de-rol as that in Alabama."

"In Kentucky, they stroke their beard once or twice, and the other places his thumbs in the waistline of his pants."

"Now *ain't* that fine? And me without a beard. I like to accommodate Kru Krux Klam," said Commercial Appeal, being sarcastic, "and grow a beard to stroke—you seggest how."

"I asked Uncle Jim about that once, but he said a body should treat it like a garden, put manure on his face, and water it with a sprinkling can two or three times a day. Thinking it over, I don't believe he was ser—"

Commercial Appeal was staring over my shoulder, at the woods behind, and his face had gone sort of gray. "Oh, Lordy, Lordy," I heard him groan, and all of a sudden he wilted down to the ground and wriggled behind the sycamore.

I turned around slow, and there was Uncle Jim, sitting quiet on his black stud horse, Satan, watching.

I swallowed and tried to say something, but I couldn't hit on just the right subject, so I kept still.

He rode on up, very slow; I couldn't recall that I ever observed a horse so deliberate; and always before, this Satan had been as quick and mean as a snake.

Uncle Jim dismounted just as deliberate, hauling out his left foot from the stirrup and sliding down belly-to, the way some of those cavalrymen do. Then he said,

"Any explanation, Davey?"

That was me.

I hadn't planned to open my mouth, but before I knew

it, I said, "We weren't doing mischief. That's all I care to say."

"*Care* to say!" For a minute, he straightened up, as black as a thundercloud; then his face smoothed out and he eased himself down onto the log. "Sit down, boy, sit down," he said. He reached around and picked up Commercial Appeal by the trousers seat. "You come on around, too, Mersh."

That was what he called Commercial Appeal, because he once said he wouldn't dignify any newspaper on earth that much, no matter how good it was. He was against naming darkies names like Commercial Appeal, and Constipation, and Posthumous, and Almighty Who Art in Heaven, and Sunday May Ninth, and Lena Ginster, and Priapus, and Watermelon Patch, the way a lot in our neighborhood were.

"I figured you'd mull over the ruckus tonight, and I figured you'd come here. You meant to steal the costume. Wasn't that it?"

For some reason, I felt blubbery—I might have known Uncle Jim would see through everything and be kindly—so I said, "If you cross those murderers, you'll end up being hung. I've heard it talked about in town."

He lit one of the long, skinny black cigars he'd got in the habit of from the Mexican War, that my aunts claimed would poison him sure, and said, "There's a thing I want cleared up. I had your word you wouldn't mention our conversation of this morning."

"It didn't apply on Commercial Appeal," I said. "We don't have secrets, and we don't tell any, neither."

"Very interesting, and very pretty, too, particularly as to grammar. Now, you, Mersh," Uncle Jim said, swinging around to face him. "What if the Ku Klux Klan grabs you up and says Boo!"

Commercial Appeal's teeth were cluttering but he spoke out and said, "Kru Krux Klam kin saw off my laig, but I ain't fixing to give out comfort, Mistuh Jim," and it was easy to tell he meant it, too. "You my kith and kin," he added, to nail it down.

"I'm obliged for the connection," said Uncle Jim in a dry kind of way. He looked us over, trying to make a decision. By and by he said, "Listen, now, and you better mind me, hear? Forget this ugly business. Drop it. Go on back to Grassy"—that was where we lived—"and play with something your size. Spin a top. Go fishing."

Then he gave me a stare that seemed to have a question in it, and when I didn't answer, he flushed up red. I thought he might box my ears, but he got up on his horse and sat there without moving for a second, holding the cigar in his hand that was resting on the pommel.

"By *God!*" he finally broke out, having to say something incomplimentary or bust, I reckon, "I never *saw* such a grimy pair of scissorbills. Where's your shoes?" he said to me, and then he asked Commercial Appeal, "Boy, you're all over mud—doesn't Clarissa take a wet towel and scrape off the topsoil now and then?"

"No, suh. Not frequent, Mistuh Jim," said Commercial Appeal, with his spunk back. "I doesn't take kindly to it. It appear to give me the lombago, like."

Uncle Jim clucked at his horse, as if he was disgusted about something, and yanked its head around sharp. I giggled and saw him almost stop, but he clucked again and dug in his heels; then he trotted off out of sight under the pines.

"Mistuh Jim mad," said Commercial Appeal.

4

WE WENT into town to see what was doing, and everywhere there was a feeling of something about to happen. You know how it is—people talking in undertones, standing here and there beneath the store awnings in the shade; work almost stopped; little groups of men looking suspicious at other groups, and an uncommon number of hard-faced strangers around, mostly on horses, riding in and out, or lighting at the tavern. I heard one mention that it was nice weather for a lynching, but I heard a man in another group say it was a shame, that nothing good would come of this.

During the late evening, one of those brickbats with a message had been thrown through the window of the newspaper, and it got into the paper on time, which was printed last night and out today. People everywhere were reading it, though I saw some of the better citizens, on the order of Major Bowyer, who ran the general store, looking angry and disgusted, as if they'd been made fun of.

I got a paper—lifted one from a counter where it wasn't working—and read the notice, but it was so lowdown and uneducated I couldn't follow it, and anyway, it didn't come out and say anything sensible. I heard Major Bowyer say it was "typical," but he didn't look pleased. It went:

"DOST HEAR, DOST HEED!

Grand Cyclops, Sepulchre, Nitro Glycerine, Den Mortals, Avenging Swords, Hear!

Gaunt Spectres Give ear. Bloody bones draw nigh!

Sons of the Bloody Dagger Prepare!

Short work!

23

Carpet bags beware! The good die first, the bad must follow. No more concessions! Revenge is sweet.

It must come!

Build the Monument—the ghosts of departed Klans will nerve you.

The spirit of the living will assist.

Pharaoh's Drowning Host!

Moons of Burning Souls! Avenging swords! The River of Stix, Philistines Down!

Whet the Swords of extermination! Slay all traitors! Cast the worthless scabbard aside!

Forget not your oaths, your bindings!

Thrice again shall vengeance reek, until blood shall flow in every creek."

At the top of this hogwash was a skull and crossbones, and at the bottom, for a signature, was the figure of a black coffin, with three K's around it, like this:

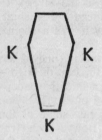

Somebody said it was the most elaborate one yet, that they must have had a cut made up for the printer, but Major Bowyer said "Humph!"—meaning, I judged, that everybody knew the editor of the newspaper was a member himself.

Commercial Appeal and I went over to the Courthouse, which was red brick and set all around with nice shade trees, hoping to pick up some news, but people mainly hushed up when we got there.

Three or four men were pitching nickels at a line drawn in the dirt, and a couple of mumbledy-peg games were going. I had three cents I got for not saying "ain't" all day Sunday, so I entered a game with two farm hands, penny a game. I did palms, and backs, and both fisties, left and right, and had worked on up through spank-the-baby and was about to jump the fence, when Uncle Jim strolled along. Seeing the money on the ground, he leaned over, picked it up, and put it in his pocket.

The farm hands jumped to their feet, but there was something so offhand and unconcerned about Uncle Jim that they didn't do any more than say, one of them, "See here, who do you think you are?"

"Shouldn't gamble with children, Coley," Uncle Jim said. "It isn't nice."

The one he spoke to, a big fellow with coarse black hair growing low on his forehead, said, "You Burnies have played it high and mighty around here long enough. For two pins I'd—"

The easy smile kind of faded off Uncle Jim's face; he took the cigar out of his mouth with his left hand, and stood waiting.

"Come on, Coley, leave him be," said the other one. "His time'll come soon enough."

When they walked off, Uncle Jim said, "My confreres," and turned away himself.

I was a little sore. "Wait a minute," I called after him. "I as good as had two cents won. I don't need—"

"Shut your yap and get home," he snapped in such an unexpected and savage style that I concluded we'd better not pursue it. Commercial Appeal and I went to the wooden horse trough and got a drink and stuck our feet in when nobody was looking; then we went to the old black iron one on three legs across the square, and did the same thing. After that we headed for Grassy.

When we got there, my aunts collared me and took me into the sitting room and gave me a lecture on delinquency and moral tepitude, which they said was in my blood on account of my mother; and my Aunt Effie, who was the worst, if possible, washed my ears four times in a row. I'd rather had a licking any day. She was a puzzlement to me, and always had been. She was old, past forty, and thin as a rake, but she had power in her arms like a mule kicking. Once she'd got out her crockery basin and a wash rag, and took a grip on your neck, you might as well give up. A person would have been happier if an octopus had him. It was her idea that everybody's ears were dirty, or so she said, and she tried to put the whole works right with mine. It felt like a brace and bit going through your head. There wasn't any way to get the jump on her. She had false teeth that she put in a glass of water at night—to keep from biting herself during a dream, I reckon—but the time I switched it to coal-oil she smelled it first, poured it out, and did what she said was the best job yet on my ears.

My Aunt Lou was downright agreeable alongside her. A person seeing them together would have taken Aunt Lou for practically normal. She was the one that gave me the lickings, but there wasn't any sting in them. They had a younger sister, which was my mother, but her husband got killed in the war and later she ran off with a Union officer, leaving me behind. She was dead now. She'd tried to send for me, but my aunts wouldn't let her. That was the family disgrace. Uncle Jim was the only boy in the litter, and sometimes it tugged on him pretty hard.

Well, *I* didn't feel disgraced, and said so, but they hushed me up in a hurry. They had my mother's room closed up exactly as she left it, and once a year, on the day she escaped, they went in there and took on like lunatics. You'd a thought London Bridge was falling down. And when they came out, they always gave me several lickings and washed my ears for about an hour, as if *I'd* been to blame. I tried to tell them I didn't have anything to do with it. I told them they ought to look up the guilty party, which was the Union officer, and wash *his* ears, but they wailed and lamented so, I was sorry I said it. They loaded me up with so much disgrace, and asked me how I could bear the shame of it so often, that Uncle Jim finally got me aside private and suggested that my mother may have slid out to get shut of my aunts. After that, I felt better. I didn't care if she'd run off with a Chinese burglar, so she got away.

The odd thing was, they chucked out my father's last name, and tacked on their own for me. It was nonsensical; my father wasn't involved at all, being dead in the war, so you'd a thought they might punish my mother and throw *her* name out. But no, they got the Court to swap it right back to Burnie, and said it was none of my business. And were they agreeable when I threatened to go to Court and change *theirs?* Not for a minute; they said they'd never heard of such impudence. So it rested —David Burnie.

Anyhow, they finally locked me in my room now, and made me solemnly promise not to bust out, then swear on the Bible, and while I was sliding down the oak tree outside, I concluded what to do about Uncle Jim. I hunted up Commercial Appeal, and sure enough, he'd been right about getting whipped if he listened to me. It was annoysome to think how many people played him down, especially my aunts, who said he "corrupted my speech," as they called it. He was smart, and I told him so; I didn't mind coming out and saying it.

"If I'se smart, I wouldn't *listen,*" he said, trying to find a way to sit down and be comfortable.

You see? The most of those people that ran him down, they were only jealous.

Toward dark we sneaked into the worst-burned part of the house and climbed up into the attic. I knew what I wanted, and we found them, perfectly sound, resting on the old gun rack made of deer antlers. They were my father's squirrel rifles, that got killed in the war. We lifted them down—beautiful guns with scrolly work on the metal, heavy, very long barreled, with almost no rust— and all of a sudden I felt a lump come in my throat. They said he was an expert shot, almost as good as Uncle Jim, and liked to hunt and fish as a boy. It seemed a pity he couldn't still do it, but he hadn't even got through his first battle, being the first man killed from our county; shot off his horse leading a charge up a little hill. I opened the big hair trunk and took out a picture of him, made one time on a trip to Chicago. I studied it over. A young fellow with a moustache, calm-looking, with light-colored eyes, a high forehead, and a nice smile. If my father could smile like that with his head in a photographer's iron clamp, he must have been, as everybody said, a person of rare and sunny good humor. He was Uncle Jim's best friend. I wondered how it would have been to go fishing with him, and felt my eyes sting a little. But then I remembered that they had captured the hill, so it must have been all right. The thing that troubled me was, in the picture he didn't look mad at anybody.

We tiptoed down and took the guns, together with powder, wadding and shot, to an empty shed, with a lantern, and scoured them up.

"I ain't fired these but onct," said Commercial Appeal, "and it like to knock my shoulder down where my knees is at. I ain't sure I can *hit* de Kru Krux Klam."

We'd tried them out one day when we thought nobody would care, and were anyway gone to a funeral, and the kick *was* unusually brisk. But if you could find a rest, like a sapling crotch, for the barrel, you could hit a gnat at two or three hundred yards. They were expensive Kentucky rifles, made by the best workmen, and there weren't any finer guns anywhere; Uncle Jim said so himself.

We stashed them in a good place, and I climbed back up the tree, so as not to take any chances about later, and when my aunts came to release me for supper, they were so perked up to find me in, and the house not destroyed or something, that they loaded me down with rewards.

"David," said my Aunt Lou, "you *have* decided to reform, haven't you? I can see it in your face—it's, it's transfigured, like Moses when he descended from Sinai."

"Yes'm," I said, looking at the gingerbread with cinnamon sauce and whipped cream that Clarissa was bringing in. "I've been on the wrong track. I realize it, and mean to act on it."

"Tell me, David," my Aunt Lou went on, "was it because of what Reverend Abernathy said on Sunday? Take some more gingerbread."

"I believe that was it," I said, cutting out a piece about the size of a wagon bed. "Yes, I know it was, now. It was that started me thinking, anyway."

"What particular part?" asked my Aunt Effie, acting as if she'd like to believe it for a change. She was a pretty tough proposition; she was born doubting, and never got cured.

"It's hard to pin it down."

"Try," said Aunt Effie.

"Well, you take it all around, and I believe it was the part about the Moabites." That was perfectly safe. This sanctimonious old pest was always babbling about the Moabites; you'd a thought they were planning to leave him money.

"Hm," said my Aunt Effie, but she must have been partly convinced, as she got up and allowed she was going to return my slingshot. She'd hid it because I accidentally hit the Macreadys' work bell three or four times one day and called all the field hands in during the middle of the morning.

Watching her take a stool and feel along the top of the sideboard, I wasn't hopeful she'd have much luck, and wanted to offer a bet on it. She always hid things in that exact same spot, so if you wanted them back, you knew where to look.

"It isn't here," she said, turning around slowly. "You, David—perhaps you can clear up why?"

"Ma'am?"

"Can you shed some light on this disappearance?" said Aunt Effie in just about her acidest tone.

"Yes'm," I said, very reluctant and being careful to clean up the last of the gingerbread first. "I think I can. I *hope* I can, anyhow."

"Indeed? Pray go on."

"Well," I said, uneasy. "I dislike to peach on anybody, even a bushwhacking pr—"

"On whom, for example?"

"Well, Sunday afternoon, when Reverend Abernathy came to call, and you were getting tea ready, I peeked in here and he was fooling around by the sideboard, acting mighty strange. I don't like to accuse anybody without evidence, but if you ask me, he's got all the earmarks of a slingshot thief. Uncle Jim said—"

I knew it; I should have suspicioned how it would turn out, and kept my mouth shut. She climbed down off of the stool, with a kind of weary but set expression, and got out the wash rag. It was one of the roughest sessions I can remember putting in. And afterwards, they locked me up again.

Uncle Jim had a key for just this kind of emergency, but I didn't figure he'd be home tonight, and he wasn't. I slept till nearly midnight, which was the earliest the Ku Klux Klan ever started their wickedness, then I slid down the oak and tiptoed off under the trees in the moonlight after Commercial Appeal.

I hate to write this part, because it *was* ugly, and might give a person nightmares, but in a book you have to tell things the way they happened, whether you please everybody or not.

It was one of those gusty nights, the air clear and cool, but the wind whipping up lively now and then, sliding things along the ground—trash and such—and tossing the leafy branches around like wild arms waving. Overhead, a procession of puffball clouds raced by so that the moonlight was bright as day one minute, with the ghostliest kind of shadows standing up, and the sky black as ink the next. It was scary.

I crept up under the window of Clarissa's shack and hooted like a hoot-owl. I did it very well, too. It was necessary, with Clarissa. She wasn't reliable. Back when our signal was a catbird, which didn't come easy to hit on, sometimes sounding like a bluejay, or a sick crow, she emptied a bucket of slops on my head. What's more, it was winter. And the next day she had the gall to tell on me when I placed a mouse-trap in the bread-box and caught her finger, taking off a ridiculous small amount of skin and not breaking any bones at all, except a possibility of splitting one in her little finger, which was weak anyway, and didn't need setting.

But all went well. I hooted four or five times, soft and low, and presently the door opened a crack, and then Commercial Appeal eased out, wearing a tow shirt and a pair of raggedy trousers.

Not talking much, we collected up the guns, and flew along down the road toward Ben Woods' place. Once a dog barked, close at hand under the shadows, making us jump, and another time a big night bird flapped off a tree limb directly overhead.

We made three or four turns—maybe two miles altogether—and cut across a field, and there was Ben's place, a very neat, well-kept farm and house with no busted chairs or punched-out buckets or rusty springs or crockery or anything else lying around to clutter up the yard.

We found a handy spot, in some bushes but with a good view to the front porch, and settled down to wait. It didn't take long.

In fifteen minutes or less, we heard a drum chorus of hoofbeats far down the road, but coming on at a gallop, and immediately afterward a lamp shone out, pale and yellow, through one of Ben's side windows. He must have known what was in store. I remembered he'd untangled a fishline for me once, and showed me a better way to tie on hooks.

There was a stir at the door, it was thrown open, and we could see Ben, fully dressed and holding a shotgun; but the moon ducked under just then, and we lost him.

"They goin to hurt that man," whispered Commercial Appeal. "I wish I'se home."

I waited a minute, my knees practically knocking themselves black and blue, and he said, just as I thought, "I ain't goin, though."

Then the hoofbeats swept around the curve and up to Ben's gate and stopped, with nothing but that shuffling around that a horse does when it's been ridden hard and dislikes settling down all at once. The moon shot out again, and you could see them, two or three dozen, dressed in those monstrous costumes, sitting there silent and awful.

"Ben Woods," a voice boomed out, "you are summoned to the Kingdom of Hell," or some such statement; I couldn't remember very clear, for being scared.

"Yes, sir, Mr. Givens," Ben spoke up, his voice perfectly steady. He moved forward into view in the moonlight, still on the porch. "What was it you wanted?"

One of the figures leaned over and opened Ben's gate; then he rode through, as the others watched, and dropped something white that fluttered down to the ground near the steps.

Ben stood without moving on the porch, his gun still slung over his arm, not raised or brandished. Then he turned a little and said to somebody inside—we could hear him clear enough—"Marbella, han that light out." She made a protest, half crying, and Ben reached around and snatched the lamp himself.

We saw him stoop over the paper.

I could feel my blood freezing up inside, and in the years since then, I've learned very well the kind of sickish knotting up that comes in your stomach when you know a person's about to die. But I never got used to it.

"Yes, sir, Mr. Givens. It's a deed to my lan," said Ben, standing up straight again, holding the paper.

"You've got three minutes to sign it."

Ben said, "I couldn't do that, Mr. Givens. I bought it outright and legal, after you let it go for taxes. I built it up with my hans, along of my boys. No, sir, I couldn't sign away my propity." He was scared almost white, but he didn't give way an inch.

"Two minutes."

"I got a wife an four chillen," said Ben. "They speck me to stan up lak a man," but I judged that his wife didn't want him to, because I heard her moan out again, trying to get him inside.

"One minute," said the man on horseback, holding up a watch in the moonlight, and while he was talking, I cocked my rifle without knowing it. It made a noise like a twig snapping, and caused two or three riders to look around, but none of them investigated.

"All right, boys. If there ain't any objections," said the man with a chuckle—"string him up. That maple limb'll do."

Ben's wife screamed from the doorway, and one of his boys, aged about nine, ran out as naked as a newborn jay and fastened on to one of Ben's legs, yelling "Pappy! Pappy!"

At that moment another of the riders drew his horse apart a little way and said in a conversational tone of voice, "I've got a couple"; then he lifted up his hands, which had duelling pistols in them. He knocked off his ridiculous high headgear with one of the gun barrels, and it was Uncle Jim.

"I've always been a great stickler for parliamentary procedure, especially with an outfit as exalted as this," he said, looking easy and comfortable sitting on his horse in the moonlight, "and I'll have to insist on casting two votes according to the regulations. The only point is, where do I cast them?"

I never saw anybody with such a scratchy manner when he wanted to. He couldn't have stated his case in ordinary terms. Oh, no; he had to make it just as troublesome as possible. If he'd been on his deathbed, he'd acted frolicsome with the Angel Gabriel.

"God bless you, Mistuh Jim," Ben cried, and his wife called out something from the doorway; I couldn't hear what.

"All right, Burnie," said Givens. "You've been hankering for a showdown." Raising his voice and turning in the saddle, he said, "This is the smart-aleck that hazed us through the Army, boys. The war's over; they've retired all the rich pretty-boy officers. Bill Mullins, Ab Mullins, Coley—"

I haven't exactly got it fixed in my mind what happened next, but everything exploded all at once. Givens swung round, bringing up one arm with a sawed-off gun, and Uncle Jim hit the ground with a thud when the charge came. I could see him turning over and over, trying to get behind the pump-box, so he wasn't dead yet, thanks to goodness, then one of Givens' partners, very near the pump, took careful picks with a pistol—he couldn't have missed. I skipped out of the bushes, raised my rifle and let go. It hit him near about the middle of his stomach, knocking him clear out of the saddle.

The moon ducked under, there was a rackety stamping and switching of horses, a lot of yelling, with considerable cussing, and when it shot out, making things bright again, Uncle Jim yelled, *"Watch it,* Davey, boy—on your left."

I whirled a second too late—I couldn't have ducked to save me. A man wearing a headdress that resembled a "turned-up churn," as Uncle Jim said later, was riding right down on me, aiming a rifle with one hand. But a roar went off in my ears that felt like I'd been pole-axed, and he sprawled across the horse's neck, his rifle clattering to the ground. I opened my mouth to say thanks, but another shot rang out from deep in the crowd, I heard a kind of sigh, and Commercial Appeal sank down on his knees, like somebody praying, then toppled forward on his face.

I screamed, and everything went blurred. The next I remember was Uncle Jim shaking me, to pry me loose from trying to make Commercial Appeal come back to life.

"He's dead, boy—there's nothing you can do about it. Come on, get up—we haven't any time to waste."

I looked up and saw his left shoulder covered with blood, and Ben Woods and Marbella bending over with tears running down their faces, and Givens flat on his back nearby, staring up at the sky but not seeing it, being dead, too—shot by Uncle Jim—and others killed here and there. The rest were gone. Ben picked up Commercial Appeal easy and gentle, one arm under his head, the other under his legs, and carried him inside. The raid was over, and with it our life in Kentucky.

5

"YOU CAN take my word for it; I'm in a position to know," said Uncle Jim firmly, addressing me and my aunts in the sitting room, one lamp turned on low, and the shades all pulled. "We have no other course except flight. It goes against my grain to run from swine like Coley Baxter and the Mullinses, but they'll shoot from ambush, now. They've wanted my hide since I broke Ab Mullins for skulking at Chancellorsville. And it's not only me; it's the boy. They'll get him as sure as I'm born."

My Aunt Effie spoke up in the smallest voice I ever heard her use. We all felt sniffly and low on account of Commercial Appeal, especially me, but she looked peaked and drawn, and her hair was on crooked. It was the first time I realized she wore a wig. It bothered me; I felt sad about it. A person seldom sees his opportunities till they've collapsed; the wig opened up wonderful possibilities. For example, a batch of lively, well-selected fleas transplanted from Uncle Abnego's old setter Flatus (which Uncle Jim gave him, along with ten cents a month to keep it away from the house) might have briskened life up two or three hundred per cent for Aunt Effie. Again, a thin coating of glue spread on the inside would likely have kept her mind off wash rags and ears for several days. The sight of that wig made me realize what I'd been missing; I couldn't help it.

"David stays here. Nothing—nothing—can make me believe that anybody is sufficiently depraved to harm a beardless child, even one like our late sister's abandoned son."

I didn't care for the compliment, and fell to thinking again about the fleas, and how it would be better to starve them down a few days, in a tin box, before settling them in, but Uncle Jim said:

"You don't seem to understand. This boy shot and killed a man, a cousin of both the Baxters and the Mullinses—Klansmen all—and I added a couple more for good measure. The hullabaloo will spread like a prairie fire. Word will travel up and down the river—all over the South. Even the decent members will rally to punish us, most of them. If the Klan lets this go, its authority is finished. No, we've got to scoot for cover, and do it fast. The Macreadys will see to it nobody else gets raided here, but Davey and I have to run—now, tonight; there aren't any two ways about *that*."

"Oh, dear," said my Aunt Lou, trembly and fluttery as usual. "I believe I'm about to faint. I simply can't bear—"

She was always fainting, in any kind of emergencies, but I noticed she picked out a nice soft spot for it first, or made sure somebody would catch her. Then she got a lot of attention when everybody pulled out the smelling salts, or some brandy, or cologne, or other such truck.

If you want the truth, she was little more than a common humbug. I know, because she raised up one time when I got confused and gave her a tumblerful of cologne to drink and dabbed a little brandy on her forehead, and laid about as lively as anybody, with a statement employing some language that didn't seem to fit her disposition. But when I thought it over, I decided that Aunt Lou could have been a very enjoyable person, and had an average life, if it hadn't been for Aunt Effie.

"Faint later, Lou," said Uncle Jim abruptly. "There isn't time. We're going to need supplies, and money. But what we want most is speed. Get the strong box," he said to Aunt Effie.

I figured she would hit him with a poker, because she lorded it over Grassy's accounts like a warden of a penitentiary, but what she and Aunt Lou did in the next hour set me back worse than I'd ever been in my life.

First off, Aunt Effie fetched the strong box drawer from its hole in the wall behind a family portrait of somebody's great uncle, where it was entirely safe, because any right-minded person seeing that old blister wasn't apt to come any closer than necessary; then she opened the box and they counted up and found fifteen hundred dollars in gold besides a fortune in Confederate bonds that she was keeping in case they fought the war over and it came out different.

"Five hundred dollars will give us a start," said Uncle Jim, filling up a little leather sack, but Aunt Effie shoved the whole yellow pile across.

"Take it all, James. Grassy is still self-sufficient, in spite of the oppressor's wrongs. God and our loyal people willing, we shall continue to thrive."

Uncle Jim started to argue, but she cut him off. "I want David to have every advantage." She looked down-right unhappy and said, "It was Lou's hope, and mine, to see him grow up to manhood."

It was the first time it occurred to me that these two aunts of mine weren't flat-out enemies. I'll have to admit it came as a shocker; I didn't know what to make of it. What if they *had* been doing what they thought was best? I raised up my head to study them in the lamplight, but Uncle Jim said:

"Come on, boy; come on—pack and get moving. We can't afford to dilly-dally." He took my wrist and pranced me along, over to our room, and started throwing articles like extra socks and drawers and his Army revolver and a book that he said was his "pocket Shakespeare," whatever that was—something about hunting, I reckoned—into a sea-bag he owned, and gave me another for my things. But when I filled it up, trying to use a little horse sense in choosing, on account of the weight, you know, he dumped it all out again—not only my slingshot, but my stuffed white mouse, fifteen marbles, the stink-bomb I bought from a peddler, some dried corn-silks, two rabbit traps, and my wooden whistle. When he filled it back up with clothes, we looked around the room for the last time.

It was a cheerful room, with rag rugs on the floor and faded old wallpaper, along with a mahogany four-poster bed and a trundle bed, which I'd been cramped into be-cause Uncle Jim said a firebug shouldn't occupy a four-poster while the people he dispossessed settled for lesser accommodations.

"All right, that's it, boy," he said, then he did something curious. He took a very old, wrinkled oil-paper out of his wallet and unfolded it. It was a map, with some stiffish handwriting at the left bottom, a row of what seemed to be islands strung out catty-cornered, and a seaman's drawn-in compass-rose at the top, with the direction points inked in as far as N.N.E., and the like. On one island a line of dots led from an inlet that had "Teach's Cove" written under it, and at the end, an "X," with the notation: "Directly north of natural pot-hole well." There was some additional material; I couldn't make it out, except for one reference to "Bar silver" and another that said, "Jewelry, settings and loose stones."

"Look it over, boy. Here's where we're heading," said Uncle Jim, and I could see his eyes shine in the lamplight. "If they get me, don't fail to take this map off my body before you shove. *Don't forget!*"

"Map of what?" I said, looking suspicious. Uncle Jim was a fine man, as stated, but he'd been known to go off on hare-brained ventures, and he wasn't over-finicky about the nature of them, as long as they produced excitement. That's why Aunt Effie kept the accounts.

"It was given me by a very dear old friend who regrettably fell in the Mexican War, an upstanding worthy who went by the name of Cutthroat O'Hare. I have the impression he stole it from a family in the Bahama Islands."

"What is it?"

"It would seem to be a treasure map, having to do with a place called the Florida Keys, or *Los Martires,* as the late Ponce de Leon termed them."

"They're new to me; I never heard of them."

"You will, laddie, you will," said Uncle Jim, and nobody ever spoke a truer word.

We crept back down to the sitting room, and I stayed with my aunts while Uncle Jim went out to see Clarissa. He was gone an amazing long while, considering the need for haste.

It made me so fidgety I could hardly stand still. For some reason, I was having a rough time looking my aunts in the face. Now that the moment had come to leave, I wasn't quite as anxious as I thought.

"David," said my Aunt Effie, and I could scarcely hear her, "I want you to do me a favor."

"Yes'm," I said in a voice just as small.

"You must take care of your Uncle Jim." It seemed like an odd thing to ask of a boy thirteen, particularly one with moral tepitude, but I knew what she meant. Then he was back from Clarissa's, and I'd never seen him look so before. He was dead white, besides sweating.

"What is it? What's the matter? How is she?" cried Aunt Lou.

"Come on, boy," he said in a harsh voice, and leaning over, he blew out the lamp. At the door, he told them we would write a letter whenever we could, sending it always to Clarissa, to keep from being traced, and after that we were ready to say goodbye. They'd fixed a big parcel of food—sandwiches, smoked meat, hard-boiled eggs—and wrapped it all around with two blankets, so we wouldn't freeze. Then they insisted on rebandaging up the graze-wound on Uncle Jim's shoulder. Standing there in the doorway, with the summer bugs droning away in the grass and bull frogs tuning up from the slough, I could see a faint gray in the black sky off to the east—the false dawn—so I knew it would be light soon. All of a sudden I turned around, and both Aunt Effie and Aunt Lou grabbed me up in a kind of partnership hug, while I tried to force back the tears.

"It won't be for long," said Uncle Jim, swinging his sea bag up to his shoulder, but I don't think anybody believed him. Then he yanked me sharply by the arm, and we were off on our journey to Florida.

6

Mounted on Satan, along with our plunder, we struck out at a gallop, but in a direction different than what I imagined. We headed for the river. "They'll have the highways covered," Uncle Jim shouted over his shoulder as we pounded along. "They'd pick us off before we traveled twenty miles."

Well, I doubted it; the whole idea seemed silly, but he was right about the Ku Klux Klan—they were a cruel bunch, and never gave up on a punishment, as I'll demonstrate by and by.

In a few minutes we reached the river bank, and jogged as quiet as possible down to where we kept a skiff tied up, for fishing and picnics on the island, and crossing into Missouri now and then. The night was pitch black again, an hour from dawn, and nobody was around except two boys setting trot lines a hundred yards below us, and a flatboat within hearing distance, out in the middle of the river.

We untied the skiff, then went after the oars in a willow thicket where we hid them, and I'm blessed if Zebediah didn't stick his head out of a clump and say:

"I got 'em, Mistuh Jim and Masser Davey. Don't fret yo'se'ves; grasp hold of the prow, now, and we'll trot her right on down."

He had a blanket roll over his shoulder, a Confederate forage cap on his head, and a pair of overshoes on his feet, because he was anxious about the damp, and always had been.

"Where in thunderation do you think you're headed?" inquired Uncle Jim. "Put those oars down."

"Don't you fret at all, Mistuh Jim," said Zebediah,

chuckling. "I may be ugly as a burned maul, as the man said, but I fixing to look after you the same as before. You seen the hind end of your worries, and that's a fack."

If you asked me, they were just about beginning to pile up. This Zebediah was about the tiresomest know-it-all alive, and had a saying to cover everything on earth, as well as upward of ten thousand riddles. He had been Uncle Jim's body-servant in the war, but Uncle Jim said he was so much trouble, fussing around with his bossy wisdom, that they finally found out he was in the pay of the Union Army. According to Uncle Jim, Zebediah was the only reason he hadn't got to be a general, but this wasn't altogether true. I hate to admit it, but Zeb *did* know a lot, and if he hadn't been so cocksure, he'd been enjoyable to have around.

"Nip on home, Zeb," Uncle Jim said briskly. "This is a bad business. What's worse, it's a wet business. You'll get a nose-cold and die on our hands."

"I surely obliged you mention shoes," said Zeb, though nobody had that I heard, "cause I got to ask you and Masser Davey to slip one off. Right one he preferable, but either on em'll do."

"What for?" asked Uncle Jim, and I said, "Not me," but he went ahead, mule-headed as usual, and took off one of mine and one of Uncle Jim's. Then he placed a penny down in the toe of each, and said, "There, 'at charm'll perteck you all along de way. I don' know no better. You take my advice, you'll watch out for a stretch of good luck."

"We'll have very good luck if we don't get bunions," said Uncle Jim, but after saying this, he got serious and told Zeb, "Now listen to me, and don't argue. We've got a rough passage ahead, and I don't plan to do a lot of jawing over trifles. I mean what I say, Zeb: scold around like an old woman and I'll send you packing."

"If you kinely take hol' de prow an'—Lordy above, what's 'at?"

We heard it at the same time, a clatter of horses' hooves, tired, too, from the way one stumbled.

"Get down! Back in the bushes," Uncle Jim hissed,

and started throwing our plunder out of sight; then he led Satan deep in the willows, and we crouched down, with Zeb still holding the oars.

"I don't hear anything," came a voice from up on the bank. "Shine a light here."

"They've gone a-horseback; I told you so before," said another man. "Coley looked in their barn. We're wasting time."

"Hold on," said the first man. "Let's prove it out while we're here. If you're searching for grubs, there's no sense lifting one log and skipping the next."

There was a noise of somebody scrambling down the bank, and I peered out to see two men, one with a lantern, examining our boat.

"The boat's here, just as I claimed," one of them called back. "Nobody's donkey-headed enough to start down the Mississippi in a skiff when he can sit a saddle in comfort, not even Burnie."

I waited for Uncle Jim's gun to go off, to kind of set the record straight and cure up this fellow's careless tongue, but he stood as quiet as an Injun, holding one hand over Satan's mouth.

"All right, let it go. Come on up," the spokesman on the bank cried down. "Wait a minute, though—we might as well smash that boat while we're about it."

"What with—our fists? Come and smash it yourself, if you're a mind to. I'm fixing to run that whelp to earth. Nobody shoots my blood cousin in the stomach and gets by with it." Then he seemed to think this numbskull statement over, because he said, "Or any place else— neck, thigh or shinbone."

I could see his face in the lantern light; it was Coley Baxter, who I'd played mumbledy-peg with. He'd always been considered addled in the head, and had never done anything but the meanest sort of farm work. Now he'd got his teeth into something worthwhile at last, as Uncle Jim said, and wasn't apt to let go in a hurry.

In spite of the threat, I began to breathe easier, and after some arguing back and forth—these bullies *were* in a gritty humor, and no mistake—they left in a rush of hooves.

None of us said anything, not even Zeb, but the way we worked in the next few minutes showed how serious we were. We walked the boat down to the water, tossed in our things, including the saddle from off Satan, which Uncle Jim allowed he would sell down river, and then he whacked the horse on the rump.

"He'll go home. I told Clarissa to hide him out a few days." He stood looking up in the direction Satan had gone a second or two, then he said, "All right, boys, let's roll it."

We shoved out as silent as possible, headed across river in a long downward slant, taking to the oars in earnest so as to reach the shelter of the Missouri side.

It was only a few minutes before dawn, of another nice fresh morning. When I thought back over the last twelve hours, I hardly could believe that everything had happened. And now, odd as it was, I felt tired for the first time.

We glided along, staying just outside the easy water, where it forms a back-current, you know—very helpful if you're trying to pull up river but no use to us now. Once across, we scarcely touched the oars. Uncle Jim said we would concentrate on slipping quietly out of the territory for now; then try to make up some mileage, by rowing, later. So we skimmed down on a four-mile current and watched out for snags and sawyers, which were tree limbs that were caught in the bottom and sawed the water, and deadheads, which were logs so water-soaked they floated just below the surface, out of sight.

Lights were beginning to appear in shanty windows here and there, and before long the sky lightened up with gray streaks that looked ever so pretty, and mournful, too, somehow. It was cool, but not cold.

Uncle Jim said we'd tie up when it became full day, so we could dangle some lines over the side now in the hope of laying in a catfish or two. Mostly, you couldn't get much satisfaction trolling that way, because cat—mudcat, that is—were so lazy they disliked to move to get food. What you got, then, would be buffalo or carp, or maybe an eel, or an alligator gar, and nobody ate those if they could help it, except darkies.

But this time we had good luck, fishing on the bottom with rolled-up doughballs taken from the bread we had and held down by a heavy sinker, and caught a channel cat weighing nearly five pounds. It was just right for a meal. We let him flop in the bottom, shiny and blue, with that mean, spiny fin sticking up out of his head, and watched out for a place to light.

Once we rowed into the bank in a hurry, to let a steamboat slosh by in a crossing, very near; then we pushed out again, and in a few minutes, rounding the bend, scrunched up onto a towhead, which is an island covered with willows and cottonwoods, and poison ivy, too, if you aren't careful.

But we had a stretch of sandy beach, perfectly private, nothing in sight on either bank, except trees as thick as brambles, so we stretched ourselves and got comfortable.

Uncle Jim and I pulled up the boat, covered it with branches, and hauled out our truck, while Zeb made a fire back in a shelter of greenery. Then we cooked the catfish and had breakfast, after taking a swim first to freshen up. What I mean is, Uncle Jim and I did; Zeb said he wouldn't as much as put his foot in for a thousand dollars, cash and hard money. He said he knew all about water, and wouldn't trust it; that his granny had told him how to proceed in cases of *every* kind involving water, so there wasn't any sense arguing the point.

"I knows water, up, down and sideways, chile," he said, as blowy and overstuffed as usual; then he went on to state that water had a few uses, but it had to be handled very careful, else you could get in trouble with evil spirits, and it might backfire on you. A house could be purified if water was poured on the steps at midnight, but under certain conditions it would be better to pour it on the front porch in the early morning or late afternoon.

Well, that made about as loose a program as possible, and I told him so, but he said if you poured bottled-up water on the sidewalk in the morning, it would ward *off* the evil spirits; they'd somehow get in the jug and be "absorbed" during the night.

I never heard anything so far-fetched. He said he wouldn't care to recommend any more on the bright side of the ledger, except if you put a sleeper's hand in water, he'd wake up and tell the name of his sweetheart.

"Howsomever," Zeb said, preparing to moon on, but Uncle Jim interrupted. "I think that'll do it. We'll have breakfast. What we many want to consider here is the possibility that you've got water on the brain."

We laid into the catfish, which was steaming hot and so tender it fell apart in big chunks, entirely free of bones, and had broiled tomatoes and poke salad Zeb picked and boiled in a can, and fresh white bread from home. We could have had smoked pork, too, from the big slab Uncle Jim carried, but it didn't fit into the menu.

After breakfast, we spread our blankets on the sand, in a sunny place ringed around with cottonwoods, and slept up, but we were wakened several times, twice by steamboats threshing along and once by a flatboat, carrying produce to New Orleans from someplace north. Such boats were rare now, but in the old days, it was said, they used to skitter down the river as dense as waterbugs, carrying corn, flour, cider, apples, pork, beef, whiskey, rope, salt, maple sugar, hides and such-like wares.

I saw Uncle Jim raise up and eye this last boat, thinking, and before he lay down again, he said:

"Now that's not a bad idea; safe, too. We'd better turn it over, come evening."

As things worked out, we got mixed up with flatboats soon enough, and I'll tell you how it happened. For three or four days we pursued the same course: whisked along down the river at night, rowing and drifting, and crept in to sleep during the day. You take for the most part we had enough to eat, but we did miss salt. Zeb said it wasn't necessary to have salt, that neither the African darkies nor the Indians needed it, so we should forget about it, but Uncle Jim asked him: "Did you ever see cows grazing in a field?"

"Sholey I has. What kinder question dat?"

"Have you ever noticed a small white object, say, six inches square, lying nearby, or propped up on a stick? You have? Well, that's what's known as a *salt lick,* to improve the health of the cattle. Cattle know what they need, and so do I."

Next morning before dawn he drifted us down, hugging the Kentucky side, where the bank wasn't bluff, but made a kind of pasture, with nice grass, and waited till we heard a cow moo; then he headed in so we could look for the salt. But we had rotten bad luck, because this farmer hadn't put the salt out in his fields at all. It was wired onto a stake within fifty yards of his house and barn, and before we got to it, Zeb tripped over an old washtub and made a racket fit to empty the graveyard.

Some dogs began to bark, and I heard a woman in the house say, "What's that racket?" And then she called, "Omer, bring a gun; it's those dratted weasels again."

So we figured the farmer was already up, otherwise they'd be in the same room, and we made tracks. Uncle Jim worried the salt block off the wire, then left a gold piece in a cleft stick he'd cut; and after that we aped it for the boat.

But Zeb couldn't let it rest. He was pretty soaked through with religion, and had a reputation that way, and would have turned preacher if a number of cooler heads hadn't talked him out of it. He said it was morally dishonest to steal salt like that, no matter whether we paid or not, and it would be better to go along down river, occasionally taking a lick here and another there if we needed to, along with the cattle, and avoid an outright theft. Further, he said, it might be days before the farmer discovered the salt was gone, and where would the cows be *then?*

Uncle Jim told him to hush up; he said he'd heard all he could stand. "They can't only buy two or three tons of salt with that gold piece," he said, "they can buy a salt *mine,* and get into the business. Drop salt; let it go for awhile. Take up some other condiment, if you have to— sugar, or pepper, or paprika. But I've had enough salt for now; I don't want it mentioned again."

Well, I was perfectly happy to. It wasn't very good salt to start with: coarse and bitter, and not overly salty. But it served for a couple of days, perking up the food, and then our provisions began to give out, so we knew we had to stop off at a town to fodder up.

"It's chancey," said Uncle Jim. "Dens all over the South have got our description by now, and they'll be on the watch-out, but we're bound to risk it—it's the only way. Besides," he added, "I'd sooner be a corpse from gunfire than from starvation. I always promised myself I'd die on a full stomach."

This naturally raised a howl from Zeb, because he said it was the worst kind of luck to speak of corpses in that offhand and disregardful style, and he said, for example, if a person dreams of a coffin he will marry rich but will die a short time after the marriage. This didn't have any connection that either of us could see, as Uncle Jim stated. But then, to get even, Zeb asked me a riddle, and said, "Why do they bury people in Harlan County with they heads pinted toward the West?"

I figured it had something to do with the high water, and spring rise, to keep the deceased from washing away, which would make a troublesome situation, but he said, "Because they's dead, chile, that's why."

I thought Uncle Jim would die laughing, and I made a note to square things up with this nuisance, but he asked another riddle that was so easy it put my mind at rest, and made me feel like letting him off.

He says, very brash and smiley: "Twelve crows settin on a fence. One tuk a notion to fly away. How many's left?"

I couldn't wait to get the answer out. If there was one thing I knew, it was crows. I'd studied their habits from way back, and I said, *"None,* by Jiminy, because if a crow flies away, the whole pack'll follow as fast as shooting; they won't waste a second on it. So there."

"All on 'em, honey. He just tuk a *notion;* he didn't fly."

This time, I thought we might have to get a doctor for Uncle Jim. He seemed kind of choked for awhile. But then he got straightened out, and I determined I'd fix that smart aleck if it was the last thing I did. I'd work up something *special.*

That night we decided to hole up about midnight, so as

to get some sleep before going into town. Uncle Jim tried to figure out how far we were down the river, and he got out a map he'd brought, but it was a vexatious tough job because of all the crooks and bends. Some places, the Mississippi flowed along in a pretty straight line, but this wasn't one of them.

"As nearly as I can calculate," he said, before we made out a likely island in the dark, "we're getting down toward Arkansas. To be specific, we might make Carruthersville, Missouri, in the morning early. In some ways it's a tolerable town; that is, it's no more boneheaded than most. Carruthersville'll do. I've been there. We'll provision up and lay our ear to the ground. Frankly, and I don't mean this to sound impolite, I wouldn't mind branching out a little for a few hours."

I didn't much like the sound of this, because Uncle Jim had a mighty free and easy manner, even in strange towns, and I didn't want him to get us in trouble just because he was feeling good.

Anyhow, we pulled into the island a little after midnight, had a cold bite to eat, being too tired to cook, as well as reluctant to start a fire on such a black night, and set up camp in the same old way. And then, after I heard Uncle Jim and Zeb begin to snore, I got up, quiet as a mouse, and put a loop of tarred fishing line around Zeb's right foot, where it stuck out of his blanket, and tied the other end to the nearest cottonwood. I did a good neat job, and felt satisfied. It's funny how peaceful a body can get if he knows he's done his duty. My Aunt Effie used to say that, and mostly I never believed her. Before I tied the line, I'd been wide awake, tired as I was, but now I was drowsy as a cat. But I knew why I had to stay awake, and it took a plaguey long time—round about an hour—then here came one along, lit up like a jack-o-lantern, furnace doors open, blowing out sparks, decks gleaming like ropes of jewels even this late, and bows grinning with white teeth. Conditions were just right.

"She's afire! She's afire!" I yelled, throwing off my blanket, and Zeb jumped up like he'd been snake-bit and headed lickety-split for the boat. But he didn't get very

far, on account of the line, you know, but took a header into the sand, landing on his chin.

Uncle Jim sat up and gave me a very long, hard look; then he went over to Zeb and inspected his foot.

"You tie that line on there, Zeb?"

"No, suh! I never touched it. Witches done this mischief on me, and I'm glad it happen, cause now maybe you'll believe—"

"*A* witch," said Uncle Jim, and hauling out his knife, he cut a twig off a small, springy willow.

It didn't bother me any, but was worth every whack. The only off note in the whole evening was that Zeb persuaded Uncle Jim to stop practically before he got started.

"Boys'll be boys," he said. "They's inclined to be prankish. In de case of Masser Davey, his min' ain't apt to develop up to de human stage for eight er ten years yet."

I was glad to be let off the licking, but I wasn't overjoyous about the tribute, so when we went back to bed, I popped out with a riddle myself, the only one I knew, but raspy enough to take this fellow down a peg, and show him whose mind was who.

I said, "If a calf skin makes the best shoes, what makes the best slippers?"

But when they gave up, I'd forgot the answer, confound the luck. I couldn't think of it to save me. I pulled up my blanket to drown out their laughing, and tried to get to sleep. I didn't pin it down as banana peels till they were both snoring again, so I concluded I'd spring it in the morning.

7

Now I've GOT to tell about how we went into town, and what happened, because I see I've been dawdling along, not getting down to brass tacks, but putting in too much conversation, and failing to "advance the narrative," according to Uncle Jim.

Well, when we reached the town, it wasn't Carruthersville at all, but a place, faded and seedy, called Pembroke, and by George if it wasn't in Arkansas! So we'd made good time.

We pulled up against the sloping mud bank, hauled the boat out a little way, and removed the saddle. Uncle Jim allowed we'd sell it; he said it took up too much room, and we were already on as familiar terms as he'd care to get.

At first, he said Zeb could watch the boat, because there were some shifty-looking loungers about, but then he changed his mind and said Zeb needed a "refreshment," too, whatever that was.

So we walked on up the bank. Three or four shantyboats were tied up at the landing, along with the usual number of skiffs and scows, and a smallish houseboat built on a flatboat instead of logs. It was painted with fancy lettering, something to do with a "Dr. Snodgrass," and looked out of place there amongst all those wrecks. All in all, Uncle Jim said, the scene fell short of uplifting. But when we got into the town it was worse—nothing but a mud street between straggly rows of unpainted stores, porch boards warped and worn, raggedy awnings in front of some, a slab bench or two full of loafers, dogs enough for all, railings to tie horses to, a trough in the middle of the street, with a hand pump, and several wagons in town even this early.

Everybody eyed us pretty curious as we passed, and I could feel Uncle Jim getting his back up. You could tell it by the way he walked a little more deliberate and stared back a trifle longer than was necessary. He lit a cigar, too, out of contempt, I judged. Ordinarily he was the politest fellow alive, but I'd seen him match the worst kind of rudeness and come out on top.

What set the tone of our whole visit, you might say, was when he approached an overgrown ox standing on a store porch with a beaver hat on and asked, "Would you mind directing us to the livery stable?"

This hayseed, a tolerable-looking man in some ways, was stretching himself, and when he finished he stared down at us and made an answer that struck me as off the track.

He says: "I feel so good I could fight a bear with a switch."

Uncle Jim studied him a minute, while pulling on his cigar, then said: "I wouldn't advise it. I understand they've got a law against fratricide in this state."

The man started to say something like, "Hey, wait a minute, now——" but we proceeded on, considerably slower now that Uncle Jim was sore.

The stable was at the end of the street, set back aways. We found the proprietor, a long-faced man with a vest on and a gold chain with a tooth hanging from it, currying down a lathered-up mare.

"Care to buy a saddle?" said Uncle Jim shortly, motioning Zeb to throw it down. "Top grain leather, Mexican silver mountings. Original cost was a hundred dollars."

The proprietor knocked off swabbing and came over, seeming perfectly friendly and courteous, which made a nice change in that town so far. But he was so gloomy I thought he might break into tears.

"What with? I haven't took in only four dollars and thirty-five cents this week, and a dollar of that was produce. Between you and I, and I wouldn't want this to go any further, if things don't look up soon, I may let the whole business go—land, buildings, horseflesh, tack and manure."

I could see Uncle Jim ease up a little.

"That is certainly regrettable. What appears to be the trouble?"

"I'm glad you asked. I dislike to be critical—it's easier to be critical than correct, as the fellow says—but the trouble lies in the present nature of the town. Boiled down, it ain't worth a puke."

"Indeed?" said Uncle Jim, raising his eyebrows in astonishment.

"Make it half a puke and not split hairs. No, the population's gone to pot, and the structures along with it. Tell me honestly now, did you notice a certain lack of civic spirit as you walked along?"

"On the contrary," said Uncle Jim, beginning to enjoy himself, "the town struck me as among the authentic garden spots of the nation. And the people themselves—urbane, courteous, graced in every—"

The proprietor interrupted with a guffaw that I thought might split the walls; then he took out a plug of busted-leaf tobacco and offered Uncle Jim a chew.

"That's the first genuine, outright horse laugh I've had in six months. And me with a stable," he added as an afterthought. "What happened was, the place has turned so no-account the steamboats won't stop by any more. For awhile, they'd put passengers ashore in a launch, dollar a head—mostly lawyers headed for the county seat, that would hire a rig—but they quit it because so many got dog-bit. I hate to admit it," he said, looking the gloomiest yet, "but there's been talk at the bank of throwing me off into bankrupt."

"No!" said Uncle Jim, thunderstruck.

"My old Daddy would turn over in his grave. It was him built it up. Well," he said, brightening suddenly, "let 'em. Let 'em go ahead. Sue a beggar and you get a louse, and so they'll find."

"It may not come to that," said Uncle Jim. "But since our time here is limited, perhaps you can tell me who might buy a saddle. With my apologies for changing the subject."

The proprietor knitted his forehead for a second, then he exclaimed, "Why, Arney Spottswood's your very man. He's rich, and his own saddle was thieved not a week back. Gonad"—this to a colored boy forking out hay— "scamper down and fetch Colonel Spottswood. You'll locate him playing pinochle in the tavern."

In ten minutes or less, the boy trotted back in and said, "He coming, Mistuh Sam. He sober, too, and mighty tempery."

Not far behind him, leading a barebacked gelding with curious gray spots, came that selfsame ox that had refused to give us directions. If this fellow was a colonel, I was commander-in-chief of the Zulus, and Uncle Jim he looked the same.

"Well, well," he said when he walked in and looked us over, "if it ain't the stray lambs. What's the account, Sam?"

"That there's a mighty spruce-appearing saddle, Colonel," said the proprietor, pointing. "Seeing as yourn was thieved, and your uncle dying and leaving you a thousand dollars, I thought—"

"Your *bought* saddle?" said the ox keenly to Uncle Jim; then he spit a stream of tobacco juice that just barely missed our feet.

Uncle Jim studied him, up and down, along with the tobacco juice, and said, very relaxed and polite, "My saddle—to your question. As to your spittle, keep it clear of my boots."

I could feel the old trouble coming, and saw Zeb shift around uneasily, out of the corner of my eye.

Taking no notice, the fellow leaned over and inspected the saddle; after which he said, flicking a silver buckle, "Trumpery Mexican gewgaws. Fancy, very, but will it stand up to pounding? Sprinter's a good dog, but Hold Tight's a better. What's your price?"

"Drop an offer," said Uncle Jim.

"It's your saddle, or so you claim; you ort to know its worth."

"It's *worth* a hundred dollars; that's what I paid, but I aim to sell it second-hand. Drop an offer."

Suddenly the ox roared out, in a fit of anger, "I don't

chaw tobaccer but once"—referring to answering questions, I reckoned—"and I spit where I please," whereon he spewed out another soaker, just missing by inches.

Uncle Jim removed his cigar from his mouth with his left hand, and shifted his weight on his feet; but he only stood there instead of doing anything.

It was as good as a play to watch them, and might have gone on forever, but the man evidently wanted that saddle, for he bent over to have another look. When he straightened up, he said, "Taking everything into account, the doubt of it being a *bought* saddle and all—three dollars."

I put my fingers in my ears to drown out the explosion of Uncle Jim's gun, but none ever came.

"In the circumstances," he said, "maybe it would be better if I bought your horse."

"*This* horse? Three parts Apaloosa pony and one part A-rab. There's quite a few wish they could afford him. Drop an offer," he said, as mocky as could be.

Uncle Jim knew horses—everybody in our part of Kentucky said so—and he went over this specimen like a man that had lost a flea. He got down to examine hooves, knees and fetlocks, peered in its mouth, measured the length of its teeth, poked in its ears and had a squint at the tail section, aloft and alow. Then I'm a speckled hyena if he didn't straighten up and say, "Taking everything into account, including suggestions of fistula, ringworm, heaves, swayback, glanders and spavins, *and* if you can produce papers of ownership, which I doubt— fifty cents."

I might have known.

The Colonel stepped back a pace, two or three shades paler, and snatched down some heavy harness from a peg. But just then a sour-looking stringbean wearing an eye-shade and garters on his sleeves appeared at the far doorway, with several others at his back, and called out, "Arney, let me see you a second."

Still clutching his harness, the ox wheeled and stepped out, and they held a confab, keeping their voices low but glancing up at us a time or two. The stringbean, who had about the same sappy appearance as the editor of our newspaper back in Hanksville, was holding something—a dodger or circular—in one hand.

They broke it off, and the ox walked in slowly to face us, whilst the others watched from behind him. And now, I'm blessed if he didn't very deliberately *take the left lapel of his coat and shake it,* while all the time staring hard at Uncle Jim.

I knew well enough this was a recognition signal of the Klan, and wondered what Uncle Jim might do. Well, if there was one thing you could be sure of, in a situation like this, he'd do what seemed to give the most offense to all hands.

So *he* leaned over and spat, and it wasn't any bad shot, either, but lit, most of it, not counting spray, right between the ox's feet. It was the first time I'd ever seen him cut loose like that. Commonly he swallowed it.

There wasn't a sound; dead still. Even the loafers back out of range waited without a word.

Taking another hitch, the ox *ran his thumb around the inside waistband of his pants.* He did it two or three times, keeping an eye on Uncle Jim's face, as before.

"If you're feeling itchy, scratch," said Uncle Jim, trying to be helpful. "And if you're troubled with body lice, I'd recommend you peel down your clothes and boil them. It's the only way—*Colonel.*"

"This is the fellow, boys," the ox sang out. "The cub fits, too. I think we know what to do. Leave off now and hew to regulations."

He made as if to go, but Uncle Jim whipped his Army revolver out from under his coat so fast you couldn't really see it and let go a blast at the top of the barn. A folded-up measuring stick with a hole through one end plopped down at our feet.

"That thing's been bothering me all along, peeping over a beam-edge," he said, putting up his gun. "A carpenter must have left it sitting on the beam. Come around and see me any time, boys—" he called out to the group in the doorway, but they scrambled off. They seemed in a hurry, because one of them ran out from under his hat, leaving it on the ground; I reckoned they had business somewhere else.

The ox backed out, pushing his horse along behind him.

"We'll meet up soon, sonny," he told Uncle Jim. "Don't have any worries on that score."

"Oh, I know, I know. But you'd better come at night, according to custom, and sneak up at my back. You'll feel more at home that way."

"You just wait," said the ox, and left.

Zeb and I took a big breath and the proprietor, looking as if it was the first time he'd ever showed any spunk in his whole life, walked over and shook Uncle Jim's hand.

"There's some that's tired of their bulldozing, and I happen to be one of them. They may punish me for it, but I'd like it known, open and clear, that I'm glad to make your acquaintance."

Uncle Jim acknowledged this speech with a nod, then said, "See here, do you want this saddle? You can have it, for ten dollars—on credit. When you get the money, send it to Grassy Plantation, Hanksville, Kentucky. But take your time about it."

The proprietor looked as if he was about to jump out of his skin for joy. "By George, this may make all the difference! I can raise fifty dollars on that saddle, and buy a horse."

"You mean to say you're in the livery business and haven't got a horse?"

"Not a blessed one. The last I had, Fauncher—light bay mare with a pustulating ear—fell in harness six months back."

"But how—?"

"Stabling—fodder, curry, water and stall, fifty cents. Weekly and monthly rates, of course."

We shook hands and left. I thought we'd certainly rush out of this ratty, rundown town, and Zeb said, "I ain't had such an appetite to haste in I don' know when; em men's bad clean through," but I'm hanged if Uncle Jim didn't declare that we'd get a square meal first, if it was possible without being poisoned. He was in such a contrary humor now he'd have found some way to show off if they were coming for him with a hearse.

So we tramped back down the street, with everybody looking on from both sides, and went into The New Imperial Hotel, a frame two-story building that was kind of tilted over on one side, as if a corner had sunk down in the mud. It had a room which was called the "Banquet Room," but there wasn't a soul in it except a man that was eating soup with his hat on.

We took two chairs at a table for four, and Uncle Jim had Zeb stand by, with a napkin over his arm. It was about as outrageous a sight as I ever saw, because Zeb still had on his forage cap and overshoes, and the rest of his clothes weren't in what you'd call ballroom condition, because of the boat, you know, and camping out. No matter how you lie, they *do* get a little ripe after you've slept in them for a week or so; there's nothing you can do about it. When a waiter finally turned up, scratching himself underneath, and seemed about to complain, Uncle Jim said, "My valet customarily tends my table after the food arrives. The fact is, he usually brings along a dog, too, to try things out on first. But we're in transit, by skiff, and have to make concessions to space."

Naturally, the waiter failed to make anything out of this idiotic drivel, but looked around in puzzlement at a number of people who had their faces pressed against the window, so Uncle Jim went on briskly:

"We'll have the *table dote* dinner, clear soup, sole, saddle of venison, a cheese soufflé with champagne, and, I think, some fruit and coffee to end up on. That's all, my man. You may go."

The waiter stood there, with his jaw hanging down, but finally he appeared to get a grip on himself, and said:

"There's hog meat and hominy; take it or leave it."

Uncle Jim started out of his chair, saying, "We probably got into the wrong room"—he glanced around and shook his head. "Of course we did, I was wool-gathering. What we were after was the *Banquet* Room, a mecca for jaded palates that I've heard sung up and down the river. Go to The New Imperial Hotel, in the watering resort of Pembroke, they say, and try the Banquet Room—"

By now, the waiter had caught on to all this sarcasm —any fool would—and had begun to get a little sore.

"This is the Bankit Room."

"Hog and hominy?"

"You heard me the first time, Mister."

"They go together?"

"You call for one and you get the other."

"Three orders of mahogany."

"Hog and hominy. What's the third one for?" the waiter asked, giving Zeb a suspicious look. "We don't serve niggers in here."

"I eat two," said Uncle Jim. "It's my favorite dish. Keep this under your hat," he said in a low, confidential tone, "but the truth is I came to Pembroke for the hog and hominy."

They were a painful long time getting the orders out, and when they did—in three old cracked bowls, along with some gray-looking bread that had green mould spots on it—it was about as untasty a dish as you'd care to find. And tough? Boiled rhinoceros hide would have been an improvement.

By now, the manager of the hotel, I figured, was watching from the doorway, besides all the people peering through the windows, and by jingo if Uncle Jim didn't summon him over. He kept him waiting awhile, too, while he held up and carefully examined a piece of meat from the bowl.

"You keep a cat?"

"Naturally. We'd be et out of house and home by rats otherwise."

"I'd like to see that cat."

"What do you mean?"

"I'm a cat-lover," said Uncle Jim. "Always was. Born and raised."

I was getting so jumpy, with all this tommyrot, that I couldn't swallow real good, and Zeb was standing on one leg and then the other, muttering.

The manager hung up a minute, then he went and fetched a sorry-looking cat, with burrs in it.

"That's all right, then," said Uncle Jim, brightening right up. "Clean bill of health," and he fell to eating with a good appetite.

"Say!" began the manager, reddening up, "I've got a good mind to—"

"Not a word," said Uncle Jim, waving good-naturedly. "I did you an injustice. I don't mind owning up. The cat's on deck, whole and hearty. Some more water," he said, lifting his glass.

"By God!—" burst out the manager, and left. Uncle Jim passed up the third bowl to Zeb and said, "Fall to."

"Now, Mistuh Jim. I don't min' standing here and listenin to the dog-drattedest nonsense ever I heard," said Zeb, "but I'm blowed if I be a party to anything this troubley. You can't take and push people *too* far. I know that for *sure*."

"Eat it, eat it. I regret your upright position, but it may aid digestion. People sit too much, generally."

Seeing Zeb gobbling away there, and he *was* tucking it in, the manager came rushing back and yelled: "What's going on here? We told you we don't feed niggers. I don't care if you *do* pack a gun, by God—"

"Don't excite yourself. Nothing's untoward here," said Uncle Jim. "I always take my valet along as taster. It's as much for your protection as my own. I know you wouldn't want to poison me—you don't look like that sort of man. Believe me, he isn't eating; he's tasting."

"*Tasting!* Why, he's already tasted up a whole bowlful. You don't—"

"Yes, devotion like that is rare in a servant these days. What about it, Zeb? All right? No," said Uncle Jim to the manager, "he feels he ought to taste another bowlful. He isn't sure yet."

"Listen, Mister, you better pay your bill and get out of here."

Uncle Jim sighed. "Just when I was getting fond of the Banquet Room. I'd hoped to take a suite at the New Imperial and stay on for the rest of the hog and hominy season. Well, so be it—"

He threw some money down on the table, and we left, but outside we busted into a perfect hullabaloo. People were running toward the river, all worked up with excitement, but looking happy and satisfied, too, so Uncle Jim judged that somebody must have had an accident.

But he was wrong; they had collared a very nice-appearing old gentleman with a handsome white hat on and a white suit, and a nicer young girl of about eighteen, and were whooping things up pretty hot. This old gentleman was the owner of the houseboat, that had "Doctor Ewing T. Snodgrass: Health Cures Effected, All Diseases" painted on the side. He operated a medicine show, while his daughter played the trombone, but his practice had run into rough weather, for two or three reasons.

An angry, red-complected man wearing an apron was standing on the bank, shaking his fist, and said Dr. Snodgrass had tried to sneak out without paying for a skiffload of provisions. But that wasn't the worst. On another trip down the river, when Dr. Snodgrass stopped off at Pembroke, a number of his cures had failed to take hold. In one case that could have happened to any doctor, and was purely an accident, he ladled half a bottle of his leprosy cure, Essence of Distilled Spooju, into a man suffering from delerium tremens, and the fellow went right ahead and died, probably out of spite, as Uncle Jim said. It struck me as a fuss over nothing, because they said this patient was ninety-two years old and had been in bad health, or drunk, for twenty or thirty years, but Dr. Snodgrass took the blame. The bottle was labeled wrong.

Dr. Snodgrass wasn't *always* right, as we came to find out, but he did do a lot of fine work, up and down the river. He was clearly in the wrong, for example, in giving one Pembroke citizen a bottle of Indian Snake Oil for what he diagnosed as Buckboard Rump, when the man had a piece of bone chipped off of his hip, where the wagon had hit a rut. Even so, I think Dr. Snodgrass could have got by with these trifling mistakes (and others) if it hadn't been for his remedy to keep coal-oil stoves from exploding. Now there wasn't a particle of danger in this preparation, which was called Nix-Combusto, being pure sand, without any quack additions, but a Pembroke widow that had a mania about fires put three or four times too much in her stove and the whole works blew out the side of the house, taking most of her furniture with it, along with her dog, which died.

Anyhow, they now had Dr. Snodgrass and his daughter, and were aiming to tar and feather them. It was the happiest event that had taken place in Pembroke all year, somebody stated. In the hurly-burly over these two unfortunate and maybe misguided victims, everybody mostly forgot about us, but one of the ringleaders of the crowd at the landing was Colonel Spottswood, and as soon as he saw us, he shouldered his way forward and says:

"You ain't forgot. Indeed not. You can stand by, as a spectator, for now, and see what's apt to happen to riffraff in Pembroke."

I had a bad feeling about this scene; it made me uneasy, because Uncle Jim had ceased being smart-alecky and was standing wholly quiet, but different, somehow, looking on.

"Here comes the tar and brush!" a man sang out, and sure enough, several of the country jakes were rolling a big black iron pot, waltzing it right along, down the street to the slope, and another had a basketful of chicken feathers covered over with tow sacking to keep them from blowing. They already had a whopper of a fire going, with a green stick to hang a kettle on, and they didn't waste any time rigging things up then throwing in several lumps of tar, which was in brick form and hard as rock.

"Strip 'em down!" somebody cried, and another said "What—the girl, too?"

There were several women there who had looked spiteful and mean before, but now they softened down and said, "It ain't right. The child's not to blame. She only blowed the sliphorn." For all their gossipy ways, women never can stand to see one of their own breed mistreated by a man, particularly a girl.

"Well, she played it might poor; she's lucky she ain't hung for it," a fellow answered, and all the men laughed, saying it was a champion good joke.

I was watching so close—scared, and disgusted, too—that I didn't notice Uncle Jim had left. I looked around, and he'd jumped up on Dr. Snodgrass's boat, which was tied to a derelict scow. He was standing on the front deck, with his revolver out, and now he said, in a voice that carried out over all the heads:

"Take your hands off those people." There was a cocking noise, as he pulled the hammer back with his thumb, and the crowd sort of gave way. All but Colonel Spottswood and two or three others. These people had counted on a tar and feathering to brighten up the dull times—it was a sport that couldn't possibly do any injury to them, and consequently was popular—and they hated to let it go.

"Release them," said Uncle Jim. "Stand aside so they can come aboard."

Everybody waited to see what the Colonel would do.

"And what if we don't?"

Uncle Jim fired a shot—threw it, almost—at the fire, and a number of blazing sticks zoomed up like rockets bursting. People nearby scrambled out of the way, so as not to get burned.

"Get the skiff," he told us, and Zeb and I hopped to work unfastening it, putting it in the water, and tying it onto the houseboat.

"Now, doctor, if you and your musical daughter will kindly step aboard—"

As they were crawling, pretty fast, over the scow and onto their houseboat, Uncle Jim delivered himself of a few insulting remarks:

"*Aren't* you a brave lot of scoundrels?" he said, looking them over slowly. "And *wouldn't* it have been an accomplishment to tar and feather a helpless old man and a young girl in her teens? It makes me sick to look at you. I've been in a fair number of towns in my day—north, south, east and west, as well as Mexico and points below —but this pimple on the posterior of the universe strikes the lowest note in my experience. If you want a suggestion, take a leaf from history. Follow the example of Caesar when he left Carthage. Don't just haul down the buildings—plough the ground up and salt it. No, don't thank me," he said to a fellow that was about to speak up and do no such thing—"anybody would tell you the same."

There was a lot of angry muttering, but nobody did anything, with that gun pointed at them, so Uncle Jim said, "Push us off," speaking to a couple of red-faced rustics nearby.

"Not me," said one of them, with surprising spirit.

A bullet kicked up mud about two inches from his left boot toe.

"Push us *off*," said Uncle Jim, but Dr. Snodgrass spoke up to say, "I beg your pardon, sir, but with all allowances for my gratitude, and that of my daughter, I have not, in fact, paid for these provisions." He pointed to a pile of tins and parcels heaped on deck at his feet. "Not to do so, to leave under any imputation of fraud, no matter how slight, would place a strain on my conscience that might prove an intolerable burden."

"I can well imagine," said Uncle Jim in a dry tone.

"However," continued Dr. Snodgrass, looking happy and energetic, "I think I have the perfect solution. Bereft as I am of cash at this moment, I can still make restitution in a worthier coin." He disappeared amidships for a second, then came back with a wooden carton.

"Twelve bottles of Dr. Snodgrass's celebrated Swamp Elixir, a specific for pneumonia, consumption, ulcers, cholera, catarrh, hepatitis, dropsy, fits, hemorrhoids and headaches. Internal or external use, good for man or beast. Hand it down, will you, son," he said to a young saphead at the bank, and then added, "If you don't mind my saying so, you look liverish. Take a pull of the Elixir; it'll work wonders for you, wonders."

As we drifted slowly away, with Zeb working a sweep in the stern, Colonel Spottswood fired a parting shot.

"You won't get fifty miles down the river, Burnie. You'll curse the day you set foot in this town."

"Oh, I was doing that ten minutes after I arrived. It's an unusually easy town to curse."

"Take a piece of advice," continued the Colonel. "Stay out in the middle of the stream; don't get close to a bank. Don't land, and don't go to sleep. Aside from that, have an enjoyable trip."

Uncle Jim waved and we drifted out of sight.

8

ONCE WE GOT around the bend, Uncle Jim assembled us on the forward deck, and said things would be happening fast, now.

It was late afternoon. We'd killed nearly the whole day in that town of Pembroke, and already it seemed like a bad memory. This craft was a crude flatboat with a likely structure erected on it amidships—one large room—about thirty foot long overall, with a stern sweep and one on each side, port and starboard, and could easily be handled by two people, if the river was normal and not rampaging along at flood.

In the fading but still hearty sunlight we had a chance to study each other for the first time. Dr. Snodgrass was upwards of seventy, I figured, tall, very robust and spry, with apple-red cheeks, whitish yellow hair that fell long over his shoulders, bushy black eyebrows, and a merry but concerned expression, as if he'd just dosed somebody with creek water but preferred to believe it was medicine.

His daughter Millie was beautiful, and had a companiony look. She looked *interested,* if you know what I mean, and didn't give you the feeling, when she was silent, that she was only waiting to shove in her oar, the way most females do. She had black hair done up in braids like a little girl, blue eyes, very white, even teeth, and a slim, strong body that Uncle Jim said was "full-blown," or something along that line. He said her father ought to take and truss her up, above the waist, because she hadn't any more on than a cotton frock, and she'd outgrown it. But she was one of these regular tomboys, and didn't like to wear any more women's clothes than necessary.

Anyhow, Uncle Jim told them part of our story, and said they needn't feel obliged to travel with us, because we might expose them to danger. But Dr. Snodgrass insisted. He said they appeared to be in some danger themselves, and would feel more comfortable if we went along for awhile "in tandem." I got the notion that trouble maybe wasn't any stranger to Dr. Snodgrass, but was apt to raise its head nearly any old time he stopped on either bank of the river. A doctor who makes his living like that—buying a houseboat, floating down the Mississippi, selling out in Orleans, and then returning to do it all over—is apt to find quite a few patients laying for him, with things like bull whips and tar pots. It's what they call an occupational hazard, and is common to all professions, in one form or another. Especially in Dr. Snodgrass's case, Uncle Jim said, when all of his remedies were "still in the experimental stage." "It has yet to be proved," he said, "that swamp water and cane syrup will cure anything but a love for swamps."

So Uncle Jim took command of the expedition about an hour out from Pembroke, and you may not believe it, but he put us across river to land above the first village we sighted. Then he sent me in after a bundle of oakum. When we were under way again, he said he could anticipate what was coming. Pembroke was at the upper end of a U-bend so sharp the river almost doubled back on itself, and would probably cut through, leaving that part stranded, by and by. "In the old days this was a prime spot for flatboat-sinkers, and I expect they've still got their hand in. We'll take pains to be prepared."

Dusk came on before we finished the bend, then dark settled down, with only a speck of lantern glow here and there in cabins off in the woods. We daren't land while it was light because the word would have spread on both sides by now, so we hadn't any choice except to run most all night, and get shut of this area. If a steamboat came along, we'd have to show a light, else be smashed over, but for now we were as dark as a pocket. Once in a while you could hear the water scush along the sides, when a breeze blew waves up against the current, but there wasn't anything else to tell where we were; we'd might as well been on the moon. Unless you looked up at the sky, that is. Looking up, a person could make out the outlines, down below. I don't know how that happens, but it's so.

Well, all of a sudden Zeb sang out:

"I heerd somethin, Mistuh Jim. I heerd a paddle dip, over yander."

He was always hearing something, or seeing something, or suspicioning it—especially if it offered some hope of a calamity—so I didn't pay much attention, but Uncle Jim seemed to believe him for once, and said, "Look sharp now, everybody. If they come, they'll bring people able at seeing in the dark, so they'll have the advantage."

It was just about then that I stepped into the house for a drink and felt the water. I yelled, "We're sinking! Water's coming in the bottom!" Uncle Jim skipped down in a second and cried, "Light the lantern low and keep it under wraps," then he tossed me the oakum and said to start looking for holes. Taking out his revolver, he scampered back on deck and commenced staring up at the sky and then down, to try and spot small boats, and sent Millie to give me a hand.

We went over the bottom, shining the light very faint, and found three places where water was bubbling up, so I jammed in oakum while she wedged it tight with a hammer and chisel.

Dr. Snodgrass had an old flintlock rifle that he'd taken in on a case, where he'd absent-mindedly treated a Chinese peddler for yellow jaundice, and Uncle Jim gave Zeb another revolver; we weren't too bad off for arms. But the water was coming up, in spite of all we could do, so I called Uncle Jim down again.

"Look alive, now," he told us, and you could see he was having a wonderful time; "let's catch them in the act." And the second a new bubble appeared, he fired a shot down through the bottom. There was a sound from below, a kind of choking noise followed by two or three heavy thumps against the boards and then silence.

Millie looked a little sick, but Uncle Jim said, "Now I doubt if they've brought another under-water swimmer for *that* work, so maybe we're beginning to see daylight." And after that he whipped out his knife and whittled a pine plug to stop up the hole. Before he was done, two or three shots rang out from above, we heard a kind of crash, and Zeb began crying for help. When we got on deck, the sky had lightened up some. We could see Dr. Snodgrass down on his back and Zeb fighting—jabbing with a pole—a man trying to climb into the boat from a skiff. He was doing very well, too, being astonishing strong in the arms and back, though usually timid, but the man had a good grip on the pole, and his companions —we could see three in the skiff—were starting aboard, too.

"Quick, Davey boy, with the lantern! Crouch down!" cried Uncle Jim. I fetched it in a hurry and held it over the side, the sickly glow flickering out over the water, but expected my arm to get blown off pretty fast.

Then there followed a perfect riot of shots from their side and ours, and a man from the skiff called out, "I'm hit bad, Merle; shove off, for God's sake!"

It was right here I dropped the lantern, for reasons that we found out soon enough. You could hear it plop into the water with a solid, splashy thunk, the way a rock does.

"They gone, Mistuh Jim," yelled Zeb. "I see 'em dreft off, but they ain't sprightly. They's two hit for sure."

"We've got problems of our own," said Uncle Jim, grabbing me as I started to keel over. I was shot in the arm, high up, clean as a whistle, and hadn't felt a thing before the dizziness set in. But that was only one of our misfortunes.

Dr. Snodgrass was lying dead still, his head all dabbled with blood on one side and his rifle resting butt-upward across his neck.

When Uncle Jim lifted him up a few inches, he whispered faintly, "Essence of Spooju."

"Forgive me for being blunt," said Uncle Jim, "but this is a case for a regular physician. Colored water may not fill the bill."

"Spooju," said Dr. Snodgrass, in a slightly stronger tone.

"At least make it brandy, or whiskey."

"He only swiped, Mistuh Jim," said Zeb, bending over with his nose almost on the deck. "He ain't skull-cracked or punctured."

"Prepared after an ancient formula of the Aztec aboriginal," said Dr. Snodgrass, still more weakly than usual, "the Distilled Essence of Spooju is, in fact, rich in those ingredients which have endeared *spiritus frumenti* to the more vulnerable elements of the human race." Taking a bottle from Millie, he tilted it for a hearty pull, reducing the contents about a third. "In a word, it's forty-three per cent alcohol. Efficacious for—"

"Oh, be quiet," said Millie, bursting into tears.

Late that night, we made the head of a large, wooded island and tied up. It was as much as thirty or forty miles below Pembroke, and practically safe. They'd patched up Dr. Snodgrass's head and swabbed out my arm, which was throbbing and hurting now. Zeb found some cobwebs, and soot off another lantern, and made a poultice, which he said would stop the bleeding. It did, too, but Uncle Jim said it would have stopped anyway. He very politely restrained Dr. Snodgrass from giving me a dose of Swamp Elixir, saying that I had none of the diseases previously mentioned, and he'd rather wait till I got one.

The boat was hauled out and repaired. Uncle Jim told us that flatboats were often sunk like that, used to be, with the oakum pulled out from below, and a few scoundrels were still at it, mainly around Cave-in-Rock, and Pembroke, and Fort Massaic, near the mouth of the Tennessee.

Still, he told Dr. Snodgrass and Millie that the raid would never have happened if the Klan wasn't after us three. He offered to leave them in peace, and we'd go on in the skiff, as before. But Dr. Snodgrass said it was the first time he'd had any real protection for Millie, and with his sort of practice, it was sorely needed. He begged us to stay on.

"Frankly, it would be a service," he said. "Do you happen to play a musical instrument, sir?"

"I'm afraid not," said Uncle Jim.

"I thought as much. You have more the look of an

outdoor man. Would it greatly inconvenience you to beat on a tin kettle while Millicent plays the trombone and I sing 'We'll All Go down to Rowsers'? I assume you have a sense of rhythm?"

"None whatever," said Uncle Jim.

"A pity," replied Dr. Snodgrass; then he explained that it would have been agreeable to "expand the unit," as they were "lacking in musical depth." But Uncle Jim persuaded him it would be risky to give a show for a few days anyhow, and by then, he said, we'd see what could be done.

For a week or more we ran nights, and tied up in the daytime. Then we switched, feeling out of the danger zone, and began to float along in the usual way. It was pleasant. It was about the end of June now, and the weather grew warmer as we made our way south. They had a little stove in one corner of the house, with a rickety flue and a piece of sheet-iron underneath, and the girl made the tastiest kind of meals on it. They rigged up a curtain across the middle, with another dividing the doctor's half, so we were comfortable. It beat skiffing, because you could walk around while traveling; neither did you run the chance of sleeping on wet sand if a rain came up during the night. We were under way by dawn nearly every morning. The river has a good smell then; wet, and fishy, and cool, but sometimes a little too fishy, if it's dropping and dead ones are left lying along the banks to rot. Whenever we could, we found a creek or slough to tie up in, because of the cleaner water.

Ordinarily we laid out trot lines each night. Zeb and I ran them in the skiff. A trot line is about fifty feet long, with hooks every few inches, and has a weight like an anchor on the outboard end, with a line fixed to a bottle or jug above, so a person can lift it out. The best bait is liver. It was a slim day when we'd only get two or three fish; mostly we snagged as many as half a dozen—cat, nearly all, and tender and good fried deep in pork fat.

Every few days we put in to buy produce—salt, and butter, and meat, and such-like—and once in awhile Millie and I picked a few things from fields, if a farmer's crops appeared overloaded and need thinning out.

Uncle Jim told Dr. Snodgrass and his daughter we were on our way to Florida, and said he hoped to get there before we were too old to enjoy it. The thing we planned on, he said, was to proceed on to Orleans, taking a paddle-wheeler as soon as it seemed healthy, and book passage from there down the Mexico Gulf to an island named Cayo Hueso, that the people now were calling Key West.

Dr. Snodgrass looked thoughtful. At last he sighed and said, "What kind of place is it, sir?" (He always either addressed Uncle Jim as "Sir" or, mainly, "Major," which Uncle Jim said was the easiest promotion he ever got, and he only wished Dr. Snodgrass had been his Commander in the war.) "Is the climate salubrious, or is it a low, marshy area in which the people might be given to pneumonia, consumption, ulcers, hepatitis, catarrh, cholera, blue b—"

"I've never been there," Uncle Jim said hastily.

We skimmed on down river, past Osceola, past Pecan Point, past any number of shabby little "landings," slipping by at night because it was such a known center of Klan work. And then, when he couldn't stand it any longer, Dr. Snodgrass stated that we'd better sell some medicine; his funds were getting low. His head had healed up, and so had the wound in my arm. But I had a very nice scar that they said would continue on, and be a pride to me the rest of my life. Comparatively few children had scars in their arms from the Ku Klux Klan, Uncle Jim said, and he said it might make me celebrated after the Klan was stamped out, for both he and Dr. Snodgrass agreed that this would happen.

We came to know Dr. Snodgrass better, also his daughter. Dr. Snodgrass was a gentleman born and reared, you see, and had gone to a medical school in Chicago for awhile, but he was a mischievous kind of boy, and had what they call a sense of humor. He left the school because he considered most of it humbug, and also after he prepared a potion to reduce nervousness in middleaged widows. It did reduce it, too, but it turned a number of them into drunks, being largely grain alcohol, so the university decided to let him go. According to his daughter, the people that ran the place were mournful about his departure, because they claimed he had the best bedside manner in the history of that school. They said he was a natural to go on out into practice and make a fortune, whether he knew anything or not.

But he was mightily relieved to get his freedom, according to Millie, because his uncle that cared for him died along about then, and Dr. Snodgrass was no longer beholden. He'd told her all about it. He could indulge his love for showmanship, and bolster it with what he had picked up in school, which was meagre, aside from the bedside manner. Altogether, before he quit, he'd run off with circuses four times, on each occasion being grabbed by the authorities and hauled back to duty.

He'd married young, to a very well-connected snake charmer (her mother was related to the Bullocks, of Georgia), but she died with her boots on, so to speak, having been bitten by a rattlesnake that they thought was charmed but wasn't. Later in life Dr. Snodgrass had married a lady cornet player, but she took a fondness for Essence of Spooju, which caused her to lose her lip, and eventually she went off to New York with a salesman. She was dead, now.

So you can see that Dr. Snodgrass's scramble up to his present fame hadn't been any bed of roses. He was a self-made man, and when you come right down to it, that's the best kind. The establishment of a practice like his, with many patients fighting their way up through crowds to kiss your feet, and others trying to get in a lick at you with a hatchet, takes some very special skills. Uncle Jim said so himself.

Millie was the daughter of Dr. Snodgrass and the second wife, the one that got a strangle-hold on Spooju. For the first fourteen years of her life, she went to a convent school in Chicago, and was highly educated. She could speak French, or so she claimed, and knew a lot about geography and history, including considerable material having to do with some Egyptians that spent all their time building tombstones. She told me about it now and then. But she was like her father in some ways, so when he finished his internship, which was conducted from the tail-gate of a wagon, and put his office on a houseboat, she skipped out and refused to go back. There wasn't anything they could do with her, Dr. Snodgrass said. She bucked like a steer when the school authorities turned up, and bit one of the head nuns on the finger. If Dr. Snodgrass hadn't dosed the woman with Spooju, and put her in a better humor, there's no telling what might have happened.

I don't want to show Dr. Snodgrass in what Uncle Jim calls a flippant or whimsical way, because he had his serious side, and was a fine man, taken all around. We were set back a good deal to find that he *believed* in those remedies, at least partly. That is, he had what was called theories. He said most human ills arose from boredom or unsatisfaction, and if you put the mind at rest, the body was sure to follow. Distilled Essence of Spooju was composed of forty-three per cent alcohol, as stated; water—pure if possible, but if not, something dipped out of a slough would do, because of the purifying effect of alcohol, you know (though he was very upright and careful to seine out things like water bugs, spiders, and pollywogs); cane syrup to make it taste good; and a kind of bright green coloring. A lot of people bought it on the strength of its coloring alone; it was beautiful.

Swamp Elixir was a different kettle of fish, having a tidy dollop of paregoric in it. Uncle Jim stated to us confidential that paregoric was nothing more nor less than opium, but Dr. Snodgrass contended that it was a proved medicine of good standing, and had been endorsed by leading physicians everywhere. He always tried to provide a base of fresh pump water for the Elixir, but it wasn't easy, of course, because people might see him, in little towns when supplies ran low, and wish to ride him out in the country on a rail. So he just went ahead and did his best. He had some other remedies, but these were his staples. He told us a good deal about his early struggles, and how his career stood or fell on bottles. It was troublesome to keep a stock that hit exactly the right note. "A bottle, to engender a sense of therapeutic confidence, must be the right shape and size," he said. "I could put

Swamp Elixir in whiskey bottles and not sell a spoonful from St. Louis to Orleans. A doctor's lot is a hard one —never forget that."

The only flaw in Dr. Snodgrass's equipment was his love of showmanship. It was there that his theories slacked off a little. As Uncle Jim explained it, Dr. Snodgrass had "an overflowing abundance of jwah de veev, along with a lively sense of the ridiculous." He never could resist perpetrating hoaxes on the human race—if they were harmless, that is. To tell you the truth, there were times when even we, who got to know him well, couldn't separate the serious doctor from the traveling medicine man having a picnic of a time.

Anyhow, here we were, all five together, cooped up on a pretty small boat, and it made an interesting situation. Dr. Snodgrass had been used to talking most of the time, before, but now he found it uphill going, because of Zeb. What's more, they disagreed professionally. If Dr. Snodgrass recommended his Golden Anodyne Nutrient for pernicious anemia, Zeb claimed it wasn't in the same class as a toad skin boiled in the sap of a juniper tree.

As the days slid by, Dr. Snodgrass kept agitating to stop and put on a show; he was flat broke for cash, and it made him nervous. He was a very proud man; honorable, too. Uncle Jim offered to loan him some money, but Dr. Snodgrass said it wasn't in his nature to take credit without putting up honest security. He said he'd be willing to let Uncle Jim have several cases of Spooju, and he more or less unconsciously started his spiel, but Uncle Jim turned it down.

So, in the end, we agreed to put in at a one-horse burg named Bosky Dell and sell some medicine. Nothing else would do. Uncle Jim wasn't really for it, but Dr. Snodgrass got so fidgety, it seemed like the best thing. He had one whole corner of the boat piled high with cases, so there was plenty of products on hand.

After an evening of bustle and meditation, from which you'd a thought he was maybe getting ready to play a violin concert in New York, he said he believed he'd push trusses.

"In the present area in which we find ourselves sequestered, sir," he said to Uncle Jim, "I have in times past allayed all the common diseases, along with some baffling cases of leprosy and sleeping sickness, but I have not, according to my notes, struck a blow against hernia."

"How do you know there's any hernia around?" asked Uncle Jim.

"On such occasions as I am supplied with trusses, there is hernia," said Dr. Snodgrass firmly. "It may be un-manifest, it may be incipient, it may be dormant, but there is hernia. It is my duty, the wearisome burden of a physician, to create an awareness."

Well, it didn't seem very sensible to me, and Zeb only snorted, but we left it at that, then turned in early for the night.

9

WE WERE UP even earlier in the morning, and floated around a bend toward Bosky Dell. But three or four miles before we reached it, Dr. Snodgrass asked us to put in on the Mississippi side; he wanted to check a case that he'd treated on the last trip. "They live on a farm very near to this landing," he said. "I'll return within the hour." But it was almost two hours before he got back; then we proceeded on to Bosky Dell, a small town without much in the way of trees or shrubbery, and a very poor landing. The river'd been rising, and things were all mud. Taking a hitch on his spirits, Dr. Snodgrass said we'd have to hire a hall. It had been his hope to tie up to a steamboat dock, and work from there, but this was impossible. The dock was rotten, besides being slewed around at an angle. What's more, the slope, as I said, was nothing but gumbo now, and not fit for any decent citizen to walk down.

"You take the average man with hernia," said Dr. Snodgrass, "and he couldn't make it. Or if he did, he couldn't get back up the bank. He might be compelled to spend the summer here."

"Even a case of incipient hernia," said Uncle Jim sarcastically.

Dr. Snodgrass paid no attention, and we went on into town. The people were cheerful enough, though idle, the way it generally is in those towns farther south. Later on, we learned that they had a feldspar mine here, so most everybody was pretty well off, thus could lounge around as they pleased.

Dr. Snodgrass rented a large empty store-room with a rostrum and a busted-out window, paying off with half a case of Liquid Vermifuge, one of his rarer medicines that he generally used only for the last stages of tuberculosis. He said the room was ideal, with the rostrum and all, including the broken window, that he said would admit a little ventilation, which was necessary in these towns that weren't strong on bathtubs, and also having a rear exit in case there was a riot. It had been used for a month by a traveling evangelist that had converted nearly everybody in sight six or seven times and then got them to sign a temperance pledge, after which he passed out cold—drunk. They rode him out of town on a rail, of course, but after they did, a loafer told us, it was found that a girl he converted, working with her private several nights after meetings (she being a tough case), was in the family way, so they were sorry they'd been so hasty to get rid of him. "He was just about the right cut and size for a shotgun wedding," the loafer said.

We helped Dr. Snodgrass carry up a variety of medicine, along with a large box of trusses, and a case of spectacles for good measure. Uncle Jim tried on a pair and said most were nothing but window-glass. A lot of them didn't even have glass in them, but were only rims.

Well, we set up shop, arranging things on the rostrum, while Dr. Snodgrass went around town and tacked on signs. By and by I slipped outside and looked them over. They were downright embarrassing. On one, fixed to the outside of the Post Office, it said, "Dr. Snodgrass's Celebrated Supportatory Trusses—for Men Who Feel Fatigue Upon Arising in the Mornings." On that basis, I needed one myself. Everybody felt tired when they got up in the morning, unless they were crazy. There was considerable more stuff about how you stood a good chance of losing your leg if you let a hernia go too long. Also, it said most people had a hernia but didn't know it. And then, on another sign, I'm a coyote if he didn't come out and include women. "Ladies' Hernia Problems Attended Privately—Trusses for One and All, Constructed After a Design by the 140-year-old Choctaw Chief, Wah-Wah-Too-Se."

Well, I happened to know that he only had one kind of truss, so I figured he was planning to peddle them out just the same to men and women. It didn't seem like good practice, somehow.

When we assembled back on the boat, before the performance, Dr. Snodgrass seated himself on a stool and went into deep thought, very dramatic, with his chin in his hand. Now and then he shook his head and sighed. It was perfectly plain that some idea of importance to the doctoring business was taking shape, and it was beautiful to watch.

Then he straightened up briskly and said to Millie, "After the trusses, I think we'll do the Lotus Bud routine."

"No!" she said in a low, passionate voice, looking quickly at Uncle Jim.

"It's necessary. I wouldn't consider it otherwise. We've covered the region with Spooju; and Swamp Elixir went begging in the next village on the last trip down. Also, if you recall, it attracted that tiresome protest from the fellow with the boat-hook. We'll sell a few trusses—bound to, unless I lose my voice—but I'm obliged to confess that this is a pretty spry looking group of males.

"Their problem, and I'll stake my reputation on it [Uncle Jim sort of gagged here, as if he had something in his throat], is reproductive. While the men look bumptious, the women have a hangdog appearance, *and you don't see enough small children around to wad a shotgun with!*"

"I *won't!*" said Millie, almost in tears, but Dr. Snodgrass went on as if he hadn't heard her: "This bears out a favorite theory of mine, and it coincides with a monograph on the subject by Dr. Heinrich Gotz of Vienna—"

"Working the Danube?" inquired Uncle Jim.

"—that sexual vigor is often in inverse proportion to muscularity. You take a man who makes a fetish of chinning himself on a bar, hunting, climbing trees, fi—"

Millie got up here and rushed out, and to tell you the truth, I didn't understand what all the fuss was about. Anyhow, Dr. Snodgrass said we must take over five cases of his Men's Kickapoo Gooser, and we got ready for the show.

When everything was assembled, Dr. Snodgrass had

Zeb stand outside the hall, wearing a white gown, like a nurse, with a sandwich sign over his head, saying "Cure One, Cure All—Step Inside," and beat on a tin pan with a spoon. In fifteen minutes or so, a fair crowd had collected. Some of them were roughhousing a little, and others looked sour, as though they might have been stung a time or two in the past.

Uncle Jim sat in a rocker, smoking a cigar and looking on, entirely removed from it all, but I'd promised to pass out trusses and spectacles and bottles and such, for what Dr. Snodgrass said would be a "very substantial emolument," or words to that effect.

Well, when the place was full, including both darkies and whites, and a good number of women, Dr. Snodgrass stepped out from behind a black velvet backdrop he'd rummaged up from his things—not ordinarily included in a doctor's kit, as Uncle Jim commented—and began to speak. He was dressed, head to foot, in a beautiful white Indian's costume, along with a headdress and feathers. It didn't make any sense to me, because he'd advertised himself all over town as "Dr. Ewing T. Snodgrass, D.C., M.P., Ph.U.," and if that sort of name could be identified with any particular Indian tribe, it had escaped my attention so far.

Almost his first words cleared it up, I'm glad to say. They weren't *quite* his first, for he led off with several sentences of humbuggery Indian talk, during part of which he looked toward the heavens, or, rather, toward a hole in the ceiling where a strip of tar paper hung down —chewed off by rats, likely—and raised his arms aloft, then went into a very loud chant. It appeared to me he was asking for trouble, because a little more noise aimed in that direction might bring the whole roof down on our heads, and end the meeting.

Anyhow, nothing happened, so he broke into a sunny smile and said, "Good, and ailing, people of Bosky Dell, I address you in Choctaw, as a fitting preamble to my remarks this afternoon on the subject of health, cures, prevention of disease, and eradication of symptoms. A goodly number of my formulae, yes, the greater majority, were early supplied me, a beardless child captured by marauding redskins, through the kindly offices of Choctaw medicine men who for hundreds of years had passed them down from father to son—"

"How'd they happen to give them to you, Doc?" asked a big sleepy-eyed rube who was a kind of leader of the roughhouse group.

"I'm glad you asked me that, sir," said Dr. Snodgrass gravely. "It's a relief to me to find that you're awake. For a minute, I thought somebody had let a horse in here and he was asleep on his feet."

Well, the roughhouse group practically broke up with hilarity, slapping each other on the back and shoving, but the man that spoke turned mighty red and looked sore for a minute. Then he gave out a sheepish grin, and let it slide. He was a good sport.

"In answer to your question, and it's a *good* question," said Dr. Snodgrass, with a comradely smile, to show it was all in fun, "I was a sickly child, with most of the known ailments plus two or three they hadn't thought up names for yet, so naturally the medicine men buckled down over my case. You could almost say they made a career of it. In the end, they saw that, in being cured, I had absorbed virtually all the medical knowledge held by that tribe, so they decided to go the whole hog and give me the rest.

"Yes," said Dr. Snodgrass, wheeling suddenly toward the other side of the platform and limping very slightly, "you might not believe it to see me now, *but I was totally unable to walk till I was twenty-four years old!*"

Well, they *did* sit up and take notice! Even the ones that had been so comical before, pushing and gouging, looked serious and thoughtful.

"You ask what did it?" cried Dr. Snodgrass. "I'll be happy to tell you," and he threw open his Indian Jacket, showing that he had two of those ridiculous trusses strapped on, one on each side. I never saw such an outrageous sight.

"*Here is the secret!*" he shouted. "Trusses designed, after suggestions from the medicine men, by Chief Wah-Wah-Too-Se himself. I'd had a compound double hernia all along, with complications of fibrosis, osteo-jaundice, and yaws."

Dr. Snodgrass dropped his voice down to a sincere, confidential level, and said, "Friends, I wish you to believe that I was walking, nay—I was running, leaping streams, and participating in the Indian games, *within a week after I put these trusses on.*"

I thought he was going to break down, and I'm not ashamed to say that I had to blink pretty hard to keep the tears back myself. A boy like that, sitting on all fours for twenty-four years, suddenly finding himself as able and spry as anybody. It was enough to work on the emotions of a Hottentot, and I saw several women swabbing at their eyes.

Dr. Snodgrass then told the crowd a little about hernia, and I was glad to hear it, because I'd never exactly realized what it was, before. He explained how the muscles in the outside stomach, or peritonitis, got inflamed from eating the wrong kind of food, and caused an inner swelling not visible except under a microscope, where the legs joined onto the body part. The sockets didn't heave and haul right. At the least, a person felt tired now and then, and maybe irritable or depressed, and at the worst, your legs fell off.

You could see it was a satisfaction to the people to hear about this, because it was entirely new information to most of them, just as it was to me. And Uncle Jim, later, said it broke fresh ground in his experience, and would probably come as a piece of original pioneering to the whole medical fraternity.

"It happens," said Dr. Snodgrass, "that I have on hand a limited number of the Chief's appliances, for both men and women, and before our regular clinic gets under way, I'll be willing, though reluctant, to let them go, one dollar each, straps and instructions ten cents extra."

As many as a dozen men swarmed up and plunked down their money, while Dr. Snodgrass turned down a few that wanted to pay off in turnip greens or catfish, and there was a scramble of adjusting and tightening. The only hitch came when a very neat, well-shaven man spoke up to say, "I thought trusses were meant to be worn *under* the clothing, Doctor."

"Another good question," sang out Dr. Snodgrass. "This particular design, not duplicable anywhere else on earth, except in the lodges of Choctaw tribes that shall remain nameless, can fit either under or over. They're meant for emergency use, and I don't mind saying, though it may perhaps strike a note of mild indelicacy, that it's many an Indian brave I've seen in the summer wearing *absolutely nothing else*. No, some of them gained the notion—incorrectly, as it turned out after exhaustive research by myself and my colleagues—that any further impedimenta might hinder the function of the appliance."

Dr. Snodgrass stopped, with a kind of frown, and I could see his mind toying with the possibilities. Sure enough, he was unable to resist adding a footnote that sort of gave the whole thing a black eye, it appeared to me.

"If you don't think a group of otherwise healthy Indians stamping out the annual corn dance while wearing nothing but trusses provides an unusual and eccentric sight, then you good people of Bosky Dell are even more widely traveled than I'd thought."

He sold thirty or more trusses to men, and you could see right off that they made a big hit. The patients hitched up their legs, and strutted back and forth, saying, things like: "Now that *is* better!" and "The Doc's right —I had a hernier all along," and "This is the first time I've felt really able in fifteen years." Still and all, these fellows *did* seem odd, outfitted so, and I saw that clean-shaven man look disdainful, as if everybody in town had suddenly turned into a lunatic.

But he got a worse jolt when Dr. Snodgrass raised his arms again and shouted that if the women in the house would step behind his velvet partition, they'd be taken care of by his young female assistant, a Chinese specialist just arrived from Hong Kong. I sneaked back for a minute, to see what was going on, and he had Millie dolled up in a white-and-gold Chinese costume, with side slits way up the legs, and a fit as tight as paint. What's more, she didn't have another stitch on, according to Uncle Jim.

He said she would of looked decenter naked. Her eyelids were blackened up, to make them seem narrow, with little lines running out from the ends, and her eyelashes seemed longer than is customary. They could say what they wanted to; I thought she was beautiful.

She fitted several trusses to women that complained of having backaches, or shooting pains, or what they called being "off their feed," or grouchiness, or childbirth, or another of those female complaints, placing them outside their clothes, but one woman insisted on hitching up her skirts for an inside job, and they saw me and shooed me out. She said what were they running here, some kind of peep show? It was humilerating.

When I went back out front, Dr. Snodgrass had uncovered his box of spectacles and was lecturing on the importance of good vision. As I stood watching him, I realized that we were maybe inclined to laugh him off too much, particularly Uncle Jim. He was a real doctor. Another man, a faker, might have gone ahead and peddled that window-glass as fast as possible, thinking only of the money, but Dr. Snodgrass explained the whole eye business first, and he did a bang-up job of it, too. He knew what he was talking about. To lead off, he told about the different parts of the eyeball, the iris, the cornet, and the retinue; then he went into considerable technical detail, known only to doctors, and first-class doctors at that, saying that, "The vitreous body, or *humour,* is surrounded, as I need hardly tell you, by both the superficial fascia and the opthalmic canal, into which empties the tarsal plates. Ordinarily, this need not cause concern, unless there has been a dislodgement of the optic stalk. It can happen to anybody; don't worry about it. The condition is easily correctible, and at a minimum cost. What we *don't* want to do," he went on, looking virtuous and noble, "is put anybody in spectacles who doesn't need them. It wouldn't be right, it wouldn't be proper, and, indeed, it would provide a downright violation of my Hippocritic oath—"

That clean-shaven man burst into laughter here, then turned on his heel with a snort and walked out.

"Judge Travers seems dead set against you, Doc,"

somebody called out, but another said, "Oh, shucks, he's always spoiling things around here. It was him that stopped lynching before they flogged out a confession first. Perfect kill-joy."

"In every clinical group," said Dr. Snodgrass soberly, "there is always a voice of dissidence, a skeptic, a retarder of progress. It has been so since the invention of curative medicine. Pay it no mind; the man is very probably sick. Zeb, quick, here! Take this bottle of Liquid Vermifuge, find that fellow, and present it to him with our compliments. Now, then—to business."

To weed out those that didn't need spectacles, Dr. Snodgrass set up one of his "charts," which had several lines of lettering on it, ranging from big down to small, and put a chair facing it across the platform.

"All right—first man," he said briskly. A young country-jake, with straw-colored hair tumbled every which way, sat down, grinning, and read off the top line, then the second, and after that, the third.

"Now the fourth," said Dr. Snodgrass.

"Why, there ain't no fourth; or none that I can see."

"My friend, you need glasses. David, will you be so good as to fit a pair of spectacles to this good man?"

When I got through, I looked back at the chart, and by George, if it *didn't* have a fourth line, now. But it didn't before; I'd been up close and seen it perfectly well. Somehow or other, standing there alongside, he'd switched them. It gave me a peculiar feeling about the whole clinic, but I reckoned he knew what he was doing, so I didn't say anything.

Upshot of the session was that he sold spectacles to about half the people in the crowd, or until he ran out of the kind that had glass, after which he sold the rims to a number of darkies, explaining first that they needed glasses, all right, or would soon, but that their faces weren't yet conditioned to the feel of them, and this would take care of it.

I should say that five or six people held out very strongly against buying glasses; they refused to budge, and said there wasn't a particle of use in it, so Dr. Snodgrass gave up on them, but since they were wearing glasses already, it didn't reflect any on his diagnosis.

What Dr. Snodgrass had called his Lotus Bud routine was the most astonishing part of the show. When he had milked out the last dime for glasses, he had Millie tiptoe forward, very pert and Chinesey, fluttering a fan, now, and introduced her as Dr. Lotus Bud Chan, formerly a person of high birth, in a mandarin's house, but now an authenticated doctor with a thriving practice in Hong Kong, unless she was on a "sabbatical," which she was now, assisting Dr. Snodgrass. Then he asked her to tell her story.

I have to admit that Millie talked very well, although she seemed to wiggle around a good deal, besides falling into a singsongy kind of tone that sounded like a person playing a musical saw, but needing a few lessons, too. What's more, she addressed herself chiefly to men.

She explained how China had got into terrible trouble during something called the Whang Fu Dynasty. The birth rate dropped down to practically zero, so that there was a lively chance the entire place would be wiped out. (This certainly didn't jibe with what they'd taught me about China in school, because they said the country had always been so overrun with people they were reduced to eating birds' nests and bamboo.) Anyhow, the Emperor was worried, as he naturally would be, with a chance of losing his situation, so he offered thirty million yen, or two thousand dollars, for a remedy to restore what they called "vitality in men."

All the scientists got to work right away. It was a tough nut to crack, because this kind of medical problem was brand new. Everybody had just about prepared themselves to see the race die out when a new young scientist that hadn't any standing at all—He Wee Tuck —came along with a discovery that solved the whole works. It was practically a miracle, Millie said, jouncing around on her tiptoes and fluttering the fan.

By now, the crowd in front of her was really interested, so they shoved up to hear the rest. According to Millie, this fellow Tuck had been prowling around in Inner Mongolia and ran across a lot of small, frog-like animals.

Every now and then a striped one turned up amongst them, and Tuck made an investigation, collecting several thousand altogether.

"What scientist discover," said Millie, twisting herself around in what Uncle Jim said later was a brazen and wanton way, "was that striped frogs were *males,* in proportion one to fourteen-hundred females. Great scientist velly velly excited—what was source of vigor these males possess?"

Well, she went on, Tuck lit into this thing with both fists, keeping a number of textbooks handy, and found that the males had a small, curious sac at the base of the spine. He named this the Queeli Queeli sac and extracted quite a few, grinding them into a powder. Then he got on his horse and dusted out of there for the Emperor's court. The first man they tried it on was the Emperor's uncle, who was eighty-seven years old and in rotten health for his age. With the whole assembly of nobles watching, the old man ate some powder, straightened up, threw away his cane, cried out *Yang Foo-kee!,* which Millie said was the Chinese version of *Hurrah!,* and lit out down the corridor after a fifteen-year-old temple dancer.

To sum it up, Tuck's powder saved the nation. It worked wonders, resulting in China's overpopulated condition, and Millie, as Lotus Bud Chan, a direct descendant of the mandarins, had the secret formula.

"Yes," boomed out Dr. Snodgrass, walking over beside her (but not limping this time), "we have been fortunate enough to manufacture a limited amount of Queeli Queeli powder, which, after the Chinese wish, bears the American trade name of Men's Kickapoo Gooser. We are temporarily in a position to let it go at a dollar-fifty a bottle, guarantee assured."

"Mister," cried out a woman in the rear, working her way forward through the people by main strength, "is that the stuff you sold me last year at Dobbsville?" When she reached the rostrum, we could see she was expecting a baby, and pretty soon, too, from the looks of her. She seemed happy.

Dr. Snodgrass gave her a keen, though kindly, inspection, and said, "Why, I believe I *do* remember. You're Mrs.—ah, don't tell me, now—Mrs. Par—"

"Mrs. Clyde Perkins."

"And your husband was bedfast, weighing ninety-two pounds, with nervous exhaustion and a shriveled prostate? Yes, I recall the case well. It seemed hopeless."

"Mister," she said, "I'd like five more bottles of that remedy, and I've brought in cash to pay," upon which she plunked down seven dollars and a half, silver.

"I don't know," said Dr. Snodgrass, musing. "Ordinarily, we only permit two bottles to a patient, but no, forget it—in your case we'll nullify the rule. David, provide Mrs. Perkins with what she requests. Careful you don't drop them, now."

After that, the ice was broken. Nearly everybody there fought for the Gooser, and I noticed about as many women buyers as men. That amazing old humbug sold every bottle he had on hand.

We were just ladling the last out when there was a noisy commotion outside, and several people rushed in to cry, "A man's broke his back, down on the wharf. You're needed there, Doc."

Well, says I to myself, let's see what you can figure out *now*. Here was an authentic case where a poor devil really needed treatment, and it wasn't anything that could be fixed with Swamp Elixir, either.

Dr. Snodgrass had the decency to look rattled for a minute, then I'm blessed if he didn't snatch up a black-leather kit he had—filled with worthless nostrums, like enough—and bray out: "Lead the way, gentlemen, and do it in a hurry. It may not be exactly in my line, but my Oath precludes me from hanging back in any medical emergency."

But when we got there, with half the town running helter-skelter down the mud street toward the river, and a number of children, and dogs, cats, chickens and pigs squawking to get out of the way, a professional-appearing gentleman dressed in black was bending over the victim on the wharf, so it looked as if there was a real doctor on hand already, thanks to goodness.

It was a pitiful sight. The man was gasping his last, I

reckoned, while his wife bent over him, slapping his wrists and moaning. They were new residents, living up river, and were canoeing down for provisions, but when he tried to climb up onto the wharf, he fell with his back divided over a boat roller.

The professional-appearing man was a doctor, from the next county, who had happened to be passing through a-horseback, and had seen it all.

He shook his head sadly, then placed one of those heart cones to the man's breast, which had practically stopped moving, and said in a whisper, "There's nothing can be done. I'm afraid our unfortunate brother is about to join his Maker."

The wife broke into a perfect torrent of sobbing, and most of the men took off their hats. The women were swabbing at their eyes, saying things like, "Oh, that poor, poor thing," and "It's too cruel, at her age," and such like, and then the doctor looked up and saw Dr. Snodgrass standing there, saintly and impressive with his goatee and white-yellow mane.

As soon as he was noticed, Dr. Snodgrass bent over and said, "Vertebral severance? Or a hiatus in the vital fluid?"

"I was unable to locate a major severance, sir," said the man. "Indeed, the case is extraordinarily puzzling, though there's no question of deep spinal involvement." And then, half standing, as if he'd just heard Dr. Snodgrass's question, "Why bless my soul, are you a doctor?"

Dr. Snodgrass nodded gravely, while taking a closer look at the victim, who appeared to be dead, now. "Yes, a poor but struggling practitioner in the vineyard of Aesculapius. Dr. Snod—"

The man sprang to his feet. "You aren't, you couldn't be, Dr. *Ewing T.* Snodgrass, the worker of miracle cures?"

Dr. Snodgrass looked embarrassed, but proud, too, and I began to take back all the bad things I'd been thinking.

"Then you might have at hand a bottle of your celebrated Golden Anodyne Nutrient. For God's sake, say you have! It's our last chance."

Dr. Snodgrass stood tugging at his goatee, muttering,

"I don't know; I just don't know." Then he barked out, "Millie, that is, Dr. Chan, fetch me a bottle of Nutrient, and make it quick!'"

He and the other doctor lifted the patient's head up and forced some liquid between his lips, then did it again, and, in a minute, a third time.

You never heard such a cheer go up. That fellow opened his eyes, batted them a few times, and said, "What happened?" *And then he got up and stood!* He swayed a little, and put one hand on a bitt, but he stayed upright.

Well, everybody just went to pieces. His wife threw her arms around Dr. Snodgrass's neck and kissed him three or four times, and so did most of the other women. A number of men slammed their hats down and stamped on them.

"In the entire course of my professional career," said the doctor from the next county, "I have never seen a more dramatic exhibition of therapy. I've heard of your Golden Nutrient—indeed, what reputable physician hasn't?—but I'd never realized its full potentialities before. Marvelous, marvelous!"

"See here, Doc," one of the men in the crowd spoke up, "ain't you got any of that remedy for general sale? We're glad to see this fellow healed up, naturally would be, but it ain't fair, not letting it out to the public at large."

I felt sorry for Dr. Snodgrass. You could see he was in a tight spot. He didn't *want* to use the medicine unless there was an emergency, on the order of a back-breaking, but he didn't have any choice. These people were bound to have it.

At last he held up both hands in surrender. "Very well, good citizens of Bosky Dell, I'll let my present stock go, and try to prepare a new batch as I travel along. I pray to Heaven I'm able to finish it before something terrible like this happens," and he waved to the patient, who was now fully recovered.

In the next five minutes, he sold a hundred and ten bottles of Nutrient, or all that he had, and the townspeople scampered on up the hill. They seemed anxious to get home before he changed his mind.

Just at dusk, when we slid out, I had a pretty bad shock when not only the other doctor but the man with the broken back, along with his wife *and* the woman expecting a baby who'd turned up at the clinic, sneaked onto the houseboat. This last woman didn't appear to be expecting any longer, now, but was perfectly flat and trim. We had a lantern going, and Dr. Snodgrass was counting his money. He looked up, not in the least decomposed.

"Well, old friends, you did noble, noble. Let me introduce a former colleague," he said, turning to Uncle Jim. "Washington Gates, originator of the much-sung Omnibus Balm of Gilead, an absolute specific for everything, now retired for reasons of ill health to a farm six miles distant. His brother, Monroe, and wives. Colonel Burnie, of Grassy Plantation, Kentucky."

Dr. Snodgrass gave each couple twenty dollars, and they left, because they had to canoe up a considerable distance partly in the dark, and it wasn't any easy job, particularly, as Uncle Jim told them, a little sourly, for a man that had just got over a broken back.

Before we cut our houseboat loose, Dr. Snodgrass paid me the "substantial emolument" he'd promised for helping. He had a remarkably fine memory, and was wholly honest in matters like that. It was two bottles of Essence of Spooju, but when I went out on deck to take a swig, Uncle Jim grabbed them and dropped them in the river. He said there had been enough damn foolishness around here for one day.

10

I SEE WHERE I've dawdled too much again, without doing what Uncle Jim called getting on with the narrative. But I've got to tell about one more stop that changed our journey all around, and then I'll be off for Florida, though not exactly in the same old way.

It was deep summer now, and the river generally had a mist rising off it early in the morning, ghostly and still. We ran daytimes, in spite of what Dr. Snodgrass said was "double jeopardy" at the moment. That is, he claimed that besides our Klan troubles, there might be an upheaval from the citizens of Bosky Dell, because he said many medicines ran the "risk of a reaction," especially if the people found out what was in them. Even so, he had got himself back in a frame of mind where he thought he had done those lunkheads a favor, and was lording it over Zeb about as painful as anybody could stand it.

"It's psychological, you understand, Colonel," he said to Uncle Jim, who had been a captain in the war, as he often mentioned to keep from being promoted illegally every three or four days. "If they *think* a truss is efficacious, then it *is* efficacious, even if it's strapped onto a goat. And the same applies to other cures. I'll venture a sizable sum that Bosky Dell, Mississippi, is the healthiest town in the United States for several months to come. They'll *wallow* in good health."

"They take and drink that Nutriump, there won't be nobody *left* to be healthy," said Zeb. "They'll all be daid, and what ain't daid'll be creppled, from hitching on a trusk. Let a little time pass, en I wouldn't go back to that town for a pass through the Pearly Gates. It'd be too gashly."

Uncle Jim knew some people that had a big plantation near Vicksburg, and he said we must visit them. It was a Mr. Paxton Farrow, who he had fought with in the Mexican War, though not on opposite sides, if you know what I mean. What I mean is, they hadn't fought *each other,* but had fought side by side, or close by. Sometimes, with even the best writers, the simplest kind of sentence is apt to jump the fence and take off on its own. You've got to put a pretty tight rein on them if you want to keep the meaning clear. I don't mention that to sound braggy, but only to set it down for use by other good writers who may possibly be coming along in the future.

Well, we talked it all over and agreed that it might be restful to tie up awhile. Things *did* get a little cramped even on a houseboat. Dr. Snodgrass was no longer fidgety, but had some money now, or all the money that was in Bosky Dell on the day we landed, and Uncle Jim said we were probably beyond the reach of the Ku Klux Klan.

Another reason for stopping was that Millie was getting sweet on Uncle Jim, according to Zeb. I didn't notice it myself, but spent most of my time around her trying to keep from learning how Cornwallis crossed the Delaware, and such other rot. She was a nosy bother. Whenever I stretched out for a nap, or to fish, she laid into me. Uncle Jim put her up to it, partly, but that didn't make it any easier. She walked around barefoot, wearing a low, floppy blouse, and had a habit of slipping up behind you to fire questions. They'd given me some books to read, and I'd promised to swallow a little out of each one every day, but she generally caught me unawares. It was worse than going to school. I'd be just about to doze off in the sun, whilst watching the shore line slip by, with its nice pine trees and now and then an unpainted clapboard shanty in a clearing, and all of a sudden:

"What did George Washington say to his troops when he left?"

"How'd I know what he said? I wasn't there."

"It's in the book, numbskull. The Farewell Address to his Troops."

"Well, I was mulling that over, and I don't think he said anything to his troops. I think they collected up their pay and shoved. I don't imagine they'd stand around leaning on their guns, waiting for somebody to make a speech, once the war was over."

"Would you care to have me call your Uncle Jim? Maybe he can refresh your memory."

I wasn't looking for trouble of that kind, of course, so I usually allowed to try harder, keeping my fingers crossed; then she'd tuck right into it again.

She says: "We'll take up Greek history. You've read the book, I suppose?"

"I read as far as you told me. You said Chapter Ten and about a hundred lines in Eleven. I did it, and marked it," and I showed her where I'd numbered the lines up to a hundred, so as not to go over.

"Very smart-aleck. You can erase those later. Now, then, who was Socrates?"

"He was a fellow that loitered around on street corners, out of work, but he talked so much they declared him a public nuisance and threw him in jail."

"Is that *all* you can say on the subject of Socrates? Is that all he means to you?"

"He doesn't mean a thing to me. I'd a helped him if I could, but I wasn't on hand. It happened before I was born."

She said, "Sometimes I think you're the dumbest-headed fool I ever met. I don't believe you can learn *anything*."

"I guess you're right," I told her. "In fact, I know you're right, so if it's just the same to you, I'll turn in these books and go on and take a nap."

She raised her voice a little and called out, "Major *Bur*nie! Major *Bur*-nie!"

"All right," I said, "let it go. What is it you want me to know?"

"We'll take a look at the grammar. You've studied the grammar book?"

"That happens to be one I enjoy," I said. "Grammar's in my line, somehow. There isn't any use trying to catch me up on grammar, because I've got it down cold. Frankly, I advise you to skip it. Pass on to something else."

"No doubt. But I tell you what let's do—let's *pretend* you don't know it, and go over it anyhow."

Confound the girl, she wouldn't take anybody's word for anything. She was so superior it almost made you lose faith in the human race.

"First off, we'll consider Lesson 27, the different uses of saw and seen. Do you remember the chapter?"

I couldn't help but laugh. "Go ahead, try and trip me up on saw and seen. It's the easiest chapter in the book."

"All right, then, in the following sentence, which one would it be: 'The boys hadn't —— Mr. James anywhere.' "

"Mighty tough, isn't it?"

"Just go ahead and answer, without the frills."

"Very well, then—it's *saw.* Only you got it wrong yourself. 'The boys hadn't *sawed* Mr. James anywhere.' It was probably because they couldn't find a saw. I remember that fellow James, and he was as mean a man as ever lived in Kentucky. Now, if you don't mind my saying so, I'd learn the thing myself before I lit in on me."

She took a swipe at me with the book, but missed; then she said, "I'm not going to stand much more of this; you can either come up with a sensible answer next time or I'll fetch your uncle."

I didn't say anything, so she dribbled on with some rubbish about run and ran. I knew it well enough, so I hadn't any worries.

"In the following sentence, which one is it? 'Yesterday, Mary —— a splinter into her finger.' "

"I'm sorry," I said, "but that one won't work. You'd like me to say *ran,* but I'd be doing the whole subject of grammar a disservice if I did. Not me; get somebody else."

"Why *can't* you say ran?"

"I'll tell you, Miss Smarty. If the girl *ran* a splinter into anything, it'd be her foot. So what have you got to say about *that?*"

"Maj-or *Bur-*"

"All right, all right. Quiet down. I'll nail the next one. Anybody can make a mistake."

"You didn't *make* a mistake, you *are* a mistake. What's the matter with you, anyhow?"

"I don't know. I never have been able to learn anything. It makes me nervous."

I don't believe I ever saw a girl so red in the face. She was delicate; it didn't take anything to upset her. I certainly didn't want to hurt her health, so I said, "Never mind that, Millie, let's get on with the grammar."

She gave the book a spin across the deck. "I've had enough grammar. Consider the subject closed. I could teach a jackass to write essays with his hind feet before you could learn grammar. We'll take up geography, then I'm through for the day. There's a limit to what the human can stand."

That was bad news to me. I hated to see her let go so easy. It gave me an unhappy feeling about the girl for a minute or two.

"You've read the book, *Places and People?*"

"I went through it with a fine-tooth comb."

"Studied the maps?"

"Every last one."

"Well, then, where's Venezuela?"

"How do you spell it?"

"What's the difference how you *spell* it?"

"It makes a good deal of difference to me," I said, "because I want to get it right, and not confuse it with something else. There are quite a few of those V's."

"I'm going to count to ten, and—"

"Is it in Italy, with canals running through it?"

"It is *not.*"

"You sure? It's easy to get mixed up about a thing like that. Maybe you'd better check it."

"I think we'll just call Maj—"

"Then it's in South America, on the north coast, with Colombia on one side and Brazil below, with the Orinoco River running up the middle."

I thought she was going to hug me. "Good, Davey! That's good! It's the first statement you've made today that was above the mental level of a chimpanzee."

I thanked her, being naturally pleased, and said, "What else do you want to know about it?"

"Well, what's it like? Tell me a little about the country, and the people."

I have to admit it was fun in a way to make her happy, so I spoke up in a hurry. "It's pink—the whole works. Ground, buildings, trees, people, everything—a kind of light pink."

"Have you gone *crazy?* What do you mean, pink, you lunatic?"

"Look at the map. It's laid out right there before you. Venezuela's pink, Colombia's green, and Brazil's yellow. Now you needn't take it out on *me.* I didn't have a thing on earth to do with it, and frankly, I'd like to see it. I'm surprised more people don't go down there and look it over."

I failed to duck this time, drat her, and she caught me directly over the ear with the geography. It wasn't any light book, either, with all those maps, and I saw a number of black spots dancing around for a few seconds.

When I got back to consciousness, she was gone, but the sun was too far down now to take a nap, so I went below. I figured I could make it up tomorrow if the weather held good, because I really didn't think there'd be much chance of trouble about schooling for several days. The girl had worked hard, and needed a rest.

We got to Vicksburg on a Sunday, and Uncle Jim went into the city to inquire where the Farrows lived. We waited for him on the houseboat, which we tied up to the stern of a ferry that was out of business. A man wearing a patched-up old commodore's suit and chewing tobacco that kind of leaked out of the corners of his mouth was living on it, and he contracted to keep an eye on our traps for twenty-five cents a day, which he said was exactly the kind of employment he'd been looking for, being light work and also on the water, but Dr. Snodgrass persuaded him to take it out in Elixir, three bottles a week.

I noticed Uncle Jim looking on, before he left, and afterward he got Dr. Snodgrass to promise, with his hand on a Bible, that he would refrain from starting a clinic here, and maybe getting put in jail, or shot. "This is Vicksburg, not Bosky Dell, and they probably have such operations as yours regulated," he told him.

"Undeniably, it represents a challenge," said Dr. Snodgrass, meditating, "but let it go. I'll get them next trip. Have you noticed an excess of catarrhal, or tubercular, coughing, followed by hocking and spitting?"

"I wasn't listening."

"The entire populace," said Dr. Snodgrass, "is, in my opinion, suffering from a dearth of Vermifuge. It amounts to starvation conditions. I hope to correct it. The only reason I have failed to do so is that, on my last visit, about two years previous, I was met by creatures of the local 'medical' society, so-called, and escorted back to my vessel. They even had the effrontery to confiscate two cases of the Men's Kickapoo Gooser and feed it, publicly, to pigs. It is my sworn purpose to show them the error of their ways."

"But not at this particular time," said Uncle Jim, and left.

He was gone about an hour; then he came back and said that the Farrows' place, known as Belle Mead, was nearly five miles back-country, on what was known as Plantation Creek, a broad sheet, partly a back-water slough, that flowed down to the Mississippi. He'd hired a buggy, from a private citizen (because there weren't many public livery stables or hotels in big Southern cities around the war years, on account of the hospitality, you know) and was driving it himself. It was pretty ramshackle, drawn by a horse that any Kentuckian would have said had a ewe neck and cat hams, but we piled in, with Zeb and the luggage on a box in the rear, and rattled out of town.

It was a nice day, not too hot for a change, and the birds were twittering all along the way. This buggy had a top that was held up by four flimsy supports, so that it was open clear around, and I must say that the ride was enjoyable, though we hit a rut, or a clod, or the horse stumbled, once in a while, and shook up your insides, which kept a person from going to sleep.

We got there by and by, after stopping twice to ask, both times of bone-heads that had never heard of it, and one of them hadn't heard of Vicksburg, then turned into a long shadowed driveway bordered by live oaks with beards of Spanish moss hanging down, gray and crinkled, and wound on up to the mansion house.

This place made Grassy look like a darky's shack. It stretched a considerable distance in front, with square pillars, and a second-story porch the whole length, and by George if it wasn't fresh painted! White all over. A fan-shaped lawn spread out before it, and on one side a terraced garden ran down to the water's edge, where I could see several small boats riding. Adjoining the house were the kitchen and what had been the quarters of the house slaves, and back behind the terraced garden were the barns, cotton storehouses, tobacco sheds, stables, and cattle pens. Still farther away were the plantation-slave quarters.

Well, these people looked prosperous, but before we left we found out that they were unpopular in the Vicksburg society, and even ostrichized, as somebody said, because they'd had money banked in England and never drew it out to help the Confederacy. They claimed an excuse but nobody swallowed it.

Anyhow, they had the means to grow cotton on a big scale now after the war, and they paid a fetching price to darky help, but it wasn't their old slaves, which seemed peculiar to me. All of our people at Grassy stayed right where they were, except one, a man named Sulphur and Molasses, a feeble-headed fellow, but harmless, that had been talked to by the Freedmen's Bureau, and said he preferred to go North and run for President. My Aunt Effie gave him the money to go, at a time when she couldn't afford it—when none of the hands were taking a dime in wages—because she said she'd prefer to see Sulphur and Molasses President to what they'd got at the moment. That was several years ago, and he never had run; I don't know what happened.

When our buggy arrived at the porch, a big servant man in a plum-colored suit strolled out and grabbed our horse's head (which didn't need grabbing as he was about caved in) and then came up to Uncle Jim.

"Yas, suh, gentlemen," he said, pompous and grand as he saw our rumpled clothes, "kinely let me announce you and your business. Marster require to know who's visitin'."

Uncle Jim climbed down in a leisurely sort of way and stood gazing around for a space—he had a wonderful manner toward uppity servants; it was enough to make their teeth grind—then he finally said, without looking at the darky:

"Fetch a boy to take care of the rig, then trot in and tell your master that Captain Burnie, of Grassy Plantation, Kentucky, is being kept on his doorstep by an impertinent houseman."

In about thirty seconds, or less, a fair-haired fellow of Uncle Jim's age, dressed with great elegance in a suit of brown linen duck, with a fancy nankeen waistcoat, came bursting out of the house and cried:

"By God!—*Burnie*." Then he added, when he saw Millie, "I beg pardon, Ma'am."

Well, he and Uncle Jim practically pumped each others' arms off, and then this Farrow did the same to us. He was what you would call handsome, I reckon, with a thin, straight nose, a tanned face, and a kind of excited expression, but I noticed that one of his eyes had a very slight cast to it. A person wouldn't spot it if you didn't catch him at a certain angle.

"Now you're here, Burnie, you won't get away soon. By George, we *have* got some catching up to do, and we'll do it over the very best Madeira in the cellar. By the way, I mustered out first—what happened to old Grimes?"

"I shot him," said Uncle Jim, lighting a cigar.

Mr. Farrow was set back for a second; then he broke into a merry laugh. "It's possible, quite possible. It's just the sort of thing you might do."

I found out later that a Colonel Grimes had been their commanding officer in the Mexican War, but nobody could stand him, and several came right out and said they liked the Mexicans better, and would switch sides if things got worse.

We soon learned that this Farrow household was cluttered up by a lot of people. I never could get them all separated in my mind, so I'll just stick in the main ones, which were the old lady, Mr. Farrow's mother, who dressed always in a black material that rustled when she moved, with white lace at her neck, but she stayed mostly in her room; a beautiful girl with blond hair almost white that was his sister, named Lauriette; a collection of bony, peckish aunts, and an older sister, as black-haired as the other was pale. She was about forty, I figured. They were the ringleaders, but there were others, too, that flitted through these high-ceilinged rooms and picture-gallery corridors. I never managed to remember their names, confound the luck, but mostly addressed them as "Ma'am."

It came to me that Mr. Farrow, Uncle Jim's friend, was the only man in the establishment. Somehow it didn't seem healthy. What's more, I hadn't been in that house three hours before I realized something was wrong; these people looked worried. All of them were polite, though stiff, and exclaimed how glad they were to have us as guests, all but the younger sister, Lauriette. I didn't care for her manner, which was scratchy and sarcastic. It was the same way to everybody, mocky and over-gushing, and to tell the truth, I don't think she liked a soul on earth. It was odd, because she was the handsomest person I ever saw, including Millie, who had a clean and fresh and sturdy outdoor look, but managed to get a tomboy note into it, one way or another. Still, aside from the schooling, which wasn't her fault entirely, I wouldn't have traded her for a dozen of these deep-south Lauriettes.

For instance, they had an aunt there named Cora, a vinegary old possum that was forever complaining about her vertigo, which they said was a disease of the head. Well, along comes this Lauriette and, "Why, *darling* Aunt Cora, how charming and *well* you look! My land, you're just the living *picture* of bouncing good health. Whatever have you been taking that's worked this miraculous cure?"

You see what I mean? After that blast, the old girl couldn't any more have belly-ached about her vertigo than she could have swum up to Memphis towing a barge. She'd had all the wind taken out of her sails before she had a chance to sound off. And it was the same way this Lauriette treated them all. She pounced on everybody's weakness, it seemed to me, and made it sound worse than it was.

In mid-afternoon, with Uncle Jim and his friend swapping yarns in the library, Millie taking a nap, and Dr. Snodgrass giving a medical lecture on the porch to a fair-sized sprinkling of aunts, *all* sickly, the girl got me to walk her down to where the boats lay.

"What's your uncle's name?" she asks.

I wasn't in the humor to be bullyragged by a female, so I says:

"Which one?"

Instead of getting vexed, she burst into a gay laugh and said, "Why you *dear,* fun-loving little boy. You're joking, aren't you?"

"I've got nine or ten uncles up in Kentucky," I said, working up a lie. "I thought you meant one of them."

"Now, why would you think that, you cunning child?"

"How's that again? You'll have to excuse me," I said, "but I'm a little deaf in my port ear."

She burst into another laugh, and said, "What kind of man is he, your Uncle Jim Burnie?" So she knew his name after all.

"Well . . . I think he's better; yes, I *know* he's better, since he got out. He may be all right from now on."

"Got out of *where?*" she asked in the first serious tone I'd heard her use.

"Prison. They gave him three years off for good behavior. He strangled a smart-aleck yellow-haired girl just about your si—"

I don't know what happened, but she grabbed my elbow and spun me around, hard. "Little *boy*—what's your name? Davey? Don't say anything like that again unless you mean it. You *didn't* mean it, did you?"

"No, Ma'am," I gulped.

But she was already far away in a study, lost in some private reflection that hadn't anything to do with me. We walked on down to the water's edge, hung over dark with mossy limbs, and she told me I could use the boats, including one that she said was a centerboard skiff for sailing, entirely new to me; then we climbed back up. By the time we arrived at the porch, her old style was back again, and she dismissed me with, "Run along now, you dear, amusing child. Why don't you go back to quarters and visit your terribly picturesque old family retainer? He may be lonely."

It seemed like a good idea, so I did it.

Zeb was situated in a very clean, neat room in the old quarters for house slaves, with a family in the other part of the house. He took his meals with them. When I went in, he had his feet up on the wood hopper and was playing a mournful tune on his jew's harp, of a sort that Uncle Jim said was an African's lament over being in slavery.

"Come in, honey, come in," he sung out when he saw me. "Ol Zeb feeling mighty low."

This was unusual, because as a rule he was as smiley and cocksure as a rooster.

"I'd just as soon move along, myself," I said. "I don't like it here."

"They's trouble in this house, honey. Bad trouble. You cain't fool Zeb about things like that. We do good to git shet of here, come dark."

"It may be imagination. We've been cooped up on a small boat and haven't seen any other kind of people. Uncle Jim knows what he's about."

"*Do* he? Mistuh Jim finish up de wah a cunnel, er gineral, if he hadn't been so notional and back-sassy."

Well, that was true enough, I supposed. At least, it's what everybody said, but I wasn't aiming to let this know-it-all get by with anything, so I says:

"If you're so all-fired wise, what's wrong about the house? I expect you've got it figured out by now."

He chuckled, restored to his old braggy self. "Whoa, now. Pull 'at hoss back. I only taken it into cogitation on my juice harp. It'll come, honey; you jes wait."

As annoysome as he was, occasionally he had a very peculiar way of smelling out the truth, so I said, "That's fine, but let's pin it down farther. You must have *some* reason for saying the place is troublesome. Which of the people bother you?"

"Mighty nigh all on em, and that's a fack."

"Look here, Zeb, I want you to do me a favor. Shinny around amongst the hands and see if they've got a conjure man here. If there *is* something wrong, let's dig it out. Ask him to boil some chicken bones or something."

"I don't *need* no conjure man. I kin cogitate it out on the juice harp, if I gets the chance. People all the time coming and going; it's enough to detract the strongest conjure man on yearth."

"If that's the way you feel about it," I said, getting up, a little sore, "I'll be about my business. I don't need a house to fall on me, and never did."

"Now you set back down, honey. Have an apple. The folks here're mighty nice—generous, too, and give me an apple. It's only got part of one side chewed out. You take de rest, and welcome. Tell you the truth, old Zeb done let this place grin' on his nerves."

"Well, that's all right," I said, picking up the apple. "It's got me jumpy, too. They're overloaded with females, for one thing. I feel sorry for that fellow Farrow. I don't know why he doesn't make a break for it some night late. He could braid a rope ladder out of bed sheets."

"I was cogitating him de very minute you come in," said Zeb. "An I was gettin somewhere, too."

"In that case, go ahead. You cogitate him out on the harp while I finish the apple."

He didn't think it would work, with someone looking on, particularly eating his apple, but said he would give it a try. He commenced playing, about ten times mournfuller than before, and I judged that if the music had anything to do with Mr. Farrow, he'd might as well pick up a spade and go on out to the graveyard, because that music wasn't suited for anything but a funeral.

All of a sudden, the door flew open with a bang, we whirled around, and there was that older sister, Miss Marguerite, standing on the threshold, pale as death. She was breathing heavy, and opening and shutting her fists, so that the veins stood out on the backs of her thin hands.

When she saw who it was, she tried to get control of herself, but she said, "Put that away at once. You mustn't play that here at all." After a minute or so, she added, "I'm sorry to speak to you so, but I really can't have that instrument played within earshot. I—I'm highly nervous, do you understand?"

I said, "Yes Ma'am," and Zeb began some gabble about how he was out of practice but that she'd enjoy it once he had his hand back in, but she spoke up very positive.

"No, I meant precisely what I said. It distresses me to treat guests in this fashion, but you are not to play any further while you remain at Belle Mead. Do I make myself clear?"

We both nodded, and she left, after saying goodbye and asking Zeb if there was anything he needed.

"Now what do you suppose is eating on *that* old witch?" I said.

For once, Zeb couldn't think of any satisfactory explanation, so I got up to go. He was crushed down because he took her remarks to be in the nature of musical criticism, and stated that he was considered to be one of the best juice-harp players anywhere near Grassy. He said he'd been invited to play with a serious concert group—musical saw, nose-whistle, washboard and suitcase drum—at the town bandstand one Fourth of July, but he'd run a catfish fin through his strumming finger at the last minute. He said he didn't want to sound unmodest, but he thought that was a pretty good record, or as good as she could produce on any instrument you could name, from the juice harp right on down to the piano.

I hardly heard him. I knew perfectly well he was scared, and was only talking to put in the time. Twilight was coming on; I could see it through the window. With all those oaks and hanging-down moss, it made things ghostlier than is common. Back somewhere in the quarters I heard a baby crying, then a dog barking, and down toward the river the bullfrogs were tuning up. The locusts were sawing away, too, complaining about the summer weather, and I can't think right off of a miserabler sound, especially when you're a little down to start with.

For the first time since I came in, I noticed Zeb's room. It reminded me of Clarissa's nice old comfortable shanty, and of Commercial Appeal, and I felt my eyes water a little. The shiny new adventure of this trip had rubbed off; I didn't particularly want to go anywhere except home. I knew Zeb was studying me, so I went back to staring out of the window. For some reason, I couldn't figure out an offhand way to leave.

"Well," I said, without looking around, "I guess I'll—" and choked up. Then I felt his ox's arm around my shoulders in the kind of hug I couldn't remember from anybody except the darkies at Grassy, because my aunts weren't made that way and my mother was gone practically before I'd got out of the cradle, and I had a good cry.

"You go right ahead, chile. You let her bust loose and git shet of it. You'll perk right up. My, my, I rec'llect when I was nussin' yo' Uncle Jim through the campaigns, and we was sleeping many's the time on the ground, and without any blankets, either, my min'd turn back home, and I'd feel powerful blue. It ain't anything to be ashamed of, being homesick. It shows you *belong* someplace."

"I'd like to see Grassy, and my aunts, and everybody . . . Clarissa, too."

I could see a worried look come into his shiny, broad black face, and he said, "You may be homesicker 'n I thought. You get *too* homesick, it's onhealthy. About all I care to see of that Clarissa is her south end as she's retreating no'th. She got a tongue like a blacksnake whip."

"I don't care. I'd *like* to have her bawl me out. I'd like some of her fried chicken and biscuits."

"Each pusson to their own taste, honey. I'd sooner eat grass, and do it in peace. Now I tell you what we'll do— I'll han' you a saying to think on tonight, so as to get your min' off home. Ol' sayings is best, and they come true, too. Now, then: If a young man will eat a hundred chicken gizzards, he can marry the girl he wants. You go on up to de house, and remember that, chile; it'll come in handy."

"I don't *want* to get married," I said. "I'm too young."

"You will; you sholey will."

We jawed back and forth about it some, and I left. He

was a hopeless case; there wasn't any more give to him than there is to a crowbar. Uncle Jim once told me all those sayings were genuine, including the ones on marriage, but he said they were so complicated they were dangerous. He was dead right. I'd already tried out two, and got in trouble both times.

On the first, he told me to place a horseshoe over the doorway, and the first person that entered would be my future wife. Well, I did it, but the first person that entered was my Aunt Effie, who'd smelled smoke, and when she jostled the door, the horseshoe fell down and hit her on the head.

The second time, Zeb said: Walk backward at sunset to a fence and cut a notch, looking over your right shoulder. Do this for nine consecutive nights, then walk backwards to the house, and you will dream of your future husband or wife.

I tried it, but it rained all day the sixth day, so there wasn't any sunset, and I had to start over. On the next round, I'd got up almost to the end when they took us visiting across the river for a spell, so *that* one blew up. I decided to give it one more show, but in walking backward to the house I tripped and fell into a ditch they'd dug for a drainpipe and split my head wide open on a shovel. I was in bed almost a week, and during that time, one of my aunts accidentally got a look at that fence. At first, they thought a family of beavers had been at work on it, but Uncle Jim said he figured somebody was converting it into a picket fence. It wasn't long before they hung the blame on me, as usual, and couldn't wait till I got over my busted head so they could give me a licking.

After I slammed his door and started off for the mansion, I heard his chuckle again, and when I looked back I saw his face in the window, grinning. And then, by Jupiter, if it didn't occur to me I'd forgot all about being homesick. That's what he was up to all the time. I didn't feel mad at him any more, but was glad he'd come along. He was practically as smart as he thought he was, but not quite.

I went on up to dinner, as they called it here. Because

of us, they had it at 7:30. One thing you could say about this bunch, they did things in *style*.

Usually, there were only two important meals: a breakfast very late, by our Kentucky notions, and dinner at three in the afternoon. In the "mornings," from one to three, they had what was known as "ladies' visiting," when sometimes a cousin or two might come in—never a stranger—and gossip on the veranda, if the day was cool —or in the coolest of the parlors, if it was hot.

In the afternoons, with dinner over, most everybody took drives, and in some spanking fine carriages, too. They had two made, as they said, by Rogers of Philadelphia, and one by Brewster, of New York, and their horses were mainly Kentucky or Virginia thoroughbreds. They even had a buggy swung on big C-springs, with a pair of imported Andalusian mules to draw it.

These drives every day were necessary, because the aunts had to "take the air." They'd got it worked out in their minds that only the air along the roads was fit for human use, so when they came back they said things like, "My, how much better I feel for getting a little air!" and "I just don't know what I'd do if I couldn't get out and take the air."

I asked Uncle Jim about this, thinking that the air around Belle Mead might be putrified, but he said it had to do with idleness. He said that being towed on wheels over a dusty, rutted road gave them the illusion of doing something important. He told me to go right ahead and breathe as much air as I pleased; it was perfectly fresh, and wouldn't harm me.

The third meal, at 7:30, was what they described as informal, except on this day of our arrival. Afterwards it was in the drawing rooms served by butlers bearing great silver trays, and consisted of coffee, tea, chocolate, biscuits, sandwiches, and light cakes. Most all the family arrived in their very best dress and made polite conversation that was aimed to improve your culture. The whole business seemed pretty thick to me. Nobody talked about anything of interest, but prattled on about the latest periodicals that had got in on the boat from London or Paris or somewhere—plays and books and concerts and such.

Most of these people had "finished" their education abroad, you understand, and occasionally dropped in foreign words or phrases, wholly meaningless, to prove it.

After one go at these sessions, I ducked out. I concluded to spend the time down at Zeb's, and avoid having my culture ruined entirely. Also, the food was better. The time I went, they combed and cleaned me up and set me next to an old biddy, in a little spindle-legged chair with a rickety table out of a "nest" before me, and said load up. I bit into one of the sandwiches, but it had a commodity on the order of watercress, or plantain, in it, so I tucked it aside—shoved it under the old girl's chair when nobody was looking. She says to this effect: "Are you finding it amusing heah?"

"Yes'm, it's all right," I said, "but there's one thing I'd like to get nailed down: do the fish *ever* bite in this slough?"

She didn't answer, but appeared interested, and even trained one of those quizzing glasses on me, like a person drawing a bead on a squirrel, so I felt encouraged to go on:

"There's another point; do you generally use beef liver or doughballs for channel cat around here?"

I reckoned she didn't know, and was embarrassed, because she picked up her traps and moved over by somebody else.

Anyhow, I've got ahead of myself, and must come back to dinner, or supper, in the dining room, on our first night here. The way it turned out, it was about as peculiar an event as I can remember, right up to the present.

We sat around a mahogany table about the size of a bandstand, and ate off of what Millie later said was rare china and glass, with the best damask and linen, and candlelight from heavy silver candlesticks that had about ten branches, each one working out of another, like limbs on a tree. Every person there, including me, had a colored servant in a white coat standing behind him as a waiter, and how they'd jump if you needed something! Up above the table was a kind of fan, with several blades hanging down that waved back and forth. A boy generally stood off to one side and worked it by pulling on ropes, but it wasn't hot enough tonight. This was a machine that one of the uncles, now dead, had brought back from India years ago, and out of respect to his memory they still called whatever boy operated it a "punkah wallah," the same as in the English regiments out there, they said.

Mr. Paxton Farrow sat at the head of the table, with Uncle Jim at his right hand, and his mother, stiff and murky and unsmiling, at the other end. They had that rattle-headed sister, Lauriette, next to me, but Dr. Snodgrass was on her other side, thanks to goodness, for I didn't have to talk to her as he spent the time telling her antidotes about the Choctaw nation, where he said he was the chief medicine man emeritus, whatever that means.

This supper was beautiful, if you stood off to one side and inspected it, but the conversation scooted along in little spurts, like leaves in a gusty breeze, then almost fell off entirely—becalmed. I kept watching Uncle Jim out of the corner of my eye, whilst waiting for Lauriette to turn and say something mocky, but he didn't appear to catch anything in the air at all.

But it was there. The old lady never said a word; didn't eat, either, but waved back dish after dish that her waiter brought, and turned her wine glass upside down. Still, she was the picture of calmness compared to Miss Marguerite, who was as jumpy as a bobcat. She kept trying to fill in the talk with things that had to do mainly with Mr. Farrow, it seemed to me, as if she was recalling them for both him and Uncle Jim. But the going was uphill, and finally she played out, too. And after the aunts ran through their ailments, Uncle Jim took over.

He puzzled me. Ordinarily, at Grassy, he never put himself out particularly to be handy with small talk, but often preferred to smoke a cigar while giving the others a show. People always said he was a "good listener," if he wasn't in some kind of mischief, like shooting down the Ku Klux Klan.

But now he took charge altogether, I never saw him so easy and graceful. Maybe charming is the word, no matter how sissified it sounds. He told about our trip, in very humorous detail, with friendly sallies about Dr. Snodgrass that caused a general laugh and brought about some witty remarks, also friendly and serene, by Dr. Snodgrass, and then of course, Lauriette had to tune up and say:

"But what persuaded you and this darling boy"—waving at me—"and your lovable old darky valet to leave home in the first place? There are so very *few* of our good families traveling down the river by skiff these days."

"Why, we had the misfortune to find ourselves in a tangle-up with the Ku Klux Klan, Miss Lauriette," he said. "To drop into the vernacular, they were, they still are, after our hides."

"Mercy sakes, how romantic! But then, you're a fighting man, aren't you, Captain Burnie? Still, though, that doesn't quite explain to little old stupid me why you chose sides so *peculiarly.*"

"It's a long story, ma'am."

As quick as her answer came, it wasn't quick enough to conceal a sort of tightening-up that went around that table. She was ready to pursue it, but she happened to glance down at her mother, at the same time I did, and there was a black, beady glitter in that old lady's eyes that would have squelched a magpie.

And I'm a tadpole if Uncle Jim *still* didn't notice anything. It was the first time in my life I realized that he didn't really have much sense. Those words come hard, about a man that's always been practically a hero, but they were true.

No, sir, he babbled right on, telling stories about the Mexican War, now, and taking more wine whenever the waiter offered it, having an all-around royal old sapheaded good time.

"By the way, Pax, I miss those jew's harp concerts of yours. They made Mexico almost a delight, Grimes or no Grimes. How about giving us a tune after dinner?"

Leaning forward, Miss Marguerite said, "Oh, no!" very quickly, as if it was important, but Mr. Farrow laughed and exclaimed, "I haven't touched it since the war. The fact is, I took an aversion to it, and haven't even got an instrument at the moment."

I'd told Uncle Jim about Zeb and Miss Marguerite, but since he didn't speak up, I started to say I knew where I could borrow one, but I chanced to catch his eye and it was just about the same feeling as being slapped in the face with an oar. I shut up in a hurry.

"That's often the case," Uncle Jim said smoothly. "The things we've enjoyed most in the past suddenly lose their flavor for no reason, and we leave them behind. Pity."

He was about to go on, but something was happening to Mr. Farrow. His face had taken on a feverish look, and now he leaned forward, in a trance, his eyes glazed, his body trembling, and saliva working out of the corners of his mouth.

One of the women half rose in her seat, motioning to a servant, but Mr. Farrow sat back, the trembling gone, and broke into a very loud and disgusting song.

Nobody moved a peg while he sang a verse and chorus, having to do with a lady that was employed in the lower part of Natchez, working nights, as I got it, and kept time by beating on his wine glass with a fork.

When he finished, Miss Marguerite started to say, "Captain Burnie, if you'll—" but Uncle Jim went right on and resumed his antidote that had been interrupted in the middle. From first to last, he never turned a hair.

"—so neither of us was responsible, for once, but a wild ram of a fellow, and a corking good soldier, Alan Shelby—you'll remember Shelby, the straw-haired kid from someplace up North, Illinois or Indiana?"

"Yes, a most attractive youth, ingenious, too," said Mr. Farrow, smiling. He was fully recovered from whatever it was, and the whole company, including me, sat back in their chairs, more comfortable.

After dinner, as I was walking up from the river, I passed Uncle Jim and Mr. Farrow, both smoking cigars to keep off the mosquitoes, and after they went by, deep in talk, Uncle Jim called to me and sauntered back.

"I wanted to remind you, Davey," he said in a normally loud voice, then almost in a whisper:

"Be at Zeb's shack at midnight. Tell Dr. Snodgrass and

Millie. I'll join you there. *On no account permit your-selves to be seen.*"

My insides froze up with the chills. I hadn't any idea what was going on, but I knew that tone, and it was usually the preliminary to some unholy jamboree.

11

"DOUSE THAT LAMP—put it on the floor in the corner and rig a quilt over it," Uncle Jim told Zeb when Dr. Snodgrass and Millie squeezed in through the door. "I don't want even a peep of light leaking out. Draw that curtain tighter. Good. Now, keep your voices low, and we'll get on with this."

The room was nearly dark; I could see their faces in pale outline. For once, neither Dr. Snodgrass nor Zeb said a word, and Millie slipped her hand into mine, waiting.

"It's time I explained why we came here. As you may have guessed, it's more than a visit to an old friend. I wish things were that simple."

"If you don't mind my saying so, Captain," said Dr. Snodgrass, demoting Uncle Jim again in his concern, "this Mr. Paxton Farrow of yours is a very strange man."

"Ah, but you see," replied Uncle Jim, with a thrill of excitement in his voice, *this is not the fellow in question at all*.

We all gasped, and Millie sounded as though she was about to get the fantods.

"You are perhaps suggesting that he has undergone a mysterious change of character," said Dr. Snodgrass. "Twice during the course of my prac—"

"What I mean is, the man here representing himself to be Paxton Farrow is somebody else, another person entirely. I expected it to be so when we arrived, and it is so. I'm not certain yet about the deception being practiced in this house, but I mean to find out everything, make no mistake about that. Farrow was my friend—we shared the hardships and the joys of a soldier's life—and I will find him, even if blood has to run again in the streets of Vicksburg."

I knew it; it was always his way. First off, run down two or three thin leads, and then get the guns going. Nobody could walk softer, or speak gentler, but when he decided that reason had thrown in its hand (and it didn't take long) the bombardment commenced. It made me uneasy. It had caused him a lot of trouble, and everybody hoped it was over. I suspicioned he would mosey on up to the house now, ask this humbug Farrow a courteous question or two, and then blow his head off. But I misjudged him—maybe I was overly scared—because he said in an unbloodthirsty voice:

"I'd better give you the background of this business. Farrow and I were comrades. After the war, we corresponded, oh, say, every two or three months, a pleasant exchange of reminiscence and news, with the usual promises to visit—something that never took place. Then there came a lapse of a year. He had described the members of his family, and eventually I wrote a note of inquiry to his mother. In time, I had a reply from the sister, Marguerite, who said he had embarked on a leisurely trip around the world—the 'Grand Tour.'

"Well, this wasn't unusual but he'd never mentioned it before, and for some reason I couldn't put it out of my mind. I had no letters from abroad, so after two years went by, I wrote again, this time to the sister herself. Well, lo and behold, his old correspondence resumed, and from Belle Mead, too. But not *quite* in the same handwriting. Oh, it was close, very clever indeed, but it was not the handwriting of the man I knew. I have the paid opinion of a Memphis expert on that. And the contents, while accurate in the main, appeared to me to be chiefly to show that the writer knew of certain happenings that might establish his identity.

"Time went on, I meant to act, but the war came along, and other things were forgotten. I tried to trace him through the Army, but hadn't any luck. When I got out, I resolved to look into this curiosity, at the very first chance. That arrived, courtesy of the excellent Ku Klux Klan, and here we are."

"Major Burnie," Dr. Snodgrass spoke up, restoring his old rank, "now that you've seen the, er, incumbent Farrow, what are your reasons for declaring him a fraud? Are the two dissimilar in appearance? How can such a substitution be made in a plantation society where everybody is known to everybody else?"

"They are absolutely identical. But you see, Paxton Farrow was wounded in Mexico—a bullet creased his forehead. This fellow wears no such blemish. There are other points; I'll mention only one, for the moment. You may recall that, at dinner this evening, I rambled on about one Alan Shelby, a member of our regiment?"

"Yes, it struck me you were anxious to put him on the record, especially after that singular fit of ep—"

"Yes, yes," said Uncle Jim, cutting him off pretty short, it appeared to me. "Well, no such person as Shelby existed. I merely threw him out as bait. You heard the response? Our precious Mr. Farrow of the moment *knew him well.*"

"Then, in the name of all that's holy, who—"

"Later. Right now, I need your help."

"Sir, we shall back you to the limit," said Dr. Snodgrass, grasping his hand, and it was easy to see he meant it. "Fraud and deceit can not, must not, be counten—" —he took another hitch at it—"Of all the human vices, frau—" then he gave it up, and said, "Let us by all means find the rightful proprietor of this establishment; we must see that justice is done. Fraud and deceit are condonable on some levels, but not on others, if I make my distinction clear, sir."

"You do, doctor," said Uncle Jim, without any sarcasm, for once. He liked Dr. Snodgrass, and once told me, "Don't let his bamboozling of the public fool you. Down underneath, that old reprobate's got a streak of integrity a yard wide, as well as the guts of a government mule." Such a statement was rare with Uncle Jim, and I hadn't forgot it. Still and all, I didn't know what it meant. I guessed it meant Dr. Snodgrass hadn't robbed a bank yet, or poisoned anybody for the insurance.

"Zeb, you'll have to be the key fig—psst! What's that? Blow that lamp out—*jump!*"

I did so, and Uncle Jim crept to the door, then burst it open with a heave. Somebody was there, all right; the door whacked into them; then I heard a patter of running feet—bare, it sounded like. The night was blacker than ink, so there wasn't a chance of seeing the person, and Uncle Jim caught my arm when I started to slide out and follow.

"Not yet, not just yet. We've got to tread carefully. What I'm interested in is the welfare of a friend, not in an open rupture."

"Those footsteps weren't headed toward the house," I said, "they were headed toward the quarters."

"Let it alone for now."

But when he told Zeb what he wanted, Zeb set up a howl.

"White folks' biznuss. I get to messin in it, they take and snatch my head off. In addition, I'm too old to go traipsin aroun the country after dark. I apt to fall down a well."

"See here, you woolly-headed idiot," said Uncle Jim, and I could tell he was sore, "you're the same age I am. Exactly—same year, same month. I'm tired of hearing you talk about being old—'Ol Zeb this;' 'Ol Zeb that'— It's sickly. You've taken on an Uncle Tom complex. What's more, it's disrespectful of *me*. *I'm* not old."

Well, all that was true enough. Ever since I'd known him, he'd considered himself elderly. Right from the start. He was always making excuses because of his age, even when he was under thirty. He'd done it so much, by George, I'd begun to *think* of him as old.

"Fust thing I learned in slavery wuz to keep clar of white folks' biznuss. My pappy seen to *that,* and I ain't forgit it. Ol Zeb—"

"By Godfrey, there it goes again! You heard what I said—figure out some other way to describe yourself."

"But dog it, this here's the only way I know. I *used* to it."

"Well change it to 'Young Zeb.'"

"*What?* And be laughed out of town? People'd think I'se talking about a baby, and I ain't got no children; you know dat."

Then Uncle Jim did what I'd never heard him do before in my whole life—referred to himself in practically a favorable light.

"Look here, Zeb; is the Ku Klux Klan *all* white folks' business?"

"How you mean?"

"Is Ben Woods' business *my* business?"

Zeb thought it over, and said, "I wuz goin' to do it all along. They wasn't any question of *doin'* it; the main point was *when*. I wasn't ready before, but I *is* ready now, and as far as taking a header down a well's concerned, I can tote an eight-foot pole, flat out to de ground. That way, you hang up instead of splunking on down to de water."

The truth is, he was babbling like a wild man, not making any sense at all, but he was mighty scared, and I didn't blame him, so Uncle Jim said I could go along, and at daytime, to make things look good. We'd be exploring the country, and could do it in our rig, except at the very end.

"And for God's sake, drop all that drivel about the pole. That *would* look nice and normal, wouldn't it? Now, these darkies aren't Farrow people, not a one unless I miss my guess. *Some*where in this region, you'll find a family that belonged right here on Belle Mead. They'll be cautious, but they'd also like to see the truth come out; I'll bet on that. My suggestion is, make your final approach to an old man. Very old colored people don't care so much what happens to them. Nearly all the bad things have happened already."

Dr. Snodgrass and Millie slipped back to the house, stealthy and quiet, and by and by I did the same. Next day, Zeb and I had our hired rig hitched up and rattled off into the countryside, headed in no special direction. We took a lunch along, after I'd swallowed my pride and asked one of Lauriette, who gave me a funny look that sent shivers down my spine.

It was a nice, hot, dry sort of morning, and driving along these dirt roads was pleasant, even behind a horse that kept stumbling.

Casting around for a means of getting people's ear, I

figured we could go up to darky shacks and ask for a drink. Zeb could say his master, which was me, had just got over a sickness while visiting in Vicksburg and needed the country air. People are always ready to believe in somebody else's bad health; it helps keep them from getting sick themselves.

We ran on for several miles, with Zeb going up for a drink five or six times. If he got the right opening, he was supposed to mention he once had kinfolk at Belle Mead, and see what happened. He told me everybody he met was friendly, and urged him to drink as much water as he pleased, so that after a while he'd drunk all he could hold, and maybe a little more, and gave me a warning about it, so we were out of business for awhile.

By now, I'd got my own appetite so whetted up about this mystery I couldn't sit still. I'd *got* to find a way to sort it out. But we didn't get anywhere that day, or the next, and the one after that was hog-killing day at Belle Mead, so we all stayed there to watch.

The whole plantation force was out at the hog pens with their knives sharpened. Stripped down to the waist, they looked like pictures I'd seen in schoolbooks, where African tribes were fighting each other or dancing, you know. Uncle Jim said that some day, when things leveled off in this country, whatever that meant, these people would be our best athletes, for they were about the only ones that weren't living soft.

Anyhow, one after another of the boldest spirits, watching their chance, dashed into the hog pens and slashed a throat, with a quick thrust, and then scampered out, for a bunch of maddened boars and sows can be pretty dangerous, smelling death.

You never run across such a hullabaloo of squealing, feet flying, dust raising, yelling, and laughter.

When a hog was down, they'd wait their chance, and drag him out and plop him into a kettle of scalding water. Then the women, and even the children, commenced scraping the hair away, and as soon as he was clean, with the bare skin showing a kind of speckled blue and white and red underneath, naked and flesh-crawly, they'd string him up to the beams, head down. Now the oldest women brought tubs and put them underneath, to catch the blood, and a buck or two slit him and reached right in to haul out the purple guts—yard after yard of tubes and pipes, and lots of other objects, too, but none of them very agreeable to look at, separated from their natural home.

They made this hog-killing day at Belle Mead a kind of ritual, as Uncle Jim said. The rule was that all the family, including the faintest-hearted women, if any, should stand to one side and watch. It was supposed to show that down underneath the whites were as tough and knowledgeable about unpleasant things as anybody, but had risen above them.

So there they were, a row of fluttery and humbuggy pain-racked aunts and the like—not fluttery, now, but standing perfectly steady and unmoved—watching, keeping up the appearances before the hands.

Well, I got one setback out of it, anyhow. All of a sudden, I noticed Millie, beside me, breathing heavy and clasping and unclasping her hands, which were pressed tight against her bosom. The skin of her forehead was glistening, too, as if she'd been sweating, except that the morning wasn't that hot. And when one big strapping fellow with very bloody, tight trousers ran in and stuck his knife into a squealing hog, I thought she might have a spasm. I could hear her moan, then see her tighten and untighten her muscles behind, so I said, "You don't *have* to watch this ruckus, you know. Why don't you go up to the house and drink some cold lemonade?"

She practically hissed my head off: "Shut up, you numbskull! Leave me alone."

It went to show that women were *all* crazy. There wasn't a thing to choose among them; all alike, and troublesome as snakes in the skin-dropping season. *I* didn't know what she was excited about, and didn't much care, so I went over to stand by Lauriette, who was deathly pale. I did it to get even, shucking her off for the worst nuisance on the place. But Millie didn't even notice.

When the killing was done and the cooled-off hogs stretched in long rows, they lit open hickory fires and started other boiling pots, and this was the part I liked.

The hickory smelled sweet in the early morning (for they performed this operation after sunup, before things got hot and the flies turned out) with its blue swirls rising up from a dozen fires, and everybody was busy and happy. The excitement died down, even on Millie, who looked washed out but peaceful, and everybody slacked up in an astonishing way.

I was handed a pig-tail to fry over the coals, and a bladder to blow up for Christmas. And afterward, we stayed to watch them make lard and grind sausage. It was educational. I wished the principal of the school back home could have seen it; it might have pried his mind off the Golden Age of Hercules for a change.

For days after those hog-killings, the whole place has a regular picnic, eating, with not only tenderloins and spare-ribs for breakfast but cracklin and about every other kind of pig-meat you can name. Uncle Jim said the skin of every darky there would shine like polished ebony with hog's grease for a week or more. We had hog-killing at Grassy, but it was done different, without all this style; also, my aunts didn't care for it, and kept me busy at the house.

Well, Zeb and I picked up our search the day after, and hit pay dirt on the first whack. Rattling along a nice shady road through thick pine woods and occasional fields that opened out, we encountered a shanty set back a ways with a well in front. By now, I was thirsty myself, so I said we'd *both* go up and get a drink, and we did.

Not a soul in sight except two or three pickaninnies rolling an iron wagon-tire hoop, so we knocked. Presently a neat, comfortably filled-out woman with her head done up in a red bandana—just like the Northern picture-posters—came to the door and studied us over with a shrewd look.

Zeb spoke up, lifting his forage cap in a ridiculous flourish, and says: "Yes, Ma'am, me and the young genleman respectively wukked up a thust—"

"The dipper's yander, hangin by the well," she says, and then to me, after studying us some more, "You druv far, suh?"

For some reason, I decided to let caution go and take a

stab right out and open. This woman was smart; she was satisfied we were strangers interested in more than water.

"We're visiting Belle Mead, the Farrow place," I says. "Mr. *Paxton* Farrow's place."

I wasn't mistaken. Her eyes narrowed a little; she looked different.

"My uncle was a friend of Mr. Farrow in the Mexican War."

"Mistuh *Paxton* Farrow?"

"And Zeb, here, had some kin living there once, but they don't seem to be there any more."

She just waited.

"Uncle Jim thought maybe we could get a trace on them whilst sight-seeing on buggy rides. He hated to disturb the Farrows about it."

I went out to the well, with Zeb trailing behind, and let her mull it over. When I returned to say thanks, the pickaninnies had knocked off hoop-rolling and were plastered to her legs, peeping around, two of them sucking their thumbs.

I said, "We're obliged for the drink. I guess we'll be getting along. We've got a lot of ground to cover, if we ever locate those kinfolk relatives."

She was trying to make up her mind; finally she said, "If I'se sight-seeing, I turn right down about half a mile er so. Where they's a rusted-out bed-spring restin against a tree. It's right purty on towa'd the crick."

"That's fi—"

"An if you gits lost, you kin alwuz ask ol man Uncle Ned Pete." She waited a second, and added: "He's a curiosity."

I was on fire to get going, so I mumbled thanks, and started to fly, but she called me back:

"You, boy," she said.

"Yes'm, Aunty," I answered, feeling easier with a natural form of conversation.

"You *ask* him, hear?"

"Yes'm."

"He's the onliest one; the uthers uz sold to New Orleans before de wah. But Uncle Ned, he couldn't be sold; he wuz set free by Mr. *Paxton* Farrow."

"Yes'm, Aunty," I said again, not able to think of anything real smart, but when I made a motion of leaving, she said, "But I never tol you, hear? I'll gainsay it, time it comes out."

"Yes'm, I'm obliged again, Aunty."

She'd been looking pretty fierce, her face screwed up in fright, over what she was telling, but it smoothed out now, and she said, "Mr. Paxton Farrow done a good thing for my man once. We wouldn't be here, else."

Then she turned and walked inside. We were off in a minute, the horse kicking up a cloud of dust, and seeming surprised, too, at a whip being laid across his rump.

"By jingoes, we've *got* it!" I exclaimed at Zeb, but *he* was getting a fit of the holy terrors, now, though he was still game enough. White man's business scared them, and it was easy to understand. Uncle Jim said they'd lived in a "flinched" condition for more than a century.

We hit the crossroads, saw the bed-springs, and turned to the right. Within a mile, the road started sloping downhill, all leafed over overhead like a tunnel, then it meandered along another broad creek, or slough, and finally passed a homemade houseboat, tied up beneath some low-hanging branches.

"That's it! That's where he lives; I'll make any bet on it."

Zeb grumbled, not wanting to stop, but I drew up and wheeled off to a place out of sight, letting the reins drop so the horse could eat grass. There wasn't a chance of him running away; the only danger was to keep him from lying down. He was a mighty poor excuse for a horse, even a buggy nag.

"Uncle, we've come to talk to you about Mr. Paxton Farrow," I said when he came on deck, a little shriveled monkey with a face wrinkled like dried mud. "His friend and my uncle, Captain James Burnie, of Kentucky, wants to know. He's a good man." I couldn't figure out any other way to say it; the words just popped out.

They said later he was over a hundred, but he stood erect, and his eyes hadn't that watery, dull look you see in most old people. These were sharp and alert, watching first one of us then the other. He lived alone on that boat, and fished in the creek for his fodder. He had a skiff and could row it. He made corn bread in a skillet, and darky neighbor families brought him greens from their gardens. To pay back, he gave them catfish. But they didn't expect it, and a woman young enough to be his granddaughter, but not young, either—past sixty—came to check him nearly every day. With a man that age, you forget how old his children's children can be.

I explained us to him, and did it entirely above-board. He listened as sharp as a person of twenty. But when I finished, two small tears from old, nearly dried-up wells rolled out slow from the corners of his eyes. Then he said in a voice as dry and brittle as a yellowed-over newspaper that's been shut up for years in a trunk, "I wanted it to come out befo' I passed."

But he was shrewd, for all his age and good feeling, and declined to let us come in and talk just now. He said we must return after dark and not to be seen, as Uncle Jim had suggested, so we had to stir up our horse, which was full of grass now and about as active as a bale of hay, and stump off. Nobody saw us; that's what I honestly believed.

Well, it was a nuisance and botheration to put in the time till dark, because we could hardly go back to Belle Mead, then rig up all over again. Somebody would spot us sure.

In the end, we decided to jog into town—it wasn't far —marking the road so as to find our way back, and take a snooze on the houseboat.

But when we got there, we couldn't believe our eyes. It was gone, and so was that ferry. It didn't take long to locate the houseboat, though; it was tied to a half-sunk scow, and when we inquired round for the ferryboat, a man said it was back in business again. The owner, who'd been crippled off and on for years with a combination of lumbago and imagination, suddenly got well. The man said he'd been taking a new medicine, and it hauled the kinks right out of him. He'd thrown aside a cane he'd been using and gone to a fiddle dance with a woman half his age. The man that told us said nobody had heard him complain in three or four days, which they said was some kind of record.

So there you were. Dr. Snodgrass was right all along. All a person had to do was believe in those medicines of his, and you had a running start toward recovery.

Anyhow, we bought two catfish from a fellow that ran trot lines, went aboard our old craft, and cooked up a whacker of a meal. It was the first satisfaction I'd had to my stomach for nearly a week. Some people may be able to get nourishment out of watercress and conversation; I'm not one of them.

Zeb turned in for a nap, but before I joined him, I gave a darky with a horse fifty cents to deliver a note to Uncle Jim at Belle Mead. Without coming right out, I hinted we'd be held up late, and while I didn't say why exactly, I put it so he'd know. Then I went back and took a long nap.

In the evening, we fooled around town, looking in windows, and about nine o'clock headed for Uncle Ned's. It was full dark before we arrived, and down the creek road it was spookish and scary with movement. I could have sworn I saw, or *felt,* a dozen monsters, but probably it was Spanish moss dancing in the breeze. I began to get the jimjams inside, and Zeb was so quiet it was painful. I never knew him to be silent like that before, except once when he had a toothache and they tied up his jaw with rags.

The truth is, it was so dark we couldn't see the horse; we just let him have his head, and stumble on. Presently he stopped, and I reckoned it was the same place where he ate grass before, because I smelled the creek pretty strong, cold and fishy, and heard gurgling ripples where the current split on a snag or something.

When we climbed down, my knees sort of buckled, and I heard Zeb say, "Lordy, lordy," and then, again, "White folks' biznuss."

The most annoysome thing was that the crickets and locusts and cicadas and bullfrogs, which had been droning and sawing and booming away like a sawmill, all knocked off work the instant we got out of the buggy. I never realized you could miss them; I felt like I'd been shoved out naked on the main street of Memphis at high noon.

I don't know what we expected to find inside. By now I was so rattled I wouldn't have been surprised to see that crinkled-up old man hanging from a beam.

No light showing, and not a sound on the boat—enough to grate on a gorilla's nerves. He kept his shanty-boat tied to an overhead branch, and ran a long plank from the deck to the bank, taking it in at night, because they said he was afraid of ghosts. But it was something else that worried him; I found that out soon enough. Well, the plank was down, so he hadn't forgot.

We tiptoed up, and I gave a light rap on the door. When no answer came, I pushed it open and said, softly, "Uncle Ned? You in here, uncle?"

All of a sudden, more accustomed to the pitch-blackness, I saw two greenish glows—like a cat's, over in one corner. I could feel my heart, along with various other objects on duty in the neighborhood, jump up in my throat, and when I started to turn and bolt:

"Shet de do'."

It was the same brittle worn-out voice, thank heavens, and it went on to say, "Strike a light." Zeb lit a sulphur match and then a lamp, and we saw the old man sitting on a stool, with a rickety shotgun patched together with wire and plaster-tape lying across his knees.

"I fixin to see it was you, and not somebody else I could name."

The astonishing old man had fished at night so long he could *see* like a cat, in addition to his eyes looking that way. I can't explain it, because darkies' eyes are brown, not green, and so were his, mostly. But they looked different, even in daylight, and at night they shone. I don't know the reason, but it was so.

"Fetch in de plank," he said, and when we did it, he said, "Snuff de light," and Zeb blew it out. Then we sat in the dark and waited.

12

"MISTUH PAXTON the goodest man what ever lived. Everybody happy when he's aroun', alluz. But Mistuh Paxton daid, ben daid sence befo' they fit de Yankees."

He went ahead and I could imagine him in the dark with probably more old tears rolling down his cheeks, and felt sorry for him. He talked nearly an hour, and I won't try to put it all in his words, because the darky speech down here was different than around Grassy and I couldn't peg it down to sound just right. Even with Zeb it wasn't easy; sometimes he said "de" and sometimes "the," and other things see-sawed back and forth, the way white people do. Nobody talks the same all the time.

I got the main points as he went on letting it pour out after a good many years, all his stored-up angriness and grief over a pleasant life that got smashed up because a few people were mean and greedy. Now and then when he got excited the words tumbled out so fast or the speech went back to so near African that I lost the drift, but I soaked up enough to know what I needed. I couldn't wait to get back to Uncle Jim.

"They git me sure. I daid, too, now. They came and tol' me often enough, makin threats. Back when it happen', they sol' everybody off to different places south—babies snatched from mothers, man and wife cryin and sobbin goodbye—a thing Mr. Paxton cut off he hand befo' he do —but they couldn't sell *me*. I uz free; I wuz de oldes'—I spec I'se older'n God, mighty near—and Mr. Paxton sot me free. He say nobody ought to live that long belongin to somebody else. He say he sign a doc'ment I belong to myself. It wuz the fust propity I ever owned, but it depreciate considerable here lately."

125

I commenced to get fidgety because there was no telling how long he might ramble on, now he'd started. He had waited a long time for this moment, and I hated to ruin it but it was time to go. I told him he'd be all right, that Uncle Jim would fix everything, and for now he must pull in the plank when we left, and keep his shotgun handy. Then Zeb located a box of carpet tacks and sprinkled them around on deck, in case anybody tried to swim out and sneak in barefoot, which was a jackass idea, but I let him have his way.

If possible, the night had closed down blacker than before. We had to edge along, feeling every step down the board to shore, and found the buggy only because the horse nickered. Its outlines were in no wise visible at all.

I swung myself up to the driver's seat and reached for the reins, but somebody was sitting to one side, and had them already.

A familiar-sounding voice said, "Tell the nigger to get in the back," and Zeb did it, but I heard him moan a little. He didn't have to guess what was coming. Another person was in the back, too, and more were nearby, sitting quietly a-horseback.

For a second, I thought of grabbing Zeb and making a jump for it, but a thin hand fastened hard on my arm, and the owner said, in a pleasant voice, "Don't do it—my impetuous friends might spill your brains on the ground."

Well, something snapped; I don't know what. It hadn't anything to do with courage, because I've backed out of things less troublesome, but I sprang up in the seat, still clutched in the grip, and yelled, "Watch out, Uncle Ned! They're here!"

The words rang out in that still night like church bells. I reckoned you could heard them half a mile.

Something struck the back of my head, and I knuckled under in a heap on the buggy floor. But I wasn't cold-cocked: I still knew what went on, and even in the fluster of horses' hooves and curses, I heard Uncle Ned's door slam, and after that a splash, and the sound of oars working in rowlocks.

"He's cut for the other bank! Get him, quick!" somebody sung out, and two or three riders, spurring their horses down the bank, let go five or six shots over the water. And then, if you believe it, there came a shotgun blast—likely aimed at the flashes by that spunky old fellow—and one of the scoundrels gave a gasp, which was followed by a heavy thud, like a bag of pork being dropped to the ground.

"Rollie's hit—" Then a sound of dismounting, and "Holy Mother Mary!—his whole side's blown away by a scatter-gun . . . he's *dead!*"

"Come on, come on," said the voice at my side, with as much concern as you might get from a spider, "We've got work to do. Take care of him later."

He whipped up the buggy, and we streaked off down the road, followed by the men on horseback. I don't know how long we rode—perhaps only a few minutes—but when we pulled up, a rail gate was flung aside and we clattered through and into a big building—a cow barn or stable. The door was swung shut after us.

"Show a light."

In the lantern-glow, I looked around and all these men were wearing black masks not quite like the Ku Klux Klan's but close enough for discomfort.

My seat-mate, a slender, dandified fop who even though masked was a dead ringer for the present proprietor of Belle Mead, swung himself gracefully down and said, "Now, we'll teach you what happens to meddlers. String them up."

"You mean *hang* 'em?"

"Stretch them out for a flogging, you fool. We can't have the whole of Vicksburg on our necks. Flogging's one thing—it's the normal form of rebuke hereabouts—but murder's another. People seem to boggle at it."

"Well, can't we hang the coon? Nobody'd mind *that*."

"It's a silly practice—it gives them a distorted sense of importance. Better to snake some manners into his sooty hide."

They grabbed Zeb, in a half-fainting condition, and strapped his wrists to an iron peg on a rough oak pillar, leaving nothing but his toes touching the ground; then I saw my chance and wrenched free.

There was a hayloft, and I scrambled straightaway up

the ladder. My foot slipped between rungs, and somebody grabbed it, but I kicked him in the face and threw myself over the top. As I did so, I rolled onto a smooth-worn hay-fork handle, and you can bet I grabbed it like a long-lost brother.

Then I stood on the edge and jabbed it down, dancing like a crazy person. I was so mad, and scared, too, that I babbled, but yelled, "You lay a hand on him and I'll throw this through the middle of your belly! What's more, when my Uncle Jim's told, you'd better say your prayers."

"Never heard of him," said the fop. "White or black?"

"You can take off the mask, *Mr.* Farrow," I said. "I know all about you, you miserable cowardly humbug. *Your turn's coming!*"

He made a motion to one of the masked bullies, and a heavy braided whip lit into Zeb's back. I could see dust spurt out of his homespun shirt. His knees buckled, and he moaned again, and cried, "Aah!"

"Throw it down—you'll both be let off easier."

"Come and get it."

The biggest of those villains—there was something familiar about him; I couldn't put my finger on it—started up the ladder.

"Now, sonny, we'll see if your money and uppity airs can solve *this.*"

I waited till he was one rung higher, then drove the fork down. I reckon they thought I was bluffing, because he let out a surprised howl—painful, too—with two prongs sunk an inch or more in his shoulder—and then landed in a heap on the floor.

"By God, we're paying heavy for this night's work," another swore. "One dead and one stuck like a pig by a shirttail boy—"

"You haven't even started yet," I screamed, blown up like a rooster with success. I felt so cocksure I failed to notice that one had edged into the shadows, so I didn't realize anything was wrong till he seized me from behind and tore the hay fork out of my hands. He'd climbed up the chute while I was clapping myself on the back. It usually happens that way.

They hustled me down in a hurry, not too gentle, either, and strung me up alongside Zeb.

"Before we start," said the fop, "this is what you will get, multiplied a hundred times, *if you ever repeat a word of what you heard tonight.* Do you understand?"

Neither of us answered. The first bite was so fierce I cried out like an animal; I couldn't help it. I felt something warm run down my back, and then it lit again. I don't know how long it went on, but by and by I saw Zeb hanging perfectly limp and unconscious, with saliva coming out of his mouth, then things began to blur.

Very dim, a long way off, I heard somebody say, "That may be enough. I think the nigger's dead—he had a dozen too many."

But the fop's voice spoke up, cheerful and happy as a lark, and said, "Fetch the tub of coarse salt."

One of the men whose voice I didn't know answered, "See here, I'm all for punishment, also I'm beholden to you financially, but there's a limit to what I'll see handed to a boy. It may be fine for you, and for these northern trash"—I wasn't too far gone to wonder at that—"but I've seen enough tonight. Frankly, I don't know as I'll be able to look at myself in a mirror for awhile."

"With your face, I don't blame you, my friend. Fetch the salt. Or would you prefer to see your wife and brats turned out into the road?"

The next thing I knew, I was screeching and crying and twisting around in the straps, and Zeb was doing the same.

"Rub it in. Rip off the rest of their shirts, and grind it in every stripe. A lesson learned halfway is a lesson to be learned over. Let's do them a favor and finish the job in one sitting."

Off to one side, water seemed to be running, and a night wind blew on my face. I felt grass against it, too. My wits began to come back slowly. Groaning, I tried to push myself up to my hands and knees. The sky was still dark, but a pearly glow off to the east told that dawn was coming.

"Lie back, chile; let him hep you."

It was Zeb, though I couldn't exactly see him, and then the old man, Uncle Ned Pete, coming back from the creek with a poultice made of nobody knows what. It was very fiery, then wonderfully cool and soothing.

"Don' move," he said. "Let it wuk, else you be left with bad scahs."

"Zeb," I said, rubbing at my eyes with one fist. "I thought you was dead."

"I mighty nigh daid, honey, mighty nigh. I wished I *wuz* daid, there for awhile." And then—"White folks' biznuss." That was all he said, but it was enough.

"I remember, and I'm sorry. Uncle Jim'll try to make it up. I know that."

"Chile, I wished he didn't. I'se scared to think what Mistuh Jim'll do when he hyars. He goin to kill somebody for sure."

"Let him," I said, and meant it. "I hope he kills the whole bunch. I'll help him."

The old man shushed us, saying they might come back, and after that he left to get our horse and buggy, which was grazing, or part of it was, nearby.

That dried up little tough prune of a hundred-year-old darky had rowed across the river, then rowed back, upstream, and followed us. If a person was looking for a case of outright rashness under fire, this was it, because he'd come clear up to that barn and peered through a crack, watching everything and then trailed along afterwards to where they tumbled us out on the creek bank. And, as Uncle Jim remarked later, he had nothing to gain but his neck in a rope over a limb. He was a splenderous old man, but I thought lying there with his poultice cold on my back that he was in a *real* pickle now. Something had to be done, and I wanted to get home and begin it.

Being an orphan, with my mother and father checked out early, I never much learned to cry, but I couldn't help it during the ordeal of getting up in that buggy. Zeb, too. Our backs were torn to tatters, and the slightest movement stretched the skin and started the bleeding up. But it had to be done.

"Jog, don't resh. An' don't set up to drive. That horse'll fotch back de same road."

I asked him where he was bound.

"Into de bushes, boy. I been there befo'. You want me, you go to 'at same woman's. She'll know. Giddy-ap, now!" and he spanked the horse's rump with his palm.

We got there just as dawn had fresh arrived, and the horse stood near the front door, kicking at the ground, but we couldn't have climbed out of that buggy if our lives depended on it. All I did was whimper; that ride half killed me.

I tried to think up some way to attract attention; then I heard Zeb tune up on his juice harp, and it turned the trick. There was a sound of slippers scuffling on the up-stairs veranda, a door slamming, and then running feet down below.

Lauriette. In nothing but a night dress. I could see her pale face staring at us as we lay stretched out in the buggy. She had one hand clenched and pressing against herself.

"What is it? What's happened? Oh, my God, your back —"

Her cries rousted the place up, and I don't remember anything else for awhile.

When I opened my eyes, I lay on my stomach on the big tester bedstead in my room, with nobody there except Uncle Jim and Dr. Snodgrass and Millie. He had shut the rest of the family out, not very gently, they said. He hadn't shaved, so I judged he'd been up all night, and I didn't care for his look.

"When you're strong enough, tell the story slowly, from start to finish. If you get tired, stop. Hold on, wait a minute."

He stepped to the door and opened it, and by gum, I could see that monster, Farrow, standing there, as cool as you please.

"Have my man, Zebediah, carried up here and placed in the other bed," said Uncle Jim.

Farrow smiled and replied, "We don't make a practice of letting darkies sleep in the bedrooms at Belle Mead."

"There'll be an exception in this case."

Their eyes battled a minute, then Farrow gave a little

frown of annoyance, and said, "Nothing's too much for a guest to ask."

"And be damned sure he's handled carefully."

For a second, I thought they might have it out right there in the hall, but Farrow finally shrugged, and left. I didn't blame him. I'd sooner tackled a buffalo than Uncle Jim in the humor he was in.

They brought Zeb up; I took a deep breath when the door was slammed, and made ready to begin, but Uncle Jim said, "I'll save you as much as I can. In the first place, this fellow's an identical twin; he was mentioned to me once or twice. Second, he's got epilepsy, and he's no good. Now, what else went on here?"

"A good deal," I said, talking mainly into my pillow. "I don't understand it exactly—I couldn't make out the old man's speech—but—"

Zeb spoke up to interrupt, as he naturally would; I don't know how he'd kept his mouth shut that long:

"Dey darky talk down hyar is coarse and ignerint and ain't pure the way it is up to Grassy—Masser Davey's right. He *wuz* hard to make out."

Uncle Jim clucked, impatient, so I went on:

"This fellow isn't only no good; he's a feend. A long time ago, long before the war, he got in bad troubles, for one reason after another, and finally went too far. They were going to lock him up in prison, in Natchez or someplace, but the family and their doctor made an agreement to shut him away in a private asylum. Well, about 1858, according to Uncle Ned, Mr. Paxton Farrow took the fever and died, right here in his room.

"Now I'm a little hazy, but I *think* what happened was this: The old gentleman, Mr. Farrow's father, willed Belle Mead down to his only decent son, because he didn't trust a blessed one of the others, and hated his wife like the furies. So he'd left a provision that if anything happened to Mr. Paxton—'dead or incapacitated'—the next in line was the old man's brother in Chicago, to 'run Belle Mead as he saw fit until one of the children proved worthy of succession'—that's the way Uncle Ned told it."

"They brought this madman out and made a substitution," said Uncle Jim. "God knows how they expected to get by with it. Everybody knew Pax hereabouts; they must have."

"The doctor gave out that his mind was left affected by the fever. He was delicate, and unsteady, and they'd represented the other brother to be dead, a long time beforehand. Then they sold the slaves, because darkies *will* talk, you know, white man's business or not, and kept to themselves. The fact is, they hadn't *ever* been sociable around here. The old lady's French, from New Orleans and looked on these Scotch and Irish as trash, and often said so, until the Vicksburg people didn't care to hear it any more. If you ask me, she's the worst monster of all, except for the daughter Marguerite, or three or four of the others. I'd like to see them *all* behind bars, including that wasp-tongued Lauriette—"

"No doubt," said Uncle Jim. "But the next item to consider is the ugly event of last night. Give it to me step by step."

I told him, but snuffled a little when I came to the whipping, and he got up and paced around. I could see Millie with her color high and eyes blazing, and Dr. Snodgrass fixing his attention for once directly on something besides doctoring. He looked pale, as if he could use a pull of Spooju.

"All right. Are you *sure* it was this fellow Farrow?"

"He had on a mask, but I'm sure. Who else had a reason?"

"He'll be taken care of—don't fret about it for an instant, but I intend to put the whole business here straight. I can do that for a friend. Now, are you quite certain Pax died a natural death?"

"The old man thought so. He didn't have any doubts about it."

"Well, I want them *all,* including the ruffians that helped out in this lashing. If I jump Farrow now, they'll scatter. We'll play it innocent for a day or two, then I'll settle the score. Meanwhile, it might be over-charitable to let him rest easy. Call him in, will you, Doc?"

Dr. Snodgrass opened the door and told a servant, in the first hard tone I'd ever heard him use: "Go fetch your master. Colonel Burnie wants him here at once."

In a minute or two, Farrow sauntered into the room, wearing a kind of mocky smile. He seated himself airily on a sofa.

"I understand that I've been summoned."

"I want your help, Farrow, in running down the cowardly skunks that hid behind masks to flog this boy and this darky. A person who'd do a thing like that is either crazy or criminal, or both. And certainly he's as low down as the foulest scum ever born, a slimy, sneaking, craven toad who ought to be stepped on and squashed. Do you agree?"

Farrow had risen half up at the first words, the color drained out of his face; now he stood with his hands working at his sides. In a minute he got his control back and said, "Most regrettable, but I don't know the boy very well. Perhaps he found himself—by accident, of course—trifling with something dangerous. The times are touchy, and passions easily inflamed. The Ku Kl—"

"But you see," said Uncle Jim easily, *too* easy for him, "I'm vouching for the boy—taking full responsibility for his actions. That puts us back where we started: how to track down the polecat that whipped him. It's going to be my pleasure to stomp him personally. If he were a notch above the level of common scoundrel, I'd call him out to duel. A gentleman can't duel with a toad. You can see the predicament I'm in, can't you, Farrow?"

We held our breath, because he *was* pitching it in pretty hot, and there might come an explosion at any time. But nothing happened, not yet.

"Why, old friend Burnie, you don't seem to be calling me 'Pax' any more. Surely you can't hold *me* responsible for this outrage?"

"Now, I do beg your pardon," said Uncle Jim. "It may be I'm upset, and didn't recognize you for a moment. Nobody, even me, could call Paxton Farrow a toad in my hearing. He'd have a fight on his hands."

The fellow hung up a minute—things were getting over-thick—then he turned on his heel and headed for the door, saying, "You're right, of course, we must make every effort to find them. However,—" he hesitated— "and it's only a guess, I'll wager the boy got involved in some old wives' tale of the darkies hereabouts. Such stories are risky—and often slanderous."

"I'm relieved you're going to help me find those villains," said Uncle Jim. "My mind's greatly eased. I'll check with you every hour or so, to see how you're getting along."

Farrow studied us from the doorway. Dr. Snodgrass had risen to his feet, and Millie's face was so hostile I thought she might throw something. But it was Uncle Jim's attitude that warned him off. If ever I saw a man anxious for an excuse to do murder, he was it. And Mr. Farrow wasn't fooled. So he let things go, and left.

Well, in the next day or two we found that even the worst of the Belle Mead women, including Marguerite and the old lady, were shocked by this happening, though maybe for the wrong reasons. The house was sunk into a kind of sullen quiet, with the servants tiptoeing around, and doors shutting very soft; no noise anywhere. Marguerite had their doctor, a nervous, elderly red-faced man with steel-rimmed goggles on, come out and stay on the premises.

He fussed around, but his hands shook so he dropped nearly everything he touched, and Dr. Snodgrass remarked afterward that he appeared to be suffering from a *mania a potu,* whatever that was.

Anyhow, our backs began to heal up surprisingly fast, more because of what Uncle Ned put on than what the doctor did, I expect, and we were up walking within three days. But we felt mighty stiff and sore, and were wobbly on our pins.

Uncle Jim was absent most of the time. I heard he'd driven into Vicksburg to see somebody, and I caught Mr. Farrow and the old lady whispering about it, in one of the shut-off parlors.

The time ticked on, and everybody wondered what might take place, particularly the family, I reckon. There was no question about us knowing the truth of that household now, and the only thing that remained was to see who'd make the first move, them or us.

Theirs, of course, couldn't be anything legal, but might be violent, so Uncle Jim gave Dr. Snodgrass a pistol and left him on guard in the daytime, and locked us in nights. Zeb had a revolver, too, so we were all right. In addition, and very insulting, Uncle Jim told Mr. Farrow he'd require to have a servant outside our door, to taste all the food coming in. It was the same as back in Pembroke, only this time he was serious.

"You never can tell," he said, with the old raspy manner. "Those scoundrels may somehow have gained access to your kitchen."

So the trays were brought up, the taster came in, and Dr. Snodgrass directed him from one dish to another. It was right in his line.

"Fine, fine, that takes care of the corn—no stomach cramps? No paralysis of the limbs? Respiration normal? Very well, let us pass on to the okra. I have a feeling we may hit the bull's eye on that."

I couldn't help but feel sorry for the darky, because every bite he took he figured would be his last, and while he never did get poisoned, his insides were tied in such knots by fright that he had undigestion every meal, so they had to give him soda, and then castor oil to unstop him. He only lasted two days on the job; they yanked him off more dead than alive, and warmed up a fresh starter.

Dr. Snodgrass really threw himself into this thing. Aside from his humbuggery, he was a kindly, genteel man, with plenty of courage, as Uncle Jim said, and his treatment of Mr. Farrow was about as abrupt as Uncle Jim's. I honestly think he'd have shot it out at the drop of a hat; he was that aroused.

In addition to the pistol, which he wore with the polished butt sticking out of his belt, in perfectly plain sight, as a declaration of possible war, he'd taken down a Horstmann saber from a pair on the wall downstairs, and wore *that* tied to a rope outside his frock coat. He was a sight.

Before a week was over, I was so restless I took to slipping outdoors, against orders. Uncle Jim heard about it and caught me; then he gave me a lecture, after which I promised to stay close to the house in the daytime and not venture out after dark. Zeb was established back in his quarters room, with the family that occupied the other half tending him. He was healing up, too, but he was mostly treating himself with his own remedy. Dr. Snodgrass looked in once or twice a day, and they had a pretty hot argument over procedure. Zeb was the main doctor among the hands at Grassy, and considered himself as legal and qualified as anybody, but I heard Dr. Snodgrass tell Uncle Jim in private that his methods were so "primitive and antiquated" that he was little better than a quack. Uncle Jim had the good sense to give him a withering look, but it bounced right off.

One afternoon, so hot and dull that nobody stirred, I decided to take a turn in the centerboard skiff, which that Lauriette had showed me how to sail. It was the only thing she'd done since we got there that didn't saw on your nerves like a file.

This craft was balky and cantankerous, very apt to tip over if you went to sleep and caught a puff. Still, if you got a good breeze it was fun to run it down before the wind and then zigzag back. It refreshed a person, and blew away the cobwebs.

When we first arrived, the creek-slough was more of a creek than anything, with a lively current, because the river level was lower. But now the river had risen several inches, backing the creek water to a standstill. So it was a slough again, and fine for sailing.

Zeb was asleep, Uncle Jim had gone to town as usual, Dr. Snodgrass was in the library reading a book about saber-dueling, Millie was off somewhere, and the family were scarce as hen's teeth. In this kind of weather they generally let the driving hour slide. Instead, they stripped down to their shifts, stayed in their rooms, and set up a howl for lemonade.

So I climbed into the boat, hoisted the sail, and made off for a place I knew upstream, where the family had a little summerhouse, circular and up-curving at the roof, on the order of Chinese. They used to go there for picnics, on days when the mosquitoes lay low.

With the wind at my back, I made good time. The water sloshed along the gunnels, and the canvas bellied out full and unrippled. It was nice. When I reached the place, I grounded the boat and walked barefoot toward the summerhouse, which was on a spring-fed pond they'd cleaned up, making a little beach, for swimming. I thought I might take a cooling-off dip, up as far as my back, then poke around searching for water moccasins, which is a pleasant entertainment, if you don't commence day-dreaming and get killed.

But before I got there, on the crooked path through thick bushes, I heard voices, so I slowed down. I figured it might be wiser to turn back, considering the fix I was in, but I crept on; I couldn't help it. Eavesdropping *was* one of the natural instincts of the human race, as Uncle Jim often said, and useful, too. For my part, I disliked to be rude; and to deliberately not listen when somebody was talking was downright offensive. I've heard Aunt Effie say so herself.

I eased myself on, trying to place those voices. In a minute or two, I could peer through the bushes, and there they were, in the clearing beside the pagoda—Mr. Farrow talking like the slimy plotter he was, and two burly men with their backs toward me, listening. They had on ignorant, workmen's black hats and rough clothing; they appeared to be farm hands, but there was more to them than that—you might say they looked like sworn avengers from a mob. They were that silent and purposeful.

"There'll be no killing near the plantation; make no mistake about it," Farrow was saying, causing me to wonder if I'd misjudged him. "We've protected this place too long to risk it on a toss of the dice."

One of the strangers said, "Now we've come this far, we aim to finish them here, holler all you please." I knew the voice well enough; it was Coley Baxter, and when the other fellow turned around, I recognized him, too. Ab Mullins. There wasn't any sign of his brother. "More'n twenty Dens throwed in to chase him down, and I spoke out for the job. He hazed me and others through the Army. This is grudge work."

"We're in perfect agreement on the end; what we've got to settle is the *means*. Also the place," said Farrow, and I was glad to hear it. I'd built him up in my mind as a villain, and didn't like to see it fall down again. "By the way, finish off the boy if you like, but Burnie's my property. I'll take care of *him,* and enjoy it. Now what I suggest is this: let's do some figuring, and meet back here tomorrow, same time. I'll have it worked out—don't worry."

"The Dens said they got to be punished, no matter how long it takes. Me and Mullins was delegated, and paid. Ain't they got a waggle-jawed medicine faker along with them? And a black-haired titty girl?"

"Dr. Snodgrass, and his daughter. I told you that the other night."

"They stopped at Pembroke, and sold a saddle, likewise all day at Bosky Dell and hawked nostrums. It didn't take ary bloodhound to trace them, time we located his horse. One of the mulatter niggers at Grassy told Ab's brother."

So we had a sneak working up there. I knew who it was, a skinny, impudent complainer that had been north working in Indianapolis for a year and came back because he said (very surprised) that they weren't any decenter to darkies in the North than they were in the South. I made a note to write the MacReadys and let them know. If he was guilty, they'd help Aunt Effie hightail that buzzard off his job so fast he'd run out of his shoes.

"Tomorrow at noon," said Farrow, obviously having a distaste for this rabble, and wanting to get the interview over.

"But no funny business," said Baxter. "I don't set much trust in fancy vests. That's the kind we're after."

"See here, my man, are you threatening *me?*" Farrow had a light in his eyes like a lunatic.

"No threats, no promises. The Dens voted punishment, and I spoke out for it. He haz—"

"Yes, yes, I've heard your story. We'll fix a final plan tomorrow. Our local Dens may want a say in it."

"One way or another," said Baxter.

Suddenly I had the inspiration to shift. In fact, it occurred to me I might be a little late, because all at once they started over in my general direction. If they had a boat, it was tied up above; maybe they had horses.

Anyhow, I lit out like a striped-tailed ape down that

corkscrew path, but the first thing I did was trip over a root and take a header into the weeds. You could hear the racket in Jericho.

"What's that?" I heard one cry; then another, I think it was Mullins, said, "Cool off. It's only a squirrel. You're as jumpy as a tomcat."

I didn't wait to see how it came out, but got up and sneaked on down to the creek bank, grabbed the prow of my boat, and towed it along the bank, as deep in the tree shadows as I could and not tangle up the mast. It was rough going, with mud up to your ankles, and brambles, too, on shore, so when I'd made two or three hundred yards, I stopped and listened.

Not a sound. I pushed off, rattled up the sail, and struck out for the opposite shore.

Uncle Jim was in my room, with Dr. Snodgrass and Millie, and I burst in and shut the door behind me, leaning there a second to get my breath back. When they rose up, looking startled, I said, "I've got terrible news. The Klan's after us. Coley Baxter and Ab Mullins are here."

Uncle Jim quietened me down, and I told what happened. When I got done, he seemed relieved, and even chipper and perked up.

"Capital, capital—we've bunched them. I'd been wondering how it might be done. Tomorrow may be a gala day."

Dr. Snodgrass had his saber and rope belt lying on the bed, so as to sit comfortable, but he got up now and put them on again.

"Not this time, Doctor," said Uncle Jim firmly. "It isn't your quarrel; we thank you all the same."

"I'm distressed to hear you say so, sir. Your decision comes at an unfortunate moment, as I have spent the better part of two days delving into Lazlo's 'Practical Hints for the Aspiring Duelist.' I have no wish to be fulsome, but I believe I may now regard myself as a skilled all-around swordsman—foil, épée, *or* saber."

"Keep the book close at hand," said Uncle Jim. "We may have to call on you."

I lay counting sheep, too keyed up to sleep, and listened to Uncle Jim pacing to and fro in the room next door. The house was uneasy. There was a squally wind, which made the framework creak: a shutter was loose some place, besides, and kept banging. It made such a dismal racket that I concluded to find it, if possible. About half of these rooms were empty.

I slipped along the carpeted hallway in the solid dark, for the lamp that was kept lit at the stair-head had gone out; blown by the draft, I reckoned.

When I reached Lauriette's room, the door suddenly opened and a hand grabbed me and dragged me inside. Another clapped over my mouth when the door shut, but it was wholly needless: I couldn't have mustered a mouse-squeak. All the brashness had drained right out; I didn't figure on doing any more exploring for thirty or forty years, even if I lived through the night.

She said, "Where were you going, little boy?"

After a few gulps, I got some breath back and began to rile up. I jerked my arm free, and said, "What's the matter with you, anyway? You trying to scare a person to death?"

I could see her pale nightgown against the blackness of the room and smell the perfume she'd dabbed on—she was that close. I didn't care for the scent, which was sickly-sweet but with a tinge of something sharper to it, on the order of a skunk. I figured it probably cost a dollar or more a bottle, being imported, but I preferred Millie's smell, which was a combination of sweat and maybe some powder or cologne sprinkled on to keep from having to take a bucket-bath on deck in the early morning, when nobody was looking.

"Back off some," I said. "I don't like to talk in people's faces." Well, it was true, but I'd never said so right out before.

"Are you afraid of pretty girls, little boy?"

"I'm afraid of *everybody* in this house, and I've got a healed-up back to prove it."

"Why did you come here? Why didn't you leave it *alone?*" She practically hissed the words out, like a snake.

I says to myself, here's another that had better be watched, and commenced to sidle out.

"Wait! There's something—. You ought to know something."

I hung up, but figured she'd slip a knife between my ribs, so I tried to keep from getting too near.

"Things here aren't what they seem. I mean, you shouldn't make up your mind. Even very old darkies don't always—"

"You can save your breath," I said, interrupting. "I know what things are, and so does Uncle Jim. But they aren't apt to stay that way long. Tomorrow—"

"*What*, tomorrow?" She grabbed my arms like a crazy woman, and shook me so my teeth rattled.

"Speak up, little boy. For your own good. What *about* tomorrow?"

"Let it go. I wouldn't care to discuss it. Nothing. Why don't you go to bed? If I was dressed as skimpy as you, I'd stay out of people's sight."

"I once asked you what kind of man your Uncle Jim was. I can tell you now—he's a fool."

I started to rip out something frisky, but decided it wouldn't do any good, so I wrenched free, snatched the door open, and wriggled out of there in a hurry.

The lamp still wasn't lit, and the old house twisted and groaned and skreeked like a ship in a storm. It was one of those wild nights, when a body would do better to stay in bed, maybe stuffing up their ears with cotton. But I still heard banging, and by this time I'd got into a humor where it was either the shutter or me. I'd recovered my spunk back. If I didn't get that racket stopped, I'd might as well sit up and twiddle my thumbs till dawn.

So I pushed on down the corridor, feeling my way, knowing where most of the tables and stands were, and came to the wing that they kept shut off. It was the first time I'd been there, and as soon as I opened the door I was sorry. While most of the house was complaining in the wind like a whiny old man, this part was silent as a tomb. I didn't care for it, but I crept on, curious now, besides being interested in the shutter, which had quit. Even on a hot, muggy, summer night, it had a *cold* feeling.

Some of those old houses ramble back longer behind than you'd think from the front, and the wing here was a sample. I begun to get the nervous shakes again, what with that row of tight-closed doors, and when a roach scraped over the floor, I jumped half out of my skin. I turned to go back, and then, by jingoes, I caught a whiff of cigar smoke. It was a smell I could recognize perfectly well. A minute later, I heard the sound of somebody playing a jew's harp, very faint.

Well, I stood there, with my neck hairs bristling up, and couldn't help but think of Miss Marguerite on the night in Zeb's cabin.

This place was one too many for me. I decided to remove myself out of the wing and quit messing with what wasn't any of my business. But I heard somebody coming down the hall; regular footfalls, light, like a woman's.

My nightshirt being starchy white, I was as bold as a signpost, so I scrunched down behind a heavy carved chest that somebody'd carted back from a tour, I judged. If you put together all the high-priced junk that southern people fished out of Europe before the war, you could stock a hundred museums, but none that anybody in his right mind would pay ten cents to enter.

The footsteps moved past, soft and even, and I recognized the scent, too. It was Lauriette; waiting, I heard her open a door, far down the hall, then all was quiet again.

Well, I was in *this* deep, so there was no use backing out now. But when I stood up to follow, a match scratched directly behind me, and I smelt cigar smoke again, this time very strong. I whirled around, with the ginger drained out of my knees, and saw a fiery red glow, which burned brighter for a second, then swung down in a circle.

"Get to bed, Davey," said Uncle Jim in a calm low voice. "We've got a busy day tomorrow."

"What's happening in there? Some devilment's up; I know it."

"Never mind. Go on to bed. You're out of your depth here."

When I got back, I lay a long time awake, waiting for the pow-wow of trouble to start, but none ever did, and eventually I drifted off to sleep, while the house shivered and shook and the storm howled on.

13

WE ROWED across the stream, Uncle Jim and I, at a few minutes before noon the next morning. The wind had slacked off, but the sky was left drippy and overcast. After hiding the boat, we started up an overgrown path along the bank. I'd never come by land, so we had to look sharp to find the place where you turn in for the spring-water pond.

Then, as before, voices were heard before we over-hauled the owners, there in the clearing. We pushed forward slowly, parting the bushes to look.

Coley Baxter and Ab Mullins were early, I guessed, because Mr. Farrow hadn't yet arrived. As you might expect, they were making windy threats about what they meant to do when they caught us.

"I'd give a pretty to see Burnie's face," Coley said. "Likely, he thinks he's Scott-free by now. He'll turn bottle-green."

"You figure to shoot him on sight or give him a chancet to draw?"

"If I know that fine-feathered dandy, he'll be too petri-fied scared to draw. He'll grovel and beg—wait and see. I know the breed, and hate 'em all. And so did my Pa before me."

Mullins knew better than that; he seemed doubtful, and said, "Well, he didn't do much begging at Ben Woods' house. And him with only two single-shot pistols."

"That was different. Up to then he'd had his own way. He figured to run a bluff—"

"Mighty sorry bluff," said Mullins, growing angry-looking and red. "It got my blood-kin cousin killed by that cub. It's him I want. I'm bound to acknowledge I gloried in that whipping. If it hadn't been for Farrow, I'd killed him. Him and the nigger both."

So it was Mullins that held the whip. I felt my stomach sour up and came close to stepping forward and cursing him, but Baxter spoke out to say, "What's keeping that namby-pamby? Truth to tell, I can't stand him, neither. Another golden-spoon high-and-mighty. When I get finished with Burnie, I may just——"

Uncle Jim stepped clear of the bushes and said, "You're not finished with him yet. In fact, my friend, you haven't even started."

It was two against one, both with guns showing outside, while Uncle Jim came dressed in his usual decent manner, with a fresh-cleaned Panama hat from Peru, an embroidered vest, and a long-tailed coat over dove-gray trousers. But he *wasn't* smoking one of those skinny black cigars for a change; his hands hung loose at his sides. He was ready, and they knew it.

"Where'd *you* come from, Burnie?" said Baxter, making a show of grit. He was dead-white, but Mullins was pitiful. He looked about to faint. He hadn't lived all of those years near Grassy without knowing why Uncle Jim won medals in the war. What's more, he was in Uncle Jim's company, until he got kicked out with an unhonorable discharge.

"Did I understand you to say *you* whipped the boy?"

Mullins started to bluff it out, but changed his plans and said, "Farrow made me, he——" but Baxter interrupted:

"Look here, Burnie, let's talk it over. We're from the same town, and ort to stick together. Now, I'll throw down my gun if you'll do the same"—he tossed a revolver onto the grass—"and we can patch up past differences."

"Why, certainly," replied Uncle Jim, reaching in his jacket and throwing *his* gun down. Then he unwound a twenty-foot braided whip from around his waist, and said, "But I'm a great one for parliamentary procedure, as I told you at Ben Woods', and the first order of business is to even up this boy's score. Will you, or your friend, be first?"

"Coley!" screamed Mullins. "Don't let him! Go ahead, like you planned!"

"Try me first, Burnie," said Baxter, and snaked one of those little derringers out of his shirt sleeve into his hand. "Now, by God, you're going to—"

They were the very last words he ever got out. Holding the whip in his right hand, Uncle Jim flashed another pistol from his coat and fired twice—I could hear both bullets hit with a solid "thock, thock"—in Baxter's chest. He staggered backward, with a surprised look, as if it'd been Uncle Jim that cheated, and sat down. He had one hand clutching himself, and for a few seconds just sat there, staring our way. It was enough to make your flesh crawl. Then a big fountain of blood bubbled out of his mouth and nose and he rolled onto his side, slack as a bag of wheat.

"Coley!" screamed Mullins again. He kneeled down to examine him but changed his mind and wheeled to run. Before he got four steps away, Uncle Jim's whip looped around his ankles, tripping him up in the shrubbery. He rolled over and over; then, on his knees, he commenced to beg.

"Get up," said Uncle Jim, "and flatten out face forward against that sycamore."

"For God's sake, don't shoot me! They made me do it."

It was a lie; just the same, I felt a little sick.

"Fasten his hands around the trunk with this string," Uncle Jim said, and I did it. Then he handed me the whip. "All right, there's the fellow that ruined your back —those scars won't all fade out; not by any means. Serve him the same way."

I gulped, taking the whip; then I threw it down.

"I can't," I said, not able to look him in the face. "I'm not that mad at anybody, scars or no scars. One killing's enough."

"It was Mullins that shot Commercial Appeal," said Uncle Jim, studying me pretty close.

"I can't punish him in cold blood. I'm sorry."

Putting an arm around my shoulder, he walked me across the clearing. "It's all right; it does you credit.

Don't worry about it, boy. Some day the world may turn its back on violent men. At present, unfortunately, we're saddled with swine like Mullins."

Businesslike, he picked up the whip, shook out the kinks, and gave Mullins a thrashing that ripped his shirt into red pennants. He chopped his back into mincemeat, the same as mine was. For the first two or three minutes, Ab screamed the trees down; then he fell into a kind of low, blubbery cursing. It was an ugly scene, played out at high noon there in the woods, but I couldn't help watching, though I tried to take my eyes away.

Uncle Jim cut him down, yanked him up to his feet, and said, "You're lucky you aren't with him," pointing to Coley Baxter. "It's what you deserve. Now go back to Hanksville and tell your brotherhood I'll shoot you down like dogs, all of you, if ever I see you again. Hear me, Mullins—the next time I look on your rat's face, I'll kill you—do you understand?"

He gave him a push, but it wasn't needed. Mullins disappeared into the bushes at a rattling good clip, considering the condition he was in. Then Uncle Jim wiped the sweat off his head with a handkerchief, and cleaned up his hands.

"Jim," a familiar voice floated out from the pagoda. "No change, I see. The storms still gather round your head." We moved fast, and Uncle Jim's pistol glittered in his hands. Dealing with Coley Baxter was one thing, but a man like Farrow was something else entirely.

Mr. Farrow *was* sitting there, and yet he wasn't. He seemed different. It was the same face, but of a different color—pasty white and blotched over with brown. Still, he had on the same kind of clothes, with clean white gloves and a gold-headed cane.

I felt the chills run up my spine, but Uncle Jim's frame loosened up and relaxed. He put the gun back under his coat.

"So it's you," he said. "I thought so." We started forward, but the figure in the pagoda said, "Don't come any closer; it mightn't be healthy. Stand there and let me look you over. By God, you're a sight; I'm damned if you aren't."

"What is it?" said Uncle Jim. "Tell me, or I'm coming on up—nothing's going to stop me now."

The blotchy man laughed. "Probably not. You'd do it if you had to shoot me."

"I'll come, all right. Let's get this business solved for once and for all. I won't stand id—"

"You can't solve leprosy. And neither can anybody else, it seems."

"So that's it."

"You remember the Grand Tour. I dallied too long in the Islands—a girl. You might say those islands *were* the tour. Then I spent a year in the colony at Molokai, and after that they brought me home by schooner. Now you ask, why didn't I write?" He drew off his gloves, and held up a hand, showing fingers that weren't hardly any more than sponges. "But I can still strum a jew's harp, using my knuckles. And that's very good luck for me."

"Why didn't you *send* me the truth?"

"I was afraid you might come down, and they were dead set on installing Rex"—that was the brother—"to avoid losing control here."

"Something's got to be done," said Uncle Jim. "It must be! By Godfrey, I'll see to—"

"Not a thing," he said cheerfully. "The best doctors have bumbled through every stage of attempted cure—chaulmoogra oil on up, or down. With my type of the illness, called lepromatous, there isn't any at present. One progresses from lesions of the nose to thickening of the skin to 'claw hands' to 'leonine facies'—the mottled color—and, after ten years or so, to his heavenly reward.

"By the way, don't feel too hard toward the family. Their little deception—they felt they were doing their best for us all. Maybe they were right. I'd rather 'dwindle, peak and repine' at Belle Mead than in some lazaretto of rotting strangers."

"But what kind of life do you call it—all these years?"

"Not bad, not at all bad. There's little pain. I'm around, here and there, driven in a buggy, taken in the boats. We switch back and forth when times are opportune. I'm no prisoner in the room, not a bit. Think it over —they've taken their chances—every one of them. And they risked freedom by a falsified death and burial. By good fortune it's only contagious in conditions of squalor and filth. Not a soul knew the truth, not even your old Uncle Ned. Nobody knew but us."

After a minute, Uncle Jim says, "Does your charitable impulse include your precious brother?"

"Well, now, that's another matter. You'd better look sharp there. When the mood's on him, he's as blood-thirsty as a weasel. And he's mixed up with these vermin-ous hooded 'avengers.' "

"Than what do you suggest?"

"Clear off, in a hurry, with my thanks and my blessing. Either tonight or tomorrow. I talked him out of here today, for old time's sake. But I can't hold them off for-ever. They're dead set on abolishing you; I don't know why."

It was the first time I ever saw Uncle Jim at a loss. He took off his hat, then wiped his forehead again. By and by he said, "I'm sorry, Pax. I sure as hell am sorry. And I wish I could think up something better than that."

Mr. Farrow began hobbling down the path on the op-posite side, but before disappearing from sight, he turned and shouted, "Whatever happened to old Grimes?"

"I shot him," said Uncle Jim.

The laugh that burst out was as merry as a person's without a worry. Then the bushes swallowed him up, and we were left alone in the clearing, except for a dead man on the ground. All of a sudden, I wanted to get as far away from this plantation as I could.

In the afternoon, Uncle Jim and Dr. Snodgrass sold the houseboat on the quiet; then they bought tickets to New Orleans on the *Robert E. Lee,* which was due in Vicks-burg tonight. They got two cubby-hole single rooms and a nice big double one for Dr. Snodgrass and Millie. Zeb had to go deck passage and eat with the hands. But Uncle Jim gave him fifty dollars for the misery he'd suffered, and he was in a fair-to-middling humor, for him.

So little medicine was left on hand that Dr. Snodgrass sold it in a lump to that undisposed ferry-boat owner, who was doing a prosperous business again, in the very best of health. It brought a good price, too. The man was pinched for cash, so after some haggling Dr. Snodgrass took twelve dollars hard money and an I.O.U. for seventeen one-way rides across the river. Uncle Jim pointed out that this would leave him stranded on the other side, but Dr. Snodgrass said he'd likely have some more medicine by then, and could make a new arrangement, and maybe wind up with the boat. He was in high spirits; so were we all.

Packing to leave, I felt better than I had in weeks. I'd sunk so low, I'd almost forgot there were places better than this. The prospect of getting out, seeing a lot of new sights, smelling new smells, and continuing our adventures to Cayo Hueso made my healed-up back seem like nothing, and Zeb he said the same.

Our departure, toward evening, was peculiar. Things were done different at Grassy, where the people (except for Aunt Effie) were looser in their manner somehow. Nothing was seen of our main host; only two or three women showed up to see us off. The aunts and cousins had been flattened by their ailments, I judged. To our surprise, though, the old lady came downstairs, as usual dressed in black, and said to Uncle Jim, "I wish to tell you, at last, that we understand your motives for coming to Belle Mead. I thank you on behalf of my son."

Uncle Jim was by no means in a generous humor about these people, so he said, "Which one, Madam?"

"Good*bye, Captain." *That* old ramrod didn't promote him; she wasn't the kind to get his rank confused. She had a mind like a carpenter's square, and kept things in plumb every step of the way.

When we climbed up into the rig, I looked back and saw Lauriette at one of the windows. As I stared, I thought she started to wave, but she must have changed her mind, for she let her hand drop and turned on away.

Now I've got to describe pretty fast what happened when we left, because I've dwelt long enough on this part. We drove in and paid our bill for the horse, then a darky set us down on the wharf. The boat had only just arrived, but it had an overburdened lot of lumber and cement to unload from up river, and a cargo of cotton to take on for New Orleans.

It was dark before they finished, then they let us aboard, but a hitch developed after that in the form of trouble with the engine. So we checked into our rooms—and mine *was* cramped and dingy for such a gaudy big boat. But we were on our way, and that's what mattered.

Well, the time dragged on toward midnight, while the people including us went aft in little groups to look at the engineers working below in the lantern-glow. Finally, just as I suspicioned, Uncle Jim said I'd got to go on to bed. Nobody *else* had to go to bed; no, sir; only me. It turned out that way every time.

It was squeezed-in close quarters up there, with two or three pipes running along the roof over my head, so that if a person raised up from his bunk in a hurry, he was sure to dent one with his head. I never saw such a hole; things were roomier in a wardrobe.

They'd told me to latch my door, and I did it, but presently there came a knock while I was dozing off, and when I collected my wits to call "Who's there?" a voice on the outside said, "Your Uncle Jim."

I should have known better—he wouldn't identify himself in that ridiculous style but would say something boneheaded like Abraham Lincoln or the King of Australia—but I was sleepy, and opened on up. They pushed in, two of them, stuffed a gag in my mouth, snatched up some clothes, pinned a note to my bunk, hustled me out on deck, then down a companionway on the dark side. After this, we went overboard into a skiff. They had their oarlocks wrapped to muffle noise, but it was needless because of the racket in the engine room. Before we got to shore, they blindfolded me, and finally there came a rough, jouncy session in a buggy.

When the blindfolds were removed, I was seated on a bench at a rude table in what looked like a darky shack, clear enough, and across the way sat Mr. Rex Farrow. I was back at Belle Mead.

"Well, my boy—if we can't go to Mr. Burnie, perhaps he'll come to us."

"You're as good as dead. He won't let you off this time —I know Uncle Jim."

"You know him; fancy that. Take my advice and never fall into the snobbish habit of name-dropping. Now we're going to play a game, sonny. What *is* your name, by the way?"

"Sam," I said. I was so mad I commenced skating on thin ice; I couldn't help myself.

"Here's how the game goes, Sam. You tell me where your uncle was heading, or my friend outside"—he rapped on the table and a coarse-looking man with crazy black eyes came in—"will assist me in choking it out of you."

By this time, I was practically giddy, so I said, "Oh, there's no need of that—I'll be glad to tell."

"Where, then? And be careful."

My idea was, to get this fellow started off on as long a haul as possible, so I said, "Patagonia, extreme southern part."

I should have known better. I overdid it; moreover, it was Millie's fault for teaching me geography. Over-learning can get a person into a peck of trouble.

He smacked me so hard I fell off the bench, and when I got up, wiping blood from a corner of my mouth, he said, "I told you to be careful."

I sat there for a minute, then said, "Mexico."

"What part of Mexico?"

"I don't know. They didn't go into it."

"Where's the gold map I heard my brother mention?"

"Uncle Jim memorized it and ate it." It popped out before I knew it, being the action somebody took in a pirate book I read.

He half rose and grabbed my shirt, but when he reached over to hit me, a change came on him. His face froze, his eyes rolled up so that nothing was seen but the whites, saliva began to dribble from his lips, and his body stiffened up like a corpse. He was having a fit, and I jumped back out of the way to watch. Well, within a minute or so his face was a dull blue, like lead, and shortly after that he started to choke, as if somebody had a grip on his neck. Then he fell to the floor with a crash, and the coarse-looking stranger burst back into the room.

"He's got a fit," I said, so as not to be blamed.

"He's swallered his tongue. Grab his arms while I prize it out."

I caught hold, hoping it wouldn't work, but the man stuck a spoon between the jaws, then reached in with his hand and pulled up the tongue. But it wasn't easy.

In about ten minutes, Farrow was breathing regular, and opened his eyes to ask, "What happened? Did I go off?"

"You throwed a fit," said the stranger, not over sympathetic.

"Help me to bed." At the door, he turned around and said, "Tomorrow we'll attend to *your* case. And be sure of this, sonny—whether your Uncle *Jim*"—he pronounced the name with a nasty kind of bite—"comes back or not, we'll get him. As long as I'm able to travel, we won't give up, not if it takes twenty years."

They locked me in, and I fastened the bolt on my side, mainly to be troublesome, and after an hour or so, I went to sleep on a cot without any blankets. It must have been a short time before dawn when I heard a light scratching at my boarded-up window, and a woman's voice:

"Let me in, David. Hurry!"

Well, I couldn't be worse off than I was, so I opened up, and there was this Lauriette, fully dressed, in a riding suit.

"Come on, hurry! We'll need at least two hours' start."

"Where to?" I said stupidly.

"I'm leaving this house of horror. I can't live here any longer. And I'm taking you out before you're hurt further."

"How?"

"By horseback. Come on; you can talk later."

"You mean you're leaving for good? Clearing off? Not coming back?"

"Was there *ever* such a talkative brat! I'm leaving forever. That's why I asked about your Uncle Jim. But you were too busy playing the dunce to answer."

"What if he comes to get me?"

"I've left word with someone I trust. Now get a move on. Morning's coming, and they'll drag us back."

Down by the creek, she had two horses saddled and waiting, with some luggage strapped on. But when we got there I remembered Farrow's last words, and said, "There's something I've got to do. Hold up."

"Dawn's nearly here, you fool. *Will* you hurry?"

I knew what I was after, and found it—a heavy three-foot crowbar, lying against some lumber back of the kitchen; then I felt my way around to the front door. They never kept it locked. I expect they figured that nobody in his right mind would care to prowl in that house, especially after dark, but this time they were wrong.

What I had to do was the worst thing I'd ever done in my life, but I couldn't see any other course. It was best for all concerned, and anyhow he had it coming.

I crept upstairs, knowing my way well enough, and found Mr. Rex Farrow's bedroom. There wasn't a sound in all the house; nobody stirring, and no sign of the coarse-faced stranger.

I shut the door gently behind me and stood still, waiting to get used to the dark. In a minute or so I had him spotted; he was sleeping, and snoring, on top of the covers, dressed only in a nightshirt.

I took a deep breath, tiptoed over to peer down—I couldn't afford to make a mistake—and made him out beyond a doubt. Then, aiming for a spot just above his right knee, I swung the crowbar as hard as I was able.

I expected him to scream, but he gave a quick gasp that ended in a long, stomach-turning groan, a kind of sighing "Ah-ah-oh-ah!" I didn't wait, but spun around and made for the stairs. Before I'd returned the crowbar to its place, the screams began—awful and chilling—so I didn't tarry any longer. I streaked down the path to the river.

"What happened? For God's sake, what have you done?"

"Returned a favor, and slowed up pursuit," I said. "If you want to hurry, this may be a good time to do it."

She took the lead, at a gallop so fast I had trouble hanging on, and I followed just far enough behind to keep from being kicked. In the first streaks of dawn, I saw we were abreast the river, heading south, judging by the current, and before long we eased to a canter. But it must have been four or five miles until we stopped for a breather.

I felt poorly. It went hard to smash a sleeping man's leg, without giving him a chance to fight back. But when I remembered my whipping, and Zeb's, my conscience eased and I didn't care so much. Most important for us, there was one thing I knew for sure. Even if that leg healed up to be normal, Mr. Rex Farrow was out of traveling, and murdering, condition for many a long month to come. I put everything I had into that swing, and heard the bone snap like a dry hickory stick.

By and by I took to thinking: They would drop by my stateroom going to breakfast, and find that note. But what if they decided to let me sleep, and a colored steward that couldn't read came in to tidy up? He'd whisk the note right out in a dust pan without winking. If that happened, they'd be ten or twelve hours down river before they recognized I was gone. And after that, wouldn't they calculate I'd somehow tumbled over the rail? Any way you looked at it, things were in a pretty poor pickle.

14

———— ⦁—⟨●⟩—⦁ ————

AFTER THINKING IT OVER, it seems best to let the story be carried on here by a letter to my aunts. It certainly isn't a very good letter, as it contains a considerable number of lies (which the reader will quickly spot) about the author of this book, but it tells what the other bunch were doing when I wasn't there, and so takes up the slack.

In Transit,
July 25, 1869

Dear Miss Effie and Miss Lou:

Having been commissioned by your esteemed brother (Lt. Col. James Burnie), my good friend and companion of the road, to convey news of import in his absence, I must reluctantly report that your nephew David has disappeared from the public view. The concensus of opinion is, I grieve to say, that his mortal remains may lie in the muddy bed of Father Mississippi.

Without plunging into a detailed recapitulation, I should say that the expedition of Col. Burnie, your nephew, and the Colonel's valet and personal (unlicensed) physician, Zebediah, soon became encumbered with the addition of myself, Dr. Ewing T. Snodgrass, D.C., M.P., Ph.U., and my daughter, Millicent, a frail, flowerlike creature whose excess of femininity serves, I fear, to retard our progress. Like her mother before her (a musician of sensitivity, with a remarkable lip for the valve-horn), she is far from strong.

We joined forces in the tasteless village of Pembroke, Arkansas, and after a series of adventures and misadventures (during which your obedient servant managed to clean up a health crisis in Bosky Dell) we visited the Vicksburg plantation of Col. Burnie's whilom friend, Mr. Paxton Farrow. I shall not soon forget the bizarre problems that there confronted us. Suffice it to say that we were compelled, virtually under cover of darkness, to evade that foul den, aboard the steamboat *Robert E. Lee*.

Now to the business at hand. Our company being largely disposed in small individual staterooms, David was alone, and when the "rosy-fingered dawn" (Virgil) arrived, bringing with it the promise of breakfast, we decided to let the lad sleep. He had lately undergone physical reverses which I shall describe in another missive, with Col. Burnie's permission.

As there was no sign of his presence at noon, we again repaired to his room and this time were staggered to find him missing, vanished like the proverbial Arab (Longfellow), not to be located in any quarter of the ship. His bed had been occupied, we found, and his knapsack of small possessions, including a deceased and fragrant mole, reposed upon a wash stand whose water pitcher appeared to be untouched (typical in the case of boys his age, I believe). A negro steward under questioning revealed that the room was also tenantless at nine A.M., when the bed was made, and that the door was seen swinging half-open at 7:30.

Now, certain surmises are permissible without casting aspersions upon the character of this promising child. Col. Burnie has affirmed that, upon receipt of an order, any order, such as a command to retire for the night, his instinct was to do exactly the opposite, and that just as swiftly as possible. Col. Burnie has also verified that the boy, having apparently been born with a species of monkey curiosity, was an eavesdropper of rich and ingenious gifts. In addition, the mountebank Zebediah has emphatically if tearfully volunteered that the unfortunate's capacity for mischief has never been equalled in the long history of Grassy Plantation.

I hasten to say, worthy ladies, that these traits, in the aggregate, do not provide an anchor on the road to progress. On the contrary, faithfully cultivated, and enhanced, they might well produce a man of distinction—a politician; a banker; an international swindler; a great general, glorious in defeat; even a President, if the owner could divest himself of any taint of conscience.

So—we have opined that David Burnie—God soothe his active soul!—may have tumbled overboard in the course of some prying, nocturnal stroll. Who knows what could have summoned a boy thus driven? Laughter from a partially shuttered stateroom, a dice game among the lounging stevedores, an ambition to remove some nut or bolt of the darkened machinery on deck, an urge to bore a hole in the hull.

Col. Burnie went straightway to Captain Ogilvie, who stopped the engines and began an exhaustive search. Nothing forthcoming, your brother then bade us all good-bye, arranging win or lose to meet us later in New Orleans, and went ashore in a lighter. He will inquire in villages along both banks of the river, back to a considerable distance.

Meanwhile, we are, as you may imagine, in a state of deep mourning. It galls the undersigned to dispatch you such ill-omened tidings. Let us pray that my next communication may be in the nature of pealing church bells, heralding the great news of discovery and restoration. David could swim—there can be no question of that. At an island where we once tied up, he negotiated a broad deep slough and returned carrying a very substantial load of pilfered corn in a sling on his back. It would have done credit to a thief twice his age. So there is some chance, we think, that he might have made his way to shore. If that is true, the nearest community would of course be alerted, if not up in arms, very shortly. And on that note of restrained optimism, I stay my pen with every felicitation and condolence for those of you, his loved ones, at Grassy, and an avowal to keep you abreast of the intelligence as it develops.

Your respectful friend (by proxy),
Dr. Ewing T. Snodgrass,
D.C.; M.P.; Ph.U.

At the time Dr. Snodgrass was composing that idiotic note, Lauriette and I were sloping along down river, steering around towns and staying shy of people. The first night, we hid and slept in a hayloft. In her saddle bags the girl had brought two loaves of bread, two tins of fish, a long sausage and some fruit from Belle Mead. So we had a tolerable supper, with the horses tied to a tree beside a fresh-water creek, a good distance off the road.

For once, she appeared untalkative, except for bossiness now and then, like most females. What they do in the case of a boy, I figured, is work in all the high-handed orders that they're able, to pay up for being run by a husband later on. For instance, she had a couple of toothbrushes, and when we finished eating she handed one over, with instructions to scrub up. I told her I was generally in the habit of brushing my teeth when and how I pleased, and had been doing so for a number of years.

"Then let me see your toothbrush."

"I don't remember saying I had one. I lost it."

"Do you want your teeth to rot and fall out?"

"Well," I said, "George Washington didn't have any teeth. They put in wooden ones, but it didn't slow him up much. He went right on and bagged a very nice situation, according to some people's lights."

Anything along that line, any kind of argument, caused her to fall right back into her old fakey speech, so when she said, "Little boy, you're just so cute and cunning I could eat you up," I brushed my teeth in a hurry. A little of that kind of thing went a long way. We watered the horses, went to the bathroom, in different directions, and moved on.

After dark we located a farm set back by itself, and waited for the people to blow out their lamps for the night. Then we pegged down the horses to graze and crept toward the barn. But she was nowhere near as smart as she thought, for she would have tramped right on up, regardless of where the wind lay.

"No you don't," I said. "These farms have dogs, and there'll be a pow-wow if they scent us. We'll mooch up from the *other* side."

Now in the hot summer there was nothing in the barn

but a mare about to foal, but she never bothered to whinny, having her mind on her family, I reckon, so we climbed on up to the loft. A breeze blew in through the opened hay door, and the hay was clean and fresh and sweet-smelling. On top of that we had a nice aroma of the warm horse below—and there isn't any better perfumery that I know of—besides traces of other animals and fowl, on the order of goats and dogs and chickens that wandered in and out of there, and altogether it seemed like one of the best places to sleep I ever struck. But she took on as if she was about to bed down with pigs in a pigsty.

She says, "What a *vivid* stench! I thought you said barns were ideal places to stop, darling boy."

I could have argued, but didn't, only suggesting that she go on back to the grove and sleep with the horses, if she felt bottled up. The fact is, I was sorry for her, because I realized that she probably hadn't ever done this sort of camping before. They lived soft at Belle Mead.

"You'll be safe out there," I said. "They don't often see bears in this country, and those they see are generally harmless, unless one has cubs, or a bad disposition. Except for that, and maybe snakes and wild dogs, there isn't a thing to worry about. Aside from poison ivy or oak."

She gave me a mean look, as I punched out a place to lie down; then she had the downright cussedness to make me undress out of my clothes.

She said, "It isn't sanitary to sleep in your daytime garments like a tinker. We'll observe a few amenities here, no matter how gipsy-low we sink otherwise."

So I peeled down to my drawers, then called a halt. "I've got a little regard for the amnesties myself," I said, "and privacy is the main one of them. Do whatever you like, but I'm *through*. If necessary, and it shouldn't be, I'll wash these drawers out every few weeks, but as far as *you're* concerned, this is my sleeping outfit, so you'd might as well get used to it, and live with it."

She went ahead, standing in front of the hay door in the moonlight, humming, and stripped right off to her skin. Then she took a silk nightgown from her belongings and prepared to put it on, but she wasn't in a rush about it. She paid me no more attention than she would a cigar-store Indian. It was humiliating.

I gave a kind of cough, and by George, I meant it to sting!

"You sound a little croupy. We'll have to get you some tar syrup tomorrow."

"If it wouldn't place any strain on you, you might cover yourself up," I told her. "This is just an ordinary barn, not a Show Boat."

"Oh, bosh. You're not that sensitive. Haven't you got any sisters?"

"None that strut around rump-naked in front of strangers."

"How old *are* you, you precocious little cuddlekins?"

"Fourteen," I said, and turned over. Confound the creature, she'd spoiled my sleep, with all of her noisy gab.

We were up early, and stole out before anybody saw us. For three more days we did exactly the same thing—slept in barns and picnicked along the way, making ourselves as small as we possibly could. Twice we stopped at drowsy, littered-up general stores, removed from the main river route, and bought things, but only one of us went in at a time, lest the organization have a description out about a boy and young woman traveling together. On top of that, we mumbled some tommyrot about visiting in the neighborhood.

And then, on the fourth day, she said we were far enough along to continue by steamboat. So we struck back for the river and jogged along it the better part of one afternoon, or until we got to a sizable town. Then we found there was a St. Louis boat due in that night, and Lauriette bought two tickets to Orleans, fishing some yellow-back bills up from between her bosoms, right in front of everybody.

"Now, about these horses," I said, disgusted. "We can get a rousing good price for them; saddles, too, if we strike the right dealer. But you've got to be careful. Most of these fellows are as crook—"

"Not on your life. And have them traced back to Belle

Mead? We'll give them away, and do it back in the country from town."

Well, that was one too many for me. I'd rather been caught than give away two perfectly sound horses, and said so. But she was correct, as time proved out.

Even so, you never saw so many precautions. She hired us a rig, which I drove while she rode one of the horses and led the other. The boat was due at round about midnight, so we rattled back into a poor section of one-horse cropper farms, and then, at the last minute, she changed her plans.

"We won't give them away—it might arouse too much curiosity. We'll turn them loose, individually," she said. The silly fool found all this entertaining, because I imagine it was the first time in her life she'd ever done anything on her own. A person living in that frosted-over hermits' hole of a plantation might just as well have retired to a monkery and resigned.

So after a while, when dusk came on, she saw a darky farm that looked tidy and neat, with no trash in the yard, but picked up and raked as respectable as anybody's, and she turned her fine blooded stallion—an expensive and beautiful horse, though mean like her—loose in the pasture.

"They'll find it, and inquire around, then keep it, I hope," she said.

The whole rigmarole was ridiculous, of course, but I had to play along; there wasn't any help for it. We stuck the saddle in a barn of another place about three miles down the road, and then we did it all over with the other horse.

After that, she was satisfied; we rolled and bumped back to town. I never ran across anybody so puffed up with virtue. "They'll find those horses and saddles useful," she said. "I'm glad they have them."

"What'll probably happen is that some innocent, hardworking darky man, father of nine or ten sick and starving pickaninnies, will be hauled up for horse-stealing, and hung. No, I can't say you've done anybody a good turn here today."

Her eyes flashed and her nostrils kind of opened in and

out. "They wouldn't dare!" Then she thought of an easy way out, and said, "In a day or so, I'll write a disguised letter to the local newspaper and explain what I've done. That ought to fix everything."

And let me put in here, so as not to forget it later, that she went right ahead and kept her promise. She wrote a very flourishy note and showed it to me before mailing it at a landing where the boat unloaded some flour, whiskey, and iron castings. Somehow it made me feel better about her, but not for long.

At midnight, we boarded the *Jacob Gruber,* which was one of the big Mississippi packets, over four hundred feet long and having a forty-four foot beam with double side-wheels. Best of all, it was one of those new low-pressure boats and had it painted so in box-car letters on the paddle casings. Here lately there'd been a lot of explosions on the high-pressure boats (which were cheaper to build, of course) and people were happy to ride on the low-pressures for a change. They had a better chance to arrive at where they were going.

It hadn't been so long ago that anybody'd forgot the *Moselle's* boiler bursting at Cincinnati, from building up steam to beat another boat, with a loss of two hundred fifty lives. Or the fire aboard the *Ben Sherod,* racing the *Prairie* below Natchez, that burned or drowned two hundred passengers and crew. Or the *Monmouth,* carrying six hundred Creek Indians from New Orleans to the Arkansas River (shuffling those poor devils around from pillar to post, as they always did and still do) running into the *Trenton* while short-cutting up part of the river where it hadn't any business to be, and killing more than half of that tribe. Or a good many other accidents, more recent. People were scared of those high-pressure boats, with plenty of reason.

Lauriette, who claimed to know a lot about steamboating, just as she did about everything, said a man named Charles Dickens, who was an Englishman that wrote very interesting books for a living, when he wasn't too mad about something to work, took a trip on the Ohio in 1840 and expressed himself as being uncomfortable all the way. "It always conveyed that kind of feeling to me which

I should be likely to experience, I think, if I had lodgings on the first floor of a powder mill," he said. (But I heard he had a poor digestion, and was jealous of other writers, which I'm not, thank goodness, and haven't any reason to be. There aren't many good ones around.)

Well, it wasn't *quite* that bad, but we were happy to be on a low-pressure boat, just the same, and I felt peaceful for the first time since I left Grassy. If Uncle Jim and the others, even Millie with her geography book, had been along, things would have been perfect.

We had a big, gaudy double cabin with beds, not bunks, along either side and a Chinese screen in between, and a window to look out of. It must have cost a stack of money, and I said so.

"Poverty has never been considered among the unpleasant features of Belle Mead," she said in an acidy tone, so I let it drop. I'd met people that were purseproud before, including Commercial Appeal once for a week after he found a dollar, and sooner or later they got their comeuppance. In his case, he invested in two rabbits off an Indian trader, meaning to go into business and make a fortune, rabbits being inclined that way, but they both turned out to be males.

They had entertainment on this boat that people said was above the ordinary. It was on account of the Captain, a portly, hee-hawing, red-faced jackass named Boomer, who was known as a riot of fun. He very much fancied his figure, which was stuffed pretty tight into a shiny blue suit with enough brass buttons to open a store with, and he cut a lot of shines amongst the ladies, taking them in little bunches to see this wreck, and that snag, and the like—all very dangerous, to hear him tell it—so that they would squeal, dainty and timorous, and look at him admiring, then say things like, "Oh, my *goodness,* Captain Boomer, how *do* you go up and down this monstrous big river month after month? Doesn't it just scare the *life* out of you?" Upon which he'd roar out in laughter, giving them a pinch on the arm, or any place handy, and tell them no, he could run it "with both hands tied in a fog with a blizzard going."

But one noon when he'd drunk three or four glasses of

wine and told a dozen or so braggy "experiences," he went up to the wheelhouse, with the usual kite-tail of ninnies, and the first thing he did was run the boat onto a sand bar. It was stuck as tight as a brick set in concrete, and the river falling. Well, neither the crew or the men passengers were overjoyed, because a number had to row out in boats carrying anchors to kedge us off, and it took a tiresome long while, as well as involving several styles of cussing. Most of the ladies retired to their cabins; it was too various for them.

After this for awhile the Captain didn't blow so much but meeked down a little and even quit pinching the ladies, which was a good thing, for I'd noticed a husband or two looking ruffled, as if they didn't know quite what to do. About the only female he hadn't any luck with was Lauriette, who blossomed out like a morning glory on this boat, with a gown cut so low you could practically see her knees. It was a disgrace, as I told her, but she said when a woman was "richly endowed she shouldn't hide her lights under bushels"—common.

Well, that ass of a Captain ventured to give her a friendly tweak as she leaned over the rail, and she straightened up with a peal of laughter, tossing aside her handkerchief, and fetched him a clout across the chops that rolled his eyes in their sockets like marbles. He reeled over the deck on rubber legs and kind of fell down a companionway to his cabin. "You're a wonderful conversationalist, Captain," she called after him, as if she didn't notice anything wrong. "We must have another chat soon."

It seemed a little hard. After all, she'd practically invited him to gouge her, by bouncing around so, and then she had to punish him. She was a bully.

I tried to make up my mind which of them I couldn't stand worse. The next day, I saw Captain Boomer lounging around near the texas, sporting a shiner, and offered him a pair of brass knucks I got in a pawn shop, to give him a fighting chance, in case she piled on him in earnest, but he turned them down, thanking me courteously. He'd had all the wind taken out of him by that whack, and no wonder. It was vicious. This Lauriette may have *looked* soft and round, especially standing naked in the barn in the moonlight, but she was about as helpless as a crocodile. I'd found that out when we were riding on the road. She could pound a saddle for hours without tiring; she had my tongue hanging out before we'd gone ten miles.

Before long, Boomer recovered his natural offensiveness, and hauled out his principal amusement, which was a cockfight. When I saw it, I was sorry I'd offered him the brass knuckles, for he didn't deserve them, no matter how bad women beat him up. We found out that he always carried this kind of sport along, to round out the roistering and gambling in the saloon (which, by the way, was over a hundred feet long—the principal room—on the *Jacob Gruber*). He had a combination friend and employee, a greasy fellow named Lopez, darker than the average Cuban, which had a collection of gamecocks.

Well, on a ship this size somebody or other was always transporting domestic fowl, and after the Captain had shamed and ridiculed the owner, they usually gave in and agreed to fight.

On the occasion of our trip, a young farmer, red and worried (because he'd as much as been called a coward in front of a rowdy group), picked out his brassiest rooster and they got ready, on the upper deck space around the smoke pipes, forward of the saloon and sheltered by the pilot deck, generally used for baggage and open-air seats.

Everybody with a strong stomach that could crowd in was there, and a number, flushed with drink, were betting large sums. Lopez and the farmer squatted down, holding the birds, and when that fool of a Captain shot off a gun, they gave them a ruffled shove out into the center. For a minute, they only circled around, wary and suspicious, but the gamecock had been trained to kill, and seeing an advantage it leaped forward and lit on that tame rooster all spraddled out. But Boomer and Lopez had a surprise coming; the farmer's bird very clearly preferred civil treatment from its companions, and said so, along with several rooster oaths; then he kicked that gamecock about ten feet straight up.

There was a hubbub from the gamblers, because it was

mostly the professionals that lost; then somebody set up an outcry for a re-match, this time with gaffs. The farmer looked unhappy—he was a decent enough fellow and likely would never have served his flock so, but he was in a tough position—so they sawed off both roosters' spurs, put on gaffs, and, after the Cuban held his bird's head in his mouth—to "revive" it—shoved them back again. In a twinkling both fighters were stabbed through the neck and lying bleeding on the deck. But the Cuban's finally got back to its feet, wobbly and weak, and was declared the winner. There was no other way to judge it, for the farmer's bird was stone-cold dead, sprawled down in a mess of blood and feathers.

"Hoo-rah!" the Captain cried, with an impudent stare at the farmer. "Now if you've got anything better than that, trot 'em out, for you surely to God ain't showed us much yet."

"I need the rest of my roosters for when I and my wife set up to farm," the young man said, looking around, defiant. "If a hen figures to lay, she needs a rooster. And I've already lost my best worker."

"Why, you don't mean that specimen laying *there* was apt to oil up a hen's machinery, do you?"

Well, everybody like to split open, laughing, and said it was as powerful a joke as they'd heard in a month of Sundays, and the Captain was so pleased he could hardly rest. It was the first real good one he'd got off this trip, according to one of the gamblers. He said it all over again; then he sent a deck hand down to rouse up the first mate, so *he* could hear it, but he came back looking pretty sour, being asleep, and then they pushed up around the farmer and commenced to make things warm. Poor hayseed, he hadn't any idea how to handle this situation, with all these swells in fancy clothes, so he just grew redder and redder. But he tried to stick to his guns.

"How much do you ask for your fowl—all of them, my man?" said Lauriette, walking coolly forward amongst that gang of dandified roughnecks.

"I thank you, ma'am, but I didn't calculate to sell them."

"What do you want for *your* collection?" she said, turning to the Cuban with a curl to her lips.

"See here, Madam—" said the Captain, beginning to bluster in a cautious sort of way, but she cut him off short.

"Name a price."

This Lopez scratched his head, and said, "These birds *muy expensivo*," or words along that line. "In Cooba—"

"Would fifty dollars put an end to this disgusting exhibition?"

"*Sí, Señorita,* maybe. *Muchas gracias.*"

And then, by golly, she unlaced her bodice and dug down into the bank again, causing a number of whistles and catcalls, shelled out the money, pointed to the Cuban's coops, and said to the farmer: "I trust these will repay you for the loss of your bird."

He couldn't cough up a single word, but gulped several times and worked his Adam's apple in appreciation, while the rest of the people muttered a protest, angry and baffled. It appeared certain there'd be trouble, for they had hoped to see all the farmer's roosters slaughtered and the man put out of business, so naturally they felt cheated. A piece of charity like this went against the grain. They weren't used to it.

But there were good sports among them, because one fellow sang out, "Pshaw, I'd give up a cockfight any time to see another treasure hunt like *that. I'm* satisfied." And after that, others chipped in. Somebody hit on the banking idea, as you might expect, and inquired if he could make a deposit. Well, when he said that, everybody broke up all over again, and then two or three of the ignoranter element got down and rolled on the deck when a weazened-up little fellow wearing a high fur hat removed a pair of white cloth gloves, took out a long pig-hide purse, and declared that he'd admire to become a stockholder. The whole atmosphere turned good-natured, if rowdy, and a well-dressed and dignified elderly man hit the keynote when he told Lauriette, "Little lady—I've got the best supply of fighting birds on earth back home, and they're all yours for a dollar, if you'll kindly peel it off the bottom of the roll. Dig down—do."

Lauriette told him they were "coarse," and he seemed surprised, trying to figure out what he'd said, but the meeting broke up before he worked it out. There wasn't any way to solve his puzzlement; it was only the humor of the times and place; these fellows weren't accustomed to any other kind. Still, I don't think things were as bad as suggested in a newspaper article I saw soon afterward, in the *Prescott Paraclete,* that said: "The river is navigated, with but few exceptions, by a class of low-bred, ungentlemanly, and sometimes ruffianly vagabonds, who seldom, if ever, treat a person with as much respect as a well-bred hound deserves."

That may have been stretching it, the same as a U.S. Army Engineer did when he wrote, after some romantical stuff he read about pilots: "Most of the river pilots are possessed of but little knowledge beyond that required in turning a wheel."

As soon as everybody was gone, I went to the rail and dropped my brass knuckles overboard. I thought I owed the girl that much for being so disloyal about the Captain. She *was* a bossy creature, but she had some good points, too.

The *Jacob Gruber,* being low-pressure, was slower than the other kind, and took longer from St. Louis to New Orleans, but it was by no means a bad run. The average time of high speed boats came to be about four days upstream, and three down. This wasn't anything to sniff at when you consider that the river, between those two chief points, was nearly 1,400 miles long, with all its twists and turns—some of them doubling back so that a body traveled due north at times—and that the old flatboaters required 120 days to pole up, after a float down.

The *Gruber* usually made its downstream run in five days, more or less, but on this trip we hit so many sandbars the schedule got joggled. The Captain being a showoff was always taking the wheel from the pilot's cub. And the farther we fell behind, the oftener he tackled shortcuts—across "chutes," or places where the river had sliced through on itself—and the more uncharted chutes he tried, the frequenter he bulled into the sand. He hit a snag, too, and knocked several buckets off one wheel. Finally, in a burst of self-confidence, to show what he really could do when pressed, he ran us onto the rocks. Just above Natchez. This was serious, and the pilot kept him away from the wheel after that. Sandbars never damaged a Mississippi paddle-boat unless a captain tried to knock one out of the water while racing (which activity caused most of the accidents), but rocks would kill a ship in record time.

Well, when we hit this particular shelf, barely covered by water, we got out by using our spurs, which were crutches—big long poles or planks, like stilts—that they stuck down on the bottom near the bow. Sometimes they lowered one, sometimes two, depending on the size of the boat and how bad she was jammed. Once the spurs went down, a tackle was rigged from the tops to rings on deck, and then, with everybody cheering, they hauled on a windlass and lifted the bow clean out of the water. The second she was up, all steam cracked on and those paddle-wheels churned up a fury. Customarily the boat pranced right on over; after which the spurs slipped from their place and she was free. And if a person couldn't throw a chair through the hull, on she went. They patched her up in a jiffy.

The truth is, these Mississippi steamboats were treated reckless. For all their buttery shelf-paper look and brassy gewgaws, they cost very little, so Lauriette said, and if one got wrecked, it long ago had paid itself out. The machinery and furniture could usually be saved. She said in the case of the old *New Orleans,* half its cost of $40,000 was earned back the very first year. In another case, where a boat was built on a ridiculous piece of high ground, with an Evans engine installed, the river fell for six solid months and they never *did* get it floated—rotted away so bad there wasn't money enough to repair it. So what was done? Why, they took out the engine and set up a saw mill on shore. And did a whacking good business, too. That engine was said to chew up three thousand feet of boards every twelve hours. As the Captain stated, it was a superior kind of sailoring, for he wasn't obliged to learn any more river than a forty-foot cove, where he'd tied up a skiff, for fishing, and he no longer had to operate at night, because the mosquitoes ashore were too pesky. Once he got used to his steamboat running all the time in air, and filled up with sawdust, he wouldn't have swapped places with a commodore. Nobody took things very serious in the river-boating business, then.

The *Gruber* had so many frills, with that monster saloon, two orchestras, gambling, a barrel of whiskey always tapped on the boiler deck for the crew—to be drunk whenever they pleased—filagree work everywhere, and deep Wilton carpets, that I couldn't help wondering what she charged for passage. So I hinted around with Lauriette till I found out. That double stateroom cost sixty-five dollars. Up-river fares were just double what down-river passage cost, because it took longer and they had to burn more wood, stopping at country landings where wood ranks were kept filled and ready. Wood was $2.50 a cord. Cotton cost two dollars a bale to haul from Memphis to New Orleans, and a dollar from Natchez. Deck passage (which meant a pinched little hole under the boiler battery or dining saloon among the mules back aft, and a regular punching up at midnight by the mud-clerk, along with fighting and thievery from roustabouts that talked practically pure African) cost from three to six dollars, according to what humor the steamboat people were in when you bargained. Taken all around, it was worth a little less.

A person traveling deck passage on these boats got next to no show. He was looked on as down and out, with little chance to elevate himself up. The ship officers tried to be fair, though, and if somebody cut his throat while roughhousing, they sewed him into a brand new canvas—nothing ragged or brown-stained the way canvas gets pretty quick on river boats—and slid him overboard with weights on his feet. Oftentimes, they even gave him a prayer, as proper as church, if a preacher could be located on board that wasn't drunk. On the other hand, if he hadn't been killed but had only been beaten or mauled (and his possessions stole), one of the mates conducted a search among the hands, all aboveboard and proper, and told them right out and positive that they ought to quit doing that sort of thing so much. It was distracting to the life of the ship, and annoyed the Captain. Good rousta-bouts that really worked were hard to keep, with the whiskey barrel going all the time, and the officers didn't care to offend them more than necessary. Nobody ever got any stolen stuff back, of course, because if a rousta-bout delivered up an article, it was probably something the mate could use himself. The roustabouts understood it, and admired him for it.

15

WE ARRIVED IN New Orleans early in the morning of August 7. Neither of us had been there before, but almost all of Lauriette's family had, and stayed at an elegant hotel where they lorded it mighty high, but she steered us away from that so we wouldn't be traced.

Leaving our luggage at the steamboat office, we walked over the streets in the strong sunlight, past the wharves, from Canal Street to Julia, piled high with square white bales of cotton. Then we had a look at the packets tied up two and three abreast at the Girod Street landings. Farther along, from Julia to St. Louis, there were dozens and dozens of boats that made shorter trips—to the Red River, the Black River, the Ouachita, the Alchafalaya, the Tensas, and to Bayou Lafourche and Bayou Sara. These were being loaded or unloaded with cane, cotton and tobacco mostly, and a clackety bustle every place you looked. Some of the streets had just been watered, and things smelled good: fish and strong coffee and the piles of fruit for sale. Flowers were everywhere, in the window boxes of the houses, too, and negroes were singing whilst sweeping out before places of business. It was strange and exciting enough, I reckon, but it was pretty Frenchified, for me. As we progressed farther, some amazing stinks came out of little restaurants with grilled ironwork tables in front. Lauriette said it was only French cooking—getting soups and things like snails and frogs and barnacles going for lunch, you know—but I didn't entirely take to it. I'd heard before, at home, that Frenchmen ate snails' legs and frogs, but I never believed it until that morning we walked along the New Orleans streets. It wasn't ten o'clock yet, but a good many men were sitting at outdoor tables, fully dressed from high hat on down, drinking odd-colored liquids from very fancy-wrought glasses. And one fellow that I judged got tired of sitting, because he was under the table instead—was asleep with his head on a crossbar. The proprietor had removed his hat and left it in a chair, obliging and polite, to show that the table was occupied, along with the space beneath, but it wouldn't have done a person any good to sit there, for no place was left for his feet, unless you put them on the man in the basement's chest.

But the tables had more besides men. There was a fair sprinkling of darkish sleepy-eyed ladies, dressed in the gayest kind of clothes, unusually bright for this time of day, so I concluded that they were going to a party. A number of other ladies were leaning over balconies above, with very little on, almost tumbling out of their bodices, and these were as friendly as you could wish. One or two even asked me up to visit, laughing and showing their pearly teeth. Lauriette called them Creoles and said they were no better than they ought to be, but I didn't know anybody that was—the statement made no sense—so I smiled to quite a few and bowed as they pointed me out, until she gave my arm a wrench that halfway pulled it out of the socket. She was about as unsociable a person as ever lived. The nicer people acted to us, the stiffer she became. There wasn't *any* way to get along with her.

Lauriette said we should find a hotel room, then have the other hotels in town canvassed to see if Uncle Jim and the rest had arrived. I'd told her what I figured happened about my disappearance, and said they probably considered me lost. If so, they would travel on, and might have pushed ahead to Cayo Hueso by now. We had to find out if we could, and do what seemed best.

"Look here," I said to the girl. "Are you dead set on running away from home? This Cayo Hueso's a long way off, and it mayn't even be safe. You've transported me down here, and I thank you for it, but this might be the place for you to stop and turn back."

"Not on your life!" she snapped. "Nothing could make me, ever. This is the first time I've ever truly been alive in my life."

Well, it was also the first time I'd ever heard her speak out so passionate and unfrolicsome, too. So I shrugged and knuckled under. I'd got to put up with her for awhile longer, I saw, and it was better to do it with a good face.

We got a room big enough for five people in a sleepy hotel with a wide upstairs porch all around and folded green shutters with the paint peeling off. It was what she called shabby but genteel, "and it won't be apt to bring us to anybody's attention." Then she summoned the desk clerk, a young man of about twenty-four, totally bald, wearing an eye shade and garters on his sleeves; had *him* come up to *us*. One thing this frisky female got from Belle Mead was a kind of royal attitude that everybody was born to serve her. She may have differed from that family in some respects, and been better, but she was as high-handed as a duchess.

The fellow slouched up the stairs and knocked on our door, and by George if her manner didn't cause him to remove the èyeshade. And him the boss of the establishment.

"You sent for me, Ma'am?"

"I had the porter fetch you on an errand of importance."

"Yes, Ma'am, that's what he said, and said he was off to the steamboat company to get your bags. We ain't got only the one porter, and Mr. Reeves'll be knocking the place up for rum at 11:30. He can't—"

"Never mind about that," said Lauriette. "This comes first. I'd like to hire somebody to check all the hotels in the city. We're looking for friends."

The young man squinted, then batted his eyes, as if his brain was too paralyzed to comprehend it. "I don't know —I just don't know who it would be. I had a boy around here once with sense enough to run errands, but he went off on a steamboat. Then there's my brother, but—"

"Get me somebody in about an hour, if you please," said Lauriette, and handed him five dollars. "He'll be well paid."

"What's this?" He turned the bill over and over, looking at it. Likely it was as much as he made in a week.

"It's for you. Now the day's warm, and *my* brother" (*brother,* now, was it?) "and I want a bath. Instruct your errand boy to knock before he comes in."

"But I already *told* you, Ma'am. He's gone off on a steamboat. To the best of my knowledge, he'd be in Louisville around this time. It'd be downright awkward to—"

"See here," said Lauriette in about as rude a question as I ever heard, "are you altogether bright?"

"It's been claimed I ain't," said the young man with a keen look. "Sometimes I get the keys mixed up. You take last week and I accidentally sent a traveling man up to a room where there was a widder woman waiting for a boat to South America. When they informed me about it, two days later, I figured to catch old Merry Ned, but—"

"Bright or dull, your tongue clacks. Good-day to you," said Lauriette, half closing the door. "Find me somebody competent to search the hotels—preferably *not* a relative. Get somebody from outside. If you understand his speech, look further. Get a person who makes no sense to you, and he'll serve very well."

Well, I *never* ran across such a wiseacre. You'd a thought she was the Queen of the Zulu Islands, she was so uppity. I was embarrassed, and said so.

"Clodhoppers! Half-wits! It's enough to strain the patience of a saint."

"If you don't mind my mentioning it," I said, "most people strain your patience by breathing. Another thing is, how much money *do* you have to toss around in that style? It's ridiculous to be handing over five dollars to every Tom, Dick and Harry that'll consent to be bawled out. Why don't you put a half-hobble on your tongue, and give them seventy-five cents? You could save up a very respectable amount in a year's time."

"*Money!* What do *I* care for money?"

"Nothing, I can see that plain enough. But I do. I wasn't raised this way. I could have bought a billygoat with that five dollars."

"Well, that's just what I did," she said with a brilliant but superior smile, and went off to take a bath.

The man they got turned out to be passably smart, but

he reported back that Uncle Jim wasn't anywhere to be found, nor was Dr. Snodgrass and the others.

So there was nothing for it except push on. We sent the canvasser to the steamship offices, particularly the ones going south, but they had no recollection of anybody resembling Uncle Jim—they were too busy to try—and we decided that, after all of our troubles, he might have signed the passenger list with a false name. We were up against it.

Our best chance was Cayo Hueso, or Key West, as people here called it, but all the boats going out for the next month had their cabins sold out, and Lauriette declined to sleep on deck with the roustabouts. She could get picky at very annoysome times.

In the end, we worked out a tedious sort of passage, in several stages, to a place named Tampa, set back in a bay on the west coast of Florida; and the following Monday we checked out and turned up at the wharf for the trip. The steamship bunch said we could probably catch a boat —Cuban or some such—from Tampa to Key West, meaning one time or another. They acted as though we wouldn't mind laying over for a year or two. I never saw people with so little regard for haste. They closed up their offices at noon, for instance, and lolled around, sleeping or drinking and smoking, until late in the afternoon. Neither did they get up early in the morning. Breakfast was apt to be around eleven, which would give them a full and comfortable stomach for the nap to follow. The only people you saw of early mornings were the ones that hadn't gone to bed yet. Mostly, nobody went to bed in this city. It didn't agree with them. They lived at night, and lived hard.

Nearly everybody had a brownish tint to their skin. At first I thought it was the strong sun, but their color was too sallow for that, and even bordered on the unhealthy. Lauriette laid it to a mixture of races from the countries lying below, but we came to find out it was coffee. A Mr. Bradford in the hotel got tooken down sick, and they rushed a doctor up to him fast. The clerk told us about it, after a few preliminary insults from Lauriette to remind him who had the upper hand. The victim had shut himself in for the weekend, with some work to do—and kept the porter trotting up with a fresh pot of coffee every thirty minutes.

Finally he collapsed, and they called the doctor when somebody noticed that his bed sheets had turned brown. It could have been yellow janders, but they were always worried about the plague in these tropical places, and never knew what form it might take.

But the doctor said he had *sweated* the sheets brown. They came to find out he'd drunk upwards of thirty quarts of coffee in three days, and it was coming out of his pores. By good luck, the weather was just that sultry, otherwise the man would have died of acute coffee-itis, so they said.

The doctor saved him, by emptying him out and putting him on a diet of rum, but it was a very close call.

The trip we got outlined by the U.S. Mail Company would have to be broken into several pieces, as I said, but it turned out even worse than we hoped. First off, we got aboard a rusty old tub called the *Star of Baton Rouge*, don't ask me why, and mooched along the coast to Mobile, Alabama. It was different from traveling down the Mississippi, as I found out pretty quick. In the morning, we got up and had to side-pedal along the deck to breakfast in the saloon. I figured there was something wrong in the contruction of the ship because it refused to stay anything like level. You'd a thought you were on a teeter-totter, but it wasn't as pleasant as that, for after a sizable teeter, you expected the same kind of totter and it didn't come. The thing held up a few seconds, and when it did rise, a body's stomach rose with it. The deck kept sliding off, so that you had to keep your wits about you to stay upright.

And then, when we got sat down (and I thought it was suspicious odd that practically no other passengers showed up), a steward wearing a frilly white jacket brought in a first-class breakfast of mutton chops, catfish, fried potatoes, ham, creamed beef, fried eggs, bacon, grits, biscuits, corn bread, something called curry, apple pie, and coffee, and I didn't feel so good. But I disliked to be un-mannered, so I decided to try and stick it out.

After all, they'd tried to serve up a nice light breakfast that would make everybody comfortable, and I wasn't aiming to strike a bad note if I could help it. I knew what the trouble was well enough——a woman in the hotel had given me a peach, the day before, and it had probably gone bad; it had soft spots in it.

Well, I took a hitch at the mutton, which seemed chewier than usual. In fact, the more I chewed it the bigger it got, while the fountains in my mouth worked overtime. Then I tackled the beef, which appeared to unloosen my stomach from its moorings, and after that a man sitting alongside me, wearing a hat and muffler to keep the sea air off his "quinzy throat," as he said, summoned the steward:

"Discussing this coffee, now."

"Tasty, ain't it?" said the steward, a skinny white man with a bad tremble to his hands, and flicked his napkin with a beautiful flourish that squashed a fly which had settled down on the ham.

"You carrying sheep on this trip——live sheep?"

"Well, no. I wouldn't say that. I couldn't say it, because it wouldn't be true. The answer, not to be misled, is ——No."

"To take it a step further, ain't this sheep-dip that you've substituted for coffee by mistake?"

The steward inspected it, with a kind of mock-worried look, and said, "Why, no——I would have swore——" ——he tasted it——"Yes, I'm right, and I knew it. It's coffee. The sheep-dip's kept in another place."

"Then what in the blistering Hades is wrong with it?"

"It's full of chicory, for one thing. You couldn't pay me to drink it. I've got more respect for my stomick."

"What kind of a blue-bellied boar would take and serve it to *us?*"

I would have stayed for the answer, because it happened to be something I wanted to hear, but I broke one of my eggs open just then, and it reminded me that I'd better get out on deck. It came over me all of a sudden. Afterwards, they told me I was seasick, and put me in a swivel chair exactly in the center of the ship, so it would rock up and down but I wouldn't, and presently I felt some better. But not good enough to go back in that saloon.

When we got to Mobile, we had tickets on a stage line for a place called Pensacola, in the north of Florida. We could have taken a train except that the Florida-Alabama Railroad, which ran from Pensacola to the Florida-Alabama line before the War, wasn't any longer in business, and the Jacksonville, Pensacola and Mobile Railroad wouldn't be started for another year yet, they said. So we got into a rickety stage, along with a Yankee that claimed he was going into the drug business, a very pretty woman with a kind of powdery, baked-on face who somebody said was shooed out of Mobile, he didn't say why, and two or three others. It was a jangly, hot, sweaty trip, with several stops at dingy little inns, and we never got rolling for any period of time, because we always hit a rut and some of the luggage fell off. The Yankee finally blew up and asked the driver, "By God, why don't you get down to brass tacks and *tie* it on?"

"I foller the manager's orders, and I ain't been ordered to," said the driver, who was chewing tobacco all over his chin. "I don't get paid hardly more'n enough to hold body and soul together, so I'd be a durned fool to branch out, now wouldn't I?"

There wasn't anything to be done, so we went on, but everybody's suitcases were smashed up before we got there, and the Yankee allowed he was planning to sue. The driver was all for it, and said he would testify for him, if the company gave him a day off for it. I never could tell if he was joking or not. He had another of those frozen faces; practically nothing he said came out sensible. What's more, his assistant, a smelly old fellow with a gray-streaked beard, doubled over with laughter every time he opened his mouth. Lauriette said they both needed a thrashing and that if we had anybody but a Yankee along, they'd get one. The Yankee heard her but failed to respond.

In Pensacola we got passage of a mean sort on a schooner that was hauling immigrants to Cedar Key, about half-way down the Florida west coast. A lot of these boats, jammed full, were leaving because a rush of population was underway towards the South. Most such new arrivals were northerners who had heard about the Florida west coast from Yankee soldiers and sailors that were sent there on raiding expeditions during the war. The climate was so balmy they tooted it up all over the country.

Lauriette said Florida was having a "boom," which sounded to me like it had exploded, but anyway a whole fleet of schooners and sloops was sailing down that coast, stopping at this white beach or that for people to settle. Some, from the East, were traveling to Tampa by the new railroad from Fernandina to Gainesville, then down from there on a stagecoach. A man named Moses Levy, who owned thirty-thousand acres and eighty-one slaves near Cedar Key, had the idea of turning his place into a monster resort for "oppressed European members of his faith," and one of the things he did was get some people interested in starting the Florida Railroad, which aimed to run from Fernandina, on Florida's upper east coast to Tampa.

Well, sir, lo and behold, Mr. Levy, who changed his name to David Yulee (for business reasons, as they said), instead ran the railroad right over through Gainesville to Cedar Key, where he owned all that land. Moses neglected to go on to the promised land, which was Tampa, somebody told us. Tampa was left holding the bag. The citizens down there felt kind of sore, particularly because the state had guaranteed the interest on Yulee's bonds and he was granted big tracts of land for it, free. So they got together and burned him in "effigy," which wasn't as satisfactory as the real thing, of course, but would have to do until he made himself available.

Afterward, they must have forgot about it, because this Yulee, or Levy, was elected the first U.S. Senator from Florida. He never did get the oppressed peoples over, though, and a number of Tampa residents came out flat-footed and said it was a very good thing. But these were the ones still grumbling about the railroad. Most everybody's got a business reason of one kind or another, I've noticed.

Along with the Yankee immigrants were poor southern

families fleeing away from their homes because of carpet-
bagger rule. Many of their towns now were run by darkies of the worst breed, and nobody liked it. This southern bunch traveled mainly in covered wagons, drawn by
oxen or mules, and made only a few miles a day along
the sandy trails.

Part of the migration was an aftergrowth of what they
called the Homestead Act, which was passed by Congress
in 1862. The Federal Government, confound its hide,
owned a lot of land in central and southern Florida, and
when the war ended these tracts became open to occupation. Each settler was entitled to 160 acres of land if he
built a home—a lean-to would do—and swore to till the
land for five years. When all was said and done, this free
land was maybe the chief thing that drew the new immigrants down, along with the climate and the bossy
negroes that I mentioned.

Neither of us favored the schooner trip from Pensacola
to Cedar Key, because it came on to blow, and there
wasn't a dry stick on this shabby little vessel. When the
wind hit its worst, we lost a spar from the top rigging,
and it came down and struck a Cuban man that had
something to do with cattle on the head. They stretched
him out on deck, and one of the passengers, who had
meant to become a doctor but failed then decided to become a farmer instead, bled him considerable into a jar.
The man had been breathing quiet and easy before that,
in spite of the wound, but when he lost all that blood, he
died in short order. The farmer claimed he would have
died anyhow, but there was some criticisms about it.

Lauriette got off her usual sass, which didn't help any,
and certainly failed to bring the man back to life, for they
slid him overboard with a piece of chain tied to his feet,
whilst the Captain read a beautiful service, in Spanish,
which somebody thought might be appropriate. You had
to give them credit, because it's no snap of a job to dig
up something in that language right off, so in the end they
took it off a crate. But Lauriette got sore about this, too.
She said it was a disgrace, and hadn't anything to do with
burial, but was only, *"Arriba, siempre de pie; cuidado*

mojarse," which meant, "Keep this end up and store in a dry place."

When we got off at Cedar Key, wore out with all that tossing around (it had practically been one of those end of the summer hurricanes), we ran into the old business of waiting. A Captain James McKay, who ran the U.S. Mail Line, had regular boats going from Cedar Key to Tampa, but there wasn't any passage for a week or more.

Lauriette blew up, of course, and threatened to buy the line and throw Captain McKay out, but the agent laughed in her face. This McKay had a reputation for toughness and direct action. He'd started the whole business of shipping cattle to Cuba, in the late 1850's, and encountered the usual trouble with Havana grafters. The agent said there wasn't an honest man in Cuba, and from what I saw later, I reckon it was nearly true. Anyhow, early in the game, McKay let the Havana officials know where he stood, because after they tried to squeeze him for bribes, he invited them to ride on his ship *Magnolia,* took them out to a patch of water that thrashed and swirled with sharks, and tossed them all overboard. When they climbed back, a little gnawed here and there, they never mentioned grafting again. *This* bunch was cured.

That had been before the war, of course. Now, ten years later, the Cuban cattle business was going great guns. The revolution against the Spaniards had started, and the rebels controlled most of the cattle in Cuba, so the Spanish came over to Florida after beef for their soldiers stationed there. For every steer driven to a shipping point, they gladly paid a doubloon, worth $15.60 in American gold, and for each one shipped to Havana, half again that much, also in gold.

So (to get back on the track) Lauriette had to give up her windy threats against Captain McKay and look elsewhere. The only other course was to take Yulee's railroad to Gainesville, out of the way, and proceed down from there to Tampa by the stagecoach.

It was the only time I'd been on a train except once when my Aunt Effie went to Memphis after her store teeth. I was glad it worked out this way; it was interesting. Old Yulee (who they called "the father of Florida railroads") had built this line before the war, or about 1853, and it stood up pretty well with a few drawbacks. For one thing, it was bumpy. They said the track was 5-foot gauge and had 58-pound iron "Chair" rail, which was imported from England. The first locomotive, the "Abner McGhee," had been bought from a sawmill operator, nobody ever told me why. The train we got on—one coach and a baggage car—was drawn by a locomotive named the "Governor Marvin." All the locomotives on the line had names, and were so referred to, as if they were people. It was confusing. We were standing at the station when an employee wearing a uniform took out a watch the size of a gourd, and said, "Governor Marvin ought to be pulling in any minute, now." I said I was happy to hear it, because I'd never seen a Governor, and wondered how tall he was and whether he had a silk hat on, but the employee blew the whole thing up a minute later, by saying, "He'll likely need his wheels oiled, and if he ain't got a hot box, I miss my guess. Further, we'd better make ready to scrape the cattle bones off his cowcatcher."

I realized perfectly well I hadn't been around much, but I wasn't so ignorant they could fool me into believing that anybody would deliberately squirt oil on a Governor, and I didn't think he wore a cowcatcher, either. But when I mentioned it to Lauriette, she only gave me a withering look and said, "Aren't you a *funny* child?"

The route led us through scrub pines and oaks and palmetto, as wild a land as you'd hope to see, and somebody pointed out three rattlesnakes sunning themselves in a gully. We had two regular stops before Gainesville—one at Sumner and another at Venables, but as it turned out, we stopped several times.

Lauriette said people generally resented progress, no matter what kind, and it was so in this case. The backwoodsmen claimed the turpentine operations opened up by the road ruined their hog business, and they were hopping mad. So we were chugging along through the scrub, five miles out of Sumner, when all of a sudden there came a grinding crash, the seats flipped forward, the wheels slid and skreeked, and we stopped short, with steam a-hissing.

I heard the sound of somebody cussing up ahead—the engineer, or fireman—and we stuck our heads out of the window.

Directly in our path, a big pile of charred ties had been stacked up on the rails—crisscrossed one over the other to a height of six feet or more. We couldn't got through it without running a chance of busting our headlight.

Well, the engineer and firemen climbed down, along with most of the passengers. Two or three men wearing linen coats threw them off, and we started laying aside the ties.

From over to one side under the trees, though, somebody yelled, "Enjoying yourselves, boys? Hot, ain't it? It don't do to tromple things up so a man cain't raise his hogs. It's mean."

"Why don't you swill peddlers crawl out of that skunk cabbage and show yourselves like men?" the engineer roared. He was about six feet four and must have weighed upwards of 230 pounds, nor was any of it fat. "You're going to get in trouble for this sort of thing—you wait and see."

A perfect riot of laughter went up under the trees, and after that a rifle shot cracked out, clear and sharp. The bullet struck the engine, pinged off the iron, and went singing like a bee into the bushes.

We scrambled back aboard the train, and as it moved forward, nudging the remainder of the ties slowly out of the way, the engineer let them have one last blast, with just his nose showing above the window sill of the cab: "I know you—you damned trouble-making Turners, and don't think the Sheriff won't hear about this."

All he drew forth was another rifle shot, fired up in the air, I supposed, and some more yells of laughter.

If you'd asked me, we came out second best, but this wasn't all. By no means. Twenty miles farther on, at a place where a rut road crossed the tracks, the engineer hooted ten or eleven times on his whistle, and we stuck our heads out again.

It was women this time, about eight of them, all wearing sunbonnets. One was driving a mule hitched to a cart that had stopped just across the tracks. They stood in the way of the train, and declined to move.

Down we climbed again, the engineer swabbing his neck with a bandana and looking played out. He didn't mind fighting men, but this was one too many.

"Well, Mrs. Perkins," he said to the ringleader, a sharp-featured old battle-axe clutching a hoe, as if she intended to use it. "What is it? Same old thing?"

"Eight outright broken, nigh onto a dozen cracked, and the remainder likely scrambled in their shells."

"I informed the company; I told you that last time. In addition, I advised you to pack them in sawdust. And if my memory serves me right, I suggested you get rid of that mule. He's jerky; he don't throttle down for the crossing."

"Mules don't grow on trees, John Kelly," she said, and raised a kind of grumbly laugh of agreement from her sisterhood.

"Well, they've been having some mighty smart success with grafting, Ma'am," said one of our passengers, a waggish little fellow with very deep-set eyes. "It may be they'll have a tree producing by this time next year."

She said, "Fresh!" and twitched her hoe.

"Now Partheny Perkins," said the engineer, "you've halted my train here for the umpteenth time, and I'll thank you to get off the tracks."

"There ain't a single one of us fixing to budge till you've did something about my eggs—we've took an oath on it, and don't mean to break it."

"Well, what in thunderation do you think *I* can do? I'm not in the egg business."

"Begging your pardon," said the passenger, looking very serious and concerned, "I think she's requesting you to lay some more. Over there near that hummock is a good place for a nest. Under the conditions, it wouldn't be any hardship for I and the other passengers to go back to the coach and wait. Cackle when you've finished."

"You'd better get that whipper-snapper out of my way," said Mrs. Perkins, "else I'll part his hair with this sod-buster. We're bent on action, and it'll take more'n bandies from an end man in a minstrel show to stop us."

"Yes, yes," said Mr. Kelly, "he was only being facetious. Now these folks want to get on up to Gainesville, so I'm afraid—"

"We're afraid you'll have to grade up the crossing to smooth out the bumps or they'll be here till Doomsday."

Mr. Kelly sighed, then swiped off his neck again, and after that he and the firemen borrowed some tools off the women and went to work on the road. In about an hour, they had the dirt pushed up level with the rails, so there wouldn't be any bumps, but he said:

"It'll wash down again with the first rain. You know that well enough, Partheny. It's nothing but work wasted."

"To say nothing of eggs wasted."

Mr. Kelly made some kind of remark that indicated he was near about through with the railroad business, and we resumed on.

Half a mile up the line we hit a cow. It was purely an accident, in no way the engineer's fault. We were smoking around a bend, with our view cut off, and the bony animal jumped out of the bushes in our path. It was dead by the time we stopped, and when we climbed out, two raggedy boys were there, staring at the cow, shy but ruffled.

"Paw'll take it to court," said one of them to the engineer.

By this time, I'd begun to wonder if we ever *would* get to Gainesville, because I figured the engineer was about to walk off the job into the scrub and let the whole thing slide. He'd had enough.

"Oh, he'll sue, all right. He's got thirteen suits pending at the moment, including around nine for cows that were snake-bit."

One of the boys whispered in the other's ear; then he picked up a rock, sent it sizzling by the engineer's head, and they dove into the bushes like deer.

The engineer made no answer but only wrote down about the cow in a notebook, and we started up once more.

This time we made it without further interruptions and had good luck in addition, for we got right onto a stage-coach headed for Tampa. It was full, but the people were nice and pleasant, and the trip was interesting. The roads were so rough one lady got seasick, but they took her behind a tree, where she unloaded her breakfast, and at the first country store they got her some seasick remedy and she picked up.

We had entertainment all the way because of the driver's "gopher grabbing." None of the passengers had ever seen anything like it. Without slowing down, he'd leap from the seat like an acrobat, snatch up a gopher (which were all over everywhere, and not prairie gophers at all, but ordinary land turtles) then toss it up onto the baggage rack overhead. These animals were worth twenty-five cents a piece; they were fat and tasty, so people said, and darkies were crazy about them. It had got to be a regular fad in the cities.

The driver told us he usually made more from gopher-grabbing than he did off his salary, and better, it kept him exercised and healthy. He looked fine, but wore down a little toward the end of the trip, which took two days and a night. More particular, he was limping and said he'd wrenched his right knee, which was the one he landed on, and also may have jammed up a section of his spine, but nothing serious.

People complained that the Gainesville-Tampa stage was slow, but it was a wizard compared to the freight-express operating from Tampa to Barstow, as we afterward learned. For this, they used lumbering broad-wheeled tarpaulin-covered wagons drawn by three and four yoke of oxen, that were driven by hearty war veterans which used black-snake whips so accurate they could pick flies off the lead yoke. The express took two full days to travel the forty-two miles.

We got to Tampa just in time for it to cease existing. On the day the stage rolled in, there wasn't any such city —a very curious situation, as I'll explain by and by.

16

Dear Ladies:

WE ARE ARRIVED at our destination, the target of our
dreams and aspirations. In this line (as one looks about)
it may fall a few inches short of Elysium, as I do not believe that in the course of my eventful medical career I
have beheld a more pushful, congolerate, noisy, shouting,
singing, tumultuous, sweltering, wind-blown and yet exotic and many-faceted isle. Physically, it is less than im-
posing, being four miles long and two miles wide, being,
indeed, often referred to even by its own residents as
"The Rock." I am further informed that Ponce de Leon,
in his voyages of 1513, spied this out-flung bracelet of
coral sands, or "Keys," and named them "Los Martires"
(the Martyrs), out of melancholia produced by a heavy
sense of loneliness and foreboding.

But more of these descriptive pearls anon. In this my
second epistletory report (on behalf of Colonel Burnie) I
must first tell you regretfully that your nephew has not to
date been found.

To resume where I left off in my inaugural, the Colonel went ashore to institute a search, and he told me,
later in New Orleans, that both banks of the river were
combed back to a distance of one hundred miles. Nothing
of value was uncovered. In one area a hope was raised
when it was learned that a series of petty thefts had
plagued the countryside during the week past. This was
resolved with the apprehension of a carpet-bagger who
(as it were) was hauled up on the carpet of justice, then

put in the bag (or gaol) for some months to come. (It is a weakness of mine that I make these little jokes, and others even worse.)

A second excellent lead played out when Colonel Burnie investigated a constable's report of a slingshot raid on a hothouse. You may well imagine the zest, the certainty of reconciliation, with which the Colonel rushed to the lock-up in question. Prepared to embrace our missing member, his spirit was deflated to find that the culprit was a half-wit child who had escaped from a nearby orphanage.

Other hopes were dashed. A farmer with an account of vanishing chickens finally (and courageously, in view of his wild accusations against neighbors) laid the blame squarely at the door of a weasel.

A desecrated schoolhouse proved to be the work of its principal, whose nervous breakdown (his ninth) is being treated by the local physician, who feels that the ailment is occupational and not, at this stage, certifiable. (He has suggested remedial reading.)

The discovery of two squalling cats hanging over a clothesline with their tails tied together was not given much importance; it is a favorite amusement with every boy in the town.

In short, nothing anywhere had been seen of a lovable tow-headed vagrant youth, with a suppressed vandal expression. Despite these setbacks we are in uniform agreement that the boy will, in fact, turn up. It is more than possible that he has struck inland, where the citizenry, removed from the educative river traffic, are more vulnerable to those nocturnal forays which lie so close to the wanderer's heart.

Together with my daughter Millie (who remains fragile) and the negro quack, Zebediah, I continued on my way to New Orleans, the only notable part of the journey being a serious case of larceny, involving our companion of color, who was separated from a pouch containing the upper left incisor of a pregnant female lynx, a severed wishbone, three apple seeds, a capsule of powdered bull's horn, a peacock feather, a white button with four holes, a dried mullen top, seven orange pips, and a section of vertebra from a deceased albino rabbit.

As our friend claimed that these curiosities, in the aggregate, rendered him immune to misfortune, I registered a spirited protest with the Captain, getting nowhere. (I must in fairness confess to a certain skepticism myself, since the victim's recent life, in transit, has been little more than a fabric of disaster, but he hotly demurred.)

On my pressing the case, with hints of litigation, the Captain grudgingly consented to appraise the inventory, at the going market rates, in company with his officers. Their price (arrived at late in the evening) of thirteen cents struck me as parsimonious, but nothing could be done. There the matter rests. I greatly fear that deck passage must be undertaken with *full acceptance of the hazards involved*.

We debarked at New Orleans and repaired to the hotel designated by your brother, lodging Zebediah in a connective establishment maintained for the servants of hotel guests. Our week of waiting for Colonel Burnie was pleasant though dull for a physician who has, I believe, displayed unusually quick mobility for a professional man. Hence you may not view it as strange when, to while away the time (and to strike a blow against infection), I slipped briefly back into harness.

To be specific, noting that a good segment of the New Orleans population sported an unwholesome, sepia-colored, liverish complexion, and finding that our hotel had a tap running freely with excellent water (that is, discovering that all the ingredients of my most famous specific were available) I took steps to sacrifice my time to the public weal.

The spot I chose in which to ~~make my pitch~~ hang out my shingle was at the corner of Bourbon and Charles streets, where the above mentioned jaundiced condition seemed more acute than elsewhere. I commenced ~~peddling bottles~~ treatments at about five in the afternoon, when the sufferers had arisen from a heavy, drugged "siesta" and knocked down the first drink of the evening, thus being in a maximum state of receptivity.

Well, with the limited aid of my daughter, whose excess of femininity will only just permit her to wham out a hearty trombone (and no more), I made a start toward putting this deteriorated city back on its feet. Three men emerging from a saloon were dosed with Liquid Vermifuge and restored to the gutter a surprising percentage of those poisons which had brought them to their low estate. A gaudily-dressed woman carrying a parasol, swallowed, reeled, spat out a stream like a fire-hose, then emitted a string of crisp, sailorly oaths, and ankled down the street with improved celerity. In a word, my practice was booming with its usual satisfying effects when I was rudely interrupted by the arrival of two constables and a representative of the local medical group. This last was a man with one foot in the grave, as I saw at a glance, and the constables oozed jaundice at every pore. However, they refused Vermifuge and demanded to see my credentials.

Always genial, I told them I had never carried a sheepskin, as I'd never had occasion to skin a sheep, but they disregarded the jest. Upshot of the affair—an indignity virtually unparalleled in my experience—was that my daughter and I were confined to our hotel room, like common criminals, until the arrival of Colonel Burnie, who straightened out the matter with a sprinkling of judiciously placed bribes. If I have a moral to my story, it is this: The corruption and sharp practice of New Orleans are beyond the beliefs of honorable men, and will doubtless retard the city's growth. Indeed, it would not surprise the undersigned if the metropolis is eventually abandoned, as being too much of a handful for any practical use.

Now, with the arrival of your brother, alone, we mournfully prepared for the last leg of our journey to Key West, which was accomplished via the thousand-ton steamer *Galveston,* having had a passage cancelled on the *Matagorda*—both Texas vessels which call at New Orleans and Tampa twice monthly between Texas ports and Key West, Havana, and the North. The *Galveston,* on its trip up, was carrying a cargo of Texas ponies for the Florida ranges. Our run was comfortable and without incident. Loaded for the journey down with a variety of staples having a connection with the sponge and cigar industries in Key West, besides a quantity of dress goods, millinery, pottery and kitchenware, we arrived after a smooth passage and lodged in a hostelry of lacy-frame construction, run by a Cuban who promptly attempted to enlist us in a political club dedicated to the liberation of his native land. Even more urgent, he pressed us for a "donation to the cause." I was glad to be able to respond promptly, and I did. I promised him that, as soon as we had become settled, I would prepare a batch of my greatly lauded Essence of Spooju (a specific for everything) which he could ship to the rebels with my blessing. Your brother's suggestion that he give it to the Spanish, if he wished to strike a positive blow for Cuba, was ignored by the undersigned. Colonel Burnie has an eccentric sense of humor.

Cubans have flocked into Key West in vast numbers this year, we are told. Taking their place beside such American manufacturers as William H. Wall (who founded the cigar business here in 1831), they are establishing factories that should bring a high measure of prosperity to this southernmost little-known part of our republic. Perhaps the most prominent of this group is Vincente Marlines Ybor, who is in process of moving his El Principe de Gales plant here from seething and uncertain Havana.

As to the revolution, it is everywhere in the air of Key West, which in truth is as much Cuban as American in tone. Political clubs are already in existence, and several news journals are printed in Spanish. Unquestionably, the largest sums to this worthy movement are being donated by the cigar manufacturers, but a number of Americans have also been afflicted by the fervor. I understand that the local Collector of Customs may be removed from office because he has contributed $100. There is talk of filibustering expeditions, to originate here, and it is known that three ships—*Dauntless, Monarch* and *Three Friends*—have come in and out of our harbor under cover of night, bound on God knows what furtive missions.

While resting here, and waiting for Colonel Burnie to formulate our plans for the new life to come, I have possessed myself of all available historical documents concerning this strange region, and have studied them thoroughly, an enterprise in which I have been joined by my daughter, Millicent, against that joyous day (which *will* arrive, as stated) when the prodigal child returns for a resumption of his tutelage.

May I say, aside, ladies, that any close inspection of history can only fill the reader with dolor over the follies of the human race. As to Key West, it is a sad commentary, to begin with, that the islands were discovered quite accidentally by a vanity-ridden adventurer whose principal motive was to find a basin of wash-water whereby he could restore the vigor of his youth. (In modesty, I must add that this discovery was not to be made for another 350 years, when a humble physician, whose name is not unfamiliar to you, would produce his now famous Swamp Elixir, with feats of rejuvenation scientifically described in nearly every magistrate's records of the Mississippi valley.)

The local scholars inform me, over the tiny cups of penny Cuban coffee—imbibed in the coffee houses as the principal social function of the area—that the first evidences of habitation date from around 1700, when the Caloosa Indians (now disappeared) were driven southward from the mainland by numerically superior tribes from the north. The English helped complete their annihilation after Florida came into English hands, in 1763. Most were killed; some fled to Havana, where the sturdy, fighting blood now mingles with that of the Cubans.

I am certain that no part of our young nation has been tossed like a beanbag between owners as has this single Key. Ponce de Leon's voyage claimed Florida for Spain, naming it for the Feast of Flowers, the Spanish phrase for Easter; then the Treaty of Paris, in 1763, ceded it to England in exchange for Havana, which, to mix a metaphor, must certainly rank as one of the poorest samples of horse-trading in the annals of Spanish real estate.

"Cayo Hueso"—Isle of Bones—arises from the assaults on the Caloosas, for the coral was apparently strewn with the skeletons of those luckless red men. William P. Whitehead, an early settler here, writes in 1829:

"It is probable that, from the time of the first visit of Ponce de Leon until the cession of the Floridas to the United States, the islands or keys . . . were only resorted to by the aborigines of the country, the piratical crews with which the neighboring seas were infested, and fishermen. . . . The oldest settler in this part of the country, one whose residence in the neighborhood of Charlotte Harbor dated back to about 1775, used to say, that in his early years (around the commencement of the eighteenth century) the Indians inhabiting the islands along the coast and those on the mainland were of different tribes, and as the islanders frequently visited the mainland for the purpose of hunting, a feud arose between the two tribes, and those from the mainland having made an irruption into the islands, their inhabitants were driven from island to island until they reached Key West. Here, as they could flee no farther, they were compelled to risk a final battle, which resulted in the almost entire extermination of the islanders.

"This sanguinary battle strewed the island with bones, as it is probable the conquerors tarried not to commit the bodies of the dead to the ground, hence the name of the island, *Cayo Hueso,* which the English, with the same facility which enabled them to transform the name of the wine *Xeres Saco* into 'Sherry Sack,' corrupted into Key West."

And an archeologist who lately visited our island retreat writes:

"Relics of European occupation are found on Key West as well as on some of the neighboring keys—stone walls, remains of earthworks and the like, with indications that the island was well known to the pirates who frequented these waters during the Eighteenth Century and had not wholly disappeared when Florida passed into possession of the United States."

Well, to sum up, as these excurions into the past may distract your interest from the personal account of your family and friends, our British cousins (twice removed—by force) ceded Florida back to the Spanish in 1783, and shortly thereafter Cayo Hueso was presented out of hand to one Juan Pallo Salas, a young officer, by Don Juan de

Estrada, the Governor of Florida, presumably for services rendered.

Salas, an enterprising fellow, sorely in need of cash, sold his Key twice simultaneously, once to a John Simonton, of Mobile, Alabama, for $2,000, and again to a Mr. Strong, who wisely and quickly resold to a Mr. John Geddes. There followed a lively lawsuit, which was resolved when the over-zealous Salas gave Geddes a schooner and four acres of East Florida land (neither, by coincidence, owned by anybody else at the moment) to pacify the Simonton interests.

Spain peddled Florida lock, stock and mangrove to the United States in 1815, and in 1822 Commodore David Porter arrived with a naval squadron to rid the adjacent seas of pirates, who were believed slightly to outnumber the fish in these waters.

Porter's accomplishments, doubtless known to two maiden ladies of culture, were in the finest tradition of American energy and patriotism. After bottling the pirates up at the Isle of Pines (near Cuba) he attacked them with damaging results, then hounded them to their end in Porto Rico. We pause now for one of those typically depressing footnotes to American history. Spain, which had villainously protected the pirates in their profitable work, lodged a diplomatic protest with the pumpkin-heads almost continuously in control of our State Department, and Porter, who had made the mistake of pressing a war to its victorious conclusion, was courtmartialed and suspended for six months.

As our leading commodore hero (and by far our ablest sailor) he was obliged to seek employment with the Mexican Navy. Later, having given that dubious body its sealegs, he transferred to the Turkish Navy. No doubt his name will some day regain the luster which was stripped from it by our ever-timorous, weak-kneed, altogether mealy-mouthed and all-around embarrassing and incompetent Department of State.

In another dispatch, I shall mention the mixture of population which comprises our chosen abode. Indeed, Colonel Burnie has requested me to communicate our day-to-day adventures, with sidelights on their historical background, as a means of keeping a running journal on this emigration of note.

Our arrival here has occasioned no little interest. While it may be over-fulsome to describe us, currently, as distinguished residents, there are yet points of identity which set us apart from the commonalty of Key West.

Colonel Burnie is believed to be the only Confederate officer here with eleven high decorations for bravery and twenty-two official reprimands. My daughter Millicent is beyond question the only female trombonist on the island with qualifications approaching virtuoso rank. The quack, Zebediah, is the Key's acknowledged expert on Southern Kentucky medico-superstition (all of it ludicrous) and the undersigned will strike, when the time is ripe, with a series of those miracle cures which have made my name a household ~~oath~~ word from Minneapolis to Grand Isle (below New Orleans). All that is needed is an epidemic of some mild sort—cholera, yellow fever, bubonic plague —and my position will be secured. If it isn't, we can always move north a Key or two—out of range—they string out toward Florida's ~~underbelly~~ understomach in a bejeweled arc of 150 miles.

In that last regard, Colonel Burnie informs me, in strict private, that he holds a treasure map, gained from the Mexican War, which has as its locale a Key called Matecumbe, in approximately the middle of the chain. On it, I suspect, we shall eventually settle, and live from the fruits of buried gold. The prospect is entrancing.

So I close, with every expression of sympathy and regard. Let us trust that when next I write, our party shall have been reinforced, so to speak, with the arrival of your no doubt itinerant but highly esteemed nephew.

> Obediently,
> Dr. Ewing T. Snodgrass (Resident Physician, Casa Lopez, Key West, Florida)

P.S. I should add that Colonel Burnie has just read the above composition and expressed himself as satisfied with the general quality of my reporting; saying, in fact (and I repeat this in no spirit of braggadocio), "If the present florid and mendacious tone expands, this material may take its place beside the papers of Villon, De Quincy, Casanova and other leading rascals of literature."

E.T.S.
(D.C., etc.)

17

OUR STAGE pulled into Tampa (with a record catch of gophers) soon after the city had gone out of business, same as I said before. The way it came about was this: After the war, a whole bunch of wandering, rampaging, freed or long-ago runaway negroes came swarming in, and began to parade their new "equality." This wasn't the general behavior of *all* darkies, you understand, but a lot of them did cause trouble. As a visiting writer said, they "swaggered through the streets, often pushing white men and women from the sidewalks. They refused work but they needed money for whiskey. They got it by breaking into stores and homes, often in broad daylight."

And the Tampa *Peninsular* said, "Our families cannot even go to church without leaving someone at home lest on our return we find our places robbed. The inherent nature of these people is savage."

Well, the mess had to be cleaned up, of course, so a city government got going again, having been allowed to die out during the war. And what happened? Why, what usually does, according to Lauriette. The officials disremembered they'd been elected by the people, and went right ahead as if they were the boss of the universe. They put the darky trouble down all right, by electing a sheriff and holding courts, but then they went crazy on the subject of taxes.

I once heard my Uncle Jim say that taxes had caused half of the world's woes since time began. He said people generally forgot they had the power to tax or untax themselves, by turning up at elections, but mostly nobody bothered to fight. "They just settle dully into the notion that their government is something apart from themselves, higher and bigger, and full of punishments and threats, rather than a poor charity body they can yank up whenever they choose." So Uncle Jim put it.

In this case, on top of everything else, the officials decided to whack out a crusher of a real estate tax. For once, the people got up on their hind legs, as they're forced to do everywhere, I reckon, and voted those scoundrels out of business.

Instead, they elected a slate that promised to discontinue Tampa, and that's what it did, and put things in the record: "—as the City of Tampa has forfeited its charter, all property of this city shall be taken over by the county clerk."

Well, *didn't* those tax-crazy officials feel like fools? They slunk around town, or, rather, that part of Florida, hardly looking anybody in the eye, even their old friends of the happy, pre-tax days, when they all lived together in Tampa. Not only had they taxed themselves out of a situation but they'd served their city so well that it disappeared, like Pompeii in the history books. Uncle Jim said later it represented a "low-water mark for government baboons," which was already so low they had it staked out somewhere three or four foot below the mud level.

Even so, we weren't inconvenienced. There wasn't any Tampa, but the houses still stood where the city *used* to be, and the streets hadn't been took up. Things were just the same, only they didn't any longer have a name to go by.

There wasn't any question that Tampa had been, and maybe still was, a rackety place. A story in the *Peninsular* said:

"To say that our city was infested with gamblers, No. 1 blacklegs, burglars, thieves, robbers and cutthroats of every shade and high and low degree is but speaking the simple truth. One morning a man, a noted villain, was found swinging to a pine tree. A few were whipped. Others were warned and got their orders to leave. The effect was electrical. Robberies ceased. Gamblers fled."

Anyhow, we rode on in, and after some inquiries put up at the residence of a Mrs. Hawkins, who also ran a

Private School for Girls, just as a Mr. Samuel Craft ran a Private School for Boys, nearby.

But on the way, right in the center of town at the corner of Washington and Franklin streets, we ran into an odd commotion.

A man dressed like a politician, in a frock coat and high hat, was lying there drunk, and a number of people were helping him out by pouring molasses and corn over him. I don't believe I ever saw anything quite so peculiar.

Well, once they'd got him covered—and they did a bang-up good job, too, ladling that stuff out freely in a period of hard times and high prices—the pigs waltzed in and added *their* bit. For a minute, I thought they might eat him alive, for these were half-wild swamp hogs that hadn't been penned up often. Rooting and squealing and shoving and squirming to get at that fodder, they tore all his clothes off, leaving him lying there naked and filthy, still passed out.

It was easy to see from people's faces that this went farther than a low practical joke. We came to find out that the man, a Mr. Bagley, was a black Republican, born in Georgia, who'd turned coat after the war and got appointed county judge for his unloyalty. But his actions were so offensive he made enemies of everybody, and whenever they complained, he charged them with contempt. In the end, he got himself impeached by the State Legislature, but before it happened, a prominent citizen walked into his court and fired off a blast at him with a shotgun. Somebody remarked that this was about the last word in contempt, and it might have earned the shooter a citation later at the Pearly Gates, except that a court clerk struck the barrel upwards at the last minute. Bagley didn't wait to issue any papers; he snatched up his hat and skinned out of there.

One of his main weaknesses was drinking, though, and he always went the whole way and got drunk, generally picking out a prominent place to fall down, for political reasons. He hadn't any trouble keeping his name before the public that way, and they always gave him a hand, to be sure he was noticed, by pouring on molasses and such.

We hung around awhile, Lauriette not bothering to

cover her eyes, the way the other ladies did when his clothes shredded off, but staring along, perfectly brazen, and when the crowd trickled away, leaving him exactly as he was, we checked into Mrs. Hawkins'.

It was a highly respectable establishment, not much given to nonsense, and I had the notion that if we'd got out of line, the proprietor might have poured molasses and corn over *us;* she was that strait-laced. But we were lucky to lodge there; it wasn't usually a boarding house, so we tried to enjoy it.

The same Captain McKay whose boats we couldn't get on had several ships going on the Havana cattle run now, and we booked passage to Key West via the *Southern Star* for the following week. Meanwhile we rested up, for we'd been bounced around very lively on the ship and on the stagecoach, not to mention the Florida Railroad, when we were on the floor more than we were on the seats, because of all those sudden stops. Also, and I dislike to say it, we were kind of fed up with gophering. It made things jerkier than necessary, even on a stagecoach.

Daytimes we walked about what used to be Tampa. There wasn't as much of it as formerly, Mrs. Hawkins said. The city itself had been losing population since about 1860, the cause being the ending of the railroad at Cedar Key, along with epidemics of malaria and dengue, or breakbone, fever, and sometimes the dreaded yellow fever, too. During these sieges the people fled out of Tampa into the woods or to nearby communities, and some never returned. The town had a population of 885 white folks in 1860, but ten years later, there were a hundred less than that. When the war started, Union sympathizers went North by way of the refugee camps on Egmont Key or Key West, and a lot of the men that joined the Confederate Army never came back. And then, after the war ended, the rampaging negroes caused many families to move where the trouble was controlled.

This Tampa never treated darkies bad; it just didn't like being run over roughshod. We saw an example of how they naturally felt, as we walked about, from a tombstone that was put up under what Lauriette called "delicate conditions."

A very prominent elderly citizen named William Ashley died, and shortly after, a youngish colored woman who'd been his servant died, too. But she was somewhat more than his servant, as they said, meaning something or other, so that the executor of Ashley's estate, with everybody's hearty approval, buried the master and the darky in a common grave. Then they had the tombstone maker inscribe on the stone: "Here lie William Ashley and Nancy Ashley, master and servant; faithful to each other in that relation in life, in death they are not separated. Strangers, consider and be wise—in the grave all human distinctions of race or color mingle together in one common dust."

Somebody said they planned to keep that tombstone in good repair to kingdom come, for both the man and the woman were respected, and treated so. It'll be standing a hundred years from now, very likely.

Though Tampa itself was dwindling in population, while Hillsborough County increased, the times could have been worse. A number of stores were doing fairly good business, we noticed, including the drug store of Dr. Franklin Branch, which was the only shop that stayed open during the war.

Practically nobody had either "hard money" or Yankee greenbacks but dealt with the stores, and each other, by barter, the main goods for exchange being cotton, hides, beeswax, honey, tallow, sugar cane, molasses, corn, tobacco and rice (and lately, gophers).

Things *had* trickled down thin in 1867, when the schooner *James E. Price*, carrying supplies for all the stores, was wrecked on Mullet Key. The *Peninsular* called it a "great calamity" and said that "many families are out of food. We hope our merchants will remedy the situation by chartering a schooner and dispatching her as soon as possible or else much suffering will inevitably result."

The crisis slid past, and nobody starved. Uncle Jim once said he never heard of anybody starving to death in this country, so he failed to understand why people worried so much. He himself didn't bother, but I doubt if anything short of the sky falling would have worried him; he wasn't made that way. And right there's where his statement went wrong. Some people are *born* to worry; they can't help it. If there wasn't anything else handy, they would worry because they'd run out of reasons.

Now I see I've dawdled again—or so I'm told—and must get on with the story. Things began to happen pretty fast, as you'll learn soon.

It was two days before we were to take the *Southern Star* for Key West that Lauriette and I, late in the nice soft twilight of a miserable hot day, were walking home to Mrs. Hawkins'. We had been to see the Hooker mansion, where an Englishman who'd come to Tampa to organize a music academy and run the town band wrote a ballad called "When You and I Were Young, Maggie." It had caught on, don't ask me why, because it was about as gloomy a piece of merchandise as you could hope to hear, and people were singing it, mooning about the past, and so on. It was ridiculous. We heard a girl of no more than sixteen sing it at a church recital, with the tears running down her face, and if she'd been much younger, as she was braying for in the song, they'd a had to put a nipple in her mouth and change her diapers.

No, that song may be all right for some, and worth all the ruckus they made, but I'd like to bet it won't last two years. People will stand so much boo-hooing, and no more.

Anyhow, as we approached home, a man stepped out of the shadows, tipped his hat, and handed us a note. Then he scuttled away without opening his mouth; neither did I get a good look at him. We went inside, turned up our lamp, and read it.

"Oh, my," cried Lauriette, looking pale and sitting down suddenly.

"Well, what's it say? You needn't hog it yourself, you know," and I snatched it out of her hand, but after I read it, I didn't feel quite so perky. Confound it, there wasn't *any* way to get rid of them.

"My darling sister" (it went, with that kind of family sarcasm I knew pretty well by now): "Did you really think you could manage it? Wherever you are, my brave men have found you. The most loutish of our local Ku Klux Klan, they are traveling in style on my happily inexhaustible funds. You may be uplifted to know that within twenty-four hours after your companion broke my leg (the crowbar was found, with some of my flesh attached) I had begun the hunt that will see Burnie's nephew in an early grave and fetch you back to Belle Mead.

"Life cheated me, and I can't allow it to play favorites with the ones who reared and shaped me. Of that I assure you, who never bothered to conceal your distaste for the epileptic. So—the word is out in the open. We never had the courage to put a name to it, did we? Our sensitive parent, whose pride was worth more than a possible cure for his son, preferred to shut the unfortunate away and run no risk of embarrassment. And do you know, dear girl, I have been told by physicians that it could have been the indiscretions of forebears that brought on me this unfashionable quirk. Rotten bad luck for me, don't you think?

"No matter. My men have instructions to track you down, erase my attacker by the most ingenious means they can devise, and drag you home. They have no particular orders about your treatment en route. Perhaps in their coarse way they may take a fancy to you. For those who like full-blown girls with your peculiarly colorless hair, you may not be unattractive. Or so I have been told.

"As to your companion, it will be my lasting regret that I shall miss seeing his punishment. Perhaps when my leg is healed (I am informed that I shall walk with a limp) I can settle the account—with his uncle. I hope so. For now, I rejoice to tell you that you have lost. You are under scrutiny by the best, and worst, human bloodhounds I could find. Your avenues of escape are cut off. The knowledge of this, when I receive it by return mail, will ease my convalescence."

> "Your doting black-sheep brother,
> Rex"

"P.S. The antedeluvian darky has been rewarded for his loose tongue and meddlesome ways. His funeral was conducted, with appropriate honors for such a quaint and protracted neighborhood fixture, only the day before yesterday."

The letter disturbed me for several reasons; as high-flown and silly as it was, it wasn't entirely one-sided. And Lauriette went to the window and stood looking out for a long time.

"The odd thing is," she said, "I never thought of him as a person before. He was always something ugly. It's true—we shut him away." Then she turned around with the old look of decision.

"*However,* the time is long past when anything can be done for *that* fellow. No matter who's at fault, he's now a full-fledged monster, and we'll fight him right down to the end."

"*We!*" I said. "How can a wea—" I almost said "weak," but the word refused to budge. "How can a girl, no matter how bullheaded, and a boy of fourteen hope to beat that bunch of polecats?"

"Well, we've beaten them so far—to be truthful, I've enjoyed it—and we'll go right ahead. I'm sure you won't be crushed to know that I never met a male yet I couldn't out-guess."

"It may be irregular to suggest it," I said, "but why don't we ankle out of here to the police? Tomorrow, in broad daylight. It's what they get paid for, you know. If you feel so all-fired eager to lambaste people, maybe you can get on some police force yourself—later."

"*What* police? Tampa's out of business, remember?"
Blast the luck, I'd forgot it.

"Then how about the county sheriff? It might give him something to do. You take usually, they only sit around playing pinochle, or collecting up donations, or jumping on somebody down and out. They get bored."

"See here, smarty; are you *anxious* to be mutilated and killed by a gang of common Ku Kluxers?"

"Not even by somebody socially prominent. Neither am I convinced that you can whip the United States

Navy, along with Jeb Stuart's cavalry, the Texas Rangers and the Canadian Mounted Police. You're tough and you're mean, but you're not that good."

She gave me a slap that made my ears ring, then burst into tears. Maybe some people can tell what a woman's apt to do next; I'm not one of them.

"Now what was *that* for? I was trying to pay you a compliment. I meant it. Pound for pound, I think you're more than a match for any man except maybe the very top people in the Army, but—"

By George, she slapped me again. With the other hand this time. She could change off as easy as eating. It gave me a fresh outlook on her, and determined me to stay back out of firing range.

"It's what I get for trying to take you to your uncle, for living in barns, sleeping in haystacks, eating filthy food bought in horrible little country stores, and traveling in cheap public conveyances like a peasant. I should have known."

Well, there was something in that, and I felt sorry, and said so; said, "I was only funning, maybe because I'm scared. You've been pretty good, for a female, and I thank you."

I tried to smooth down her hair, but it was up a little above me, and awkward, so she put her arms around me and gave me a tight hug. I didn't mind it. She was too soft in places—downright mushy—and hard in others, but she smelled good, and while I couldn't stand the breed, I disliked to hurt her feelings by breaking away, so I let her hang on for a minute.

She wasn't being *entirely* honest, of course, because one of her reasons for leaving was to escape Belle Mead, but the girl had courage, and I'd come to like her better.

"All right," she said, pushing me away and taking out a handkerchief. "That's enough nonsense for now. We've got to move fast tomorrow, so let's go to bed." She blew out the lamp and went behind her screen. "No matter what—"

Just as she said it, there came a tinkle of glass, and a rock thumped down on the floor. She gave a cry, and I scrambled after it on hands and knees. We struck a sulphur match, then unwound the paper. All it said was, "Pleasant dreams little lady we'll tuck you in ever night from now on."

They must have been watching from under the shade all the time.

"That's *enough!*" said Lauriette, standing in the dark. As usual, she hadn't bothered to put on a stitch while we were striking the match. She had as much modesty as a monkey in a zoo.

"We'll *see* about this tomorrow. I've got a few ideas on the subject, so lock the door and window, and let's get some sleep."

"Excuse me," I said, "but part of the window glass is knocked out, so why—"

"I said *lock* them. And now, good night."

She was up bright and early, with a familiar tilt to her chin, and rousted me out as cool as you please.

"I've thought it over. We'll tell the whole story to Mrs. Hawkins. She seems both intelligent and sympathetic."

I didn't bother to argue, but for my taste this Mrs. Hawkins looked about as sympathetic as a bottle full of lye. To *me,* she had all the earmarks of a typical schoolteacher, the sort that might split hairs over whether Cape Horn was underneath Africa or South America. I'd run across her kind before.

But to do the old girl credit, she listened without interrupting, and when we finished she sent a girl to fetch her friend Reverend Muckleroy.

"Henry will advise us," she said. "He may give the appearance of the mild, befuddled man of God, but he's as hard as iron, underneath."

Well, that was recommendation enough for me. If this sharp-featured old war-horse considered him tough, he probably ate a boiled grizzly for breakfast and got his exercise pulling up oak trees by the roots.

But when he arrived, he struck the most laughable picture of toughness I ever saw. He was partially bald, with a pince-nez on, had watery blue eyes, a stringy neck, a dreamy, far-away expression with a half smile to it, very rumpled black clothes and a sprinkling of dandruff around the collar.

Lauriette seemed impatient, almost angry.

"Henry," said Mrs. Hawkins, "this lovely young girl, Miss Lauriette Farrow, of Belle Mead Plantation, at Vicksburg, and the boy, David Burnie, of Grassy, in Kentucky, are being pursued by the Ku Klux Klan, which intends to do them a mischief. They can't leave Tampa on James McKay's ship, for these dreadful men will apprehend them. But they *must* escape, and get to Key West. What do you suggest?"

"What's that, my dear?" said Reverend Muckleroy, rousing himself with a start.

Well, you may not believe it, but instead of cracking him over the head with a ruler, Mrs. Hawkins repeated all that over, together with most of what Lauriette had told her. During the last part, Reverent Muckleroy appeared to have drifted off to sleep again.

"Now," said Mrs. Hawkins, "tell us what to do. Don't pretend to be wool-gathering, Henry."

"Do, my dear? Why, they must engage Seminoles to take them south through the Everglades and the land of Grassy Waters. There is no other transportation in that region. They'll want mosquito lotion, of course—the rainy season's coming on—and I need hardly say that the Indians expect to be paid. Do you have money?" he asked, looking at Lauriette with about the directest gaze you ever saw.

We couldn't help it; we both burst out laughing, in pure relief.

"I have plenty of money, Reverend. How shall I make arrangements?"

He looked surprised, hurt, even. "Arrangements? Why, I'll make all the arrangements, of course. You aren't to worry about it." He hesitated. "There *is* one thing—it involves a certain amount of risk. Our Seminole" (he pronounced it Sem-in-olay) "brothers have concluded a peace, but they are not, ah, over-cordial. Also, the trip will be one of extreme hardship. I cannot emphasize that too strongly."

"Could it be worse than having the boy killed and myself taken prisoner to be done with as they like?"

"No, ah, well, you see—I thought of that. Yes, it went into my considerations before I spoke."

He got up and fumbled around for his hat, that he'd been sitting on, and said, "And now I must take myself off. In carrying out the Lord's work, there's a great deal to be done, a very great deal indeed." He put the hat on, a mighty sorry-looking sight, which didn't seem to bother him, then headed for the cloak closet. But when he got inside, a number of things fell down with a noisy clatter, and he came back out again, puzzled. He said, "Dear me," and took a fresh start toward the door, and this time he made it. He appeared to have forgotten all about us.

We came to find out that that doddering, mixed-up old laundry bag had been a frontier scout, an Indian fighter, a chaplain in the Confederate Army (decorated over and over) and that, in spite of all the Seminoles he had killed in his youth, he remained a good friend of several clans. They respected him, and believed what he said.

In the next two days, Lauriette herself was not wholly idle. The first thing she did, which surprised me, was to prance right down to the post office (at noon, so as to be safe) and mail her brother's letter to a judge in Vicksburg. He was a man the family had been friendly with before they withdrew from society, and he had influence. She put in a long letter of explanation, and blew the whole works sky-high, or aimed to. Believe me, she told the entire story: epilepsy, leprosy, the substitution of brothers, Ku Klux Klan, the beating of Zeb and me, Uncle Ned—everything. She said it was time that house of Belle Mead was straightened out. She went so far as to admit it might be better if her uncle took over. Her brothers could get proper treatment, and the people could quit living lies.

Well, the next thing she did, on advice of Reverend Muckleroy (via Mrs. Hawkins), was to change her reservation at the steamship company. Instead of having passage now to Key West, we were headed toward New Orleans. It seemed a smart dodge but not the sort of thing a preacher might dream up. He was as tricky as a fox.

Three more days ran by without another note or any further word from the Reverend, and then, one evening, we got word to make ready. Mrs. Hawkins knocked on our door, and said, "I have instructions from Henry. He says it's important that you carry them out explicitly."

Then she sat down on the edge of the bed, looking faint, and added, "Oh, dear, I hope we're doing right. You're a very young and beautiful girl to be thrown among red savages on a long wild trip. It frightens me."

She was a good soul, but she should have saved her pity for the Seminoles. I'd traveled a considerable while with this young and beautiful girl, and knew her habits.

The next morning, we were told to pack a few things and leave them in the house while we took our mid-day walk. And when we came back, they were gone. This addled-looking preacher intended to shake us out of Tampa without *any* chance of being followed, and he came within an ace of doing it.

The day after that, when we were about to venture into town, Mrs. Hawkins came to our room for the last directions.

"Gather up your small toilet articles, and any other little personal belongings. You are not to carry anything that might indicate you are leaving. This is your last walk. Go slowly and aimlessly to the bandstand. You will see Henry there. *Do not speak to him.* He will tell you what further to do."

She gave us each a hug, sniffled a little, and dabbed at her nose with a cambric handkerchief.

When we left, she whispered from behind the door, "Go as if it were another morning walk. Henry feels that they aren't watching these daytime outings by now, but you aren't to take chances. Now, then, you're gone. God bless you . . . write me some day and tell me you passed safely through this frightful ordeal."

18

We walked on down the street, with Lauriette holding her head high and defiant, as though she could whip the Seminoles with one hand and the Ku Klux Klan with the other. We ambled about town, taking care to stay in the busy parts, and finally wound up at the bandstand. Reverend Muckleroy, somewhat more rumpled than usual, was standing there eating goober peas out of a sack. He had a dimmish, far-away look to his eyes. We kept on walking around the park area, circling the bandstand itself now and then, but didn't address him directly. Lauriette, of course, had to demonstrate that nobody could tell her entirely what to do, so every time we passed him, she "harrumphed," in a coughing sort of way.

Nobody else was in sight, anywhere. On our third trip around, Reverend Muckleroy said, without turning toward us: "Very good. Now continue your stroll down to the Bay. Directly in front of the U.S. Mail Line Pier, you will encounter an Indian with cropped ears. He is my friend, and your friend. Do exactly what he says. He will guide you south through the Big Cypress Swamp and to the land of Grassy Waters. After that, he will make arrangements. I wish you good luck, my children."

I felt a sort of lump in my throat for this preacher; he was the first one of his kind I'd ever liked, and even Lauriette, who thought that the whole human race was born to serve her, whispered, "Thank you for this, Reverend Muckleroy."

He never moved, but continued to munch on goober peas, as vague and bewildered a specimen as possible, and said, "It's part of the Lord's work. Moreover, you'll

213

be expected to pay. But Crop-eared Charlie is an honest friend of his white brothers. All will go well. You have my constant prayers."

So we were off. At the steamboat docks, a squat, darkish man of middle age, dressed in a cloth Indian costume of bright colors in a zigzagging pattern, stepped out from behind a crate and said, "Come—please to not look behind."

We followed after him down the piers and along a shell beach to a cove where a cluster of mangroves hid a long dugout canoe—a pirogue, hollowed by burning and scraping out of cypress wood.

As we learned more of Florida, in the days and weeks and months to come, we found out about these things. Cypress is a kind of evergreen, without much foliage except air plants that cling to it in bunches, like mistletoe, separate, gaining their fodder from the atmosphere. The trees grow standing in water, and never rot, even if they're cut. You can take a cypress log and stick it in water, fresh or salt, and it will do nothing but gather barnacles or slime for the next hundred years. So you see, it makes a very good kind of wood for some boats.

Crop-eared Charlie had this canoe there, with five other Indians, a perfectly silent and fat and shiny group, as much black as red, in gaudy clothes and no more smile to them than there is to a ham, waiting. There was one more, a fellow that checked in five minutes after us, to see we weren't followed. He was wrong, but it didn't look that way at the time.

Charlie spoke English, or thought he did. He was carrying a big pack, aside from our clothes, that he said Reverend Muckleroy had put together, and turned it over to us. I may not remember *all* it had, but I do recall two large pieces of oil cloth (which came in handy soon enough on that choppy Bay); rubber hats; two mosquito nets; soap in a copper box; rubber surgical plaster; two big hunks of chewing tobacco (which we thought very queer); castor oil, which caused Lauriette to sniff in disgust; a medicine case with cholera mixture, quinine pills, carbolized sinew for sewing wounds, and colorynth pills; a pocket surgical case and thermometer; a small bag with scissors, needles, thread and buttons; a pocket compass in case we got separated from the guides, I reckon; a small whiskey flask; veils for our hats; two lead pencils; a small fishing bag containing one heavy trolling line, one light trolling line, sinkers, hooks, one large spoon, one small spoon, and six flies.

Besides this, there was a pouch with a watch in a waterproof casing; some cookery including knives, forks, and spoons (because the Seminoles seldom used any); salt, pepper; tea; coffee; sarsaparilla in tablet form (if things got dull and we needed a toot); some condensed cola-nut preparation, which a number of South Americans employed to hoist up their spirits; chewing gum with cola-nut; and an 1840 map of East Florida (the whole Peninsula part) which had been done by two army officers on orders from the U.S. Senate. I noticed it had a dotted trail eastward from near a place on the Gulf named Sanybel across the Pay-Hai-O-Kee, or Everglades, to north of Fort Dallas, on the Mi-am-i, or Big Ocean Water. It said: "Passage for Small Boats as Reported by the Indians."

Well, it seemed like an odd assortment, but it came in handy, or part of it did.

When the last man had pulled in, and grunted something to Charlie, he said, "You get in now—not look back. Is better than feel goodbye."

You take that all around, and it was about the best advice I ever got, and all since then I've said no more goodbyes than an Indian does. It saves wear and tear on the nerves.

Now I haven't an exact idea what our route was in heading out of Tampa, but I know that we carried the canoe several times, and several times camped on the banks of dark, spooky-looking rivers, a-splash with large fish and draped over with Spanish moss from the oaks on both sides.

But I'll try to trace it as near as I can. One of the worst features of the ordeal, from start to finish, was Lauriette's high-handed manner toward the Indians. You might have thought she had bought them outright, and I told her so, the second or third time we pulled into shore for a rest.

"See here," I said, drawing her aside, "you'd better ease up on this Cleopatra and the slaves business. We aren't at Belle Mead, you know."

"Oh, pooh, I'm paying for this expedition, and I expect service. They're impudent."

"*Impudent!* Why, they haven't addressed a word to you so far. They haven't even looked at you."

"That's what I mean. Except for that fellow with the chewed-up ears, they don't act like servants. They need to be put in their place."

"Well, they *aren't* servants," I said hotly. "They're guides, and you'd better get that through your pretty skull. What's more, Miss Smarty, you're walking on thin ice. These Seminoles may have quit fighting ten years ago, but they never signed a peace treaty, so watch out."

Well, sir, on one of the early stops, two guides had a confab to one side, then made a lot of jabber with Charlie, who came over sort of apologetic and said, "Mistippee wish part of pay now, say white man break promises all times."

"How much?" asked Lauriette with a contemptuous look.

"Muck-el-roy agree two hunerd dolla—all complete. Maybe one hunerd now."

Lauriette shrugged, then dug down into her bank, which caused the trouble-makers to rumble, or what passed for laughing, then one of them tried to dig his hand down, too. She gave him a very good sound whack on the cheek, and the others sitting on the ground practically rolled over on their heads. But Charlie looked unhappy about it. He smoothed things over, and we pushed on.

To go back, we shot out of our Tampa cove and struck out on a downward, or southerly, slant across the Bay, past the mouth of the Manatee River, then along the coast in shelter behind one slender, white key after another.

On the first hitch, a stiffish gale blew, and the Bay was rough, as it generally is, they said. Spray was flying around some, and Charlie covered us up with the oilskins and rubber hats.

When the wind lay from the right quarter, they rigged a leg-of-mutton sail, putting a kind of center-board keel over the side to keep us from sliding off, and we zoomed along. Later, we learned that, using sails and paddling when becalmed, these Seminoles had been known to venture as far as Havana, from places like Cape Sable and the mouth of the Shark River, below the Ten Thousand Islands. Our guides paid no notice to the weather, but paddled on while one bailed in the stern with a cocoanut shell. We made good time; it was a fast boat, and the high, curved prow of these pirogues threw the worst spray water aside, leaving us tolerably dry. Indians always make rough-water boats like that, while white people go right ahead turning out flat-bottom skiffs that get you soaked in the mildest breeze. I never understood it, and never will.

Down the coast during open stretches between keys when the Gulf rolled, we laid up, or carried the canoe if the distance was short to protected water.

The first night, we pulled in behind something called (on the map) Long Island, and made camp ashore. It was the first time I'd had a chance to really examine these fellows. They were sturdy and strong, though running a little to fat, and, as Lauriette said, "impassive." That is, they seldom changed expression, and they never used gestures. The truth is that they hardly spoke at all, something not confined only to our bunch, but was true of the whole tribe.

These men had on costumes that would have blinded a weak-eyed person in strong sunlight. The main part was a knee-length tunic of loose woven cloth, for coolness, that had bright patches of color sewed on just everywhere. There were bands that went around in stripes, braids, strips tacked on here and there, and what was called geometric designs sprucing up the lower part. It was gaudy. At the middle, they were tucked in by a beaded belt or cloth sash.

Underneath, they wore beaded buckskin trousers and moccasins. But this wasn't all. Generally, they had two or three bandanas around the neck, and a cloth turban on the head. One or two had long plumes of feathers sticking out in a graceful curve to one side; not straight up or falling forward, the way you see them in pictures of the Western Indians.

Altogether, you might call these Seminoles handsomely dressed; I had to give them that much. But when we studied the women folk, a while later, the men looked downright drab by comparison.

There was another side to this foppery, though. Besides being absolutely blank unfriendly, they smelled like billygoats. It wasn't for lack of washing, either, for commonly they peeled off and bathed in the river or Gulf after a day's run. They used a mosquito shooer of rancid fat—rubbed it all over—and I have to admit it made sense.

That first night, Lauriette and I rubbed on the mosquito stuff Reverend Muckleroy gave us, besides tucking in beneath our nets, and the word went out like a flash. The mosquitoes relayed it right along: a bunch of fools had arrived with some tasty new material. They fought each other to get it. It was awesome. A mosquito would sniff, take a few practice loops, get up a full head of steam, then tilt over like a pelican after a fish and come sailing right through the net. I never saw anything like it in the mosquito line.

Lauriette was boiling mad; she called Reverend Muckleroy a halfwit and said he'd put in the wrong bottle by mistake. She said this lotion was mosquito-nip, and could attract customers from as far as ten miles away.

"Why not try the Indians' remedy?" I said. *"They* aren't troubled with mosquitoes. I haven't seen a mosquito near them."

"Not in a million years. I'd rather be chewed to pieces than lower myself to the same class. What's more, you aren't to use it, either, not if you wish to sleep near me. I've got *some* standards left."

She was unusually small-minded that way. Now I'd once owned a goat, before it ate an umbrella handle and died, and it got mighty ripe now and then, so I was used to the air being a little blue. Medical books don't tell anything to do about a Seminole smell; it would have seemed to me politer to ignore it. It isn't genteel to go around sniffing at people and hollering "Pew!" But that's what she did. I might say that Charlie once told me, when she was off in the woods, that the Seminoles didn't care for *her* smell, either; but that was all right because she figured hers was correct and theirs wrong. It was one of her typical jackass viewpoints.

Anyhow, we made camp that first night behind Long Island, and even Lauriette had to confess that these fellows knew their business. They collected up some dry seasoned wood—windfalls or driftwood (good salt-soaked driftwood is the best fire burner on earth)—and laid them in a circle, like wagon spokes, so:

That way, when the ends burned down, all you had to do was shove the logs in farther. It saved chopping so much wood. But first, they'd laid a ring of coral chunks around the outside, to keep off the wind, and they had an iron grill to put over the logs, along with an old dented-up pot to place on top.

Lauriette was afraid we might starve to death, but the food turned out fine. One of the men shot an egret, a beautiful bird with feathers that were considered more valuable later on, and another paddled the canoe into the bay, hoisted sail and trolled for thirty minutes, using a wire hook covered with white heron feathers. When he came back he had a dozen mackerel and speckled trout, and one sheephead, a big fellow with broad black-and-white stripes, that he caught on the bottom using fish-belly bait.

They cut up the egret and the fish, including the entrails, added water out of a stream, along with other things from pouches they carried, and made a chowder. It was delicious. They had one crude hand-carved wooden spoon amongst them, and passed it around, which seemed perfectly workable to me, but no, Lauriette had to lay her ears back and balk. She made an elaborate show of hauling out Reverend Muckleroy's kit, extracting a spoon, and wiping it clean on her handkerchief. In some ways, she could be as offensive as Uncle Jim in his ornery moods.

I ought to state here that these Indians never were hostile or rude, after that first experience with Lauriette. They just weren't interested; they ignored us. It was only a few years previous that they'd retreated South—many branches of them—into the Everglades on the east and Big Cypress Swamp on the west, and knocked off fighting. But they resented the way they'd been handled, and had no regard for the whites. It was all right with me. All I wanted was to be overlooked. I hadn't ever had any compliments on my hair, but I preferred it to lie where it was rather than dangle from somebody's belt. It was more comfortable that way, and easier to comb.

Once we'd eaten, they washed out their pot with sand, then threw up an overnight chickee, or roof on stilts. They made the thatch from palmetto, and hoisted a pole floor up a couple of feet off the ground. This was to keep clear of snakes, and the open sides—like permanent Seminole chickees—were to prevent the house from blowing away during hurricanes. They had lots of those storms down here.

Lauriette raised a yowl about bedding down on the same platform with Indians, but nobody paid any attention except Charlie. Very meeky and mild, he said she might prefer sleeping outside with rattlesnakes crawling over her. He could fix it if she insisted, he said, and told her they had a fine remedy for snake-bite which usually worked in as many as three cases out of four. After that, she eased up on the noise. But she got peeved all over again when two Indians picked up *their* traps and went to sleep in the boat, after she'd sprayed herself with perfume. They couldn't stand it, they said; it made them sick. I told her it served her right, and I had a notion to join them, but she said, "Oh, shut up!" in such a brisk tone that I thought it wiser not to pursue it.

We did our communications with the guides by way of

Crop-eared Charlie. For some reason, he liked white people, and as a matter of fact, that's how he lost his ears. It was shortly before the end of the Second Seminole War, during what came to be known as the Colee Massacre, in the New River section of South Florida. Charlie, who was a young boy then, liked the Colee family and heard his elders planning to destroy not only the Colees but the whole settlement there.

Well, very plucky, he passed a warning, though nobody believed him until the attack began. Even so, most of them were saved because of the boy, and afterwards the Indians found out who upset their surprise. They held a tribal council (as Seminoles do about everything) and took his case under advisement.

As it worked out, he got off practically scot-free on account of his youth and previous good record. The Seminoles always were a fair-minded people, and conduct better courts than the white men; I've heard a number of people say so since.

So they cut off his ears and banished him for life to an Everglades island so scraggly that nobody else wanted it. But he had a girl that liked him, and by and by she talked the chiefs into letting him come back into the tribe again. Being a young man of good sense, he wasn't mad at anybody, so he went right ahead associating with whites. In addition, his ears, though missing (probably used in a stew, or given to some deserving child for a plaything) never bothered his hearing. If things were tuning in fuzzy, not having a backboard to bounce off, he simply swiveled his body at an angle, to let the sound get a straight shot at him.

Charlie became well known around the settlements, particularly later on the East Coast, and I reckon he'd hit it off especially well with Reverend Muckleroy. Once you got used to his looks, and he *was* a shocker at first sight, he was as enjoyable as a person with all their parts intact. Something else you might say for him, I suppose, was that he'd been converted to a religious Christian, and carried a stick which he notched every day, to observe Sunday.

Well, on the sixth or seventh evening, when we pulled

past Charlotte Harbor (on my 1840 map) and onto the beautiful island called Sanybel—cluttered up with the handsomest kind of sea shells, spotted and whirling—I realized that something was up. Mistippee, who was boss of the guides (after Charlie), collected the others together and did a lot of talking, for a Seminole. Charlie listened in, then came to us with the result.

One thing they'd jawed out was our route to the Shark River and Cape Sable (from which we'd sail over to the Keys). Naturally, we'd agreed to stay clear of trading posts and Forts. Two or three now wished to travel up the Calusahatchee River and into Lake Okeechobee; after that, they knew the hidden waterways down through the Everglades and across the Grassy Waters.

Mistippee preferred to strike south from Sanybel into the Big Cypress Swamp. It would be shorter that way, and a couple of our fellows had been here before, during the wars; so they knew now to navigate, in a general sort of way.

The argument arose because of the difference in Seminoles. All of them were Creeks, of course, driven out of Georgia and Alabama at different times in the old days, and afterward mixed with runaway negroes plus a few renegade Spanish. (King Phillip, for instance, who'd been their head chief, was the son of an authentic Spanish duke and a Creek woman.) But the tribes remained in two factions in Florida. One branch, that liked to hunt and fish (and fight) for a living, took up residence in Big Cypress, which was about as easy to find your way around in as the South Pole; the other went to live in the main Everglades, south and east of Lake Okeechobee, meaning Broad Water—the giant fresh-water lake in the center of south Florida that flows steadily down over thousands of square miles of grassy flat lands to the sea.

Now the funny thing was that the Big Cypress bunch, called Mikasukis, spoke a different dialect from those in the Everglades, who were known as Muskogees, or Cow Indians, because they liked to live off cattle and cropraising. The two could scarcely understand each other's speech.

Our argument arose because this bunch was Muskogees, except for the one named Mistippee, and most had a healthy respect for the Indians of Big Cypress. The Mikasukis were fierce, and no mistake. *They'd* never wanted to quit fighting, and as recently as 1858 their Billy Bowlegs was raising cain, and had jumped a party of would-be Government surveyors and shot them full of holes. Of course, the surveyors had destroyed all the Indians' gardens first, purely out of meanness. They trampled down row after row of corn, beans, pumpkins and bananas, after taking what they wanted for themselves.

But it was bad judgment, because they'd penetrated Billy Bowlegs' domain, built on high ground, or hammocks, here and there in Big Cypress, and were out of their element. So when the Indians voted to strike back, and did, the Government decided it was a poor idea to attempt a survey of the swamps after all, and called Billy Bowlegs a menace. Naturally, nobody considered the Indians' side of it—a season's crops ruined for nothing—but only belly-ached about the shooting.

Anyhow, to get back on the track, we tried to make up our minds which way to go. We had to solve it right now, because from Sanybel on down the coast it was entirely open Gulf; no more key-chains to shelter behind.

Charlie himself was wishy-washy, mainly because he figured everybody would behave and be nice, no matter where we were. That's the way he was himself, so he always looked for others to be like that, too.

It seemed an odd stand for a man without any ears, particularly since the white people he'd warned tattled on him to the Indians and the Indians carved him up to chip in *their* brotherly bit. He'd got it from everybody, you see, but he still believed in them all, as well as any strangers that came along. It's a pity there aren't more like him.

We hashed it over, and Lauriette settled, with Mistippee, on Big Cypress. His reasons were simple: he didn't care to do any more paddling than necessary. As to Lauriette, she wanted to get the trip over on account of her delicate nose, and the mosquitoes. Full of impudence, she asked Charlie to tell Mistippee, who she was sure would understand, as they had those opinions of their own about perfume. So that was settled.

The other thing they brought up was that we were being followed. On our fourth night's encampment, beside a creek on the mainland, two Indians crept out of the scrub and talked with Charlie and Mistippee, and the next day we left a man behind. For this service, they laid a demand of ten dollars extra from Lauriette, for the visitors to canoe him, and she coughed up without any comment for once.

Well, they didn't tell us why then, because Charlie disliked to scare us, but now, with our missing guide returned, we heard the whole story. It was two black-bearded white men and a couple of Indian paddlers, in a much lighter outrigger dugout. They were coming on fast, and looked as though they meant business.

"Bad Indians, most," Charlie said. "Mikasukis, not caring damn if white people live or die."

This was rip-roaring bad news, and came as a very unpleasant surprise. I thought we'd shook them off.

We explained the situation to Charlie, stressing how dangerous it was, and he said the men were likely very good fellows, and maybe missionaries.

"Missionaries your grandmother," said Lauriette. "They're murderers. They want to kill this boy and capture me. Now what do you propose to do?"

One thing positive; she always hit right to the point. There was never any beating about the bush with her.

Charlie seemed uneasy. Being sure we'd got away unseen, he was now upset at the thought of violence. But he'd promised to deliver us whole, so he held a conference with Mistippee. When he came back, looking sorrowful, he said:

"Mistippee kill men five dolla a head. He say he no budge down on price."

"That's ten dollars for the two of them," said Lauriette, musing. "What about the Indians?"

Well, I was bowled over. There wasn't any limit to her coldness. She could talk about this with no more concern than if they were fixing to squash cockroaches. So, I said to myself, they're all the same in that family; I'll just keep a little closer eye on you, Miss Know-it-all.

"Once white mens killed, Se-min-olees no care any more. All happy. Very safe."

"Now wait a minute," I said. "Why don't we just run into Big Cypress and lose them? What's the use of an execution? I know they're villains, but I was brought up with some idea of fair play, and this is shooting from ambush, isn't it. . . . No matter how other people were brought up," I added, giving her a pointed look.

"Fiddlesticks. Let's get rid of them. Quite obviously my brother Rex has hired the best men he can find—as he said, he's got unlimited funds—and those Indians aren't apt to get lost in their own nasty swamp. We'll do it my way."

"Wash me out of it," I said in a voice loud enough for all to hear. "I'd like it on the record: I'm not a cold-blooded murderer, and I want it remembered later."

She never batted an eyelash, being deep in thought.

"No," she said, with a brief shake of her head, "I guess it won't work. You couldn't trust them that far."

"*What* won't work?"

"To offer to pay them double their salary to go back and kill Rex. It's a good idea, an inspired idea, but we simply couldn't depend on it."

Well, that was enough for me. I went ahead and turned in for the night. When a person comes to a point where she'll consider killing her own brother, I'm through. They could solve it any way they pleased. As for me, I resolved to strike out on my own the very first chance I had.

But I never got an opportunity. Nobody told me what they finally decided, and I didn't ask. We pushed off early the next morning and paddled up the Calusahatchee (which means "river of the Caloosas," a tribe of giant men who'd been here before the Seminoles). It was one of those regular coppery-dark Florida rivers you see everywhere you go, deep and winding, shell or mud bottom, depending on how close to the sea, and surprisingly sweet to the taste, considering all the vegetation rotting there.

The day was hot, and on one bank where the sun shone alligators basked, motionless till they heard us, after which they slid off with a grunt or a hiss. Charlie said they weren't dangerous unless food was scarce, but you must never get between a female alligator and her eggs. By good luck, they only got hungry once or twice a week; then they ate a duck or some fish. It's odd, but some of the biggest animals on earth require the least fodder. Uncle Jim once said it was because they don't move around and burn up anything. Then he went on to tell about a chap named Buddha who had the peculiarity of sitting on the floor and staring at his navel. The fixture seemed to interest him. Well, this Buddha, who was probably feeble-minded and couldn't help it, got to the point where he moved so little he was eating a grain of corn a day. Nothing else—no soup, no dessert. I spoke up and said it was about the dullest program I ever heard, and he'd ought to got out more and seen some people, but Uncle Jim said I'd missed the whole point. He declined to go into it further, and appeared a little sore.

Anyhow, the female alligator will charge you immediately if you cut off her eggs. Charlie said there were crocodiles down on the under-coast, at the edge of the salt water, which would attack anybody any time. He knew a family that had lost a child which was washing herself on a creek bank. I never really believed him till later; *our* schoolbooks said the crocodiles lived in Africa.

We made a portage in mid-afternoon and transferred to another, smaller river; then on the third day we struck Big Cypress Swamp itself.

The whole look of the countryside changed. Now, instead of traveling along rivers, with an occasional carry across dry land of palmetto, cabbage palm (which has a bud you can boil and eat like cabbage), mangrove, scrub oak and slash pine, we were always in swamp except when we landed on a hummock, or high island. These curious knolls, sometimes several miles around, were spelled "hammock" and meant "garden place" long ago in an Indian tongue. When we stepped onto the first one, to rest, it was different than any land I'd ever seen—what was called "fully tropical" by Lauriette.

Nobody lived here, but had shoved farther south into the swamp. The soil was rich and black, and high cocoanut palms grew in clusters. Some said they were seeded long ago by birds from the West Indies. We could see the remainders of Seminole chickees, also gardens where they'd grown such things as corn, pumpkins, sweet potatoes, beans and bananas, but this wasn't their main diet, as we found out soon enough.

Nearly everywhere around these hammocks stood cypress trees, stiff and gaunt like gray dead people, with creepers trailing from their arms, their lower trunks and roots in water that flowed quietly southward. Now in September the water was three to four feet high, covering the sharp saw grass most places, but as endless and mixed-up as the Sahara Desert. It was no wonder white troops never made any headway with the Seminoles down in these gloomy swamps. It was awesome. Sometimes you'd glide along a water-way where you had depth and room; next minute, the marshy, grassy bottom rose up to hem you in all around. Unless you knew your business and found the channels, you had little chance of making your way out.

Neither did you see any signs of life, except for birds and fish and alligators and occasional snakes that slithered out of the way pretty fast. Wading birds—wood ibis, blue and white herons, egrets, spoonbills, anhingas—were everywhere one day and nowhere the next, depending on the wind—and circling birds like hawks and gulls and bald eagles and turkey buzzards could generally be seen soaring against the low, puffed-up, stormy looking clouds that rode the horizon hereabouts. Now and then, a pink flight of flamingoes flapped along, in a slow, clumsy formation, and if they flew close you could see how spindly frail they were. The color of some was practically red; they were flashy.

Taken by and large, though, I never saw a place so dismal quiet and unpersonal. A broody, prehistorical hush lay over it and gave me the jimjams. It was as if humans didn't count in these parts; the swamp didn't care whether you lived or died. It made no difference to anything except the turkey buzzards and such, and not very long to them, only enough to pick out your eyes and other juicy parts, leaving the rest to the alligators and the carrion game or fish.

By nightfall, we reached a big hammock where two Seminole clans called the Otters and the Frogs lived together. It was confusing. Even though, since then, I studied it out with a traveling English schoolmaster at our Key, who'd lived among the Mikasukis, I haven't rightly got it straight yet. Maybe no white person has, because of the peculiarities in Indian tongues, which run more vexatious than comes out in books about Indians.

These Otters where we landed never married up with the Frogs, who they considered different some way. Mostly, the Big Cypress Seminoles were organized into clans, each one taking a totem for its name, on the order of Otter, Frog, Panther, Wildcat, Tiger, and Snake. (This last bunch was mixed heavy with negroes, it was said.) But they boiled it down further, too, in a kind of family way. That is, they also had a loyalty to what the schoolteacher called a "sib," which was a kin that descended from the mother's side, rather than the father's, as we do. The Otters and Frogs lived together in every way except marriage and had several hammocks nearby where they raised crops and hunted.

Well, the first thing I noticed, when we pulled up our dugout and walked in, was that nobody paid us any attention. The Indian women sitting at work on the ground never lifted their eyes in our direction; not one. Several men lying on the platform of a chickee talked to Mistippee but treated Charlie like a traveling hawker. It was embarrassing. Still, they permitted us lodging, and that was better than nothing.

But *wasn't* Lauriette sore! She was used to a hullabaloo being raised wherever she went (being honestly handsome) so when even the women ignored her, she got her dander up. Moreover, she was having some kind of trouble underneath, from sitting so long in a cold, wet canoe. I didn't understand it very well, but she was suffering pain.

Well, when she finally swallowed her pride enough to tell Charlie, he said he'd speak to an Otter doctor. Just before sundown, a medium-old man carrying a deerskin bag and a bamboo tube with feathers on one end came over, not very eager, and addressed Lauriette in a crackle of words that made no sense at all. But Charlie translated and said:

"Doctor say he know troubles, can fix."

"How? By mumbling chants and jumping up and down?" asked Lauriette, as ungracious as always. Here she was, getting free medical advice, a house-call to boot, and she had to quiz the man like an amateur.

"Doctor say take off clothes, spread bodies down over log, facing east, he fix." Charlie said the doctor must first blow his breath—his "ammunition"—on the unhealthy part through his medicine pipe, and after that he'd treat it with *acini* and *cakani*—cedar leaf and sassafras.

"He *will* not! I'd rather suffer all the way to Key West. Tell him to go blow on somebody else."

Charlie shrugged, then explained the situation to the doctor, who shook his pipe a few times, looking angry, and left. He didn't like the way the case had gone at all. You take the most of his patients, they were probably decent and obliging. If the doctor said strip off and lie face-down on a log, they did it, and likely thanked him for it.

But before Lauriette crawled up on the chickee platform they'd assigned us, Charlie said, very timid and shy, "Muck-el-roy give tobacco?"

"You saw it as plainly as we did. Unless you're blind."

"Not for smokes, not chew."

"What, then?" Lauriette asked, her face slightly pink.

Charlie untied one of our pouches and took out a long tobacco stick. He rubbed one end over with fat, and handed it to her. Beet red, she snatched it out of his hand and disappeared into the bushes. She was one too many for me, but her temper improved a hundred per cent in the next few hours; there wasn't any doubt about *that*. One way or another, there's a lot of relief to be got out of tobacco, at bottom, and don't let people tell you different.

The Otters (like other Seminole clans we met) had one large chickee for cooking and the women gathered there to prepare the clans' meals on a grill over one of those wagon-spoke fires. They had two main things to eat, a kind of porridge made out of grits, called *sofkee*, and hunks of fried fresh-water fish that Charlie said were bass, blue gills, catfish and blackfish (or mudfish).

When the food was ready, it was carried from one family chickee to another. The pots they had were all iron or stone; at one time they'd used copper, but they had a plague of copper poisoning and a lot of people died. That's what they thought it was, anyway. Well, this was a good dinner, and even Lauriette tucked in and ate like a gormandizer.

You could carry on all you pleased about savages, these Seminoles ate very well. They cultivated a plant called coontie, or arrowroot, and made starch and flour from it, and produced their own grits by dropping shelled corn into the hollowed-out end of a log then grinding it with a wooden pestle. On other hammocks, the Otters hunted possums, turkeys, rabbits, tiny deer no bigger than goats, coons, and sometimes bears in the late autumn, when they were sluggish from storing up fat for the winter. Also, these Indians caught a good number of turtles and prepared them in various ways. The meat was tasty, though hard, on the order of veal cutlet in a restaurant.

Their gardens overflowed with vegetables and fruit in this soil that was thin but very rich. Besides the ones I've mentioned, they grew squash, beans, sugar cane, melons, and, of course, cabbage palms; and they'd planted a number of fruit trees on the order of guava and several kinds of citrus. Some of the families were bee-keepers, too, but most seemed mortal swollen about the neck and hands. I don't know why, but Indians and bees don't mix; it may have something to do with the way each other smells.

In that line, I should tell the most popular crop they had was pigs, or hogs. Cattle ranged on some hammocks, but not in the same numbers as hogs. I never saw another sight like it. Hogs overran the place, in and out of everything. They were as cool as you please about strolling into your chickee and gobbling up whatever lay about, and if they didn't eat your shoes, you were lucky.

The reason was, Seminoles made pets out of hogs, as whites do dogs, and allowed them to sleep in their beds. Now it's an open secret that a pig's habits fall short of tidy, and not many make an effort to spruce up and re-

form about the house. It was annoysome. You'd be about
to drop off to sleep when there'd come a grunt and bur-
rowing and some Otter's pet would be climbing up to join
in.

It almost drove Lauriette wild; she said her interest in
pigs was limited to the roasted variety, with an apple in
its mouth. She said she'd never before appreciated the
ceremonial hog-butchering at Belle Mead, but if she ever
went back, God forbid, she'd enjoy each execution with
relish. She kept a heavy stick in bed, to discourage pig so-
ciability, and she kicked hogs now and then in the village,
too. It attracted her mean looks, as it naturally would. I
asked her how she'd like it if visiting Seminoles kicked
her dog, but she said she had never cared for all "the ridiculous pomp and circumstance" about hunting back
home, so they were welcome to go up and kick all the
hounds in sight. She'd give them a note, what she called a
"laissez passer." This girl was a tough nut.

Mostly, Otter hogs weren't as fragrant as the kind
white folk keep. They fed largely on pine mast, back in
the pine woods, rather than on swill, and the mud they
wallowed in was maybe a little cleaner, being shell and
sand and marl, which is a kind of crumbly clay. The pigs
got moved around some, from hammock to hammock,
along with the Seminoles themselves. When the soil
played out in a place, the Indians gave it a rest, ambling
on till it recovered. They were smart about farming,
Charlie said. For instance, they grew corn on one patch
for two years only; then they laid off that crop for several
seasons.

We stayed on this first big hammock two days, or until
Lauriette could sit; then we continued our journey, heading southwest to trick our pursuers, who were now a day
and a half behind. Mistippee'd checked up while we
loafed. He was puzzled how they could still be following,
because we had taken to little known water-ways, where
trailing was next to impossible.

Well, after lunch of the first day out from the Otters,
we shuffled ourselves around to even up on the paddling.
I was placed near the stern, before a young fellow who'd
never given us a glance since we started. I believe he was

the surliest buzzard I ever met. We ignored him. He wore one of those knee-length tunics, with patches and stripes and the like, and when he climbed in, I noticed that some of the patches were missing. It was odd, because Seminoles keep their clothes in good order.

Somehow, I couldn't push it out of my mind. As we skimmed along, with birds circling overhead, saw-grass all around except in narrow channels, hammocks like oases in the desert showing off in the distance, and rolled-up clouds on the horizon, I found myself glancing backward out of the corner of my eye. It was the first time I'd paid that Indian any attention. And then, between paddle dips, he quickly tore off a piece of red patch and dropped it over the side.

So that was it. He'd been dropping them all along. Even a dunce could follow markers like that, for the red cloth would catch onto saw-grass and stay visible all along the way. Trying to think what to do, I became so fidgety I could hardly sit still. But I had to wait all through the afternoon and until we stopped for the night; I hadn't the least idea how many might be in with him.

First chance I got, ashore on a deserted hammock, I drew Charlie aside and told him what I'd seen. In his usual saphead way, he thought the man might be playing a game with fish. He didn't know him personally, but had acquired him through Mistippee, who was a wonderful guide with no record of hating whites. That is, he hadn't killed any lately, as far as was known.

"Listen here," I said, as out of sorts as Lauriette. "For once, get this through your skull. That fellow's dropping off markers—it's why we've been followed this far. Now what do you plan to do?"

He looked sad, uncomfortable, as if the whole human race had blown up in his face, but he promised to talk it over with Mistippee. Well, that paid dividends in a hurry. *Mistippee* didn't think he was attracting fish; he figured just the way I did, and held a private council with the other guides, after this skunk went to sleep. I crouched back on the edge of the camp fire and listened. I couldn't understand a word, but they were exercised; make no mistake about that. I got the impression they settled on something, for they fished out a skin bottle and passed it around for all to drink. I thought it was whiskey, and calculated we were in for a rackety night, but I learned better from Charlie the next day. It was their black drink, called *asi,* brewed from the leaves of the yaupon shrub. It's a religious potion, to make people brave and bind them in friendship—taken at all great decisions, such as going off to war. It also makes the person hawk up his dinner and maybe a few meals before that, along with the lining of your stomach—to get him purified, you know. I could hear Mistippee and the others whooping away on the ground, having a religious good time long after I'd gone to bed. While doing so, they called out, in a low voice, so as not to disturb the backslider (who was asleep in the canoe) something that sounded like "Yahala." I said to myself, I wouldn't be in that traitor's shoes for all the white man's money on earth. Religion can be a mighty blessed influence, especially for those that haven't any other entertainment, but you want to watch your step if it starts getting out of hand. History's full of trouble like that.

The following morning we started off as usual; no spats, no accusations, nothing to make anybody suspicious. They put the suspect in the stern, same as yesterday, only now they had Mistippee in front instead of me. I came after that, and kept a careful watch.

Well, an hour or so ran along with everything serene, and then, pretending to look up at an eagle, I observed our friend tear off another piece of patch. Not a flicker of an eyelid from Mistippee—a person might have thought he was deaf and dumb; he had kept right on paddling. But a few minutes later, when the fellow dropped the cloth over the side, all hades broke loose in an instant. Mistippee let out a yell, backwatered the canoe around, and left us staring at the bright red rag drifting away.

Quick as a wink, the traitor tumbled overboard and aimed for the bottom. But the channel was shallow here, and he'd got to come up sometime, so when he did, trying to wrestle his way through the edge of that cruel sawgrass, Mistippee raised his rifle and shot a hole in the back of his head: dead center. It made a thunk like hitting a pumpkin. He never moved a muscle, but floated off slow, downstream, his hair stringing out behind like seaweed and a dark stain spreading over the surface. Already the bottom fish were interested, and turkey buzzards had started to circle overhead. It was as if a lookout had whistled a signal. The carrion eaters aloft and alow were collecting for the usual janitoring job. Somebody had to do it, so there was no sense in despising them.

It wasn't pretty. Lauriette had both hands to her face, looking shocked for once, and Charlie seemed about to cry.

But we hadn't any time for sentimentalizing. We pushed on, taking a sharply different course now, and congratulated ourselves we'd thrown them off for good. These channels fanned out in a hundred directions; it was a perfect network, like the veins in a doctor's chart. As long as you stayed in midstream, and avoided breaking grass, one man's guess was as good as another's, even an Indian's.

We paddled until late, stopping to eat a cold supper in the canoe, then going on by startling white full moonlight. I had the creeps, the light was so bright all around. I dozed, and caught myself, and straightened up, then did it all over again, as many as a thousand times, I reckon. Sleepiness, when you aren't in a position to sleep, *is* the wretchedest torture on earth; I knew that from school, because I don't recall ever being wholly awake there at any one time.

It must have been three o'clock before we holed up, with Lauriette so tired I persuaded her to chew some of the cola gum. She did it, and then, to show it was all her idea, ate one of the cola pellets besides. But it had exactly the wrong effect, making her as suddenly frisky as a colt. Her worries vanished, she told me; she didn't care whether the white men caught us or not. "I'll show *them*," she said, and giggled.

Well, I should have expected it. Nothing she did followed the normal course of action. It was just the reverse. She felt talkative, and while the Indians slept—disgusted, likely—she chatted away like an idiot. She said she thought she'd buy some new clothes soon, and go dancing. She couldn't recall how she'd come to take up canoeing on quite this scale; she had never particularly liked it before. "I'm a horse traveler," she said. "Always was, always will be. You didn't know I like to ride horses, did you? Come to think of it, there's a great deal you don't know."

I asked her to shut up, so we could get some rest, because I'd heard Charlie say, after collaring Mistippee, that we'd be underway before dawn. One more day would put us clear, they claimed.

"They got horses around here? You get a horse and I'll show you. Any kind of horse."

"Now that's very likely, isn't it? On an island three hundred yards long? A wonderful place to ride. Yes, I'll fetch you one right away."

"Oh, piffle. What do *you* know about our beloved friend and companion, the horse? Nothing. Think of a saying with horse in it. You see?—blank. That's a horse on you. A horse! a horse! my kingdom for a horse! Shakespeare, or Bacon. Never look a gift horse in the mouth. No, don't ask me why; I never knew. Maybe he'll spit in your eye. *HOWEVER,* do not, under *any* conditions, swap horses in the middle of a stream. My old granddaddy did it, and was drowned in the process. He just swung out of the saddle, got down, and never came up. But he wasn't able to ride; worst damn rider [that's what she said] in Vicksburg. Served him right for not learning to ride. Or at least swim. He—"

Well, she was delirious, what they call hysterics, so there was only one thing to do. I slapped her cheek, pretty hard, and with that, by George, she hit me back so solid I came within a hair of blacking out. Then I heard her crying, and put her head on my chest.

She whispered, "I'm sorry, Davey," and I told her to forget it and go on to bed.

"I know a good judge of horseflesh when I see one," she said, "and you're it. *Never forget that.* If everything else fails, you can always go out and judge a few horses. Good night, and God bless you for your interest in the king of domestic beasts." I laid her back on the palmetto, and she was asleep in a second.

19

Dear Ladies:

DESPITE THE unhappy fact that your nephew has not thus far arrived, or turned up, I must inform you that we are making headway in our land of adoption. Major Burnie (with a display of energy surprising to the undersigned) has decreed that, if we are to live in dignity, and not rot, we must find gainful occupation. Misunderstanding him at first, I purchased a quantity of gum camphor, oil of eucalyptus, and turpentine, opened a tap of our apartment (they have excellent cistern water here in the season) and prepared to put the population back on its feet. But he feels that we should branch out in a new direction, compatible with our opportunities of locale. Also (and you will find this painful) the Major has expressed certain reservations, based on ignorance, about the remedial virtue of my formulae. Medical progress is, and should be, slow (except in the case of physical pursuit by the authorities), and time will no doubt show him the error of his judgment.

There are several avenues open for investment and enterprise here; namely, a potential salt works, fishing, sponging (in the sense of gathering sponges off the bottom of the Gulf), cigar-making, wrecking, piracy, and smuggling. The last-named, which has been mentioned with favor by Major Burnie, is, of course, dangerous, involving a lively risk of incarceration. As to piracy, Commodore Porter (mentioned in my last dispatch) all but stamped it out some years back. It is a curious fact that your brother appears to take this personally, for he states that, from boyhood, he had planned to be a pirate, and it now looks as though he may never get the chance. (Thanks to Porter, that is, whom he professes to abhor as a busybody and spoil-sport.)

One of the best remaining trades is wrecking, although it, too, has seen its palmiest days (a figure most appropriate in these parts, I believe). You may or may not be aware that, in 1840, the quiescent Seminoles swooped down in seventeen war canoes from the Big Cypress Swamp, through the lower Everglades and the coastal mangroves, across Florida Bay (which separates the mainland from the Key chain) and fell tooth and nail (and tomahawk) upon Indian Key, which is a part of the chain, about midway down toward Key West, a green-clad coral clump of twelve acres, the county seat of Dade County.

I paint this background as a necessary complement to our life here, as I believe that this is the region where we shall eventually settle. The Indian Key Massacre, as it came to be known, for it resulted in the deaths of several persons, brought about changes that greatly enhanced the wrecking business.

Foremost among those slain was Dr. Henry Perrine, the Key's most distinguished citizen, a kind of tropical Johnny Appleseed, an Illinois horticulturist and physician who had every hope of obtaining Government aid in producing hemp from an introduction of sisal seed into Florida. Perrine had been a pioneer in many directions, having given up his Illinois practice after dabbling with an arsenical quinine cure that proved nearly fatal to him. He was appointed American consul in Carapeche, Yucatan, where he spent nearly all of his time beating the bushes for exotic plants, a pursuit not ordinarily included in the duties of a consul, who, I believe, confines his activities mainly to insulting the traveling Americans who call requesting help or advice. The Yucatan officials indulged Perrine in his frenzied tour of the shrubs because he also fought cholera and yellow fever, and generally strove to improve the health of the natives.

Heavily loaded with seed, Perrine arrived at Indian Key in 1838, fresh from a successful petition to the Congress. He, and two partners, had been granted 24,000 acres, for experimental purposes, halfway between Key Biscayne and Cape Sable, or, in brief, in one of the wildest and least promising areas of the universe. The report of the Senate Committee on Agriculture, supplied me by the local "library," might be of interest:

"If the suggestions and experiments of Perrine shall be successful, the arid sands and the arid rocks, the mangroved thickets of the coast, the miry marshes, pestilential swamps, and impenetrable morasses of the interior, may all ultimately be covered by a dense population of small cultivators and of family manufacturers. Tropical Florida will thus form a well-garrisoned bulwark against invasion in every shape and shade."

In any case, Perrine's new grant being virtually uninhabitable, except for Indians, alligators, birds and fish, he took up residence on Indian Key, which was dominated by a scoundrel and bully named Jacob Houseman, wrecker, trader, speculator, storekeeper, and proprietor of the Tropical Hotel, which was complete with (and I quote from a leading journalist) "Bowling, billiards and booze."

Houseman's treatment of visiting Indians was so notorious—he tossed several tipsy young braves into a privy and locked them fast for two days—that suggestions spread out through the Everglades to separate him from his scalp at once. He kept a private militia of twenty-four men and had lately made the Government an offer; that for $200 a head he would kill or capture all the Seminoles in South Florida. The Indians' ire was further aroused by the treacherous conduct of our Secretary of War, Joel R. Poinsett, whose name is now affixed to a brilliantly handsome red plant, which he brought into this country from Mexico at an earlier point in his career. Poinsett, as was usual with officialdom of the period, had just reneged on a pledge of adequate living room for the Seminoles in Florida. Rather, he was encouraging the practice of rounding them up to be shipped to unsuitable lands in Arkansas (where many had been sent at the "conclusion" of the Seminole Wars).

So—to condense this distasteful episode and return to my narrative, a warrior chief, Chekika, set forth from Big Cypress with seventeen canoe-loads of Mikasukis, thinned down and inflamed by guzzling the ritual emetic of black drink, or *asi,* and determined not only to even the score with Poinsett but to perform, gratis, a barbering operation on the malodorous Houseman.

Like most Seminoles, Chekika enjoyed this sort of sport more than any other, so that upon his arrival at Indian Key, he became a trifle carried away. Among his lurid accomplishments that August day, he boiled a boy in a cistern, clubbed two white children and a negro playmate to death, tomahawked a fair sprinkling of adults, and wantonly shot down the luckless Dr. Perrine in the cupola of his home. Others of Perrine's family—his wife and children—had hastily been secreted in the cellar, which led to a bathhouse and turtle-crawl. Crouched terror-stricken in water up to their chins, they were overlooked by the now drunken and ravening Seminoles, who several times opened the trap door to peer down but saw nothing appetite-whetting.

The truth is that, at first, the Indians had no notion of killing Perrine, who had doctored and befriended them often. They wished only to scalp Houseman, a yearning shared by most white persons of the neighborhood. *That* worthy, as might be expected, got clean away. When the alarm broke, he coolly drowned his faithful barking dogs (to silence them) and sprinted barefoot over raw coral to his skiff, then rowed briskly out to his sloop. However, an encouraging footnote to his escape is that he was crushed to death, some time later, between two ships in a typically unsavory operation of salvage. He died raving imprecations, lamented by none.

After the damage at Indian Key had been reckoned up (the savages burned nearly everything flammable) our sluggard Government at last sent down, for protection from further raids, the frigate *Constitution* and the sloop of war, *St. Louis.*

My cycle has now turned full, and I am back to wrecking. With the arrival on the scene of these watchdogs, many immigrants arrived post haste from the Bahama Islands. They were, they are, an exceedingly interesting group, with a background which they curiously prefer to keep under wraps. In short, a number of them had been for generations either wreckers or pirates or both. Their reticence seems silly in view of the fact that several notable English families of the present were founded upon the gains of such sea rovers, or "privateers," as Drake, Raleigh, and Hawkins. But the industry has sunk into ill-repute, perhaps due to the mounting number of murders for pleasure, and the Bahamians feel it keenly. To "atone" for their past mischief, or enterprise, they have become religious to a degree, and in some cases live within depressing limits of propriety.

Now a wrecker is, technically, a man in an honest, permissible trade. So it was in the beginning, and so it will be, I am ~~fairly~~ sure, if Major Burnie buys a vessel (as he threatens to do) and plunges into the venture.

As of this writing, he has not yet decided, as extremism has made wrecking nearly as odious as free-booting. The first permanent settlement in the Keys archipelago was established by fishermen from Mystic, Connecticut, who presumably sold their catches in the bustling markets of Havana. Because of the abundant flow of ship traffic through the Bahama Channel and along the Florida Reef, this early group turned to wrecking. The winds hereabouts are capricious, severe gales blow up without warning, and the unmarked knife-ledges of coral form a lee and fatal shore for many an unfortunate vessel. The Mystic group (and others subsequent) were joined in wrecking by many Bahamians who came over after our Government dispatched the protective warships. It was a valuable addition, for the new immigrants had already acquired an almost suspicious proficiency at this enterprise in their own homeland.

Together with the Connecticut contingent, fishermen from Havana, a few English boats, and a representation of Colombia cruisers, the Bahamians settled here into a comfortable life of attention to other people's ships. The island of Key Vaca, with its two deep channels of Vaca Cut and Pull-and-be-Damned Creek, having earlier swarmed with pirates became a center for ships engaged in the largely legitimate business of wrecking, or salvage. There can be no doubt that a number of the unscrupulous occasionally hoisted false lights in time of dire weather, causing many a vessel to be wrecked that might otherwise have beat safely to seaward.

In the main, though, these were honest, if hungry, men, performing a useful purpose. I am informed, at the library, that in 1821 a shipwrecked passenger, John P. Decatur, praised Captains Smith and Place of the sloops *Splendid* and *Hyder Ali,* for having "so much honor and fine feelings." Five of the twenty wrecking vessels in the Keys in 1835 were from Connecticut; the remainder were from the places mentioned above.

The situation today is greatly altered. Formerly, the salvaged vessels were taken to Key West, where Congress had established a territorial superior court in 1828, and the proceeds properly distributed. Immensely lucrative cargoes of silks, laces, wines, silverware and liquor were bid on by speculators and underwriters' agents, the proceeds in years of especially fierce storms reaching $1,500,000.

Now, though the court remains, the pickings are comparatively slender, owing to the large number of Bahamians crowding the profession and because of the line of reef lights laid down by the Government in 1852. It is a melancholy fact that these markers bid fair to cripple an esteemed and traditional calling. Thus it is always with the cherished institutions of our nation; progress rolls them under one by one. Still, wrecking continues to offer good profits, for the alert and the competitive, so we emigrés may yet find ourselves a part of those dramatic races toward the succor of the distressed.

Before exploring this thoroughly, ~~Major Captain~~ Lieutenant Burnie strode into our humble abode (the Casa Lopez) the day before yesterday in company with an individual of mien incomparably shifty. It grieves me to say that both men had departed from the standard Key West refreshment of *un buchito* (a swallow) of bitter-black coffee, with *bollos* (penny cakes fried in deep lard of blackeye pea flour, garlic, onions, salt and pepper), and had, as it were, taken on a cargo of rum.

"Meet Captain Pereira," your brother said carelessly, giving his normally well-brushed hat a swirl toward a peg on the wall. It missed, and sailed on out of the opened window, to which he paid no attention whatever.

A swarthy, raffish villain with flashing teeth, fierce moustachios, impudent eyes, and a gold ring in one ear, bowed in a slightly mocking way, keeping his glance upon my innocent daughter, Millicent, and remarked: "I am pleasing, to be sure, especially Madame."

It was my impulse to seize up my cane and dust his jacket, but I courteously refrained when I noticed that he was wearing an ugly-looking dirk in his belt at the back.

"Pereira's got a salt works, or claims he has," said Lieutenant Burnie, lighting a cigar. "I bought in. Fact is, we've been playing cards for it, but it nicked me five hundred dollars in the end. Fellow's as crooked as a dog's hind leg."

"Se*ñor!*" hissed this absurd posturer, drawing himself up with a semblance of injured dignity, his hand at the hilt of his knife. "Even with to jest, the honor of the Pereiras—kindly remember!"

"Oh, stow it," said Lieutenant Burnie, clapping him in a friendly way on the shoulder. "How do you like the ear bauble?" he asked us; then, "Tell them about being a pirate."

This scoundrel first made a motion of ducking his head and clicking his heels faintly, to acknowledge what most certainly had *not* been an apology; then he gave a roguish laugh and said, "Captain Pernums is jocking all the times, but can be troublesome with a Spaniards."

"As nearly as I can gather," your brother went on, "Pereira's never done an honest day's work in his life, but now he's trying to straighten up with this salt works. We're about to drive out and see it. Half of it belongs to me. Keep an eye on him while I get my hat."

At this negligent speech, I anticipated at least an invitation to duel, if not murder done on the spot, but it only provoked a loud, offended hiss; and immediately afterward we gathered in the surrey that was tied to a tree out front. We arranged ourselves, Zebediah took up the reins, and we rattled off, with Pereira trying in a kind of prurient, snake's way to pretend there was insufficient room for his arms, so that he could drape one over my daughter's shoulder.

In the southeastern part of the island, the town has set aside, by lease, a section of land for the manufacture of salt from the evaporation of sea water. By what means this consummate blackguard managed to establish a going plant I am unable to say, but Lieutenant Burnie, as if reading my thoughts, said, "Oh, he's got it all right. I saw the papers. Don't ask me *how* he got it—slit somebody's throat, I expect."

This fortunately went unnoticed by Captain Pereira, who at the moment had abandoned the uncomfortable struggle to enclose Millicent with his arm, and had dropped it in juxtaposition to her leg, with the back of his hand jiggling at her knee.

We drove on, past the largely unpainted wooden houses (of cedar and hardwoods from the upper Keys) with their second-story porches and Captains' walks—no chimneys anywhere—past the grim and forbidding Martello Towers, built in the Civil War by the Federal Government (which held Key West and indeed all Florida port towns throughout the conflict); past tumultuous fish docks and turtle crawls; past displays of vividly tropical foliage—Jamaica dogwood, banyan, tallowood, frangipani, and buttonwood; lemon, lime, cocoanut, avocado, mango and guava trees, heavy with fruit. It is a most curious anamoly—a soporific island paradise shouting under the sun.

In due course, we arrived at Pereira's holding, a series of compartments, or "pans," each a hundred feet by fifty and separated one from the other by coral walls, the whole possible to inundate at high tide and capable of being closed off, too, by a system of gates.

We climbed down from the buggy, Lieutenant Burnie in his most antic and nonchalant humor (sharpened by alcohol), and the unspeakable owner capering and posing for the edification of Millie, who most commendably declined to be disturbed. Indeed, she even made a brave pretense of being flattered, thus removing a considerable amount of tension from the party.

"All right," said your brother, squinting at an indolent Bahamian negro who technically was keeping an eye on the operation while actually, seated beneath a tree, was eating a soft mango with a spoon, "Let's have it, amigo. Spiel-see. Parlari. What's it all about?"

(Lieutenant Burnie, mildly in drink, has a tendency to address *auslanders,* even Spaniards, in a rich mixture of unrelated foreign words and phrases, a peculiar circumstance since he fought in the Mexican War and speaks the language well.)

"Aha!" cried Pereira, who on the other hand is unquestionably the very worst linguist alive. "Here having to come in marina; whoosh out? No—with gates close— up sun coming, *muy calor*—water rise in air; look down —salt!"

"Look down where? Those things are all grown up with green slime. Never saw such a damn mess." He pulled a piece of fruit off a tree—a lemon or lime—sliced it in two with a penknife, and said, "Hand me one of your shakers. I want to test it."

In great agitation, Captain Pereira replied, *"Nots* some salt already. Three occasion with me of *mala suerte,* lousy, much worse. Soon salt everythings good, by Dios."

"You mean you never have produced any salt? What happened?"

"First, marina swell in high stormy. *Very* lousy. Come in, flood—whoosh, go out. Gates with."

"Took the gates, eh? Then what?"

"Night times, before *sobrestante*"—pointing to his "overseer," who, full of mango, was now asleep under a bush—"bad peoples visit, pick up corals, maybe build cistern."

"This is a heart-breaking story, amigo. Anything else?"
"Porpoise."

"What are you talking about? Porpoises don't eat salt."

"Marina partly high flooded, but gates stay. Porpoise swim in, knock downs new walls all around. Customarily lousy."

"Well," said Lieutenant Burnie, lapsing into the offensively sarcastic vein we know so well, "I can see that I've snapped up a bargain here. There's a fortune in this thing. Tell me, do you plan to clean the pans out? They're filthy. You ought to clean them out, and then take a bath yourself. Another point, where do you keep your shakers? People like salt out of shakers, you know."

"Not shakers! Wrongly conceived of salt business. Entirely."

Lieutenant Burnie appeared taken aback.

"You mean this isn't the kind of salt people eat? Now see here, Pereira. There are only two or three uses for salt that I ever heard of. If you're planning to produce this stuff to sprinkle on birds' tails, I'm drawing out. There just isn't the market for it."

By now, Captain Pereira had managed to gain the impression that he was being ragged, and he started once again to draw himself up, hissing. I contrived to smooth it over with hasty and complimentary questions, and the tour of inspection ended. It had had been a severe trial all around.

Next day, Lieutenant Burnie (in better condition) was filled with high cheer about our new commitment. Somehow he had gained the notion, from the farcical visit of yesterday, that in this salt works lay great promise.

We held a conference in the afternoon, all of us assembled—myself, your brother, Millie, and Zebediah—to discuss arrangements for our future.

"To begin with," he said, "we can't just pop down to Matecumbe and start digging for treasure. We're too conspicuous, being newcomers. The whole town wonders what we're here for as it is. The scurry of treasure-hunters down that way would make the gold rush look like a two-family migration. No, we've got to take it easy, and do something else for awhile. This salt thing looks pretty good. Everybody eats salt; I eat it three times a day myself. Look what they've done with Cuban sugar."

I cleared my throat and said, "Your new partner, Captain Pereira; do you place great reliance on his acumen and integrity?"

"A crook from the word go. I checked him out. He's

done a little of everything around here, none of it honest as yet, but the authorities remain hopeful. The fellow's family *were* some kind of high-caste dagoes, I believe. This specimen's a black sheep.

"For awhile, he had a very good thing smuggling in Cuban rum. Nobody minds smuggling around here; everybody does a little now and then. It's expected in a spot of such conspicuous detachment. But then he took a whack at landing Chinamen in the Ten Thousand Islands. They caught him on that and threatened to lock him up, so he went into wrecking, or piracy, but he lost his boat in a storm. Now he's got this salt works, and for the rest, he plays cards. As I see it, he's an ideal partner: there's no chance we won't watch him. One look at the ridiculous fool, and we're reminded that he's the greatest rogue unhung."

"That man *bad*. He *all* bad," said Zeb. "I don' want nuthin to do with him. I wuk somewheres else."

"I like him," said Lieutenant Burnie. "I find him very enjoyable. It's a pleasure hearing him talk. I believe it comes as close to pure gibberish as anything I've encountered, even in Mexico. The trouble is, I think, that he's been mixed up with pirates of so many nationalities he sounds like a Chinaman."

I entered a mild demurrer, Millie was non-committal, as she has been of late, and we let it go at that. Tomorrow we shall begin the work of cleaning the pans, hiring some negroes, and building additional compartments on the leasehold that Pereira's papers claim. There *may* be money in salt. It remains to be seen.

Before closing, I must add a footnote to our personal relations, an accidentally overheard encounter between your brother and my daughter on the upstairs balcony of Casa Lopez, at an advanced hour. I had retired, but the window was open and my daughter was taking the air before going to her room. Lieutenant Burnie returned from his habitual nightly ramble of the town, and, after a try or two, engaged the balcony's rope hammock for the smoking of a night-cap cigar. Again, it distresses me to say that his demeanor was influenced by spirits. Hearing a stir in a dark corner, he said, "Who's there? Pereira? Speak up, or by God, I'll—"

"Don't be so noisy," my daughter's voice called softly. "It's me—Millie."

"Oh. What are you doing out here? I can't see you very well. You aren't naked, are you?" (On the houseboat, your brother labored under the apprehensive delusion that my daughter was always about to cast off her *very* adequate clothing.)

"I couldn't sleep. I'm not naked."

"Why not? Sleep, I mean. You're young and healthy. The fact is, you're the healthiest girl I ever saw. You're bursting with it. Why can't you sleep?"

"Healthy Millie, the tree-climber."

"What's that?" (in a startled voice). "I thought that's what you liked. This place is full of trees, many of them never before clumb, climbed. You can do some real pioneering around here. Take a flag and plant it in the top of the nearest banyan. Think it over."

"I've often wondered," she said in a reflective, mature tone that I'd never heard her use before, "how you managed to become such a completely self-absorbed ass."

Lieutenant Burnie now sat up (I gathered) and moved to a bench nearby. He was silent for a moment; then he said, "I'm getting old, and a little stupid, and I'm certainly a self-absorbed ass."

"You're thirty-six."

"How do you know?"

"I asked."

"Why?"

"Except for my father, you're the first man I've ever known. I've been—waiting."

After a moment, he said, "Suddenly I can see you pretty clearly. *Not* a tree-climber."

"No," she said. "I don't think so. You may have tried, but you don't really."

"Honey" (and I have the impression he leaned forward and took her hand) "I haven't seen anything really since I was twenty-three. My girl eloped with my best friend."

"The medal-winner. I was always curious what drove you on, what you're afraid of."

Lieutenant Burnie arose and paced back and forth. The strong fragrance of his cigar drifted in through my window, contending with the over-sweet scent of night-blooming jasmine. I eavesdropped; I admit it.

"Not true. It was closed off, a good while ago. Let it stay buried. I'm sorry I told you."

"No; not closed off. Held onto carefully, watered and tended, and encouraged to bloom into a good excuse."

Your brother apparently seized Millicent by her shoulders and yanked her to her feet, facing him in the dark.

"I was wrong. You're not grown; you're just precociously impudent."

"Did you get out of her way, then, as a healthy person might do?"

There was a pause, and, "From a distance of ten thousand miles, I saw her nearly every day after that for twelve years."

"You *fool!*"

"Yes, just at this moment I seem to get it in focus a little better. It's almost as if something important had happened—how old *are* you, by the way?"

"Next month I'll be twenty years old. I've never been to a party. I've never had a pretty dress. I'm what they call disadvantaged. If my birthday comes before a man has kissed me seriously, intending the worst, I'll either kill myself or run away."

You may imagine with what foreboding I awaited the next utterance. Then ~~Lieutenant~~ Lt. Col. Burnie remarked in more than his usually confident tone. "The crisis may be past," and it was at this point that I arose and silently closed the window. Perhaps, dear ladies, I should have gone to the porch and restrained those two orphans of the storm, but my cheeks burned with a knowledge of my selfish blindness as a father. God give them joy, wherever their hearts may lead them.

Yr. chastened and contrite servant,
E. Snodgrass

20

WE WERE UP and away long before dawn, of a sharply cool, breezy day. I was relieved to see that Lauriette had eased up on horses, and didn't appear to favor them as much as formerly. She was downright snappish about it. Thinking to encourage her, I said, "They tell me there's a horse or two on this big hammock where we're heading. They'll probably let you ride, and maybe build a few jumps—rock walls, log racks, that sort of thing. You can't tell; they might have a colt to break."

She said, "Shut up; I've got a headache. You're a horrid child."

You never could tell. Some days, she was almost human.

We slid along at a good clip, even without the extra paddler, and when the first streak of dawn raised light over that swampy wilderness, we hoisted sail. The wind was directly out of the north for a change. Commonly it blew from the south, from off the big waters down there, and now and then it blew hard.

So we pushed forward, all morning, all afternoon, stopping once or twice, but not for long. We'd veered off into back waterways—channels between places too shallow for boats to navigate—where nobody could track us for sure. In winter (the dry season) the broad Grassy Waters lie only a few inches deep; in other seasons they may stand several feet high. Nobody seems able to explain it. They say the water comes from Lake Okeechobee, draining southward over an area of seven hundred square miles. The lake itself changes in height, as much as six feet, and some believe it's fed by underground springs.

Anyhow, the Everglades came about from this steady drainage, and make an annoysome route for travel. One white man that tried it wrote: "Half a mile a day over dry trails [he got lost from the channels in winter] through saw-grass twelve feet high, with no air and a d——d hot sun sizzling your brains."

The streams we took often narrowed from fifty feet to the length of a canoe, within half a mile or so. Sometimes, Charlie told me, it was better to go twenty miles around than try half a mile through, because if you had to get out and walk, you might sink up to your neck in muck. It was tricky and, taken all around, slow.

By nightfall we were safely removed from trackers, Mistippee said. Nothing but a miracle could let them find us now, without combing all the hammocks in Big Cypress, and by then we'd be well on our way.

Still, Charlie thought we ought to lay over in a sizable village, on account of Lauriette, and we hit it, by far the biggest place we'd visited, at noon the next day.

The Panthers lived here—a very large clan—in thirty to thirty-five chickees. They were friendlier than the Otters, but they refused to let us stay on their island. We could drop in all we pleased, they said, but we must sleep of nights on a hammock two miles distant.

Mistippee explained the reason to Charlie, who told it to us. It concerned Lauriette, and naturally when she heard that, she pricked up her ears. Charlie saw she was interested, so was less garbled than usual. He said the Panthers were extremely particular about their bloodlines, and while they considered Lauriette hideous—pasty and washed-out enough to make a person puke—some of the young unmarried bucks might decide to "mix up blood" out of boredom, the way "white people tie cans on a dog's tail."

Well, when he finished that sizzler of an explanation, Lauriette boxed his jaws. I knew she would; she was as reluctant a person to take criticism as ever lived, I reckon. She couldn't face facts. The truth was that alongside these Mikasukis she *was* pale, so there wasn't any sense in making a fuss over it.

Anyhow, Charlie sulked all afternoon, while we walked

around and looked things over. They had a big "busk" grounds, for the Green Corn Dance, and a ball pole at one end where they played their curious game. I never cottoned onto it, because the idea wasn't really to beat the other side. In spite of their fierceness in battle, these Seminoles ran their village life peaceable, with strict laws governing all. In the case of this game—stick ball—everybody was supposed to help everybody else. The idea was to take exercise, and be sporting.

But they weren't equals here, not by a long chalk. Another clan called the Snakes lived on part of this hammock and ones nearby. These people were practically coal-black negroes, with a little Seminole blood mixed in, and their standing was below the Panthers. It might be wrong to call them slaves, but Lauriette described them as "almost a vassal people." By now, they never performed slave services, but in the beginning, when the negroes ran away to Florida, the Seminoles housed them on what amounted to a paid domestic basis. That is, they were workers for the Seminoles, but nobody was *owned*.

Since then, I've noticed information in northern books that Seminoles and negroes embraced each other as "equal children of God." There isn't a particle of truth in it. The Seminoles held the negroes apart for years and years, and began to marry and lose the distinctions after a long passage of time. In a hundred years, or around 1980, I reckon, the differences may be ironed out. If you don't push things like that, it has a chance to straighten out naturally, with no hard feelings. There's no way on earth you can force people to like each other; it comes out exactly the opposite, more often than not.

The Panthers had two versions about how man came about. Charlie told them to us, after he'd finished being peeved. In one, the first three men God created stepped into a pool to bathe. The first came up spanking clean, and his descendants have always been white. The second chap got muddied up a little, of course, using left-over wash water, and his descendants were red. The third fellow, obliged to take the dregs, might as well have skipped bathing altogether, for he climbed out pretty grimy, and his descendants turned out black. Nobody felt there was any inferiority attached, you know; the bathing order was to blame for it all. If you ask me, it might have worked better if they'd dived in all at once. But the legend fails to mention how large the pool was, so maybe they'd a got in a fight there, the way people do, and nobody would have climbed out at all.

Another version says the Great Spirit made men out of clay. He overbaked the first batch—burned it to a crisp —and that was the beginning of negroes. So, on the next batch, He was so careful He didn't rightly bake it at all, but snatched it out of the oven before it had hardly got warm, leaving it underdone, or white. The third time around everything went perfect: He hit the right heat, and time, stayed awake, didn't get jumpy, put in the exact amount of shortening, and salt, or whatever the recipe called for, and the color came out a beautiful red, or Indians. A lot of Seminoles preferred this second version. They wouldn't have enjoyed being considered half-baked, or even over-baked, and consequently they looked down on people that were. They couldn't stomach the white, who hadn't been cooked at all, so weren't actually people, but only raw materials, but they *did* try to be fair about darkies.

They had other camp-fire fables about creation, but these were the only ones that made sense. Of the two, Lauriette said *she* didn't care for either, but there was very little about Indians she liked—that is, to boil it down, nothing—so her opinions weren't worth much.

Next morning we returned from our hammock after supplies, and I met a boy of about my own age. He was playing stick ball, and looked like he might invite me to join in sometime, so I did. A couple of men glared at us pretty mean, but he went ahead, and one of the women even flashed us a smile. His name was "Crazy Short Tail," but I didn't learn this from him, because he spoke no English at all. Charlie told me, later, along with other things about the Mikasukis. And the rest I got afterward from the schoolteacher, down in the Keys, that I mentioned before in this book. He'd gone into matters like language and customs, and knew practically everything, or thought he did, in the usual leather-headed style of teachers.

Crazy Short Tail had won his grown-up name only last year, at the ritual of manhood, according to Seminole practice. All the romantical books I've read on Indians lay it out that names, and speech, and spelling, and the like are as simple as A-B-C. Short's name, in Seminole, was spelled: *hacikocokniha:cî*, if that will give you some idea. After his initiation, he no longer helped his mother do chores like string beads and sort clothes, and he would have been insulted if somebody had given him a toy. He could still play games, but now he was able to fish and hunt and paddle a boat on his own. Life was pleasant, not harsh, in these villages.

In the afternoon he made me a signal to follow and we climbed into his canoe. Handing me a paddle, he pointed a direction and we struck out. The Grassy Waters were two feet high now, making navigation easy around that hammock, but the saw-grass, when we brushed it, was mighty painful (the cuts hard to heal, as well) so we stayed in small channels.

Well, we paddled an hour or so, and I judged I'd catch a talking-to when I got back, but it was fun being off with another boy. Often of nights I thought about Commercial Appeal, and the things we used to do, maybe crying a little, and somehow it made Lauriette seem like more of a nuisance than she was, really.

By and by, I spied another big hammock on the horizon, and we reached it in twenty minutes. I hadn't any idea why we'd come, but if there was something doing, I wanted to be there. When we landed, Short picked up his bow and went through an act to suggest hunting, which was perfectly satisfactory to me; I hadn't killed anything important since we left, though if I'd aimed a little higher at Belle Mead, I might have fetched game, but nothing you'd care to have stuffed and hanging on a wall.

It wasn't long till I saw that this island, besides being deserted, was a regular hunting ground. The Mikasukis kept a number like it, being careful not to hunt them out. We saw two alligators—big fellows—before we'd tiptoed up the bank fifty yards, and we treed a coon, with a small baby, a short distance farther on. But that wasn't what we were after. He wished to show me something, that was plain enough, so I ankled along without argument. The ground sloped upward toward the center of the hammock, and in half a mile or so we'd come to very dry ground, with big trees and rich grass, that looked like the mainland. It was refreshing, after all that water. A nice breeze blew, making the palm-fronds rustle and pine branches sigh, way up there, and you could see circling birds—white and black ospreys, or sea eagles, and hawks and others just everywhere. And buzzards, too, but they were hoping we'd get into trouble, and so provide a meal.

I wasn't worried; Crazy appeared to know his business. But when we approached the other side, with grass as high as our knees, he started getting excited. He looked up, nose a-quiver, and sniffed in this direction and that. So did I, but I failed to pick up any more than the smell of wet swamp, pines, former fish, and things like that.

We tiptoed very cautious, and before five minutes had passed, he pointed, hopping in excitement, at a place where the grass was rolled down flat, as if a long pipe had recently been laid there. It made a trail directly into higher grass, and as I stared, Short noticed blades that were springing back into place. Whatever it was had passed here only a few minutes before. It was awesome; I begun to wish I'd brought a gun.

We started clipping down that flattened-down trail, and when we hit an opened-out place, Short gave a yell and there it was—a snake over sixty feet long. It was monstrous, like demons you see drawn in history books about sailors' tales, or Scottish lakes. I felt my heart climb up in my mouth, and my legs took on a kind of rubbery action; I couldn't move. But when that devil coiled around, hearing our cry, and started back, and in considerable of a hurry about it, too, I finally went into motion. We flew. I don't think I ever ran so fast before. On top of the highest ground, Short slowed up, and I sank down in the grass. I couldn't kept it up much farther if the snake had been at our heels and beating a dinner gong.

Crazy Tail made sign talk to show that the snake was afraid of open ground. He raised a stick, pulled the trigger, and cried, "Boom!" several times, and I got the idea that braves had discouraged it with gunfire. I couldn't help wondering why they hadn't killed it. Then I took to wondering if we'd really seen it at all. But Charlie had mentioned a snake like that, in the region of Cape Sable, which wasn't so very far from here, and there must have been others. It was real, all right. A man on Cape Sable shot one not long after this. He cut off the jawbones, which were sufficiently big to pass his whole body through. I'd seen a thing, and wasn't apt to forget it.

We had a wonderful day with snakes. Tramping back to the boat, we heard a thrashing in the bush, and by George if we didn't see *another* sight, this time what was called a gopher snake, in the act of swallowing a possum. He had everything but the hind end down, and it was kicking like the furies. You could hear the front end squealing, too. It was enough to make you sick. I started to take the bow and arrow and lay that snake out for the buzzards, but Short became agitated. He had an uncommon strange attitude about snakes, which I didn't understand until later.

It was close on to three o'clock, now, so the boy removed a piece of bread from his tunic, which was curiously swollen about the middle. I gobbled my share right down. Fright *can* make you hungry; it works that way sometimes. Well, while we were eating, sitting on a fallen palm bole, this fellow fished in his shirt and came out with a blacksnake, full-grown, as scary a customer as ever I saw. I choked, then spit out the bread, for the two objects had been housed in exactly the same spot. I wasn't hungry any more.

He played with the snake, letting it crawl over him like a pet, then he signalled me to follow, and we struck out once more. I got the idea that while we were on a snake hunt, we had no intention of killing them. It was an outing of instruction, you might say.

Back in a dark, damp, shadowy region where mangrove roots coiled around like withered gray arms, he pulled up and commenced to sniff again. He pressed me to do the same. Well, this time I caught it slightly—a faint odor like a sweaty garment, and it wasn't Short's, either. He put his finger to his lips, picked up a stick, and we crept on, aiming to flush a two-headed dragon, I judged. I wasn't happy about it, but I didn't mean to back out until he did, either.

Then we heard the alarm rattle like a bunch of dried peas in a gourd and I saw the fellow's head and tail sticking up, one perfectly still, the other all a-tremble for trouble. It was a canebrake rattler, olive-colored with a pink tinge, and had a black tail. Some people call them Seminole or swamp rattlers, to tell them apart from diamondbacks and pygmies. I scrambled back on the jump, looking for a rock but Crazy set down his blacksnake and held my arm so I'd watch. Well, it was new to me, but that blacksnake waltzed in and ran the rattler bowlegged. He made a strike or two, dripping venom, but the blacksnake threw two loops around, as they fought with their main bodies nearly a foot off the ground. Then the blacksnake jammed the rattler's head down in a muddy hole and held it there, drowning him, but the rattlesnake finally slipped out and left. He'd called it a day, as they generally do with blacksnakes.

Seminoles cultivate blacksnakes, and carry them around as protectors. What's more, they won't kill *any* snake if they can help it. They have a superstition about it, which seems odd when you consider that they live in land that's crawling over with both rattlesnakes and cottonmouths. For one thing, they can smell poisonous snakes easy enough—all poison ones have that sweaty clothes stink—and for another, they can see and hear unusually well. Anybody can hear snakes, if he wishes to train his ear.

But the main trouble is the superstition. They believe rattlesnakes originally had no fangs or poison—perfectly harmless. But a bad Indian stumbled onto a mother rattlesnake in the woods one day, and killed her three babies. When she took her complaint to the chief (as snakes did then more often than now, I judged), he outfitted her with a set of false teeth and said, "The next time a man comes up like that, bite him." And ever since then, Seminoles have left rattlesnakes (and others) alone, believing that if a snake is unbothered, it won't bite.

Lauriette, when she heard this, got off some of her typical rubbage, and said "the administration problems" of that tribe must have been in good shape if the chief could spend his time whittling false teeth for every snake that crawled up with yowls about this and that. She cut a stick to carry, and said she'd kill all the snakes she pleased, whether they had their own teeth or not.

"As far as I'm concerned, a snake's a snake, and you can tell your new friend I said so," she told me. I didn't bother; you couldn't teach her anything. It made no difference how upright and logical it was, if it had anything to do with Indians, she tossed it right on aside.

Crazy's mother was a white woman. It sounds convenient for a person writing a book, but it was so. She'd been captured a long time before, during the wars, when she was only a child. The Seminoles seldom took prisoners, especially ones that had been underbaked during that original cookery, but occasionally they made exceptions. The women of the tribe fancied a child, or got a feeling of pity for somebody. The main Seminole warrior of them all, Osceola (now dead, after being captured when he came in for a parley with General Jesup under a flag of truce), was half white, though he usually denied it. His mother was an Indian and his father a white trader named Powell. This rubbed hard on the boy; it was a relief when he got his adult Indian name, which came from "Asi," the black drink, and the custom of braying "Yahola" when the drinkers were throwing up their grub, as stated. Hating so much to be white, Osceola yelled louder than anybody, hence received the name "Asi-Yahola," or "Black-drink Crier," but this later got confused with "Osceola" by the whites, so you see, he never altogether shook them off, after all.

Crazy's mother had been snatched from the northern settlements on the East Coast, and kept in the swamps from then on. She took to Indian ways so strong she quit speaking English, even after many Mikasukis began taking silly white man's names, like Tommy Doctor and John Jumper, and she never taught English to her son, so they said. During the week we stayed there, she never spoke a word of English from first to last. What's more, she was as unfriendly a person as there was in the village. All the same, I caught her looking at me with a kind of thoughtful expression once or twice, as though she wanted to ask a question or two. But she never did.

She was more Seminole than anybody, and wore about twenty-five pounds of beads looped around her neck. When a girl is twelve, she's given one strand, and others are added on later birthdays, or for "acts of virtue." So you could tell that she was a superior member of the tribe. After middle-age, the beads are removed strand by strand until only one remains, and it's buried with the wearer. But usually it takes a long time. These people were different from plains Indians, Charlie said, in that they coddled old people, rather than stashing them behind to die when they'd outlived their usefulness. Several people in that village were well over a hundred. It's by no means a remarkable age with them, because now, with the war ended, they hadn't any worries, never worked hard, found the providing of food easy, and seldom quarreled among themselves. In addition, they were lazy, and that helps a lot. The beaver, which seems hipped on work, in the particular line of cutting down trees on other people's property, doesn't live very long; but the turtle sits on a rock all day, trying to figure out a way to do it tomorrow, and lives to be a hundred and fifty.

Mrs. Crazy Short Tail Senior (I never learned her right name) had a solid bank of beads from shoulders to chin, and never removed it except at night. They said she slept very well, as she naturally would, for she was working like an ox if she only walked around trying to stay upright. Lauriette, sitting on our chickee platform the second day, and trying to wriggle out of her shoes, which were about the size of a chisel, said it was a barbarous custom, only possible among "a people totally savage and depraved." Maybe so, but I thought the women's costumes in general were pretty and colorful, with their full-length skirts decorated up by fine rows of designs, and a cape of the same color. These women took care in fixing themselves, and combed their hair into a knot on top of their head, or maybe a pompadour or bangs. Some of the women had their hair looped over a broad cardboard frame that extended from one side of the face, on the order of an oversized tam o'shanter; it gave them a dashing sort of look, somehow. The smallest child customarily dressed like the mother. In Mrs. Crazy Short Tail's case, this was a spindly girl of eight, practically as white as me, and with all the sociable good manners of a wasp. Charlie said that, now the war was over, the mother was teaching the child English, but I never heard it, and didn't believe it.

The boy Crazy was apprenticed to a medicine man named Buster Cypress, and on certain days collected up herbs and memorized chants. I learned about it some. If Crazy worked hard and absorbed things on schedule, he'd receive his medicine bundle in a few years and be a qualified shaman. This was different from Indian "doctors," who were a dime a dozen. Lots of Seminoles practiced healing, but these, the "doctors," known as *Aiyik-Comi*, are in a different class than medicine men, who have unusual powers that extend beyond curing people up. It's complicated, what they call spiritual, mainly. To make it worse, most elderly Seminoles have at least a *few* magical powers, so they belong somewhere in the doctoring line, too.

The outright unvarnished medicine man uses lots of remedies, along with chants and prayers, but he has to be careful what he selects. Also how he does it. For instance, all herbs must be plucked from the north and east sides of a bush. They had authentic cases, I heard, where a medicine man went to sleep on the job, as doctors are apt to do when their wives have a party on or something, fed a sufferer herbs picked from the south, and lost him in twenty-four hours. I asked Charlie if they took a compass along on outlying house calls, where the terrain was unfamiliar, but he didn't know what a compass was. Indians fix their position by the heavens or by the way vegetation grows in the woods.

Sweet bay leaves, or *toli,* are one of the mainstays of the herb bunch. If they fail to work in saving a sick person's life, the medicine man goes right ahead and uses them after death, to drive the ghost away, so the body can be touched. It's easy to see, then, that bay leaves never actually let anybody down, for if they don't come through in one way, they can always be counted on to clean up the mess. Cedar leaves, called *acini,* and sassafras, *cakani,* are obtained from around Punta Gorda every so often by medicine men, for doctoring up gallstones, coughing, and pains in the bladder. Snake root is commonly employed for stomach aches, particularly if the shaman thinks the ache might originate in the head, or mentally.

These were all good medicines. I saw them in action twice during our week there. In one case, a wife had a howling belly-ache when her husband brought in another woman to add to his string. He had dredged up the "bride's dowry," which is the opposite of our system, Lauriette said (being pretty angry about it), and the bride's relatives had sewed him a new shirt, which carried out *their* responsibilities, so the girl moved in after a ceremony that allowed everybody to get a little drunk on *wy-ho-mee* and work up some business for the doctors. Well, the other wife got this belly-ache and they called in the shaman, after a preliminary haggle over the fee, which was settled as two coon skins and a chicken, unless a long lie-in was indicated. But it wasn't. Snake root took care of everything, and prompt, too. Within three days, those two women were thicker than thieves and plotting against the husband, who was stingy about little things like silver-coin decorations, neither did he care for in-laws, particularly the nosey kind, and I never heard of any other.

On every hammock I saw, the chiefs grew a few sticks of tobacco, largely for their own smoking purposes, but some was used by shamans. It was a powerful shield against danger; also it knocked out the pain of such annoyances as Lauriette's sitter. She said that had cleared up, and she made an unholy row when Charlie told her the head medicine man here, who'd progressed up to the high degree of the tenth month, *Yobi-hasi* (calm moon, no wind) would fix it, permanent,—cure guaranteed, no matter where she sat—for a medium-sized alligator.

"The idiot!" she cried, with her usual tantrum. "How would *I* get an alligator?"

Charlie only shrugged; he didn't press the point. By now, he was so petrified of her he preferred to address her through me. He asked me to pass on that catching an alligator was easy, if you kept your hands out of its mouth and stayed clear of the tail. Or, sometimes, got hold of an ugly one, which would kill you, of course. Very generous, I thought, considering her savage attack, he offered to arrange her the loan of a canoe and a rope, but when I brought it up she looked so peeved I slid out and let it drop. She'd had about enough of this place. As for me, I liked it fine, now that I'd found a friend. We had a good time.

I asked Crazy some questions, through Charlie, and the shaman didn't mind. He was proud of my interest, and even said I might have made a good apprentice if I hadn't been white. They didn't mind me personally; it was only the color of my skin they objected to. Anyhow, Crazy would take instruction for seven years and then get the degree of the first month, *Fubi-hasi* (wind moon). If he went right on to the end, he'd reach *Yaholi,* which was so rare there wasn't any such medicine man on this hammock. Charlie said they had one on a big Eastern hammock named Pine Island, or clump place (*coyisoká: cokô: lǐ*) but his fees were so high that only the best hunters could consult him. In fact, he had what Lauriette called delusions of grandeur so bad that some thought it might bring on a kind of community, or state, medicine, where everybody pays the same, you know, and are killed according to an instruction book prepared by the clan.

When Crazy won his own medicine bundle, he'd be qualified to handle the old traditional war medicine, which is so powerful it's kept away from the village entirely—hidden in the Green Corn Dance grounds. As to the ordinary bundle, that's encased in a deerskin wrapper and contains everything for an Indian's well-being: pieces of horn, feathers, stones, bird dung, and dried animal parts.

They declined to tell me what each meant, and I didn't press it. The war medicine had been handed down through the clans for use mainly at the Green Corn festival, which was held in August. No human hand could touch it; it must be scraped into a pile with the quill of a buzzard's wing.

Nobody knew what it was, either, but you couldn't deny it was strong, because these Seminoles hadn't *yet* been defeated. They'd only retired to the swamp, as I said, while some consented to be removed to the Indian Territory in Oklahoma and Arkansas. I doubt if they *ever* sign a peace treaty; they're just that mulish and brave.

In reading this over, Uncle Jim says I mustn't fall into a jokey vein about these medicine men, and I don't mean to. Some of their shenanigans *were* funny, but I believed in a lot of it, too. And every word I've put down is the dead accurate truth, no matter how prankish it sounds. For instance, Cypress had a case where a man suffered from sneezing all the time, along with wheezy breathing as well as reddening of the eyelids, a stuffy nose, and dripping (where he had to hock and spit a good deal, you understand). Well, did the medicine man give him nose drops and sugar-coated pills? He did not. He set to work and studied the case, in what even Dr. Snodgrass later called a "very forward-looking and progressive manner," or what corresponded to his own notions, I reckon.

First off, the shaman went into the matter of the patient's dreams, and found that a large, furry, black object bounded in and out, and turned them into nightmares. That is, just as the black monster was about to pounce on the man, he woke up screaming. Then the shaman shinnied around among the clan (this fellow was a Snake, from another hammock) and asked a lot of questions about his background. What he learned was that all of this fellow's brothers had killed a bear with a bow and arrow when young, but he never had; he was afraid. It had haunted and plagued him for years.

Well, if you believe it, the medicine man said all the sneezing and wheezing and red eyes and dripping and hocking and spitting arose out of guiltiness covered up, so he put him on a dosage of snake root, which the Seminoles employ for troubled minds, as I stated before. In a few weeks, the patient felt much better, and stronger, and *then,* by George, the medicine man made him go out, first with a gun, and slay a bear. It like to killed *him,* rather than the bear, but he did it, and took on about it, as happy as a man out from jail, all that night.

The day after, about half of the stuffiness was gone from his nose, and his eyes were considerably less red. Now then, the next thing the shaman did was hand him a bow and arrow and tell him to fetch back a bear with *that*. I needn't go on about this any longer, because the patient fetched it, after the medicine man had blown his pipe on him, also on some herbs, and got off a number of chants and prayers, to nail down his fee. Also, he dusted him with *hoyanici,* from the willow, to give him extra added good luck at hunting.

A week after that fellow lugged in a bear, his symptoms disappeared completely. He was cured; and when I told it afterward to Dr. Snodgrass, he said the whole operation, from first to last, was worthy of the best medical brains of Europe. He said he couldn't have done any better himself, but he sort of lost interest when I let on that the fee amounted to three alligators, four fox skins, a pig, and two bolts of calico. He said that, thinking it over, there was more profit in Elixir, and it was a good deal less awkward to spend. He said he simply couldn't see going into a hotel, slapping an alligator down on the desk, and bawling for first-class accommodations.

Well, the days moved along, and I nabbed an alligator myself, practically, on a hunting trip with Crazy. We were looking for a web-footed panther, which was a rare animal in those parts, so we left long before dawn, because you aren't apt to see that kind of specimen in broad daylight. We failed to locate one, but before daylight we saw the ghost fire. Only a few ever got to see it, and those only on very dark nights. It rolled up in flaming orange waves on the horizon, a monster fire, heaving and billowing, as scary as Doomsday. We crouched down, even Crazy, for the medicine men had put an evil omen on it. I thought we were done for, but suddenly it left in a single fiery straight column that rose up to the sky, like a warning signal, then disappeared. No noise, no smell of smoke, nothing to show where it had been.

"Good golly," I said out loud, forgetting he didn't speak English. "What was it?"

"Great ghost fires, nobody knows," and when he said it, I turned around and stared.

"You spoke English!"

He swallowed, and, finally, answered. "I am forbidden. By my mother, and by the chiefs. I get in bad troubles."

"Well, that's fine," I said, "because I've got a lot more questions to ask; I've had them stored up for some time," but he refused to speak another word of anything except Seminole for the whole rest of the day. It was exasperating. As to the ghost fire, I came to find out that most people thought they were accumulations of marsh gas exploding, but not on the horizon, as it looked to us— higher up in the sky, where heat lightning set it off.

I didn't altogether believe it about the web-footed panther, but in the morning, after the light came, he took me to a deep hole full of alligators.

We glided along in the canoe, and before I knew it, he'd spotted one that was spewing water up onto her eggs on the bank—they do that to keep them healthy, somehow—and slipped overboard with a rope. In about two minutes, he'd dived underneath, wrestled that animal around, rolling over and over in the water, scattering the others like a school of scared fish—you never heard such a racket—and come up with a piece of rope tied around its jaws. He said later it was easy, because an alligator's lower jaw is fixed, but you couldn't do this with a crocodile, which has both jaws opening wide, above and below, and generally on an article like somebody's dog or a member of the family.

Anyhow, we dragged it into the canoe and he killed it on shore by running a spear through the head, which was the only spot possible. Then he gutted it, because we had a long way to travel back in the hot sun, and nothing can get riper in a hurry than a deceased alligator.

In the stomach we found the remnants of a duck with the feathers on, a turtle still alive in its shell, and a chunk of wood, which helps out in the digestion some way.

We went back to camp, and Crazy skinned out the hide. They said he would start curing it with salt tomorrow, and afterwards sell it on one of the rare excursions these Mikasukis made to the white settlements outside.

But in the meantime his mother made soup out of the tail, and it was delicious, not nearly as bad as I thought it would be. I hadn't any trouble at all keeping it down. They gave me two bowlsful before we started to our hammock in the evening.

Lauriette was in a bad humor because I'd been gone so long, and said we'd be leaving the day after tomorrow. But when I looked at Crazy, he was frightened out of his wits; he'd spotted a hoot owl hooting on top of Mistippee's chickee, and there was no worse sign in the whole Seminole list, which was considerable, and most of it bad. This was a mighty poor sign, and I'll tell you what happened, though I'd much rather not.

With Crazy, I went over in the morning to hear the Snakes sing some songs like "White Feather" and "The Night of Love" and "The Story of the Little Coon." They were having a wedding, and making a celebration out of doing the old traditional things, like singing, and dancing to the music of water drums, tortoise shells, gourds, rattles and flutes. Lauriette could have gone easy enough, but she stuck up her nose at any sort of Indian nonsense, no matter if it was fun or not, and besides, she was sewing all her clothes back in one piece.

Well, when we returned, at lunch time, it struck me as funny we didn't see any smoke, but I forgot it as we walked toward the cooking chickee. I remember it was the first cloudy day we'd had in nearly two weeks. I was thinking about the rains, which they said were late coming, and then I saw Mistippee, but he was lying on the ground. Usually, I never exchanged any words with this fellow—he was too stern—but this time I called out his name, wondering why he'd be sprawled in such an odd position near the chickee in the middle of the day.

When we walked a pace or two closer—slowly, because I'd begun to get the creeps a little; everything was too still—I saw that it wasn't Mistippee at all, it was only his head. I jumped back with a yell, and we hung onto each other for a second. And after that, I commenced to holler for Lauriette, running to and fro over the hammock. But it was no use; she was gone, and most of her clothes were gone with her.

"You've got to talk English," I said to Crazy, grabbing him by the tunic. "Those murderers have got her, and killed all our guides. You've got to help me."

Well, in a minute or so we calmed down and searched the place all around. Mistippee's head was lying about ten yards from his body, and our other guides, except Charlie, had been served in exactly the same manner. One lay face down, so to speak, at the swamp edge, with his stump of a neck still gurgling blood into the water. So they hadn't been gone over half an hour, Crazy said.

He was as sensible as anybody now, and spoke whatever English was needed. We finished our check: the guides all dead, both Charlie and Lauriette taken away in our canoe, and considerable of our gear stove in and strewn around the ground. All the corpses had bullet holes in them, from what looked like heavy rifles. It was a small point, but I was glad that Mistippee and the rest had been killed before their heads were taken off.

I figured the murderers had pounced on our camp without knowing I was absent, and didn't dare wait any longer. Probably, they'd line up at another hammock and try for me later.

So we had to move fast. Crazy scurried around with his nose to the ground, then said there were two white men—"big, with boots"—and two Indians wearing moccasins. It seemed odd they got the jump on our bunch that way, but they must have shot from ambush.

He said: "Go get chiefs," and I didn't argue. I couldn't think of anything else to do.

Well, when we came back, in a dozen canoe loads, and churning up the water, I can tell you, there was a fearful rumpus. I never saw those Panthers look so full of intentions.

But in a clan council held on the spot they decided it was none of their business. I tried to get Crazy to point out that it had happened in Panther territory, because this was one of their garden islands, but he refused to talk English in front of them.

I could see I was up a stump. I felt so low-down and miserable, I wondered if maybe I hadn't better paddle over to that alligator pool and dive in. Also, I'd begun to take on Lauriette's viewpoint about Indians. Here these Panthers had a regular butchery—four Indians murdered right under their noses—and what did they do? Nothing. Instead, they'd taken on a happy, contented, expecty look, and Crazy told me, off to the side, that they were concentrating on giving the unfortunates a stylish funeral. It had to be done up right: all personal belongings stowed with the bodies; everything "killed" like the owners—pots and pans bent out of shape, and other such tomfoolery.

I was so mad I couldn't sit still, and mooned along at the water's edge while they got ready to go back. They had to decide on a secret place for the burials, because it was not known whether these men had been entirely good, or bad, and if somebody stepped on a bad corpse's grave, trouble would dog him sure.

And, of course, the medicine men had to shove in their two-cents' worth, blowing through the pipes at the last minute, to hasten the spirits on toward the Milky Way, which was created long ago by the Breathmaker and had a city at the end where all the Big Cypress Seminoles go.

Looking down, I saw a scrap of cloth that I recognized, because Lauriette had the only dress of that color around here. I didn't wait; I streaked out and collared Crazy, who was listening to some mumbo-jumbo preparations by Buster Cypress. I took him aside and said, "You see this? I think Lauriette's dropping off markers, the same as our guide that turned bad. We can follow as easy as loafing."

Well, he was for it, which surprised me, and we lay low till everybody was gone; then we jumped in his canoe and whisked out of there, in a southwesterly direction. The Grassy Water was too high for them to buck the drift for long, so we took the sensible course, and sure enough, after exploring two dead channels, we found another scrap of cloth in the third.

All of a sudden, I felt downright tender-hearted about that girl. For all her snippishness, you could hardly call her a bonehead. And she did have spunk. Not many would have fought back in this way; most girls would collapse and go all to pieces, and who could blame them?

We sliced along, picking up a scrap now and then, feeling better, but we had a setback when we ran across some floating grass all dabbled with blood. I had a picture of Lauriette shot through her savings bank, lying near death, and felt the tears sting in my eyes.

In late afternoon, approaching a hammock, Crazy held up one hand, and we let the boat glide. He sniffed around like a bird dog, and said: "Smoke, from chickee fire."

It was a hammock where nobody lived, he said, and the fire was made out of *yaipaci* wood, that burns without smoke, mostly, so it was our bunch, all right, because no Seminole would build a fire like that unless he meant to hide. We talked it over, deciding that the wounded person had to stop, and tried to figure out what to do.

Toward twilight we crept forward; then we pushed through some dismal sharp saw-grass to another channel and landed on the opposite side. This island was perhaps half a mile wide, and we tiptoed along through palmetto and stunted piney growth, stumbling once or twice on old abandoned cane fields or gardens until we caught the glow of their fire. It was dusk now, and we moved up to see what was what.

Lauriette was seated on the ground, deathly pale, leaning against a corner pole of the chickee, and Charlie was stretched out on the platform, with one arm resting in a bark sling. He appeared about dead.

Standing at the fire were two rough-dressed men, tall and spare, with stubbly black whiskers, slouch hats, and wide belts with knife sheaths hanging down. One had a rifle he was leaning on—the longest gun I ever saw in my life—and the other was cutting a hunk of tobacco off of a coal-black twist. They were hard cases, and no mistake. I'd never seen either before.

All of a sudden, the biggest of these monsters snatched his hat off—he was totally bald, except for the whiskers —and went to swiping it left and right at the air like a wild man; he looked like a person killing snakes with a hoe. At the same time, he shouted some pretty filthy curses at the mosquitoes, causing Lauriette to stir just slightly, upon which he said, very ugly and sarcastic:

"Well, now, if the little titty lady ain't comed to life. Dog if I don't believe she ain't about to choose a bridegroom. Who's first? Don't forget now—I hollered Sunday."

Her reply was so low, I couldn't make it out, but when she raised her head briefly, I noticed that the whole left side of her face was black and blue.

Whatever she said (and it didn't sound complimentary) they only guffawed and slapped each other on the back with their hats as if it was the best joke they ever heard.

Then the shorter of these two (and he was still considerable over six feet) straightened up, sober and mocky, and said, "See here, Ma'am, you're a going to hurt my old pard's feelings, slanging him thataway. He's touchier'n a bear with a sore paw. About the next blast like that's apt to blow his trousers right off'n him."

Lauriette said something else, and the fellow started to slap her with his hat, but the big man caught his arm.

"Leave her be. I want her healt up for the handseling. I figure to hold it in two or three nights. Dog if I'll handsel a woman that can't no more'n walk. It'd be right down immoral."

Then he said, looking angry and impatient, "Where in thunderation are those coons?" (I figured he meant the Indians.) "I'm so hungry my belly thinks my throat's cut. When this job's done, I aim to tie their tails together and hang them over a limb. I'd rather travel with my nose in an asfidity bag."

The other fellow said they were hunting food on the next hammock; then he pointed at Charlie.

"What about *that* hunk of gator bait? If you ask me, he's done for. Whyn't we finish him off?"

"He might come useful as a talker. Leastways his mouth's big enough. I figure he'll make it; his stink will pull him through."

Crazy tugged sharply at my sleeve, and we crept backward out of earshot. He motioned me to hurry, and I did it. In a situation like this, I was perfectly happy to let a Seminole make the plans on his own home grounds.

Full dark would be here soon, so we scrambled back to our canoe, then lit out toward the next hammock. I never paddled so hard in my life. We were in luck, too; they hadn't finished getting food yet. We spied their boat pulled up on a shell bank at the end of a channel, and slid it out of there. I held it alongside while Crazy paddled us clear. Then we sunk it and crossed the half-mile water back to where Lauriette and Charlie were.

The idea was so brightful I could have hugged Crazy out of gratitude. As I mentioned before, these Mikasukis lived peaceable, without rivalry or strife, and brought up their children not to lie or steal or be cowardly or, later on, ever to drink too much. Those were the main things stressed for character, and they made it work, but when everything else played out, and a fight was called for, you'd better watch your step. These people knew *how* to fight, and nobody was more aware of it than the United States Army. If you don't believe me, look in your history books.

It was dark now, and this time we coasted in to land on the same side of the hammock, not far from those murderers' other canoe.

Then we just waited, out of the firelight but close enough to hear their conversation. They were boiling mad at their Indians, and one wanted to look them up and give them a thrashing. But the other said it was too dark, said he preferred to stomp a man where he could enjoy the expression on his face. After this, they got a bottle of whiskey out of their boat, and the talk became so vile— all of it aimed at Lauriette—that I felt my cheeks burn.

At one point, she tried to reach over and grab the rifle, which now leaned against another part of the chickee, but the big man kicked her in the face. She fell forward, moaning. I reached down for Crazy's bow and arrow, but he held my arm in a grip like iron; it was surprising for a boy his age.

They never ate anything, or offered Lauriette as much as a piece of cold corn bread. In an hour's time they downed all of that whiskey, every drop, and tossed the empty bottle aside. Then they had a very serious talk whether to fetch another quart or not.

"It ain't fitten; it ain't right," said the big man, slurring his words. "I was brought up Christian, where it's a mortal sin to overindulge in intemperance. My old Daddy never got falling down drunk unless there was a friend standing by to tote him home. He didn't believe in it. 'Never lay in the street like a hawg, son,' he used to say. 'You'll wind up with a bad name.' I ain't forgot it, so shut up your talk about another bottle."

"We better get it now while we can still find the canoe," the other said. "Leaving your old Daddy out of it, which seems sensible, seeing he died of delirium tremens afore I was born, it's like this: I either eat or I drink. It's my main rule of procedure. One or the other, or, when politeness is required, mix them. And since I ain't et, I'm bound to drink. Roust out that coon" (pointing again to Charlie) "and send him. I don't believe in waiting on myself when we've got a full-blooded domestic Injun to hand and serve."

"A Christian home," said the big man, addressing himself to Lauriette, "is one thing which you won't find no substitute for. Whiskey won't do it, and neither" (gazing in a general way at his companion) "will he. What's lacking there, and a fool could spot it, is breeding. My old Daddy would have put his finger on it in a minute. He— what's that?"

Drat it, I'd moved a little, to get at the mosquitoes, and broke a stick in two. It rang out like a pistol shot.

"Sing out! Name yourself, or by jingoes I'll—"

The other fellow pushed him down, muttering about how *his* old Daddy wouldn't take nothing off of nobody, either, especially insults, and said it was likely a possum or something.

They quietened down, and the shorter one allowed as how he'd catch a nap, to get his strength up, and then he would fetch another quart. His companion replied that he'd fetch it over his old Daddy's dead body, and then they were both asleep—passed out drunk, the disgusting sots.

We waited half an hour, then Crazy led us forward. I touched Lauriette on the shoulder—she was asleep, too, but looked half dead, poor thing—and clapped a hand over her mouth when I saw her startled look in the firelight. I could feel the hot tears streaming down along my arm as I helped her silently up; then she hung on for a minute.

But we hadn't any time to fritter. Crazy went to work as methodical as if he did this sort of thing every day. Without scuffing a moccasin on the ground, he collected up the two Kentucky rifles, slipped both knives out of their cases, took the ammunition, took the pots and pans, took the blankets, matches, hammer and saw, the mosquito nets, a bottle of mosquito salve—whatever there was loose—and stowed it in their canoe. Lauriette got in the middle of ours—wrapped in a blanket, and we carried Charlie, entirely unconscious, and laid him in the bottom of theirs.

We pushed off, towing Charlie, and stood out a little from shore. Then I had a good close look at Lauriette's smashed face, which steeled me sufficient, so I fired one of the rifles up in the air. We held up paddling, hearing them come crashing down from the high ground to the water's edge; the drunkenness all gone now. You could make out their outlines if you stared up at the sky then looked down over their heads quick. You can find a path in the woods that way on the darkest night.

"What is this? Who are you? You damned thieving redskinned bas—"

I interrupted, in as satisfied a tone as I can recall.

"You had to come searching. Now you've found us, and here you stay. You'll die right where you are—it may take a week and it may take a month, but there's no way on God's earth for you to get off of this island."

"By God, it's the whippersnapper. I told you we ort to have waited. Grab a rifle—quick!"

"The rifles are here," I said. "So's everything else. You're stranded, and so you'll find." Raising my voice, I yelled: "Your killing days are over, you murdering dogs! What do you think of *that*?"

He changed his tone, began almost to blubber.

"Look here, sonny. We wasn't aiming to harm anybody. Paddle into shore, now. Here's fifty dollars for you —a hundred!"

Crazy touched me with his paddle, and I got my senses back. We skimmed down the channel, but when they saw we were leaving, one of them picked up a rock and sent it whistling by my ear with a string of oaths.

Their Indians would likely cut thongs for a raft and get free, Crazy said, but there was no chance they'd rescue the whites, for the hammock was upstream and meant a half-night's paddle against the current with a clumsy raft. It couldn't be done. They were as dead as if the buzzards already had started in on the eyes. Without salve, nets or fire, the mosquitoes could finish them off on the first muggy, still night. They swarm in so bad, they clog up the nose and throat and all but choke a person to death. Charlie told of a case where a white man was caught by weather on a little key of the Ten Thousand Islands, without any equipment, and was bitten to death in a single night. At the worst seasons, there is no way to exaggerate those clouds of mosquitoes that come whining in, looking for blood. Cattle have been bitten and stung till they've run themselves to death, tormented clear crazy.

So—though it might sound hard, those villains had a terrible fate in store. They were doomed, and you needn't think they'll show up again in this story; they won't. We never saw or heard from them again. It does no good to blubber over citizens of that stripe. They weren't any good, nor ever would be, and the world's better off without them. Animals will turn a gone-bad specimen out of a pack, and so will a native tribe, and they know best, being close to nature and obeying nature's signals for survival. It might be smart if civilized white people watched them a little closer, and learned from their ways.

We paddled on down the Grassy Waters, then spent the night on another small hammock. We were obliged to turn in because the rain commenced to pour down like nails falling on the canoes—so hard it hurt your eardrums to listen.

So we holed up, dragging Charlie in out of the wet. Once again we found deserted chickees, and Crazy built a big fire under the community cooking pot. It felt good. He made a plaster of herbs and put it on Lauriette's face, which was purplish-blue now, but not broken, and then we looked after Charlie.

A bullet had passed through his upper right arm, in a place where it's usually said in books to be perfectly harmless—what the authors call a "flesh wound." But this time, it had hit a blood vessel, and he'd all but bled to death already.

Crazy bound him up with some kind of greenish-brown leaves under the bandage; this was meant to stop the bleeding. Then he went out and killed a coon, and cut out the liver and boiled it into a broth. We forced some strong brew from a bottle down him, then the broth, and by and by he opened his eyes. But he only lay there, never saying a word.

Now and then we loosened the bandage and before long gave him another dose of liver broth. Crazy set me to fishing, sitting in the rain in a canoe in the stream, and whenever I caught one—bass, mostly, or alligator gars— we cut out *their* livers. I never saw a medical apprentice so hipped on liver. But he explained that our aim was to restore back the lost blood. He was pompous about it, like most doctors—when you can get them to talk to you at all—and acknowledged that the case was nip and tuck. He said he wished he could run some blood back in him from an animal, or even me or Lauriette, but the practice was still in the experimental stage among most medicine men. Buster Cypress himself preferred to bear down more on letting blood out, and this wasn't exactly the kind of sickness for it.

In the next three days we killed two more coons and a possum, having to go to another hammock for them, because animals always skedaddle from a place where they know people are, and in the evening of the third day, Charlie began to make some headway.

By breakfast the next morning he asked for *sofkee,* in a weak voice, and when lunch came around, he got down some shredded liver meat. Crazy said we could pile it in, after this, so we hunted all afternoon and killed a female midget deer on a big hammock—attracted it up by scraping big sticks on a tree, like horns—then shot it with a bow and arrow, because another clan was living at the far end and might hear the noise from a gun. Crazy said they probably knew we were there anyway, but wouldn't investigate unless we stayed overnight. He said they weren't friendly, being something called the Big Towns or Little Towns clan, I've forgotten which, and thought the Panthers looked down on them socially, which was correct.

So that night we had what amounted to a merry time, for us in that season of our Florida adventure. We dressed out the deer and roasted hunks of meat including four whole legs (along with the heart, liver, and other parts) on a big fire, until the juice dripped down and made things crackle and pop. Crazy said this female was unusually fat, from not having to run from hunters—on a hammock where game was being preserved so as to build it up again, the way Seminoles do.

Well, when the roasting got under way, with the nice smell of buttonwood fire smoke, and meat sizzling, and coffee brewing, and yams from an old garden busting open their skins in the coals, poor old Charlie finally sat up and took notice. I never saw a person gorge so. First, he tucked into the deer's liver and finished it off in about three snaps; then he took strips of hot fat meat and gobbled them down whilst cutting each bite off with a knife as it disappeared into his mouth. He gouged out the insides of three baked yams with his fingers, dipped them in pools of bloody broth on the meat, and ate it all, then wound up drinking three cups of coffee. And after that, he went back and ate some more meat, for dessert.

And the funny thing was, so did Lauriette. She was in a rollicking frame of mind, considering there were Indians around, and was perfectly straightaway decent to Crazy. She had several teeth loosened, but Crazy looked them over, tilting her head this way and that, also jiggling them, as you would a horse, and said they needn't come out; they would firm up in a few days. But if they didn't, he'd knock them out and make her some wooden ones. It was a simple operation. From beginning to end, she made no complaints; we had a good time.

It must have been two hours we sat there, warmed through by the fire as the rain splashed off those wonderful chickee roofs they make, with broad eaves of overlapping palm fronds. Neither were the mosquitoes interested. The smoke, and smells of food going, and the heavy rainfall were too various for them.

All in all, it was the best evening I remembered since back on the Mississippi sandbars with Zeb and Uncle Jim.

Next day, which was sparkling and blue—the rain had played itself out late in the night—Crazy drew us a chart on white bark showing how we should continue in this main channel a short distance to the Shark River and then spin downstream till we encountered a big island above Cape Sable. An old man named Cooter Skaggs lived there, and Charlie knew him. He traded with the Indians when they were in an agreeable enough humor to turn up, and refrained from cheating them about furs and alligator hides and cured buckskin and huckleberries, so was held to be less revolting than most whites. He would see us on our way; he had a boat, and might likely take us to Key West himself. Or he could hire Indians to paddle us along the coast eastward, then over the twenty miles of flats and lakes across Florida Bay, from the mangrove-tangled underbelly of the Everglades to the long chain of Keys below.

So—we told Crazy goodbye, and Lauriette even kissed him. She tried to give him money from her savings bank, which the murderers hadn't got around to burgling, but he refused it. These Seminoles *were* proud. I remembered from my reading that Billy Bowlegs had turned down a Government offer of $250,000 to move him to Arkansas, and afterward shot a few people to indicate how he felt about the bribe, because he spoke no English and hadn't any other clear-cut means of expressing himself to another race like that.

I felt mighty poor seeing Crazy Short Tail go, and we shook hands. In the two weeks of our acquaintance, we'd already fallen to calling each other by our first names, though I really preferred mine to his, if you thought it over. I said I would come back to visit him someday after we'd got settled, in the season when the Grassy Waters were sluggish and low. In return, he surmised that he might come to the Keys with a boat full of fishing Indians, one of these years soon. We left it at that. He was the first friend I'd had since Commercial Appeal, and while both had an uncommon mulish streak, they were generally enjoyable, too.

21

Dear Misses Burnie:

I RESUME my narrative (after first stating that your nephew David remains absent though not abandoned) with an account of our venture in the production of salt, and other employments.

As to the first-named, we fell to, working side by side with the aid of several extra negroes, and constructed three more pans, employing the usual coral walls, then admitted sea-water. It must be stated that a number of skeptics from the town drove out to watch, and their comments, ribald and derisive, were hard to endure under the pitiless sun. Several brought sandwiches which they hoped to salt from our works, they said, and others came with bottles of "aguadent," or *aguardiente,* the chief strong drink of the region.

Well, when all was complete, and the water evaporating with that natural celerity provided by the laws of physics, we left our trusty Nubians in charge and repaired home. Should all go well, we expected to have salt in two days, several tons of it, and would commence another batch immediately.

I need hardly say that the supply is inexhaustible. Each gallon of sea water contains 0.2547 pounds of salt, and it has been computed (by the undersigned, after extensive research) that if the entire ocean were processed through our pans, the yield would be slightly in excess of 4½ million cubic miles of rock salt, or about 14½ times the continent of Europe (above the high-water mark).

So you may see that, barring an unexpected jump in the population, there is sufficient quantity of salt on hand for all ordinary purposes.

(I should add, Ladies, that we started with no concrete intentions of running the entire ocean through our works; we haven't the facilities for it.)

A brief word in retrospect about our solar plant might be of interest. Normally, the sea is admitted to the pans, then concentrated to a specific gravity of 1.21, at which point the impurities are removed and the salt remains. But Colonel Burnie stated that this would not be necessary for consumption in Key West and Havana, because the citizens are generally too drunk to care what they're eating anyhow. Captain Pereira concurred in this, but I am convinced that, due to the language barrier, he was ignorant of the discussion's real meaning and was under the misapprehension that somebody was offering him a drink.

The mother liquor ordinarily reaches a specific gravity of 1.26 in a second pan, where the second grade of salt separates. A residual known as "bitterns" is thrown off here, and is easily salable to France, India and some cities of America for use in the manufacture of potash, bromine, Epsom salts and magnesium chloride. But here again, Colonel Burnie, with Captain Pereira assenting (I think), decided to produce only one grade of salt, saying that a touch of Epsom, etc., would be very efficacious in the cases of most people he knew.

So—the product from *our* pans, rather than be separated into table salt and chemical salts and, in a third pan, bath salts, was to be amalgamated into an entity, which the owners decided to market under the name: "Burnie's E. Pluribus Unum Condiment"—an excellent cognomen, in my view, and states the case.

I must confess that, as a lifelong dispenser of miracle cures, I was very much taken with your brother's insight into this matter, and I derived deep satisfaction from reflecting on the probable sight of our neighbors, after a well-seasoned meal, hiking for the backhouse with potash, bromine, and magnesium chloride, the whole operation to be followed by a luxurious bath in their own juice, so to speak.

The salt from each crystallized pan is generally raked into rows, allowed to drain, lifted from the pans, washed, and finally dried.

Well, we had reached this glorious estate—rows and rows of gleaming white riches, draining—and had retired to our menage when, late at night before the final step was to begin, I awoke to hear an ominous drumming on the roof.

Yes, the heavy rains had come. In the darkness, we rushed out to the salt works, but, alas, nothing could be done. The entire harvest was ruined, and no more could be produced until the winter months, when serious precipitation had ceased.

Now it must be said that many townsmen had advised us it was too late in the year to begin producing, but such was Colonel Burnie's and Captain Pereira's hilarious condition, that no heed was paid.

Next morning, instead of repining, the Colonel, in excellent spirits, traded the works—pans, chemicals, coral, rakes, lease, and one somnolent negro—to a Cuban for a fore-and-aft-rigged sailing vessel, somewhere between a sloop and a cutter, called a "smack," very popular hereabouts.

Colonel Burnie has conceived the idea, with possible support from Pereira, of outfitting an omnibus work boat, which will be capable of sponging, fishing, turtling, and, I fear, "wrecking." (I say "I fear," because if ever a man had an evil, piratical look in his eye, that man is Pereira.)

Construction began forthwith, again to a chorus of laughter from the locals. Bait and fish wells were installed, several boxes for the storage of fish, a turtle crawl, and a rowboat for both fishing and sponging.

Colonel Burnie informed us that he had talked to a number of professionals in all these fields (in a saloon), and felt perfectly competent to go into business. Indeed, his zeal was so keen that I forebore to ask searching questions. He said he had never had much of an occupation, aside from soldiering and running a large plantation which had come to him through no efforts of his own but by inheritance. So he has begun to take a lively interest in the possibility of earning his own way in the world.

There are further considerations. For one, his funds, he says, have fallen to a low level, due in part to the gambling by which he puts in much of his time. I am unaware of his precise condition, but I gather that his need of a livelihood is pressing. (I should add that, through a fortuitous epidemic of hernia in the village of Bosky Dell, Arkansas, I am fully capable of meeting our requirements out of my private purse for some weeks to come.)

Another, a very significant factor in Colonel Burnie's wish to succeed has been made known to me only by a series of rather comical hints and implications. You will excuse me if I tell you that your brother is, in fact, behaving almost like a schoolboy.

"Doc," he said only yesterday (for he has thus abbreviated my professional title), "they say two can live as cheaply as one. How about it?"

"Quite true, as long as one doesn't eat," I replied, employing the popular joke.

"Well, I may have some news for you soon. Meanwhile, I'd better hustle and stake out a living, eh?"

I gave an appropriate chuckle, clapped him on the back, and said, "My dear boy, I am ever ready to be your confidant on any matter of importance," and we let it go at that. But I think I may safely say that a welcome announcement will be forthcoming soon. As to my daughter, Millicent—well, perhaps we had better wait till she speaks for herself.

To resume, the boat was made ready, and we put to sea, all of us, on an expedition of sponging. We had availed ourselves of several long poles with three-tined hooks affixed at a right angle on one end, together with a water-glass through which to study the bottom.

It was Colonel Burnie's notion that the easiest method of locating the beds was to follow the other sponge boats out. Well, what was his dismay, and ours, to find that our presence in those waters was unwelcome. The word is perhaps too mild. In order to sponge, a small boat is lowered, with one man as rower and a second to handle the above-mentioned three-tined hook. He is, incidentally, known as a "hooker" (an appellation more commonly used, I believe, in connection with another, older profession).

So—we put to sea—rather, to the sponge beds—in the wake of the fleet, and dropped anchor in less than thirty feet of water. But no sooner had we set the dory over than there arose a hue and cry among the other vessels, and a shot rang out, ripping through our upper sails.

Colonel Burnie uttered a short, descriptive protest that tended to associate the shooter's mother with the animal kingdom, and roared out, "The next one of you buzzards that cocks a firearm's got a gun fight on his hands."

"Clear off, you warmints," a cry came echoing back. "We sowed out these beds. Quit follering us around."

It was, I confess, not until later that we found that the sponge beds are indeed tended, and kept in a state of balance year by year. The fishermen affix to numerous tiles pieces of cut growth, each of which develops into a new sponge. Supplementing this mechanical aid, some of them in the native element attach themselves as buds, breaking off at the end of the branch to fall down and grow into a complete organism. For sponges are, of course, the cleaned skeletons of the creatures that live attached to the bottom of the sea.

Your brother disregarded the warning, and we continued lowering the boat. He was to row, and Zebediah, violently protesting, was to wield the hook. When the second shot came, from a nearby vessel with as rascally-looking a crew as ever I beheld, Colonel Burnie whipped out a pistol and apparently sent a ball through the loose-fitting shirt of a man holding an old-fashioned musket in the bow. A howl of rage went up and the boat veered off. But the fracas was by no means finished.

"Collect up some sponges, preferably large ones," remarked Colonel Burnie, resting on his oars to light a cigar, but the response he got was far from cooperative.

"Dang if I *see* any spongers. There ain't nothin down there but colorish rock. Spongers take an hide when we arruv. An that ain't all," said Zebediah. "This rocky-horse water rile my insides. It pukish. What's more I don' relish bein shot at. I done bin through one wah and that's enough."

There followed a spirited argument between your brother and his servant, of a kind that we have come to know well; then Colonel Burnie took the waterglass himself to have a look.

"Out *watching!*" cried the impossible Pereira, whose speech, though better, continues baffling in the extreme. One of the mother boats, unnoticed by us, was bearing down directly on our dory, and its tiller was put over only in time to avoid a frightful smash-up. As it was, the dory turned turtle, and both Zebediah and your brother went headlong into the deep.

When Pereira hoisted anchor (he *is* a master sailor; we must give the fool that) Captain Burnie was struggling in the water to discharge his pistol, which certainly would have established some kind of precedent, but it became entangled in his clothing.

We rescued the men and the damaged boat, but the hook and the water-glass were irrevocably lost. Moreover, nothing could be done. Vengeance was futile; we hadn't even a clear notion which mother vessel was responsible.

After he dried out, Colonel Burnie remarked with very good nature, "Oh, well, if they planted the beds, they're entitled to reap the product. No use working up a peeve about it. *However,* if I catch the jackass that dumped us, we may have a word or two."

We returned to Key West, amidst some jeers as we sailed into the harbor, and resolved to study up on sponging, then locate our own beds the next trip out.

But I must tell you that it, too, proved a failure. Several factors combined to thwart us. Chief among them no doubt was our inexperience at this highly specialized occupation. Then, belatedly, it developed that Captain Pereira, all along had been ignorant of our mission; he thought we were searching the bottom for gold, hence the look of cupidity on his raffish face. (He lost all interest when it was somehow conveyed to him that we were after sponges.) We got little for our pains but scattered information and some oddities from the ocean floor. It is certain that, on our second trip, we had far greater knowledge of both sponges and sponging, but we came a long way from having enough. Key West has a virtual monopoly on this industry in the United States, having begun it and sent the first shipload of sponges to New York in 1849.

Turkey, we learned, produces perhaps the best sponges currently in use, but Colonel Burnie commented in his usual flippant style that our boat was not equipped for a voyage of that length and that he moreover doubted whether the Turks would be any more hospitable than the Key West fishermen. He said the only thing to recommend it was the fact that we might have an excellent interpreter in Captain Pereira, whose speech was very possibly Turkish, since it was nothing else classifiable with precision. (I should add that this provoked a furious hiss and what sounded like an implied threat to duel.)

But that is only idle chaff. We aimed to seek not only the Florida Wool Sponge, but the Reef Sponge, Glove Sponge, Velvet Sponge, and Honeycomb Reef, which species, though not as expensive as the Fine Turkey Cup, or even the hard Greek Zimocca, are the most commercially acceptable.

We memorized the looks of these specimens, and set forth again, independent of our Key West colleagues. A very brisk chop was going on the reef, and Zebediah first of all refused to get into the dory. We lay offshore for two hours, during which period my daughter Millicent (with Pereira leering over her like a faun) cooked an excellent lunch, which was eaten, and thrown up, by all of our party except your brother and Pereira. For my own part, I do not recall when I ever felt queasier, and had it not been for a bottle of Swamp Elixir which I keep secreted in my jacket for emergencies, I might have been seriously inconvenienced.

The weather moderating in early afternoon, we persuaded Zeb to get in the dory, by the simple device of dosing him with Elixir and giving him five dollars. Even so, he wore an antiquated life preserver around his neck like a formal collar and tied himself to the dory on the end of a line.

In two hours' search, he (with Colonel Burnie again rowing) had lifted from the bottom—and we must give the faithful fellow credit, for he worked hard—two large crabs, a jellyfish which stung him on the hand, a rotted-out corset, a blowfish, a trolling line with multiple hooks, and a cannonball.

I confess that we were mildly set up, for this was our first expedition, and, it augured well for the future. If we could raise those articles from the ocean floor, there was no telling how great a killing we might make if and when we encountered sponges.

Well, to bring this part of my narrative to a close, we did indeed find sponges, the very next day. We returned in triumph with no less than thirty-five, and made plans to clean and grade them by size, then string them in bunches, according to the local custom. (They are subsequently sold at auction to representatives of wholesale houses, who prepare them for market by additional cleaning and clipping.)

But our spirits were somewhat dampened by the coarse and raucous shouts that greeted our catch on dock, for it appeared that the acquisitions were Needle Sponges, wholly useless to man, and that our labor must be its own reward. This is not entirely accurate, for Zebediah prepared not only the blowfish but the crabs for his dinner, and we sold the cannonball to an antiquarian for fifty cents. So, as Colonel Burnie computed it, we lost only $4.50 in the two days' venture. He said there was no reason why we should rule out sponging as a livelihood, but we must be careful not to do it too often.

The decision was made that night to change over to fishing; it seemed the wisest course. Again quoting your brother, "Any damn fool can catch a fish," and we put to sea early the second morning afterward.

A lot of our remaining capital was laid out for heavy cotton trolling lines, wire leaders, metal squid hooks, gill nets and the like. We already had "wells" for both bait and fish, excellent devices by which a catch may be preserved without ice. These are constructed of two- or four-inch lumber, according to the size of the boat, and the seams caulked. At the base, the four sides fit snugly to the boat's contour and converge toward the top like the "frustum of a pyramid," as one of my learned colleagues in town has said. The floor of the well, which thus fuses with the hull, is pierced with many small holes to permit an inflow and outflow of water while the boat is under way.

We had with us our dory, repaired now (at excessive cost), and Colonel Burnie, with Zeb, was to fish independently from it, one man rowing, as before, and the other handling the lines. They trolled two lines, in which there had been tied slipknots; when one of these pulled out, it indicated that a fish had been taken.

We made directly for the reef and baited up, but the wind had died to a whisper and the hooks kept fouling on the bottom. Even so, miraculously we commenced to catch fish identifiable (by means of an illustrated booklet) as kingfish and Spanish mackerel. These specimens, which in the former case occasionally weighed upwards of twenty pounds, we dumped into our well, and you may imagine our jubilation at the way things were going.

Then Zebediah hooked onto something that rather altered the complexion of the day. Besides the trolling lines, they had dangled overboard a heavy shark chain with a monstrous hook, the rig baited with a large mullet, in the hope of catching a "jewfish"—a species that weighs up to 600 pounds and is salable, as a member of the grouper variety, at a modest profit. The operation had been described to us, in solemnity, by one of the few friendly fishermen of the town.

Well, something snapped up the mullet, the chain (its boat end fastened to a cleat) tautened, and the dory heeled over like a toy. "Off chopping! To cast or hove—pronto!" cried the offensive Pereira, but it was impossible for them to disengage themselves, and we watched the dory point its bow toward the open sea.

We cracked on all sail, rolled in our lines, and followed, but we were heading directly into the breeze, so must make shift with tacking to keep pace.

On the occasions when we came abreast, we espied Zebediah tugging in frenzy at the chain and Colonel Burnie, his oars shipped, leaning back in comfort with a cigar.

"A beautiful day for an outing," he called at one point when we were within hearing range, but his servant only grumbled in aggrieved contention.

What had happened, we learned later, was that instead of hooking a jewfish, which remains static—a dead weight on the bottom—their bait had been seized by what was estimated to be a 1,000-pound sting ray, just as our "friendly" informant in town had hoped. The marine chronicles of the region are replete with just such adventures, and we had been steered to a fishing ground where it was most likely to happen. Only lately, the newspaper reported a case wherein a ray of twice this size had towed a 35-foot sloop!

Well, again there was no help for it. With an allowance for drift, I calculated that they were towed seven miles to sea before the ray tired. Then it eased up enough for the chain to be slipped and allowed to sink to the bottom.

Zebediah, when we pulled him aboard, was in perhaps his worst humor of the entire journey down the Mississippi, but Colonel Burnie said, "By Jove, this is the only way to live—free, too. Any reputable seaside resort would charge a hundred dollars for a ride like that."

By now the day was so far advanced that we headed for Key West to sell our considerable catch. There is only one wholesale house at the docks, and the fishermen, who generally operate company-owned boats, all sell to it.

Despite the mobile nature of the outing, our spirits were high as we approached the docks. But when we dug into the bait well for the purpose of transferring our fish to the weighers, the entire catch was found to be dead.

Nobody had thought to tell us that kingfish and Spanish mackerel, among others, do not live in confinement. These are cooled on board fishing boats that buy ice from the ships that call in Key West to trade.

So—we were obliged to sail out a distance from shore and jettison our cargo. It was heartbreaking; even Colonel Burnie seemed thoughtful as we came again to our berth empty-handed. The odious Pereira was occupied, as usual, in toothy attentions to Millie, and Zebediah was complaining in terms of returning to Kentucky.

For a few days we tried reef fishing, for the vividly-colored specimens that bite from the bottom, but with indifferent results, for every variety had inexplicably disappeared, or quit taking bait. These things happen; nobody seems able to explain it. The professionals in town came in day after day with no more than a subsistence catch, and the gloom was general.

We made one nocturnal try for Spanish mackerel by the use of gill nets, made of fine thread, into which the fish push their heads and then are unable to back out because of their fins. But our luck was indifferent. It was promptly discovered that to keep these gossamer seines from falling into the most frightful snarls was nearly impossible. Also, try as we might, we could hit on no means of keeping Zebediah awake for the important phase of gathering in the fish. He said he was accustomed to sleep at night, and was dangbusted (sic) if he could understand why the fish didn't do the same. He failed to germinate any excitement over the pursuit of a fish that declined to be caught in the daytime, in the regular way. He said he might go so far as to put out "trot lines," and run them around nine or ten o'clock in the morning, unless it was raining, or too hot, but he remained obdurate against night fishing. To top it all, he said the lights we used to attract the schools hurt his eyes. He accused us of trying to blind him, upon which Colonel Burnie exploded in one of his rare bursts of temper, and called him "a whining, flappy-mouthed, mush-headed old woman." He pointed out that all of us were working especially hard (true) and that he (Colonel Burnie) was obliged to do the thinking for both himself and Zebediah besides. Then Zeb claimed he had "protected" Colonel Burnie (from his superiors, not from the enemy) throughout the Civil War, and your brother, looking reflective, stated that his remarks had been too harsh. At this, Zebediah said he'd decided he liked night fishing, and wished to do a good deal more of it soon, but Colonel Burnie replied, and I quote, "The hell with it; I'm sleepy myself." They ended in an affectionate embrace, and we took good heart to see these life-long companions reunited, if only for a moment.

All in all, we were persuaded to drop fishing for a conference as to the future. It had occurred to us, once more, that we really knew very little about an enterprise which calls for sound knowledge and some experience. We attempted to hire a fisherman from one of the boats, but the personnel of the fleet were solidly aligned against us.

We come now to our single excursion into wrecking (and to the end of this already-too-long letter).

Boredom, which I have noticed works like a maggot in Colonel Burnie's brain when times grow dull, settled down now in earnest. The serious rains had come, the fishing had dwindled away to nothing, and I feared that the old employment of gaming and drinking might start up once more. He even appeared apathetic toward Millie. But he and Pereira finally put their heads together (it happened to be the only time in my life, barring an examination of a two-headed idiot at a circus, when I concluded that two heads were worse than one) and called us to council that evening with a proposition to expand our fortunes.

"As you know," said Colonel Burnie over the lamplight, "wrecking has ceased to be an important trade hereabouts. The infernal meddling Government has erected lights that warn ships off the reefs. They seem to be fixed, too, and don't wander around the way they used to when our Bahamian friends ran the business. However—"

Pereira hissed loudly at this, and made violent motions which I took to indicate bloodthirsty demurrers over the loss of what I assume was his original calling of piracy and murder.

"In the past, we've run this group as a democracy, with each member entitled to vote, so we'll take soundings on the sentiments about wrecking. Prizes still *are* taken, and salvage claimed, and one good haul could set us back on our feet. All wreckers aren't rogues; not by a long shot. The stormy season's at hand, so all we'd have to do would be to tie up at Key Vaca and wait. Well, what do you say?"

"No siree! You ain't gon get me foolin aroun no wrack. I alluz had a habit uv stayin way from other folks' propity. I votes no," said Zebediah. "If it come to dat, I'd ruther fish at night"; then he added, "But I ain't fixin to do at neither. I change my min'."

My daughter Millicent now spoke up, gazing steadily into Colonel Burnie's eyes, and said, "Is this to be a legitimate wrecking operation, or is it something worse? And if it's wrecking, what makes you think *we* can do it? Does it call for less skill than what we've tried already? I'm tired out with all this ridiculous amateurism. It's humiliating. Everybody's laughing at us on the street. I vote no myself."

I cleared my throat and offered the ensuing lucid, and even eloquent, opinion, as the senior member present: "In view of the less than lucrative results of our maritime ventures to date, including the gathering of 'sponges,' i.e.: corsets, and cannonballs; and not neglecting commercial fishing and/or towed voyages by courtesy of an outsized sting-ray; and taking into account the negative attitude of my colleagues who have previously held the floor, I must cast my ballot in the negative. That is, no; I'm against it."

"Pereira?" said Colonel Burnie. "Any unscrambled thoughts on the subject? Or on anything, for that matter."

Captain Pereira lowered his arm from the back of Millie's chair, arose, removed his ghastly Cuban hat (which he wears both indoors and out), tossed a coal-black cigar through the window (with some danger of burning the edifice down) and made the following unbelievable contribution: "Is wrecks not to hold piratings the same as? Hardly. No, no, no! But lights movable? Ha, ha! With reefs along Cubans inside and out. Also English, but less. Yo soy preparado, *at all time!* Why not?"

Well, this idiotic utterance was presumably a shade too thick for Colonel Burnie, for he exploded into riotous laughter and fell backward in his chair onto the floor. I must confess that I was startled; it somehow marked a subtle change in the relationship between the two men, but I'll acknowledge that it was over my head.

Pereira, of course, drew himself up, with one hand on the foul-looking knife he wears in his belt, but your brother, from a sitting position on the carpet, said "Many thanks, amigo. You've stated the case perfectly. As a matter of fact, you ought to be in Congress." Then he arose, looking solemn, banged a cane on the table and said, "The decision is unanimous; we start wrecking tomorrow. Parliament's adjourned, and I never saw a prettier example of democracy at work."

There arose some fairly heated protests, all of which Colonel Burnie urged Millicent to write down, as "exceptions," but she said, "You make me sick, you big bully!" and flounced out of the room.

Next morning, we shifted our vessel to Key Vaca in a heavy rainstorm, and tied up alongside other ships in the deep-water anchorage there.

Despite the slump in this industry, as many as half a dozen vessels were berthed here, the crews idling away their time, awaiting an onshore blow and a mishap to some luckless ship beyond the reef. By custom, they would lie up at night when the weather worsened and cruise the reef by day, seeking a ship in distress.

Well, we spent five inactive days, their tedium relieved only by the fishing we did to gather provender for Millicent's galley. Even at this small venture, we did not prosper conspicuously. Our usual catch, on the ocean side (not in Florida Bay which separates, by twenty miles, the Key Chain and the lower Florida coast of Everglades), consisted of small, noisy fish called grunts, after their frog-croaks of indignation when once in the boat. "Grunts and grits" provide a staple diet in these parts, and can be tasty and nourishing unless indulged in to excess.

On the evening following the fifth day, the barometer fell, the wind rose to a shriek, and a great cry went up toward midnight, "Wreck ashore! Down Matecumby way."

We tumbled out, sleepy and addled, and succeeded (with difficulty) in hoisting our mainsail and jib; then we cast loose from our mooring. It was touch and go in a stiff southeast gale, with the seas running high, and Captain Pereira's face showing plainly that he relished sailing far more in daylight, in a quiet sea.

A few hundred yards clear of the anchorage, we spied

a yellow rocket that looped up into the sky then dropped in a slow, ominous arc—a ship's herald of bad tidings. It lay to our left, and we headed off in its general direction, after reefing down the mainsail, which threatened to give way before the storm.

It was important that we try to arrive first on the scene, upon which we would be designated "wrecking master" by the Court and receive extra compensation for directing the operation of salvage.

Alas! it was not to be. We were within sight of the victim—a three-masted square-rigger which, west-bound, had strayed too near the reef, in a natural desire to avoid the five-mile current of the mighty Gulf Stream—when there was a grinding crash, our centerboard snapped like kindling, and we jibed, the main boom cracking like a cannon-shot.

In an instant, the mainmast broke off at its base, its rigging went over the side, and we were helpless on a lee shore.

As the lamentations of terror went up from Zebediah, from Millie, and, perhaps, from the undersigned, Captain Pereira had the presence of mind to fire off a rocket of our own. By God's mercy (for we were drifting rapidly ashore), the hindmost of the eager wreckers abandoned its share of the three-master (which would have been meagre) and came to our succor. After circling twice, she threw us a line that we made fast, and then she beat to windward, hauling us off the reef.

Daylight saw us in a most anomalous position. We had started forth on a profitable errand of wrecking; instead, we were being towed into Key West as a *wreck*.

Our humiliation had reached its peak. You may imagine that the jeers which formed a rich obbligato to our sponging and fishing were as nothing to those that now greeted us in our plight at the end of a cable.

Even in my depression, I have a single vivid impression of that early dawn scene. The wind having shifted, the square-rigger's small stores were spread out upon the surface of the sea. These were, in the preponderance, crackers. Numberless boxes of crackers had loosened their seams to sow a thick snowfall on the dark blue waters. Crackers were everyplace one looked. I doubt if I shall ever see such a sight again.

Three hours later we were in the United States Salvage Court, where a very abrupt and offensive "referee," or judge, awarded the schooner that had saved us the following ludicrous payment: our damaged vessel or $300, the choice to be made by us. It was, of course, an outrageous assessment, from a native Key Wester whose dislike of "foreigners," which lumped us with Cubans, negroes and all others not born in the city, bordered on a maniacal frenzy. (I should say that, shortly thereafter, he was summarily removed from office.)

To wind up, Colonel Burnie cheerfully paid the bill, after remarking that wrecking was the most lucrative profession in Key West, if a person was on the right end of the cable.

The malodorous official thereupon *fined him five dollars for contempt of court!*

Your brother strolled back up, after being sternly admonished to extinguish his cigar, and laid down a bill. The clerk then leaped to his feet and called after him. "Here —this is ten dollars. What about your change?"

"Oh, that's all right," said Colonel Burnie, over his shoulder, "I'll take it out in contempt."

We crowded through the exit as the Judge, red-faced, was banging his gavel and crying, "Arrest that man!" Presumably he changed his mind, for nothing came of it.

Later, your brother advised me that his inspiration with the ten-dollar bill was borrowed from an old but rather notable foe of his youth—Abraham Lincoln.

So, ladies, I regretfully end this overlong report on a note of melancholia. Our spirits remain high, our funds low. But the uses of adversity are sweet (as stated by the Bard ["As You Like It": Act II, Scene 1]) and our misfortunes will yet be turned to gain.

> Yr. versatile servant,
> Ewing T. Snodgrass
> (Emeritus Sponger, Fisherman, Wrecker, etc.)

22

"I cain't say's I favor company, prefer hanimals," said Mr. Skaggs when we found his patchwork house. We'd slid down the Shark without a hitch, camped one night on a bank where the mosquitoes like to tormented us blind, and searched over the long island from the river's mouth. The house, which stood at the far end, was made from what Lauriette called "flotsam and jetsam," taken from the sea, and had a yacht's mahogany railing around a sagged-in porch of cocoanut logs covered with tin, and a beautiful door with a brass knob, that had rode in from a sunk freighter, I reckon. The rest—two rooms—was in the same crazy pattern, and the whole, with a palm and tarred canvas roof, stood on stilts that leaned inward, from the last hurricane.

Mr. Skaggs himself was in a little worse condition than his house. I judged his age to be around seventy, but he had black, grizzly hair, a weathered, wrinkledy face, deep-set eyes beneath tufty eyebrows, a high-bridged nose, and a strong, wiry, lean frame of less than middle height. He was dressed in buckskin trousers very frayed in the seat, a homemade canvas jacket, torn and rent, and a felt hat on top of a wrapped-round bandana handkerchief over part of his head, like a pirate.

In a cove around a mangrove neck from his house, he had a centerboard schooner, with sails so filthy they were exactly the same color as the boat, which was peeled brown. Drying after the rains, they flapped and slatted, with long rips showing where lines and grommets had pulled free from reef points.

In one corner of his "yard," which was nothing but shell, with undergrowth removed to discourage snakes (and give a view of the Gulf, so he could retire inland if intruders sailed up when he felt unsocial), Mr. Skaggs had a big heaped-up mound of buttonwood burning, and allowed he was in the charcoal business.

"Hit don't pay, and Hi'm weak in the 'ed to support it —it and the wessel both," he said, and added, with a side-wise glance, "I'm uncommon 'poverished." I wondered if he thought we meant to rob him, for Charlie said he was known as a great miser. And he bore this out by saying, with another shrewd and careful look, "What pittance I've got is 'id in the ground, I've forgot where. The person hain't been born that could thieve me. Torture won't produce blood from a turnip—so never mind."

"Never mind what?" said Lauriette, always ready to take anything up.

"Hit were the porest place on hearth to settle."

"Then why do you stay here like a hermit?" said Lauriette, who didn't like him, as usual.

"I ham a 'ermit, and glory in it. I never met a hooman person I cared whether they lived or died. Not many can say that," he told us with some pride.

Studying Lauriette over, he said, "You say you've abided with Hindians. You still a wergin?"

She blushed, for reasons I failed to understand, and muttered something about a "dirty old man," but he paid it no mind. After telling us we could have a drink, if we didn't take too much, because the Shark here was tidewater salt and his cistern might run dry, he went out to tend his buttonwood fire.

He was the crankiest old fellow I ever met, and had the curiousest speech. He said his father was from the "Behamies," which meant the Bahama Islands, according to Lauriette, but his mother was Spanish, from Havana, where they used to live, and weighed three hundred pounds. I didn't get the connection, but he rambled right on, whilst poking his fire, and he said he'd run away from home on a wrecker, "account of" his mother beat him with a lignum vitae club. It was because of his English blood. When she saw it cropping out, she tried to beat it back into place. His father was less violent, though, and in return only cussed him for the Spanish part. At nine, the boy was made a regular battle-ground, and ever since he ran off, at eleven, he'd been a hermit, whenever he could afford it. You could hardly blame him.

On his buttonwood fire, he had nearly ten cords of wood stacked up in a cone, all covered with grass and sand that made it air-tight except for a vent at the top. Around the bottom were several openings to provide a draft, which would fire the wood, drive the gases up out of the vent, and, in the end, leave charcoal. Mr. Skaggs said he had been a month cutting the wood, and figured to lose about a hundred dollars on it all told, counting his labor. Moreover, he said, the fire would probably get out of control and burn right up, in which case he'd lose everything. At night he plugged up the holes in the bottom, so it would smolder, because he hadn't any extra hands now to tend it. An Indian worked for him, previous, but while the fellow never said anything, or laughed, or even smiled, out of regard for his boss, and slept a mile or two back in the scrub, Mr. Skaggs said it made things crowded on the island.

Charlie told us, to one side, that Mr. Skaggs did very well with his buttonwood, and in fact made a potful of money from it. One cord of wood produced ten bags of charcoal, and a market for it was always handy at Key West, where the ocean-going ships put in.

"Dirt look ruffled there?" said Mr. Skaggs, pointing to a rough patch of shell on the way back to the house. "Appear to be something buried?"

"Yes," Lauriette answered, hopeful to cause trouble, and fixed a look on her face as if she might come back alone and investigate.

"Dig. I'd welcome it. I don't know where it's at myself. Choking wouldn't help."

Mr. Skaggs was suspicious of us partly because he shied off from Charlie. They'd been acquaintances for years, but the mystery of Charlie's ears never had been solved in Mr. Skaggs' mind, or so he professed. All he knew was that Seminoles customarily crop slivers off the ears of liars, a small slice for each lie. He didn't seem aware that Charlie lost his ears for warning a white family about an Indian attack. Not telling the truth is the wickedest sin of all to a Seminole, and that's why they detest the whites so. None of our Government agreements with Indians had ever been kept, of course, whereas the Seminoles, when they signed a paper, meant to go right ahead and carry it out. As I said before, their splendidest warrior-leader, Osceola, was captured after General Jesup arranged for him to come to a parley under a flag of truce. Osceola walked in beside the flag, the Army grabbed him while they had the chance, and he was thrown into a mouldy jail, where he died soon after.

And it's in those relationships, Uncle Jim says, where people fall out, for lack of understanding each other's ways. It comes natural for a white man to lie, particularly governments. I've noticed that when they intend to fire a man—a minister or a high muckety-muck secretary in charge of some filing cabinets—they hold a meeting the day before and deny it. So then the newspapers realize that the man's about to be hauled out of the public trough, and write a story to that effect, getting the news to the people, who deserve it. And then next day, right on schedule, they bounce him.

Without any schooling and all, the Seminoles find this puzzling. Likely they'll grow into it later, when they're given the white man's advantages. With a little help, they'll learn to lie as easy as anybody. They've got good stuff in them, and aren't stupid.

When we mentioned the chance of passage to Key West, Mr. Skaggs said he didn't know whether he could "carry" us or not. He was pretty busy right now, also he needed to go clamming after the charcoal was sacked, and besides, he wasn't by any means crazy about the weather (which was perfect). He sniffed at the breeze, then held up a leaf and let it flutter down (looking very satisfied at this, as if he'd suspected all along it would fall, rather than rise up), and said he reckoned a hurricane was coming, which would drive up the price five dollars more, or fifteen altogether.

When Lauriette said, "I was prepared to pay forty," he grumbled and fumed and took on and said it was the most extravagant outrage he ever heard of; he would sit there and rot before he'd support it. If there was one thing that made him glad he was a hermit, it was people that threw money around.

"I won't sail for a penny over fifteen," he said. "Take it or leave it."

"When?"

"When I'm ready."

Well, he wasn't ready right away, so we had to wait till he was.

For a couple of days, we helped him dig clams, at low tide in the shallow water, and the next day, some Mikasukis came in with fifty alligator hides, for which he paid sixty cents each. He said he'd lose a good deal on them, because the market price always dropped at the exact moment when he bought some. There practically wasn't any line of business this old man didn't have his fist in, and none of it suited him. He grumbled at everything. However, he put us in comfortable beds in the two rooms, and bundled himself up in a quilt on the porch, then said it was the worst imposition he ever heard of.

Every morning when we first met him, he drew back in great surprise, and indignation, and said, "What—you still here? I might as well give up on priwacy; hit's in the natur of a stampede."

But if we pressed him to take us on to the Keys (which were only fifty miles away), he grumbled worse than ever, and said we were leaving him in the lurch. The truth is, in spite of himself, he got a kind of scratchy pleasure from having us there, particularly Lauriette, and disliked to see us go. But he wouldn't have admitted it for a tree-house surrounded by a moat in the interior of Brazil.

On our third day, he proposed marriage to Lauriette, and said that, if he racked his head, he might be able to dig up one small can with a trifle of money in it. What he called "pocket change." But a minute after he said it, he added that he wasn't *sure* there was any such can, so she'd probably better forget that phase of it.

When she turned him down, after exclaiming, "I declare you must be out of your mind!" he acted as if it was no more than he expected. He laid it all on poverty.

"See here, Mr. Skaggs," said Lauriette with considerable heat, "how old are you?"

"Call me Cooter."

"I *will* not. Cooter! What kind of a name is that? It sounds common."

"Hit were my mother's family. The Cooters produced a rare lot of notables."

"What sort? *I* never heard of any."

"In the bulk, pirates. Two of 'em were 'ung. One by his own men, for cheating, and the other right out in public. They give him a ceremony fit for a royal duke."

"Well, it's no wonder you're a proud people, with a background like that. May we presume to ask why you failed to pursue the family trade? Speaking as a prospective bride, I mean."

In some ways, this girl reminded me a lot of Uncle Jim; they could be just that offensive.

But Mr. Skaggs hushed up, and refused to talk any more along those lines. The truth is that he *had* been a pirate, as everybody knew from the Keys up to Chokoloskee Bay, and now and then he'd let slip out references to people with very awesome names, like Gasparilla, who kept a stockade full of beautiful white women on an island near Sanybel, so that it's still called Captiva Island to this day, and Black Caesar, who some say hid treasure on Sanybel.

That part of Mr. Skaggs' activities were in his pre-hermit days, but I judged he still liked to think about it, and once took me aside to say:

" 'Ow'd you like to get your 'ands on a boxful of *esmeraldas?*"

He had a habit of using Spanish words for things once in a while, which was the result of his mother's training, he said. She clubbed him for speaking English, and his father, as I said, cussed him for speaking Spanish. So for a long time, he spoke more Spanish than English.

Anyhow, I asked him what they were and he was mighty exasperated because I couldn't speak Spanish myself, but said: "Emeralds. They'd spill out your pockets."

"Whereabouts?"

"In the Dry Tortugas, but I 'aven't got a map 'idden in

a can in the wicinity of the chinaberry tree. You'd waste your time to search."

I asked him, "Why don't you go get them with your boat, Mr. Skaggs?"

"A receiver of stolen goods hain't a particle better nor a thief." He looked as pious as a deacon, and added, "Religion done it. I was conwerted from a 'eathen, and it stuck."

It was true; we heard so afterward. But when he turned upright, it seemed to take something out of his disposition. From all accounts, he'd been tolerably happy as a pirate. But it grates on most people to be honest, and I reckon that's why they've got laws.

Somebody told us that Mr. Skaggs had spent several terms in jail off and on, when he was young. He'd been convicted for this offense and that, having to do with small pirating, or wrecking, and usually wriggled out light on account of his youth, his sunny outlook, and the fact that he always promised to straighten up.

But he had the courage of his convictions, and kept right on being a pirate until a ship he was with captured an English merchantman that had a preacher aboard. Well, nobody killed this man because of his cloth, as they say, but let him live and continue working amongst the pirates, while they conducted raids. It was a Cuban ship, and being Catholics, they had respect for religion, and saw to it that the preacher received extra little tidbits at the table, and good treatment all around.

He was handy to have on board, too, being often called on for prayers when captured passengers were murdered.

Upshot was that he persuaded Mr. Skaggs to give up hellish living and come to God. They say very few of those cases work out, but Mr. Skaggs stuck to it, as he told us, and became a wholly devout and straightforward man. Also miserable.

The pirates at first were inclined to be sore, losing a good hand that way, but they eased up when the preacher threw his frock and collar overboard shortly afterward and said that this was the life for him. He turned pirate, and evened up the score.

Mr. Skaggs had certainly enjoyed a full and rich life, and one of the main things that pointed to his character was that box of emeralds in the Dry Tortugas. I *believed* he had a map when he said he hadn't; he was just that honest. He liked to reflect about it, and realize he had risen above fetching the stones and living off of the proceeds. For awhile, I thought I might do a little digging around the chinaberry tree, but refrained because I disliked to remove this important source of his strength. He was a mighty admirable old man, if you weren't around him too much.

Mr. Skaggs had one room off his house that was a store, with a wooden awning and a sign "Gnr'l Merch'dise, Provisions." He sold grits, for five dollars a barrel, jerked venison seven cents a pound, and bacon the same, along with other eatables like gophers from Cape Sable, which he kept in a crawl, and whooping cranes when he found time to go after them. Also vegetables from his garden—like cassava and sweet potatoes and starch from coontie root. Most things, though, he bought from Indians or on trips to Key West. Fishermen and hook boats put in there for fodder now and then, and a number of people lived up the coast toward Chokoloskee Bay.

The boatmen generally ran out of coffee, and complained at Mr. Skaggs because he never had any ready-ground. But his coffee mill was lost in a hurricane. They had to buy it green, parch it in a frying pan, and beat it up in a sack or tin can with a marlin spike.

A few feather hunters had settled up toward the Ten Thousand Islands, but Mr. Skaggs refused to sell them anything at all. Now that he'd had religion for forty years, he disapproved of killing birds for commerce. He said it was worse than killing people, and for a short time in his campaign against it, he had a sign tacked up in his store: "Top Prices Paid for Human Pelts. Good Condition Male, 50¢; Female, 35¢," but some people made him take it down. They said they would come and live beside him if he didn't, so he had it off the wall within an hour.

The hunters were chiefly after egrets, but they never turned down any roseate spoonbills or flamingos. The method of gathering these plumes *was* cruel, for the birds were killed at nesting time, when their feathers were most brilliant. The hunters shot the birds off of nests and left the eggs unhatched; either that or, if they'd already hatched, left the young birds a prey to snakes, hawks, and the like. So that, all in all, the entire flocks were in danger of dying out.

The demand for these feathers, from New York hat markets, was great enough for the prices to stay very high, and the scarcer the birds became, the higher the prices rose. The practice was hard to stamp out. A Society of some kind put a warden at Chokoloskee, but the hunters waited till his wife was in the nesting season and then shot him, as a kind of joke, like, and it was hard to find a replacement.

Mr. Skaggs said he once tried his hand at this enterprise, but after he'd killed several egrets off a nest, a flock of crows flew in and ate the eggs before he started to leave. When he saw that, he never did it again.

But the slaughter continued on. The Cuban cigar makers took a fancy to red birds, for locking up in cages, and paid as much as a dollar and a half apiece for them. As a result, you'll seldom see red birds in the Keys, and there aren't any to waste on the mainland above, either.

In view of the criticism, a pair of brothers named Lopez started a bird ranch, with the idea of trapping the pretty ones, feeding them up, and removing their plumage at nesting time without killing them. When things got booming, it made a noble sight, people said, that ranch with all those bright-colored birds walking around and comparing notes. But it proved to be a financial failure, because the birds ate the ranchers out of house and home. The principal diet they liked best was grasshoppers, and the brothers had all the children in the area out beating the bushes with nets and cigar-boxes, but they never could find enough. Moreover, the grasshoppers got sick of being pestered and moved out bag and baggage. They must a thought people had gone crazy around there. One month, they were perfectly happy, hopping around minding their own business and spitting tobacco juice, and the next, everybody was after them like maniacs.

Uncle Jim said it was just the opposite of a Biblical plague, with the people on top for a change.

A person doesn't realize how much a bird eats until he captures one and tries to feed it. If you think it over, they don't ever *stop* eating, so the next time a person uses the saying, "eats like a bird," you maybe ought to mention the Lopezes' ranch. It was put out of business by appetite, pure and simple.

Mr. Skaggs said the best example of this was his pet pelican, what he called an *alcatraz* in the Spanish, that ate more than a hog he kept. He said he'd weighed their fodder and, even aside from what the *alcatraz* rummaged on its own, the hog wasn't anywhere in the running.

One morning he said he wanted to take us on an outing, to see something he'd found, but Lauriette called him down, saying, "Now see here, Mr. Skaggs, we've been waiting six days to go to Key West. You don't seem very busy to *me*. Why don't we just get in your boat and start off—now?"

For once, he didn't fuss, but stated that he had arranged to take us tomorrow, when the Gulf quietened down after a blow. He looked almost human about it, though sad. But he briskened up, and shook his shoulders, then said: "I'll be mortal relieved to get back my hiland. Hi'm near dead with the noise, particular if I h'ain't liked. I don't need a 'ouse to fall on me."

"Why, we all like you *ever* so much, Mr. Skaggs. Who could dislike anybody so merry and bright and cheerful? You've done us all *worlds* of good!"

"There's a preacher to Chokoloskee," he said. "I'll slip on my coat with the brass buttons. It'll be fitten—it was took hoff the capting of a lugger."

She'd got so she couldn't resist ragging him, so she said, "You mean it's somebody *else's* coat, Mr. Skaggs?"

"Hit won't make a farthing's difference to 'im; 'e's been building up coral these fifty year."

Lauriette was shocked, and put her hands to her face, then said she could never marry a man who had killed a fellow creature for his coat. "Why, you're no better than Joseph's brothers," she told him. "Aren't you afraid of eternal damnation?"

I thought he might have a tantrum again, but he finally got a self-righteous look and said, "Hi've never saw a solitary soul walk the plank. Hit were poppycock. Take my word hon it."

"Well, in that case, I'll think it over—in Key West. You're sure, now—no plank walking?"

"Hit weren't humane," said Mr. Skaggs with a pious squint.

"Shot or stabbed was better?"

"Or choked. We had some main fine garroters—from the darker races, on the order of *A*-rabs and Chinymen."

"What a lot you've seen, and *done,* Mr. Skaggs."

Upon that he closed right up, and told us, by George, that he'd read it all in books.

Then he fixed a lunch and we hiked back into a mangrove swamp to look at an ancient Indian burying ground he'd dug up. We trudged nearly two miles, I estimated, then came to the marshy ground, but by stepping along on paths he had made, went in it a considerable distance. It was darkish there, and gloomy, and I wished we hadn't come.

But when a small clearing opened out, where some palms had blown down in a hurricane (and still lay with big clumps of earth at the bottoms), we saw the trenches. It was enough to make anybody take notice. There were seven skeletons in a row, in a sitting position with arms clasping knees, and a tooth of what Lauriette said was something like a "mastodon" in front of each. The largest tooth weighed seven pounds, and the tallest of those skeletons was nearly eight feet.

There was lots of other stuff, some of it under a palmetto roof that Mr. Skaggs had fashioned to protect it from the weather: a conch shell dipper, war clubs, balls of twine (still in fair condition, but starting to rot now, out in the air), false faces, a deer skull, a wolf skull, and a piece of jewelry that Mr. Skaggs said came from Peru.

No matter how much of a sweat we were in to get along to Key West, this place was interesting. From her reading up on Indians, in Tampa, Lauriette said these graves were Caloosas all right, that had been here for centuries before the Seminoles came. There wasn't any way to tell how old the graves were. The Caloosas lived in the part of Florida south of Cape Canaveral, and the Timucuans the part north of it. Most people who'd studied them up said they came from Central America and Yucatan, or maybe farther south. But that's only a guess. From writings and from opening mounds here and there, some details were found out. A Spanish historian named Cabeza said in 1528 "I have seen (a Timucuan) shoot an arrow buried in a poplar stump a good foot and a half." Their bows "were as thick as an arm, eleven to twelve hand spans in length" and could shoot at two hundred paces with "so much sureness they miss nothing."

Everybody agreed that both the Timucuans and Caloosas stood a head higher than most men. They were fierce, and had odd customs. For one thing, they managed to kill Ponce de Léon without too much trouble, and Uncle Jim stated that the lucky fellow did in fact find the Fountain of Youth, for he got practically no older after he arrived in Florida.

The Caloosas and Timucuans tattooed themselves, sacrificed their first-born and dined on rattlesnakes, possums, deer, turkeys, and occasionally the breasts of young girls —on feast days, when the chiefs wanted something special, you know. They also engaged as beasts of burden what was called "hermaphrodites," not either man or woman, or maybe both, it was said. These people were dressed like women but were treated like a poor specimen of men. So it was claimed; I never saw any such myself.

Anyhow, here we were with seven Caloosas lined up in a row, sitting there on the road to Heaven. It gave a person the shivers. Charlie didn't like it here, and said we were foolish to open the graves; it would bring bad luck. He took out a piece of tobacco, which wards off danger for a Seminole, and went around waving it in everybody's face, until Lauriette snatched it away and threw it in the bushes. She could only just stand so much Indian tomfoolery, and no more.

We scratched around some. Mr. Skaggs said another main feature of their diet was oysters, and that the shells from these were piled up to make burial mounds. Such cemeteries could be found all up and down the coast, but not so much in the Everglades, because there's very little to make a mound out of, of course. The Indians there buried their dead and left curious wooden markers on top. This cemetery of Mr. Skaggs' had likely been a mound, once, but got leveled off by hurricanes and high water.

I stooped down to examine the wolf's head, since it wasn't attached to a wolf, or hadn't any meat on it—that is, dead; and something whistled by my ear and went thunk! into the bank. I bounced out of that pit like a jack-in-the-box; I didn't wait.

Lauriette screamed, Charlie let out a howl, and old man Skaggs hit the ground, then scuttled backward under a bush like a crab. I don't believe I ever saw anybody of his age move so fast, especially hind-side to.

"I *saw* them!" Lauriette screamed, stumbling to the opposite side of the graves. "He was looking right at me with white lines around his face—it was one of those we—"

Mr. Skaggs clapped a hand over her mouth and yanked her back under the bush. Then we laid low, waiting. It was so silent I could hear my heart bumping, shaking my whole chest. We were on one side of the burial place, and the Indians were on the opposite somewhere.

In a way, they'd run into bad luck, because if I hadn't reached down just then, they would have caught us by surprise and killed us all. But I couldn't feel sorry for them, somehow. Presently a bird piped up, as sweet as if it was real, and another answered from about fifty yards away, so I knew where they were, but not exactly. I wondered why they didn't rush us—a girl, a boy, and an old man, and a non-military Indian without any weapons. But the trouble was, they'd heard about Mr. Skaggs, and considered him dangerous. Pirates acquire that reputation, whether they deserve it or not. It's the old business of give a dog a bad name.

But in a couple of minutes, I began to understand about Mr. Skaggs. I saw him resume his scuttling—backward as usual, and before long he'd snaked out of there and disappeared. He had a knife in his hand, and seemed happy to be back in harness. There was a lot more to this old peckerwood than met the eye. He had secret depths. When you thought he should be the most miserable, he'd brighten up as merry as a pig in swill. I reckoned he'd gone back in his mind to the pirate days, because he didn't look in the least afraid of these fellows, despite the fact that the odds were all on their side.

I had on a hat, to keep off the sun, and I suddenly had the itch to raise it on a stick. So I did it, and it was within a whisker of the last thing I did on earth. The arrow that zinged by was aimed at my *head,* not my hat, and Charlie hauled us off to another place in the bushes pretty fast. He whispered in my ear that no Seminole alive was stupid enough to fall for that trick, so I didn't feel so smart any more, but got down to normal.

By and by, Mr. Skaggs came back, crawling head forward for a change, and beckoned us to follow. He was carrying a long pole he'd cut, with the large end rounded off and the small one sharp as a spear. It was an aggravation to crawl along there in the dark amongst creepers and marshy spots, with maybe snakes or alligators waiting, but I knew better than argue. As we lit out, going as fast as possible, the bird piped up again, so I judged they heard us shifting.

Well, we continued till there was nothing but a thin path of firm ground, with black muck thicker than soup on either side. I was all of a tremble lest we tumble in, and I could hear Lauriette breathing heavy, as if she meant to cry. She was filthy, too, her dress muddied and rent and her face and arms scratched by brambles.

In about five minutes, Mr. Skaggs hauled up, then he pointed to a tiny knoll of ground almost hidden in the shadows to one side. About four feet of muck lay between it and the path. He hopped across as spry as a sparrow, him and his pole both, then motioned Lauriette to try it next. But she laid back her ears and balked, so we were stuck. "Look here," I whispered, "I'll show you; it's easy," and I launched out in a leap, felt my feet hit the bank, and toppled over backward. I went in clear to my chin, sitting up, and there wasn't any bottom. I kicked around this way and that, but each time I shoved a foot down, trying to find something solid, my head sunk just that much further. Then I felt a hand grab my hair, and I got whisked out of there quick. It wasn't a second too soon. I was so scared I gulped in big lungfuls of air, rasping it in, half sick, because I'd been right on the point of taking my last one, and it left me panicky.

Seeing I was alive, Mr. Skaggs made some gestures to Charlie, and I'm blamed if that skimmed-milk soul didn't rise up to action and *throw* her over. He just grabbed her, swung her off her feet, and let fly. It was the first time I'd realized that this Indian could perform in an emergency; then it occurred to me that if he hadn't been adventuresome, he never would have taken on the job in the first place. It wasn't any simple job, either, if you gave it some thought.

For once, Lauriette didn't yelp, but she failed to make it, too, and was pulled out as black as pitch all over. She started to cry, but stopped when Mr. Skaggs put a finger to his lips, and she even reached out a hand to help Charlie.

While I was trying to decide how we were better off, trapped on this pin-point of land, Mr. Skaggs jumped back, with a leafy branch, and swept the ground clear on the path. He had his nose almost in the dirt, as he mopped up footprints, and he'd no sooner returned, with all of us crouched down hidden, before the first of those bucks hove into view. He was the first Seminole I ever saw not covered from head to toe against the mosquitoes. He hadn't any costume on above his waist, and I recalled that they'd likely had to swim for it, if they failed to make a raft. So maybe they ruined their tunics.

Anyhow, he was painted with white stripes all over his face, as scary as a Halloween mask, and a lot more real. What I mean is, he was something to be scared of, so the mask worked, which was how war paint originated in the first place—made to scare people out of fighting. When he saw the place Mr. Skaggs swept, he grew excited and bird-called to his partner; then they got down to read up on the signs.

At this exact point Mr. Skaggs sailed into action. Taking very careful aim, as they faced the other direction, he whacked both in the back with that heavy pole, one after the other, and sent them spinning off headfirst into the muck.

When he saw them plunge, Mr. Skaggs let out a very piratical yell (as if he'd sunk a ship loaded with women and children, Lauriette said) and jumped onto the path with his stick. He stood there working as calm as a man chopping a weed patch with a hoe. Each time an Indian grabbed at the path, Mr. Skaggs gave him a helpful boost back with the pole, usually in the face. He flattened one fellow's nose on the first push he made. It was awful to see. Those Indians were no good—even their own tribes had banished them out, as Seminoles do for crimes, Charlie told us—but a death like this frazzled your nerves. They screamed and clawed through my sleep for months after.

We stood there five feet away, watching. Mr. Skaggs never said a word; the only thing you'd hear, as those poor devils thrashed in the mud, was an "aagh!" or a howl like a dog when the pole struck. The scrappiest managed to get one hand on the shaft, and then the other, but was Mr. Skaggs put out? Not at all. As cool as you please, he hauled him in, whipped out his knife, and sliced the nearest knuckles to the bone. After that, it was over in a jiffy, but it seemed like a very long time. At the end, they lost all control, clawing and pedaling, and sucked themselves under for good. The last thing I saw was a head that appeared briefly, coming back up, and an opened mouth full of muck, as the man fought to breathe. But it was too late. His breathing tube and nose were choked clear full, like a pipe clogged with concrete; he couldn't even make a noise.

We stood there miserable in spite of the fact that we'd got off scot-free. Mr. Skaggs tossed his pole aside, brushed some dirt from his clothes (which wouldn't have won any prizes to start with) and remarked: "Hit were Providential they jumped us down near the puff-mud. I don't mind owning up I was diverted."

"You are certainly a great fighter, Mr. Skaggs, and we owe you a lot," said Lauriette in an acid tone, "but I doubt if you'll ever have any close claim on Providence. The opposite number seems more likely."

"If a man in his life has made friends of b(B)oth, in the right order, and spelling the B two ways, for respect, he's been uncommon lucky," said Mr. Skaggs with his customary sanctimonial look. "I walked with the Devil, and I've walked with the good Lord Jesus. In outright candor, I prefer the Latter. I'm a Jesus man, staunch and stout; I glory in it."

Lauriette muttered in disgust, and we trooped back to the house. True to his promise, he sailed us to Key West the next morning, very early, in the crustiest kind of humor. He said we were leaving him high and dry, and if it wasn't for crowding him almost to distraction, he'd recommend that we stay. Well, this made as little sense as possible, so nobody worked up the spirit to comment.

We went aboard his schooner, which was a champion for stink and disorder, with tarred ropes lying about in snarls, barrels with the hoops busted, and a thrustful smell of garbage from below.

'What do you use the boat for, Mr. Skaggs?" asked Lauriette sweetly. "Sight-seeing parties? It's very attractive."

"Trim, ain't she? Note how she lays dead plumb level. Most wessels have a list. I carry products froo and toe Key West. What I mean ter say—to and fro."

Like all the Bahamians we came to know, he had trouble mixing up "v's" and "w's," along with additional things, and hearing people do them the other way occasionally got him addled. He never could say to and fro right.

The wind was from the wrong quarter for his harbor, he said, so he upped anchor and towed us out by a skiff. When we got clear of the point, he came alongside, clambered aboard like a monkey, and tied the skiff tight to the stern, with its bow riding out of the water. Then we hoisted sail and left.

The run would take six hours, because we were obliged to tack our way over. Mr. Skaggs said he usually waited to cross till he had a northeast breeze which would carry him to Key West direct, but he was so anxious to get rid of us now that he didn't mind doing extra work.

A few miles after we passed Cape Sable, the wind

swung around, freshening, and a nasty westward chop rolled in. The water got really high, and we pulled the skiff aboard, to keep from losing it. We were all over spray. Well, Charlie took down seasick, and so did Lauriette, and Mr. Skaggs told them to go below. There were two bunks, he said, and they could stay perfectly comfortable, also dry. So they did it, but she was back up right away, green with seasickness, but angrier than anything else.

"See here, those bunks are filthy. They have bed-bugs in them. I was bitten twice," and she held up her right arm, which had two welts inside the elbow, which is a favorite pasture for that species of pest.

Bent over the tiller, Mr. Skaggs seemed pained, and said, "The wessel's kept spic and span clean; I'm famous for it. The bugs must a bin 'idden in your clothes. If it ain't too much trouble, I'll ask you to peel down and hexamine yourself from truck to keelson."

There was a marlin spike handy, and for a minute I thought she might crack his skull, for she laid a hand on it with a look of speculation. But she only said, "You horrid, insulting old—*buccaneer!*" and flounced off below again.

In spite of Mr. Skagg's peeve, he changed course when he saw how sick they were, so that we veered in from open water and passed through Vaca Cut, between Matecumbe and Key West, then sailed a starboard tack up on the outside, along the reef that lay off shore. Beyond it, the Gulf Stream coiled its deep, blue-black waters eastward around Florida and, eventually to England. It kept England from freezing to death, according to Mr. Skaggs, but he favored letting it freeze. He had a grudge against Englishmen, because he said the Behamies were neglected by England during the Civil War, and almost starved to death.

As we neared shore, preparing to pass through the deep-water Cut, a number of boatmen hailed us, with a kind of good-natured chaff. There were shouts like, "Hey, Cooter, when'd you take to company?" and "Well, if it ain't old man Skaggs in for his monthly grouch!" and "Hoist the Jolly Roger, boys; here's one of the brotherhood." Pirates had laid up here, on account of the anchorage, and wreckers still congregated in this region, then took their salvage to Key West for judgment. But now and then an outright pirating still occurred, a fast ship swooping into these waters from Havana, or the Bahamas, or Colombia, or even from the Keys or the Dry Tortugas, and made a merry time of it for the Government. There was a brisk movement of ships down the Bahama Channel, so that the pickings had always been rich.

We passed Washerwoman Shoals, inside Sombrero Key, and scudded into the half-gale within close sight of the dozens and dozens of green-tufted islands that lay in a line toward Key West. What with one thing and another, it was four o'clock when we sighted the Martello Towers, which had been built but never used in the War, and half an hour later, we eased into the harbor, after some rough water around the point. I'd never seen any place so busy except New Orleans. Boats were everywhere, going in and out, and it took a good sailor to miss them. There was considerable cussing, in several languages, and a very rank smell of fish in the air.

Mr. Skaggs said he was itching to get away, because the town and everybody in it, including us, was offensive to him, but he said his contract wouldn't be fulfilled till we had located our kinfolk. That turned out to be easy.

As soon as we walked into town, we saw a shouting, shoving procession tramping down Duval Street, with a prisoner in tow, and it was Uncle Jim. He seemed at ease, and was smoking a cigar.

Casa Lopez
Key West, Florida
October 18, 1869

Dear Misses Burnie:

I write you what may be the last of these sprightly reports (I may say that a publisher has suggested that they be expanded to book size, with strong intimations of an advance) since I have news of stunning import. The narrative henceforward will be continued by—yes, it's true —your esteemed and energetic nephew, who has turned up in excellent health, with a singular cluster of companions, including a gotch-eared Seminole, a beautiful young girl from our Vicksburg interregnum, and an antiquated ex-pirate, untidy beyond any words of mine to describe, and probably homicidal.

You may imagine the tender and touching scene of reconciliation, which took place under unusual (and even depressing) circumstances, though they were nothing to worry about.

In brief, we were en route down Duval Street, the principal thoroughfare hereabouts, bound for the city jail, where a group of misguided citizens had insisted on lodging your brother, James.

We heard a cry from one side: "Uncle Jim! Zeb! Dr. Snodgrass!" and the whole procession stopped, so genuine was the ring of appeal.

"It's me—Davey!"

Your brother whirled around, shaking off his escorts, and let the cigar drop from his lips. It was the only time I've ever seen him confounded.

He cried, "By God—*Davey!*" strode over to that curious group mentioned above, and swept the child into a great hug that lifted him off the ground.

"I *knew* it! They couldn't lick you, could they, son? They couldn't put down a brat with all that mischief in him. Or did you go gallivanting off on your own? Do you need to be praised or strapped?"

"I wouldn't be here if it wasn't for Miss Lauriette," said your nephew, brushing the tears from his eyes with his sleeve. "Nor for Crop-eared Charlie, either, or Mr. Skaggs."

"Well, now, we're obliged to you all," said Colonel Burnie, looking them over keenly. "As for you, Ma'am, I hope you'll forgive me if I say I'm surprised."

The young lady drew up her tattered skirts and snapped, "I don't care a fig what you *are*, sir. I want a bath, and a chance to shop for clothes."

Colonel Burnie lifted his hat and said, "Why, of course. Let me accom—" but the procession of angry citizens now recovered its poise and somebody cried, "Hold on there! No you don't. A charge of piracy on the high seas ain't no laughing matter, and so you'll find."

"It's a mortal sin, specially wexatious to the blessed Lord Jesus," spoke up the disreputable old scoundrel who was unaccountably attached to your nephew, but several people laughed, and said, "Oh, sure, Mr. Skaggs," and "Listen to who's talking," and (from several) "Shucks."

Colonel Burnie merely replaced his hat and said to the young lady, "It appears that I have a prior commitment."

Now I think it's time to clear up some of these mysteries, so I'll say very quickly that, my daughter Millicent being absent visiting friends, I took Miss Farrow to our boarding house (where I am penning these hasty lines), while the others elected to remain with your brother. As David himself is setting those facts down, I shall relate only that, after being kidnapped from our steamboat at Vicksburg, he fled with Miss Farrow down the Mississippi, sailed to Tampa, Florida, and from thence was obliged to undertake a terrible journey through the dark and malodorous Everglades Swamp, from which one Cooter (!) Skaggs transported the boy (and Miss Farrow plus an Indian guide) to Key West.

Thus, all's well that ends well, or, in the Bard's immortal words, "Out of the nettle, danger, we pluck this flower, safety."

So—we have arrived at the ignominious posture of Colonel Burnie, who at present has only just managed to avoid the local *calabozo* ("jail"—Spanish) by a hair's breadth, and no more. The events preceding this error in no way compromise him; he is purely a victim of circumstance. You will recall that, at the conclusion of my last dispatch, the sailing vessel jointly acquired by Colonel Burnie and the popinjay, Captain Pereira, had failed not only at hooking sponges, but also at fishing and wrecking. (It appeared that these enterprises required somewhat more than Colonel Burnie's offhand nonchalance and Pereira's simpering idiocy but, in fact, called for skill and hard work.)

With the last of Colonel Burnie's funds, we repaired the vessel, and again tied it up at Key West, hoping to hit on some plan for its use. There was a brief discussion about sailing to the Dry Tortugas and turtling, but Colonel Burnie decided against it. He said that, in the very unlikely event we caught any (by accident or if they came forward and gave themselves up), they would probably mutiny and seize the ship on the way home. He said he wouldn't care to chance it. He stated that, in general, we should try and hit on some use for the boat that had as little as possible to do with the sea.

That was two days ago. Yesterday morning, when the Colonel and I strolled down for our daily inspection, the boat was missing from its berth. Puzzled (to put it mildly), we made inquiries among people at the harbor, and two men recalled having seen it heading for sea the previous night, running under the jib and with Captain Pereira at the helm.

So at last the blow had fallen! The snake had struck when our defenses were at their lowest ebb of the journey.

At noon of that day, a monstrous hubbub broke out at the docks, a crowd of angered citizens made their way toward our domicile, and we received the ill tidings. A dory containing three Cuban residents of the town—fishermen in good standing—had limped in with a frightful story of piracy and violence. Their smack, harmlessly in pursuit of its trade, had been attacked by a vessel that unquestionably was ours—the name *Inauspicious* (a whim of Colonel Burnie's) stood out clearly—and the crew was overpowered in a struggle against half a dozen dark-skinned strangers bearing firearms. Besides these, Captain Pereira was positively established as one of the boat's complement, and all three Cubans unctuously swore that they had seen Colonel Burnie as well.

In a dense fog out there, they'd made their escape in the dory, then rowed twenty-five miles to Key West.

Reckless cries of "Lynch him! String him up!" and the like arose from our lawn, and the neighborhood degenerated into a bedlam. It was as disgraceful a scene as I can recall, and I flatter myself that I have been the central figure at some extraordinary samples of mass hysteria.

On their way to the house, nearly everybody grabbed up some utensil with which to assault the supposed culprit—a boat hook, a loose wagonspoke, pieces of coral and rope—but they all, to a man, seemed marvelously reticent and unthrustful when Colonel Burnie appeared on the porch, carelessly dangling a pistol in one hand. On the contrary, a spirit of deep courtesy appeared, and those in front, feeling that they had usurped the choice vantage points too long, insisted on exchanging places with their less fortunate colleagues in the rear.

"Speak your piece," said Colonel Burnie, "but don't be too long about it, because I'm ready to take my afternoon nap."

He cocked his pistol and stood waiting.

Oddly enough, nobody seemed eager to articulate their grievances, until a man well hidden in back yelled, "You were seen pirating, and we've got the proof with us," upon which the three Cubans were shoved forward, hats in hand.

As the editor of the newspaper said, for these sturdy sons of the brine to hurl charges of piracy was paradoxical in the extreme, because most of them had been pirates themselves at one time or another, and their families, in the main, had been in the trade for several generations.

At the appearance of the Cubans, the mob took heart and began again the wild cries of accusation, coupled with demands (from those in the rear) for immediate punishment.

There is no telling how long this embarrassing farce might have endured, if a shout hadn't gone up, "Here comes the Sheriff!" To my surprise, a tall, dignified negro wearing a Panama hat and a gold watch chain came into the yard, followed by two white deputies.

I had forgotten that the Republican administration following the unsettled Reconstruction era brought not only a negro Sheriff but a negro Magistrate to Key West. The former of these is well spoken of by even the most rabid of the white superiority enthusiasts, but the Magistrate is deplored by all, white and negro alike. He is a surly, witless, drunken, dishonest oaf with no more claim on his important office than the vindictiveness of the times and the fact that his color is black.

"Here, here, you folks all het up," said the Sheriff. "This man ain't proved to do anything, leastways not yet."

"Stay out of this, Sheriff," somebody spoke up. "We've got our own ways of dealing with pirates, a nice little jig on a piece of empty air."

"Why that sure is pushish of you, Mr. Goings. Wasn't it your grandpappy that sailed into Charlotte Harbor with Little Gaspar? So it's wrote down at the Library. I never heard of anybody stringing *him* up. He settled down and bought a farm."

Several people laughed at this, but out of the wrong sides of their mouths, as if they'd bitten into a green persimmon. One man, slightly bolder than his fellows, stepped forward and said, "Well, what *be* you planning to do, Sheriff? Turn him loose?"

The negro sighed and said, "I reckon we'd ought to tromp down to the Magistrate's. I ain't eager, but there's nothing else kin be done."

A lot of people laughed *very* heartily now, and said, "Oh, yes, to be sure. That's *just* the ticket, ain't it? Call on the Magistrate, of *course,* if you can grub him out of the saloons."

In any case, the Sheriff took Colonel Burnie by the arm, but in perfect courtesy, as if they were walking the street together in friendship, and the motley procession headed down Duval Street toward the combination lockup and Magistrate's Court. Your brother acquiesced with good grace.

Frankly, I thought the Sheriff's controlled manner remarkable, in view of the humilating restraints placed on the negroes of Key West in times past.

In 1832, when the City Charter was incorporated, a tax was established on real estate and a per capita tax on free negroes, mulattoes and slaves. Also, negroes, slave or free, were excluded from the streets after 9:30 at night, when the town bell was rung; neither were they permitted to "play the fiddle, beat a drum or make any kind of noise after bell-ring without permission of the mayor or alderman, under penalty of being whipped or put to labor on public streets."

Needless to say, all that has later been mitigated.

So, ladies, we have now arrived at the point where (previously) I described to you the sudden and joyous materialization on the scene of your esteemed and absent nephew. Our hearts are gladdened to welcome him back into the fold, but I am downcast to consider that, for all purposes of advancing our narrative, these reports are now finished. I have related our separate adventures, and David will resume the collective story later in detail (though not, I fancy, in what modesty prevents me from alluding to as an eloquence transcending the usual physician's prose style). I will, of course, write you the outcome of our present dilemma, but it shall not, I am informed, be included among the chapters of The Book.

> With thanks for your forbearance, (and
> standing ever-ready to treat, *in absentia,*
> any of those perplexing fringe ailments for
> which my preparations have proved so specific:
> i.e., shingles, wind, croquet elbow,
> delirium tremens, lunacy, etc.)

> Yr. peripatetic correspondent,
> Ewing T. Snodgrass,
> (D.C.; M.P.; Ph.U.)

23

WHEN THE CROWD closed in again on Uncle Jim, the Sheriff led him off down the street, and we followed; all but Lauriette. Dr. Snodgrass showed her back to our house, as wet and ruffled as a hen caught in a cloudburst.

Well, the voyage with Mr. Skaggs *had* been moist, but not that bad, and we'd only taken a very little rough water in the last hour, while coming around the point. A wave or two had soaked over the bow and dampened her down, knocking her to the deck a time or two, but nothing serious.

Anyway, we ankled along after everybody, with the mob just howling for blood, and when we got there, Zeb demanded to be taken in with Uncle Jim. He laid his ears right back like a donkey. He said he had nursed him all through the war, in worse trouble than this (when they were about to shoot him for one thing or another) and he hadn't any idea of running out now.

The Sheriff patiently explained that Zeb hadn't been accused of anything, and it was ridiculous to add him to the bag, so Zeb picked up a brickbat and heaved it through the Magistrate's window; then they said that made it all right.

But there was an awful commotion inside, for the brick had knocked a half-full bottle of rum off of the Magistrate's desk, out from between his feet, where he was sleeping off a drunk. He was so mad he couldn't rest, and organized a preliminary hearing right on the spot.

We went in and sat down, and the Sheriff put Uncle Jim and Zeb at a table in front, and presently the Magistrate came in, sort of tacking along, as if he wasn't entirely steady on his pins. He was fat, and had gray kinky hair and gray mutton-chop whiskers, and very stylish clothes, and they said he had an education out of a college up North that was as broadminded as northerners intended to make the South, now, and took in a few darkies every few years, but he didn't sound like it. His face had a mean scowl, ugly and a little sick, too, I judged, and suddenly he banged his gavel on the desk and roared, "The prisoner will arise for inspection."

Uncle Jim got up with a nice smile, and Zeb started to rise, but Uncle Jim pushed him down. The Magistrate then looked around the room with a wicked glance out of his little yellow blood-shot eyes, and shouted, *"Silence!"* though nobody'd said anything. "What's the charge?"

The Sheriff now got up and said, "I couldn't say there *was* no formal charge yet, Your Honor. This hearing may be a little previous. These people done a right smart hollering about piracy, but—"

"Hold your tongue. If you ain't got anything to say, don't say it. I'm the Court here, and the sooner people realize it, the better. Is the prisoner represented?"

With a look I knew perfectly well, Uncle Jim said, "I'm representing us, Your Worship."

"What do you mean, *us?*"

Uncle Jim waved at Zeb. "This man, Zebediah Burnie, is technically charged with wanton destruction of property, to wit, half a bottle of Your Lordship's cheap rum, but in reality he's one of the most dangerous villains ever captured in Key West. You've heard of the notorious Black Caesar?"

"Ain't that the pirate?"

"In person. Note the low, beetling expression. Also the giant hands that knot and un-knot—itching to get at somebody's throat. This man has probably killed as many of his fellow creatures as anybody alive today. And that isn't the worst; he keeps *a stockade full of innocent young girls in his foul lair near Sanybel.*

"Your Lordship's running the gravest sort of risk: *This scoundrel ought to be in chains!*"

Well, several people let up and guffawed outright, with both the Sheriff and Zeb tugging at Uncle Jim's coattails, trying to get him down, but he was going pretty good now and hated to stop.

The Magistrate was too feeble-headed and drunk to take it in exactly. He sensed that something was wrong, all right, but he couldn't puzzle it out.

"See here, are you trying to sass the Court? I thought Black Caesar died forty or fifty years ago."

"That was another one, and anyway he was in Rome."

"Quiet in the Court!" He banged his gavel again and said, "Where do you get off being so high and mighty about *him*? Wasn't you took up first?"

"I was speaking purely in my role as legal representative for Black Caesar."

"*For* him! Trying to get him hung's more near it."

"It's for his own good, Your Honor."

"There's something fishy going on here. Are you claiming to be a lawyer?"

"Sir, I was formerly a member of the Supreme Court. Both here and abroad."

The Magistrate finally blew up, as I thought he would —he was actually overdue—and roared out: "Then what in the name of God Almighty are you doing in Key West pirating ships?"

"It's only a hobby."

Thanks to goodness, a noisy commotion burst out in the rear, and this nonsense got over in a hurry. Otherwise, people said later, Uncle Jim might have gone to prison for as much as two hundred years, the Magistrate was just that ornery at being balked. And when you pile on the ten or twelve years they'd add for bad behavior, Uncle Jim wouldn't be any chicken when he came out. But the Magistrate's days of bullyragging the Key Westers were over at the same exact instant of this commotion.

Captain Pereira strolled in, accompanied by a tall, fine-looking man with gray hair and a new white linen suit on, and in back of them were four Cubans with their hands shackled. Captain Pereira seemed different, not so flashy as told about in the letters; he looked downright human to me. Dr. Snodgrass had just got back and was with them, but he didn't appear any less befuddled than the Magistrate.

"Well," said Captain Pereira to Uncle Jim, walking forward, "so they've caught up with you at last. This is certainly a red-letter day for Key West"; *and he said it in absolutely straightaway speech,* without all the garbagy babble of before.

"Crime doesn't pay," said Uncle Jim; then he turned to Dr. Snodgrass and the rest of us and said, "Meet Joe Pereira, of the Havana police. We were in the Mexican War together. He's in the pay of the federals, but he has a revolutionary spirit."

"Not so loud," said Captain Pereira. "Anyhow, it wasn't a matter of sympathy. The Americans offered more money and better accommodations."

"Sir," demanded Dr. Snodgrass sternly, "do you mean that all that turkey-gobble was an imposture? If so, I resent it. The one thing in the world that turns my stomach is a fraud."

Captain Pereira looked sheepish and said, "Your Mr. Burnie can't resist a practical joke. He gets bored. I try to do my best to please him."

"I wasn't bored," said Uncle Jim. "Talk some more. It's fine—same way he used to imitate the Mexican generals."

Captain Pereira's Cubans were a smuggling ring he'd rounded up, after loafing around on the lookout for several months, doing other things on the side, and when he explained it to the Sheriff, who knew part already, they also captured the three men who'd rowed in with the lifeboat.

Then the tall, gray-haired man stepped forward and served a paper on the Magistrate, who was jumping up and down with his gavel, because nobody would pay him any mind.

"What's this? That's nothing to me. If I don't get order in this Court, I'll have everybody in the room reminded to jail."

"Sir," said the gray-haired man calmly, "you are relieved of your post. The formal charge, issued by the Governor, is malfeasance in office, and I am appointed to succeed you. You are instructed not to leave Key West."

Well, a hooray rang out that rattled the windows, along

with hand-clapping and cries of "Thank God, we've got rid of this skunk at last!" and a number of men shook hands and offered each other cigars.

"It's a lie!" shouted the Magistrate. "Everybody in town's against me, and always have been, because I'm black. I'll show you white trash who won the Civil War —Sheriff, take this man into custody!"

But the Sheriff said, "You better cool down, Jedge. You're in a peck of trouble. They ain't against *me*, and I'm blacker'n you are. Folks like you jest naturally against themselves. You better start movin out of the office, and not cause any more fuss."

Then I noticed a curious thing. Nearly everybody headed off towards the saloons to celebrate, and the very ones that had been on fire to lynch Uncle Jim before were the most anxious to buy him a drink. They said they knew all along he wasn't guilty, and one man said if they'd hung him by mistake, they'd a taken handsome care of his relations afterward. There wasn't anything mean or small about them, and they wanted him to know it.

But Uncle Jim said he had an engagement with some other friends, so he took the Sheriff and Captain Pereira and Dr. Snodgrass and the new Magistrate to a Cuban saloon and bought them a drink instead.

As for Charlie and Mr. Skaggs and me, Uncle Jim paid a boy to show us to the Casa Lopez.

I felt kind of addled.

Mr. Skaggs wanted to get away this same night and go home, sailing in the dark—sounding where the channels were by the way the centerboard hit bottom. He hadn't recalled, he said, that Key West was quite as bad as it was; the place had gone downhill considerable since he visited here a month ago.

Charlie reckoned he'd go with him, then catch a ride on up past Chokoloskee and Sanybel to Tampa on some kind of boat or other.

Before we sat down to a meal at home, Uncle Jim and the others came in, with Captain Pereira looking uncomfortable for some reason. I reckoned he hadn't been forgiven yet by Dr. Snodgrass, who did, as he said, detest fraud in any line. But Dr. Snodgrass was in for a worse shock yet, because he went upstairs then came down, and he held a letter in one hand.

"This was on my bureau; I must have overlooked it."

And when he opened and read it, he sprang to his feet with an angry flush on his face.

"By God, sir!" he cried, and it was the first time I'd ever heard him swear, "this is intolerable! It's monstrous. I—I can't take it in." He staggered to a chair, and Uncle Jim helped him, with an expression of honest worry for once. Usually he figured that Dr. Snodgrass was the equal, if not considerably more, of any situation involving humans, but this time he actually seemed disturbed.

Well, they got a little brandy down him, after his face had turned from red to deathly pale; then he handed the letter to Uncle Jim.

"Maybe *I*'d better read it," said Captain Pereira in a low voice.

"Does it concern you?" asked Uncle Jim in about the flattest tone I ever heard him use.

"It must. I'm afraid it does."

Uncle Jim handed it over, and Captain Pereira read, after a couple of weak starts: "Dear Papa: This is to tell you that I'm not really going to stay overnight with the Cannons but to elope with Captain Pereira, who is the best and most thoughtful man I ever met." [The Captain had the decency to gag here, and chew his words awhile, then he continued on.]

"I hate to break it to you in this back-door fashion, and indeed José (for that is his first name; I doubt if you knew that, did you?) badly wanted us to come to you and to Captain Burnie together..But I know how bitterly you detest him, and have no intention of seeing my mind changed, even by my wonderful father.

"I am grown now, a fact of which I believe you are unaware, and wish to be a woman in every way that Nature intended.

"Please try to understand. When some things are cleared up—soon, I hope—I do not think you will dislike José any longer.

"As for Jim, he's a dear, good man—exciting, even—

but I sadly fear that he will never be the kind who settles down. In many ways, I grieve for him. He has a restlessness that marriage cannot cure. To avoid boredom, he is doomed to wander aimlessly (or foolishly, or hilariously) over the earth, seeking the kind of violence and adventures that will disguise the fact that he is running away from himself. In spite of his nonchalant manner, he is deeply unhappy.

"I don't know whether I am in love. I think so; certainly I am in love with the idea of being in love, and my husband says he can make those two things become one.

"We shall never be far from you, dear Papa, and while I know that to lose this last member of your family is a blow, I feel that, at last, you are surrounded by real friends who will always be anxious for your welfare.

"(Please don't be cross.)

> "Your loving daughter,
> Millie"

By the time Captain Pereira finished, Uncle Jim was sitting with his chin resting on one hand, and Dr. Snodgrass lay back as if he was asleep, or sick.

"I wish you all to know," said Captain Pereira slowly, "that I would have preferred a better method. But my wife's wishes are my wishes."

"Then you are married?" inquired Dr. Snodgrass without opening his eyes.

"We are married, sir."

"If I am capable of laying my hands on a gun, my daughter shall be widowed before nightfall."

"I'm sorry you feel that way, Doctor," said Captain Pereira. "I can understand it—a Spaniard, unknown to you, perhaps alien in instinct and culture. But I promise you most faithfully I shall make your daughter the best husband of which an old and honorable family can be capable. Further, I hope to please you as a son-in-law."

"The girl is a living replica of her mother," said Dr. Snodgrass thoughtfully, his color warming up a little as his mind strayed back to the past days of medicine shows and skedaddling away from the authorities. "That was the cornetist who lost her lip and fled with a salesman in hosiery. Like mother, like daughter—the fatal weakness of character, the bad seed. To think that I've nurtured a second serpent at my bosom these past twenty years! It's hard, hard."

"You're wrong there," said Uncle Jim, and he sounded tired. "Your daughter's a good, honest girl ready to begin living. I only wish I'd had sufficient wit and energy to do something about it before it was too late. I admit it freely."

Captain Pereira started to say something, but was interrupted.

"And your son-in-law is a man you can rely on with your back to the wall. We've soldiered together, drunk together, been arrested and broke together, chased wo—, that is, campaigned together as brothers, he and Farrow and I, so if you have to damn him, you'd better damn me, too. I ask you to give them your blessing."

In the lamplight, I could tell Lauriette's face had an odd look, as she gazed at Uncle Jim, and got the feeling that maybe she thought a little better of him for his speech.

Dr. Snodgrass suddenly arose, threw back his shoulders, harrumphed a time or two, as he commonly did before starting one of his spiels, and said, "Captain, or Señor, Pereira, it appears that I have made an ass of myself. It is by no means the first time, and as I'm comparatively young—well short of a hundred—it won't be the last. Here's my hand, sir, and may I suggest that you fetch my daughter, from wherever she's hiding, then help me drink a magnum of champagne that I recently acquired (in lieu of cash) from a Cuban with a nasty case of industrial stomach. He was, by chance, in the, ah, smuggling line, but I have the impression, after today, that his time for the next few years will be taken up in quite a different direction."

Captain Pereira leaped up and embraced Dr. Snodgrass, amidst a general snorting into handkerchiefs; then he shook hands with Uncle Jim, while regarding him with a troubled look, his brows knitted up uncertainly.

"She was right, you know," said Uncle Jim to us all.

"I'd never make a suitable mate for a girl of normal habits. Or for anybody else, for that matter." He said it in an easy, offhand tone, but I noticed that he sat smoking most all night in a rocker on the upstairs porch, and the next morning he went into town early and began drinking rum.

24

UNCLE JIM says the last chapters of my book should "be in the nature of a quiet sea pastoral," but our story didn't work out exactly like that, though it came close. He said some of the other chapters sounded like penny-dreadfuls, meant only to startle and excite, but that books generally followed after life, and didn't invent it, so he guessed it was all right.

Mr. Skaggs, with Charlie, left at ten o'clock on dead low tide, and said it was no more than he expected from Key West.

"Well, I hardly think the town's responsible for the tides, Mr. Skaggs," said Lauriette. But she gave him a nice little peck on the cheek good-bye, as we stood watching in the moonlight, with the fish-boats' masts sticking up all around and the town looking like a tropical native village behind us, and offered him a substantial bonus. He refused it, preferring to stick to his original price of fifteen dollars, then said he figured he'd lost twenty dollars on the voyage. That brought his total losings for the month—from buttonwood and from sailing —to around ninety dollars. "Not counting the store, turtling, gator trading, clamming, and other wentures," he said. "I dare and welcome anybody to come and dig. It don't hexist." Then he proposed marriage again to Lauriette (without any property settlement), and went aboard his schooner, in a very testy mood.

Lauriette gave Charlie a hundred dollars extra, and fifty dollars for his wound. He said he still liked white people, and stood ready to serve us: we had only to send out the word. He bore a long letter from us to Reverend Muckleroy, and another to Mrs. Hawkins. We shook hands all around, and Mr. Skaggs edged his boat out from the dock, running this way and that like a monkey. It came over me that he must have been a wizard pirate, so it was no wonder he'd lost his cheerful disposition. Nobody could give up a trade as enjoyable as that without a number of bad effects. It went against nature. And on top of it, he'd got religion, which delivered the final knockout. It surprised me that he wasn't any crazier than he was.

The second day after, with Lauriette wearing spanking new clothes (and feeling a little less snappish), we all got together—Millie and Captain Pereira, too—and held a conference.

Uncle Jim's funds were gone; he had only the boat and a few dollars left, and he hadn't any notion of sending back to Grassy for more. Lauriette, by flinging money right and left like a drunken sailor, as I told her on the spot, was down to eight hundred, and Dr. Snodgrass through good luck had the contributions that were made him in Bosky Dell, from the numerous people there with hernia. And then, by George, if Zeb didn't turn up with two hundred! He'd saved it from his wages at Grassy, and had it in a leather bag around his neck, out of sight from thieves.

Captain Pereira said he lived mostly on his salary as a policeman, and that, with his wife's approval, he intended to continue being a policeman. The work was what he called "sedentary," and allowed time for other favorable-looking plunges, like his late salt plant. The example seemed to me unusually ill-chosen, and even Dr. Snodgrass, who liked him now, looked out of the window and whistled.

"The only thing to do," said Uncle Jim with a rising spark of enthusiasm that pleased everybody, "is go in for a homestead farm. The Government's got it all set up. There's rich land down on a Key called Matecumbe— they're starting a pineapple trade there—and we can wangle two grants of 160 acres each; I'm sure of it.

"When you come right down to it," he added, "running a farm's the only thing I've ever done successfully."

They fixed it up between them that Lauriette would own one grant, and Uncle Jim the other, and he would oversee both. Dr. Snodgrass declined to put his right name to a document; he said it had always made him nervous. In times past, when obtaining a permit or conducting a business operation, he had used one of several aliases, as he said, and he showed us some printed-up cards: "S. Twitchell Updike"; "Father Dion O'Flaherty, S.J."; "Dr. Honoré du Pont (of Paris)"; "General Robert E. Leigh"; and "The Hon. Moses Goldberg." He said he never knew what kind of group he might be dealing with, and it was better to have a variety. Uncle Jim told him that none of these would serve the Government's purposes, and he said it was all right. He'd rather function as an adviser and assistant, and return to doctoring if times got lean.

Within a week, the arrangements were made, and we hired a sailor to pilot us down to the place called, on our map, Upper Matecumbe.

I noticed a bright gleam in Uncle Jim's eye during these dealings, and sure enough, he told us, before we left, that the time had come "to lift the treasure," if it wasn't already lifted. Nobody would get suspicious now, and we could dig to our hearts' content. His cheeks had a nice spot of color in the tan, and I knew this was the moment, the high excitement, the end of the chase, that he had lived for since we left home (a good many adventures ago). I wondered how it would turn out, and whether he'd be disappointed again, as I realized he had been so often before. He was a strange man; I was only just coming to know him.

The trip was a beautiful sail, on the "outside," or ocean, from Key to Key up the chain, made on a day that would have scorched your hide off except for a cold breeze in from the Gulf Stream. The Stream moved along out there, dark and mysterious, and maybe a little rough, just beyond us, and if you saw odd shapes sticking up, maybe broken into pieces that shimmered and danced (the way they do far out on the sea), they were ships headed up the Bahama Channel toward romantical backward places like Africa and Ireland and Spain, or New York, where people spoke different languages and often went about naked, though not so much in New York.

Lying there in the stream, ships could pick up five or six miles an hour from the current alone, but they had to know their business, because the Gulf Stream shifts about, and lies in closer to shore some days than others. Big boats going west beat along between the Stream and the reef, of course, so as not to buck the drift. It was an interesting river of sea water, that Gulf Stream, and full of fish that scientists hadn't thought up names for yet. There were the other kind, too, but I never felt easy in my mind fishing out there, because if you got becalmed, or lost a spar, or had some other kind of accident, there wasn't any telling where you might wind up. And if squalls came along, its waters got mighty rough, being hundreds of feet deep.

We sailed over reef rocks as bright as rainbows, patchy and mottled with plants, and the water was clear right down to the bottom—emerald green in spots and sky-blue in others, depending on the rocks, you know. And way down there you saw ferns waving and fish so stripey and spotted they could have been painted by crayons. It was exciting.

Along shore, these Keys were green with grass under cocoanut palms that people said were seeded by birds, or by cocoanuts that floated over from Cuba. There were other trees, too—Jamaica dogwood and tallowood and lignum vitae that they pronounced vitey and was so hard it was used for ball bearings. A man told us that all the trees and fruit plants—limes, avocados, sapadilla, and the like—had been introduced by the wind, birds, or the sea, or that seafaring men had planted seeds here from ports all over the world. It was a most unusual place, these outcropping bones of coral covered with their wild mixture of greenery.

Once in a long while we saw a boat, about eighteen feet long with a leg-o'-mutton sail, and it was a fisherman or maybe somebody visiting another island, for several families lived here by now. In the Matecumbes, and others nearby, the main ones were the Parkers and Pinders and Russells and Lowes and such, from the Behamies but now called Conchs, after the "Nassau Boxing Gloves" that were used as weapons in the days when the Spanish marauded. Not everybody in the Behamies had a gun then, you understand, so whenever the Spanish landed, the ones that didn't fitted conch shells to their fists and rushed down to the beaches to fight. The big shells made tolerable weapons, with those pink and white spines sticking out, and they said Spaniards wielding swords weren't in it against them, for an expert could parry a sword thrust with one hand then smash the swordsman's face with the other.

In a couple of days we had our tracts staked out by boundaries, with the help of a family of Prindles, who loaned us some hired hands—negroes from the Behamies—and started the building of two makeshift houses made from native lumber off Big Pine Key. While the work went on, the Prindles boarded us all. Then we bored cisterns down in the rock, for these Keys were entirely without water. That is, not quite, because we came to learn the location of several "wells," or holes of fresh water that sometimes lay in places where the tide washed over. It was curious. But these commonly dried up in a long season of no rainfall, and so did the cisterns. Then the families had to buy water from ships anchored offshore to load pineapples, or even boat it clear down from Key West. Water was a problem in the middle and upper Keys.

The houses here were built on the ocean side, so as to get the cool breeze during the long hot summer. When ours were done, we moved from the Prindles and set up shop, Lauriette in one with a woman servant that got sick and left pretty soon, and Dr. Snodgrass and Uncle Jim and Zeb and me in the other. We thought it might be lonesome for her, but her house was within view of ours, and she was back and forth every day, especially in the evening. Moreover, she said it was the first peace she'd known in her life, after living twenty years in "an unnatural home of cold and scheming pretenders." Well, those were hard words, but I reckon it was so.

None of the Conch families lived very close by, and our tracts ran from "sea to sea," (what was generally called "a big scope of land"), or from Florida Bay on the inside to the ocean on the outside. They were fine pieces, though tangled with low growth so thick a body could scarcely walk it through. We were on what they called Upper Matecumbe, because Lower Matecumbe was too swampy and was, as they said, nothing but a "low swale." Here and there, on both water sides, were brown flats where the sandy marl and weed were covered with nothing but a few inches of sea even at high tide. When the tide was low, these stood out of water, with little stems of plants sticking up. To sail over flats, a person needed to learn passages or channels that the tides had sliced through, running in and out. Or maybe fishing Seminoles had done it, years before, or some Conch who, tired of sailing around, had taken a spade and made a short cut twenty to fifty feet long or so.

To get across Florida Bay toward the 'Glades,—"back country"—you had to know these passages or you'd likely be stranded on a flat up to your knees in muck. It was flighty business in a brisk wind. And you might get lost back there, if you weren't careful. Sometimes cuts were marked by crookedy sticks; again there was no way on earth to tell them except memorizing. Sizable boats never ventured back, of course, because even the ordinary waters of the Bay were shallow, but the Conchs fished there in small sailboats, for over those flats fish roamed by the thousands, looking for food. I never saw anything like it anywhere, and never got used to it. You could be sitting in six inches of water, with brown flats just everyplace, close at hand, and if you tossed a hunk of bloody trash-fish over the side, black sharks as long as a man were boiling around in a minute or less. And in the deeper places, the "lakes," between the hundreds and hundreds of unnamed Keys that lay in Florida Bay, porpoises played and leaped and coughed, friendly as always, but scattering the fish away, too, so that it made you mad sometimes.

On the ocean side there were flats near shore but also deep swift-water channels (only they called them "drains") where the tides came rushing off the Gulf Stream over the reefs and between the Keys. You seldom found a stretch of beach, because the sea broke on the reef, out two or three miles. There was talk now of build-

ing a railroad to link up the Keys and form a solid wall,
but old-timers said it was the poorest kind of idea, because when the hurricanes roared up out of the Caribbean, the water would flood right over. Since it couldn't
go *between* Keys any longer, if a railroad was there, it
would rise over and wreck everything. Once in a while, it
washed up pretty high as it was. Everybody worried
about hurricanes in these parts, and who could blame
them? Where could the people go? There was no quick
way to hotfoot it to the mainland, and their smacks or
smaller boats would be swamped if they put out to sea.
And even if some folks reached the mainland, it was only
Everglades swamp, with no towns at all clear around the
curve of south Florida eastward up to Fort Dade. And no
high ground down there, either. I heard somebody say
there would be a city at the tip some day, for northern
visitors to take the sun, but nobody really believed it.

Well, we got our houses done, and began the task of
burning and clearing land for pineapples. It was pesky
hot work in a blazing November sun. And every day it
rained some, too. We had enough money left, after the
houses, to buy pineapple slips, which were suckers that
grew off the plants, for planting a crop. Everybody—the
Pinders, Russells, and Prindles—called the fruit "pines"
and hoped to make a whopping big industry out of them;
and they were helpful to us, because the ships that lay up
offshore could use as many as anybody could raise.

But we wouldn't be ready to "break" for months yet. It
was an odd plant and could be kept out of the ground a
year, and then grow again when put back in moist soil
someplace else. What's more, it thrived in regions where
the rain never fell for long periods.

The Prindles, who were our nearest neighbors, sort of
supervised our start, and told us where we went wrong
here and there. This was better than the salt plant and
fishing and wrecking, because Uncle Jim and Captain
Pereira supervised those and knew as much about it as I
do how to be a burglar. Or maybe less.

Well, we had to eat in the meantime, so the Prindles
helped us plant Egypt corn, which is a tough kind of Indian corn—very good for the teeth, if they don't break off

first—and tomatoes and cantaloupes and sugar apples and both Irish and sweet potatoes and green pepper and okra, as well as watermelon and other vegetables; and, too, we bought things off neighbors who boated to Key West now and then. We got an old iron coffee grinder that skreeked when you turned the handle, and ground our own coffee. It was tasty but powerful.

Mrs. Prindle, a plump, motherly person, with wispy gray hair that had nine small children which owned four or five outfits between them, so that when one had on a skirt, another blossomed out in a shirt, but never hooked the two up together—she transplanted us a castor tree. She was hipped on medicine, and made Dr. Snodgrass jealous. He said she was worse than Zeb in the quackery line, but he mollified down when she consented to drink a bottle of Spooju, because he told her she likely had several internal ailments that had only recently been invented up North, in high medical circles, and hadn't found their way to the Keys yet.

So she did it, drank the whole bottle at one sitting, and it did her worlds of good. She'd been healthy before, you understand, but after she drank the Spooju, she got downright robust. And when her husband came in from the fields, she was lying on her back on the kitchen table, stirring a chowder with one hand and singing a song that went:

> "Aunt Jemima climb a tree
> They tuk a stick to bruise 'er,
> But there she stood a-throwin' corn
> An callin' a bob-tailed rooster."

Well, they said there were some other verses that became outright brisk, but Mr. Prindle hustled her into the bedroom before the children arrived. I thought he might be sore, but the next day he came over and tried to buy some more Spooju from Dr. Snodgrass, so I judged she was benefitted in a general way.

Leaves from Mrs. Prindle's castor tree were used for neuritis and arthritis, she said, but the only time Lauriette ever got me to eat one, it seemed to work out different; I don't know when I'd ever sprightened up so.

They had a lot of other remedies. When Mrs. Prindle and Dr. Snodgrass and Zeb got their peeves ironed out, and treated each other with what Uncle Jim called professional courtesy, they went over everything together.

Mrs. Prindle made her own pills, which she pronounced "pails," taking a pie plate, putting flour in it and depositing in the healing materials drop by drop. She also had fever-grass tea, with "nitre" in it to break fever; sage tea for chicken pox; catnip tea, for "lady complaints," which they made a joke about, to the affect that "it was bitter twice," whatever that meant; and what they called their miracle plant, or aloes.

It was, too. Aloes came in handy for everything, and particularly sunburn. It had green stalks with prickers on the edge and grew close to the ground. When you sliced a stalk in two, the cross-cut surface looked like green jelly, and tasted as bitter as gall. But it was a wonderful medicine, and when a person had something they couldn't puzzle out, it was customary to dose him with aloes, inside and out. If it didn't cure him, they figured he was beyond mortal control.

There was a Cuban doctor in Key West, but everybody said he relied too much on tar-oil and tallow, along with mint-bags on the chest; and a Dr. Malone was set up there, too. He was a "natural doctor" and some swore by him, as well as others at him, which is usual in the medical line, Dr. Snodgrass said.

But to get back to business, those Prindles were wonderfully good to us, just like the other Conch families. People were few and far between in these Keys, and must stick together to survive.

They helped us to make mattresses of bed grass, which was a kind of cut grass that stuffed up a ticking very well, and you could get a good night's rest on it, if you didn't turn over too much, and make sounds like a buffalo thrashing through a jungle, or if a weed didn't slip through and harpoon you in the back. But on the whole, bed grass provided a nice mattress, and anyhow we didn't have so much money left we could afford to be choosey.

We planted palms all around our houses, for shade, but a few were growing in those localities already. Somebody told us that Dr. Perrine (who had been killed by Chekika in the Indian Key Massacre) had scattered seed down this way, for "experimentation" and for the fun of it. Anyhow, both of our tracts had some very nice trees, including spoon apples, which produced big, soft fruit, a little like apples but not much, since too sweet, that a body ate with a spoon. You could make a meal on one, Dr. Snodgrass said, if you didn't care what happened to your teeth. We had lime trees that brought out wonderful big tart green limes that lime pies were made out of, with cookie crumbs sprinkled thick over the top.

A person could eat mighty well hereabouts, but he had to work for it. And that's the way it ought to be, Uncle Jim said. He said it while sitting in a rocker under a pepper tree and watching Zeb work on an outdoor oven for baking sweet potato bread. But mostly Uncle Jim worked as hard as the rest; we all did. During these months when we were clearing and planting pine slips and crowns, all of us, Lauriette as well, toiled away, and we felt good at the end of each day. Customarily, we'd take a swim, from a small sandy stretch that lay between her house and ours. Nobody had a bathing suit, but wore a pair of pants or so, and Lauriette swam in her shift, brassy as ever.

The sand played out within fifty feet from shore, and gave way to mushy bottom, going into flats, but a channel ran along shore here and made a basin four or five feet deep for swimming. After a hot day it was fine to wallow in that water, for it came in from the ocean, and always was cool. But you had to watch out for Portuguese Men-of-War; one stung Zeb and left a line of welts clear across his chest. It was four hours before they went down. He said if it occurred again he'd go back to Grassy, and claimed it happened from being talked into swimming. He said he'd stayed clear of water all his life, and now he was eaten up by a sea monster. Uncle Jim got sick of his yowling, but Lauriette put some aloes on his welts and they finally quit hurting. But he wouldn't admit it.

Sharks seldom showed up here, because the porpoises chased them away. It was hard to understand why a shark, with all of his teeth, and an appetite like a hyena, could be so bulldozed by a porpoise, but it was a fact. Two porpoises and a shark had a fight directly in front of our house one day, leaping and thrashing out of the water, and the shark made off to sea as soon as it could be arranged.

We kept our boat in a little harbor that lay in mangroves around the bend from a drain. To reach it, we must cross land undeveloped and unclaimed, but it only required a short walk down the beach. Mr. Prindle said he would teach us to handle it like experts, so as "to boat" when necessary, but in the meantime, he advised us to get an eighteen-footer, as the other families had, for fishing and use on the shallow Bay side.

So one day when the planting was well along, and the weather too rainy to do more, he sailed Uncle Jim and me to Key West, and a negro named Whiskers, with both a goatee and a moustache, contracted to build us an eighteen-foot centerboard skiff. Whiskers made all the boats in Key West, and was famous. He was also what they called temperamental, like fiddle players and plumbers, and was apt to go into a sulk if a cedar plank turned up with a knot in it. Then he'd sit on a stool in his boatyard and gaze out to sea, holding his chin in his hand. And if somebody suggested, cautious and timid-like, that he might get back to work, he'd say "I'se retired." But he built wonderful boats; they all turned out just right.

25

MR. PRINDLE reminded me of Mr. Skaggs. He was small and wiry and burned as dark as teak, with creases running every which way in his leathery skin, and he had false teeth that a boat had brought him from New York. They were so white they jumped at you out of his face.

He was always smiling. He was about the hardest working and best natured man I ever met, and Uncle Jim said so, too. There wasn't any heft to him; he couldn't have stood over five feet six, and his arms were just strings of sinew, under their tan. But he could lift fallen trees and coral rocks and things that even Zeb had to toil over. It was done by leverage, said Dr. Snodgrass, and by conditioning.

The harder Mr. Prindle worked, the better humor he was in, and nobody could impose on him enough. In age, he was about sixty, to his wife's thirty, but his hair was black and so was his beard, when it grew out for a day or two. He talked like Mr. Skaggs, only not ornery but joking, and had exactly the same kind of spryness. He wore a pair of pants made out of thin canvas, a blue shirt and a cap with a bill to it. I wondered how his face had got so burned with that long bill sticking out to protect it, but he said in his youth his cap had often blown off at sea.

He was perfectly happy to admit that his ancestors had done a right smart of "privateering," and he himself had been a very successful wrecker, mainly in the years between 1850 and 1860, when 500 wrecks, or an average of one a week, piled up on the Key reefs. In this, he was different from the other Conch families, who disliked all talk of pirates and wrecking, and seemed trying to live it down. Uncle Jim said it was silly, because both trades had been respectable at the time, and still were, in his view. Not *all* the families had pirates in them, you understand, but some did, and all were ashamed of it.

People often go just the opposite direction after things like that, I've noticed, and Dr. Snodgrass said there was "no temperance addict as fanatic as a reformed drunk." The upper Keys families, the very few that had settled into this wilderness by now, were the most honestly pious and churchy folk you'd care to meet. They held a meeting every Sunday in one or the other's home, and everybody had an organ. We went once in a while, and were welcomed, but the proceedings were so stiff and threatening, with references to the vengeance of the Lord, that I drew out. I said none of *my* family had been a pirate, and I hadn't any plan to be punished for those that had.

Most of the children were taught to play what was known as the "elmonica," because it was suitable for hymns, though raw, and one family had a "windjammer," which was a new-fangled kind of piano that a person worked with his feet, and sounded like it. They all sang, too, in that kind of falsey tone that people use in church, and several men laid back and brayed like jackasses. If pure noise could get you into Heaven, these Conchs already had a berth nailed down.

Once in a while a traveling preacher, a sourish-looking skeleton from Connecticut, named Hoskins, with exactly the opposite kind of face from the ones I'd seen of Jesus —drawn down at the mouth, smouldering eyes under overhanging cliffs of shrubbery, a high, thin nose kind of blue around the edges—came down from Key West on a boat and spent a month visiting from house to house. Except ours. We hadn't got room yet, praise the Lord, so we didn't have to put up with the old badger. But we generally went on Sunday to wherever he was preaching, because Uncle Jim said it would show me what kind of man not to grow into.

During these sessions when Hoskins was there, a particular effort was made to lasso up some converts, mainly among the children, because no other candidates were living here, and they generally picked on me. It must have been something about my expression. The fact is, I think Uncle Jim took us mainly to watch me squirm.

They had a regular church organization, with deacons and other equipment, and made a practice of passing the plate, for it was the idea of the Conch families to build a church by and by. They had a very nice wooden plate, attached to a long pole and lined with green velvet, that somebody had found in the sea after a wreck, or maybe before it broke apart, and they stuck it under your nose during organ pieces, when you were softened up. I couldn't see any benefits in having a church; just the opposite, I reckoned they would double up on me after it was done, but I contributed to the collection just the same. We all did. I gave them an envelope containing a frog one Sunday, and another time put in a water-soaked deck of cards I'd found with the Queen of Clubs missing, but Uncle Jim made me take it out.

Anyhow, this Hoskins pounced on me about the second Sunday after our planting was finished, and it seemed to me the roughest session I'd put in lately. They held church at a house up to Tavernier, which was the next big Key upward from us, and very appropriate, too, because it had been a main place for pirates once, with a tavern where they hung out, so maybe the wickedness was still in the air, Uncle Jim said.

We rode up in the Prindles' smack, a nice trip on a pretty day, not so warm, and while they were putting a few hymns in their place, this Reverend Hoskins sidles up to me and says, "Son, it's time you gave yourself to Christ. Are you ready?"

They had several rows of chairs arranged out on the lawn, under some trees, and the organ sitting to one side, in front.

Well, there was another boy somewhat younger suffering beside me, and I thought maybe Hoskins was talking to him; leastways I hoped so, so I kept quiet, but shifted to look over some people's heads at a square-rigged schooner passing along in the ocean, far out—a beautiful ship, headed for Key West, probably.

But it was perfectly useless, as I knew all the time, because the old buzzard joggled my elbow and said impatiently, bending over, "Son, Christ needs you. And you need Christ. 'Suffer ye little children to come unto me.' Yonder are the waters that cleanse—" I started to get up, here, because I thought he was directing me to take a swim, and was obliged for it, but he pushed me back down and said, "—and purify. Sprinkling, that is, *not* total immersion. Son, come to the front and be saved!"

Well, it was a long speech; he'd worked on it, and deserved an answer, so I made one. I said, "Sir?"

I could feel Uncle Jim stir a little behind me, being likely uncomfortable, because not all of these chairs were in first-class condition, but had got busted up a little while floating to shore off of wrecks.

"Are you ready for the blood of the lamb?" Reverend Hoskins shouted over the hymn, right in my ear. If he'd raised his voice two more notches, he'd a deefened me.

There was a fly on my ankle, one of those big green ones that leave a welt, and I took a whack at it with my right hand. I got it, too, though late, and held it up for him to see, knowing he'd be glad *he* didn't have to deal with it in the middle of his sermon, but he only looked disgusted.

"*Are* you ready?" he said. "Or *aren't* you, by Jehosophat!"

"Sir?"

"What I said was, and I think you heard me, are you coming up to the front? Or do you intend to go on shilly-shallying? In short, I repeat: *Are* you ready?"

"Well," I said, rubbing my ankle, "I guess not. Not today, that is. I've got this fly bite, and my mind's kind of on that. No, I wouldn't want to mislead you—I'm not ready."

He must have been out of sorts (for he *was* a godly man, and neither drank nor gambled, nor did anything that was fun), because he turned away with a snort that caused everybody to swivel around and stare. It was mortifying. Preachers at their worst are about as hard to deal with as any people I know.

Reverend Hoskins came out strong on his sermon, and left little hope for anybody at that particular meeting. Uncle Jim said it was pretty threadbare preaching, and made no sense, but he was always warped in his judgment on these things. *He* didn't care for church, so it couldn't be good, and the same went for preachers.

Me, I enjoyed it, and tried to follow the arguments, but got tangled up in the bushes from time to time, and had to hack my way out. The Reverend took his text from the Book of Nahum, Chapter I, which he said stated the Lord's case better than any other place in the Bible, and put it, as he claimed, in words that a dunce could comprehend. It didn't sound very complimentary, as he stood looking at this Keys bunch on the lawn, but it was out of my hands, and anyway, everybody seemed satisfied.

He bawled out his message, as threatening as possible, and told about God being jealous and revengeful and angry and furious all the time, and then read about the mountains quaking and the earth burning, yea, the world, and all that dwell therein.

Well, I didn't entirely believe it, because the world seemed very pleasant most of the time, so how could God be mad at it? But I wanted to see the mountains quake, of course—a person always likes to get in on things like that—so I nudged Lauriette and asked her where it went on. She told me to shut up and said I was the "only wholly committed fool" she'd ever met. She shushed me so loud a number of people turned around and glared.

Then he got off on John, though he failed to mention his last name. This John was Reverend Hoskin's favorite Biblical character because he didn't do *any*thing but rant and rave.

We were told about the scheming 'publicans (meaning Republicans, I reckoned, for Hoskins often got twisted up on such words) that gathered to hear John preach, being the first time they'd ever knocked off business, or politics, to listen for the "still inner life," which struck me as curious, because John's life was nothing but an outrageous uproar from start to finish.

Anyhow, if you asked me, his preaching came a long way from taking hold, for these Republicans were still scheming, as nasty as ever, and only lately had seized control of several districts in Kentucky that had been run, and milked decently, by Democrats for over fifty years.

Reverend Hoskins said John put in his best licks among such scum and especially among the Pharisees and Seducers. He came down on *that* bunch like a lightning bolt, and baptized the whole works. This John had a mania about baptizing. To him, a man a hundred per cent dry was a personal insult; he couldn't wait to drive him to water. Everywhere he went, his system was to scare everybody half to death, then soak them before they recovered.

Reverend Hoskins showed how John's methods of blood and thunder were superior to Jesus's. "Why, the Bible tells us that Christ baptized no more than 120 people in His entire career," he said. "What do you think of *that?*"

I couldn't make up my mind. It was puzzling. Jesus had gone around, poor gentle man, talking quietly, preaching about kindness and charity and good deeds and saying that God was love. But no sooner had he got everybody soothed down and aiming to live a quiet life than this old crabapple, John, stumped along and prodded them up fit to explode. He undid everything, it seemed to me. God wasn't love, if you listened to John; He was a holy terror. Why, you take the average worshipper, he wouldn't wait around to get burned up, or have a mountain quake on him; he'd dig out a new religion and *relax*.

No, John may have baptized all the Republicans, as they said, which was a very good thing, and needed, but he was nothing more than a noisy nuisance, the way I saw it.

Then Reverend Hoskins made a few remarks about a man named Doubting Thomas, who didn't believe anything, never had and never could, and was known for it amongst his neighbors. There was nothing wrong with him otherwise, you understand. He was a good, affectionate soul, but whatever you told him he refused to swallow it. It was raspy, and caused a lot of bad feeling. For example, Jesus stepped up and said he was planning to Resurrect. It was common knowledge among the twelve Epistles; none of *them* doubted it, but what did Thomas do? He said on the order of, "It's very likely, ain't it? Oh, yes, it happens every day, but I'd feel a deal more comfortable if you'd bring up some *proof!*" And he said it with pretty much of a sneer, that would make another man sore. If it had been anybody else but Jesus, he might have knocked him down.

Well, I've known a lot of people like that. It was on the order of a fellow back in Kentucky, that when somebody said, pointing, "There's a handsome white horse," replied, "Well, at least *this* side's white." Such trash never amount to much, and neither did Thomas. Frankly, I never figured out how he got in the Bible.

Hoskins could easily have dropped that part of his sermon, and nobody would have missed it.

But the dinner that noon and the games they played afterward made everything up. These were sensible people, not *entirely* devoted to hell-fire, and believed in having a merry time. And wasn't the food good! A lot of it came out of the sea, but not all.

First off, they had big crockery bowls full of a very steamy chowder made out of pieces cut from tarpon stomachs, from egrets and from spoonbills, and then platters of grunts (as well as groupers) and grits, cooked till the meat was falling off in white chunks, Johnny cake, sweet potato bread, sweet corn—just heaps of it, roasted out-of-doors—along with fried chicken and lobster, and pickled tarpon, too. For drinks they had coffee; nobody drank *aguardiente* here on Sunday, even Uncle Jim, till he got home, and then he had a double noggin, "to get back down to earth," as he said.

Nobody could deny that these Conchs worked hard—they had to if they wanted to live—and they laid into that food as if they hadn't been fed since last Sunday. Uncle Jim said it was religious in tone, with special reference to the preacher. That old cadaver threw aside his testament, rolled up his sleeves, and gnawed clean a space about four feet around him in every direction. A wolf couldn't a done a better job. It reminded you of the way locusts sawed through crops in Egypt, while the Christians were writing the Bible there in chains. I personally saw three or four people edge out of the way, to keep clear of Hoskins' knife and fork, because it was dangerous to be within harpoon range while that kind of fit was on him. And to do him credit, the blessing he'd asked first was only about half a sentence long, broke off right in the middle, so as to give him a chance, unexpected, to spear the fattest chicken breast, which of course was sensible, and moral, too, because if he hadn't kept his strength up, where would this group of Conchs be? And nobody minded, either, but sang out "Praise the Lord!" and "Amen!" and took the next best pieces without raising hardly any howl whatever. They were a fair-minded and very well-mannered bunch; I liked them all.

In the afternoon, a lot of grown-ups played games along with the children. They disbelieved in dancing on Sunday, or thieving, or murder, though they'd knock off praying and help a wrecked captain save his cargo, minus the percentage for salvage (if they couldn't get the whole ship), but they frolicked around like puppies after this Sunday's dinner. There was no harm in it; it served to perk them up and offset the sermon. The family here had a "flying horse," which was a tree cut off about ten feet high, with a bolt in the top, and ropes you could whirl around on. The children enjoyed it, and several lost their dinners.

They played ring-on-a-stick, and cakewalk, with co-coanut cakes for prizes, and had lemonade with the cake, later on. All of these games were fun, and the truth is, I admired all the Conch customs. They were suited to the life there. I remembered at Belle Mead we were given bladders to blow up for Christmas, but here the children played Santa Claus by jingling around with a bag full of cans. Things were different in different regions; worth noting.

We sailed home before twilight, and agreed that we'd had a fine day. Zeb made the acquaintance of several families of Bahama darkies, and promised to treat them for diseases and witchery the first time they were both-ered that way, and Dr. Snodgrass presented a free case of Spooju to a widow who was troubled with absomnier, which is what Uncle Jim said was not being able to sleep at night because of taking a two-hour nap in the after-noon. Dr. Snodgrass didn't have the medicine with us, of course, but promised to deliver it after the next big rain-fall got the cisterns back up to normal.

On the way home, Mr. Prindle asked if I'd like to fish with him. He fished twice a week for the family, and I could lend a hand and supply us that way.

The following morning before dawn, we went out in his flat-bottom skiff, sailing to the ocean side because the breeze was spanking up very smart in the Bay. First, we tried for what he called "floating fish," on the order of mackerel or kingfish, trolling with feather-covered hooks, then we hauled up bottom fish from the reef—groupers and grunts and yellow-tail and mutton snapper and such. It was sprightly but tired out your arms—those bottom fish run *heavy;* still, it was lovely out there a mile or two offshore, with a soft, pearly dawn coming up and the sweet-smelling land breeze fresh on your cheek. Down below, the reef flashed with color, rolling under us as we sailed, and the blue-black Stream moved along out beyond, with maybe a stick or two showing above the curve, where sailing ships lay hull down, partly hidden by the bulge of the earth.

Using cut fish for bait, we pulled up a mutton snapper that weighed more than fifty pounds, and we caught groupers almost as big.

About eleven o'clock the sharks swarmed around and the breeze eased off, so we sailed back to clean fish. Mr. Prindle already had gutted them because of the sun—sliced them nice and clean down the stomachs with a long thin knife and hauled out the red and purple gut-coils, heart, yellow liver, and sometimes roe in fat strips. After we landed and cleaned them, we went over to a mangrove Key in the Bay after crawfish. In some places they were piled up three or four feet deep; you wouldn't have believed it.

These crawfish were called lobsters by most, but Uncle Jim said they were inferior to restaurant lobsters he'd eaten that came from cold-water places like Maine. He said everything in New England was cold, especially the people's attitude toward spending money. Crawfish were tasty, though, and once in a while, on a bright moonlight night, they crawled right up on the beaches, or what strips of sand as you occasionally found in these Keys. Then the people walked out and got them by holding sticks to their backs and picking them up. Sea food was so plenteous in these Keys that you practically had to beat it off with clubs. A favorite saying among these families, a kind of joke, was "How about fish for dinner?"

When the tide flowed at night, we hung seines and caught all manner of fish as well as hundreds and hundreds of shrimp that scuttled over the bottom in the channels. They made good bait, but they were fine eating, too, though for some reason the Conchs didn't favor them. We boiled shrimps, then peeled off the shells and ate them like nuts. Still, they did leave a powerful stink in the house, after the boiling, so maybe that was why they weren't popular.

Every two weeks, Mr. Prindle sailed his smack to Cape Sable to go turtling, leaving his wife and nine daughters to garden. I took to going with him; we stayed over night, and always came back with a load. Turtles didn't crawl in the Keys, on account of no beaches, of course, but Cape Sable had a broad strip of sand running for miles, and was choice for egg-laying. It was so simple, it came close to being pitiful. Turtles crawl at night, and leave tracks that a near-sighted mole could follow.

Usually, we dug as many as twenty-dozen eggs, and got a number of bird eggs, too, which Mr. Prindle hated to do, he said, but the family had to eat, and we bagged three or four green turtles every trip—big fellows weighing up to two hundred pounds. Each turtle's nest has upwards of a hundred eggs in it, so if you locate two or three, you've got all the eggs you can use. The women cooked turtles and "pickled them down"—large hunks in oak barrels full of brine. It was the same way they pickled tarpon, which were harpooned in winter, if possible, when they were fat and "had gone to bed." And if somebody *did* run into a big school of sluggish winter tarpon rolling, he'd lay in sufficient for the community. There wasn't hardly any end to what these Conchs had learned to do about living in the Keys.

Well, Pounce de Lion named them Los Martires, saying they looked "desolate," but our life here was full and rich. We were busy all the time.

Sometimes, now, Zeb worked at our place, and sometimes at Lauriette's, and occasionally he stayed there, in a lean-to room they'd built on the back. He liked her, and called her Missy, and she had a curious kind of respect for him that had to do with Uncle Jim, Dr. Snodgrass said.

One night late, with the wind howling in from the sea, and lightning squirting around, too, which was rare—a perfect ripper of a night—she came running down the beach in a robe, crying, and said Zeb was dying. I heard a pounding on our front door, and opened it, and there she was, bedraggled and hystorical but looking pretty as always.

"Quick! Come quick! Zebediah's having some kind of fit. He's dying. Get Dr. Snodgrass up, and hurry!"

Well, it was a sorry predicament, because no matter how we liked him, Dr. Snodgrass wasn't anything but a medicine man, and not a doctor.

I could tell by the way Uncle Jim hustled into his clothes he was scared, for once, and Dr. Snodgrass dressed in two minutes, white as chalk, but with a set look around his mouth, as though he'd die rather than flinch away from this task, which must have been painful. He looked almost noble, with his beautiful mane of hair and light blue eyes, and erect carriage in his cutaway coat.

It startled me when we ran up the beach that he left his medicines behind—took nothing but a bottle of rum —but I reckoned he'd decided to hark back to his college years, without all the fakery.

Zeb lay on his cot, naked, mouth open and some froth coming out of the corners, with his eyes rolled up till you could see nothing but white. He made moany noises, and his limbs kept stiffening then loosening up.

"Zeb, old friend, what is it?" cried Uncle Jim, cradling up his head. "What's happened here, Doctor?"

It was the least humbuggy I ever saw Dr. Snodgrass act. He got down and listened to his chest, then felt his pulse, and examined his eyes, and whilst he was moving his head, a black scorpion six inches long slid off Zeb's neck and made for the wall.

Lauriette screamed, and Uncle Jim leaped over the bed to stomp it. We'd been warned to be very careful of these creatures, but had forgot. A big one could kill you in no time, if it bit you near the head.

Dr. Snodgrass told us to hold his jaws, then he reached in and pulled out Zeb's tongue, which had swoll up as big as a calf's. It was horrible.

"Pulse low and thready, very," said Dr. Snodgrass. "We're too late. He's dying."

"He *can't* be!" cried Uncle Jim. "It's all my fault. Zeb, Zeb, can you hear me? I ask you to forgive me."

The darky flickered his eyes for a moment, then gasped out, "What is it, Mistuh Jim? I ain't a-going?"

"Zeb, old friend, you're going back to Grassy," said Uncle Jim, crying. But after he'd said it, Zeb was unconscious again, with another fit at work, and the way he gnashed his jaws was pitiful. If Dr. Snodgrass hadn't put a knotted towel between his teeth, he'd have bitten off his tongue.

"By God, you claim to be a doctor!" cried Uncle Jim, springing up with the worst flash in his eyes I ever saw. "What's all your voodoo worth now?"

Then what happened was the best and most sublimest moment of my life, from the time I was born until now. I don't claim to understand it; and neither does anybody else, and Dr. Snodgrass least of all. He tried to tell us later he'd known for many years that he had a healing power in his hands, a sort of mysterious flow between him and some sick people, but he felt so humble about it, and cringed so before it, that he turned to the brassy sale of nostrum medicines instead.

He straightened up, not even hearing Uncle Jim, and said, "Go outside, all of you, and wait."

Standing in the doorway, with the storm about to break over our heads, we watched him bend down on one knee and say, "Lord, I ask thy aid to heal this good and faithful man," and then, "Zebediah, feel my hands upon you. You are free of pain, the poison leaves, God will restore you to your friends."

He knelt there, with one hand on Zeb's forehead and another on his shoulder, and I daren't even breathe, it was that solemn.

A minute passed by, then Zeb stirred and said, "Ain't that you, Dr. Snodgrass? I'se thirsty."

Well, it wasn't something you cheered about, but only felt thankful for, and awed by, and maybe felt strange, too. And I don't think Uncle Jim ever regarded Dr. Snodgrass quite the same again; it was the first time he'd seen something he couldn't toss off with a joke.

Since then, I've come to know that there *are* such people, with gifts outside the human limits. I read where Alexander Dumas, the French-darky writer, could lay on hands to allay pain; he had what they called "magnetic," or "odylic," or "hypnotic" powers. And once, I remember, they brought a boy to school, a traveling ragamuffin clutching some worn-out clippings about himself, and there wasn't anything the schoolmaster could write on the blackboard that he failed to solve in his head, just by looking. Dozens of rows of addition, with ten or eleven numbers each, or long division up in the millions. I was there, and saw it. It was all correct, right down to the last decimal; the Mayor was on hand, and helped check it, though what he knew about it, you could put in a hollow tooth. He couldn't hardly more than make change.

And after that they took the boy to Danville College, where he performed what they called logyrithms, and cube roots, and worse, and he told the answers right off, without blinking. Other than that, he was fuzzy in the head about ordinary things, and remembered only that in his babyhood his mother had "visions," and often awoke him late at night, and scared him.

The funny thing about Dr. Snodgrass was, you couldn't call him a religious man in general. He never mentioned religion, or God, but seemed uneasy about it. And he had no recollection, afterward, of what he said in the lean-to.

When you think it over, great musicians and people like that aren't human, altogether, but have a "gift," as they say. I reckon there are different kinds, and Dr. Snodgrass's was one of the rarest.

Somewhere deep inside him lay a bright pool of healing waters. He had a strength that baffled him more than anyone, but we were mighty glad, because it gave us back our old Zeb. As for Uncle Jim, he never said "*Doc*tor" in that mocky way again; a change had taken place—it was maybe the beginning of believing in something for Uncle Jim.

26

<hr/>

WITH OUR HOUSES all done, besides a coral-walled basin built for a small harbor in front, and the pineapple slips down, our money was very low, so Uncle Jim said it was time to search out the treasure. I've never figured out to this day how he managed to wait so long.

He got out his map, which he'd carried all this time in a waterproof pouch, and we studied it over. Printed in a coarse, bold hand, the directions said (as I told in the early chapters): "Directly north of natural pot-hole well," but there was more. The map itself, very crude-drawn, had what I knew now were the main Keys islands strung out in their arc; and the cross that marked the spot was near what appeared to be Lower Matecumbe. We lived on Upper Matecumbe, one step closer to the mainland.

"See here," said Uncle Jim, as we examined the document, all of us, on our kitchen table, "let's fetch Prindle. That family's been a little more than good to us, and if there's treasure to be lifted, I'd like them in on it. Better yet, he knows these mangroves like the back of his hands."

So we did it, got him in from his fields—he was perfectly willing to come; he'd of obliged just as quick if we'd asked him to carry us to Cuba, and without asking any questions either.

"Prindle," said Uncle Jim when Zeb brought him in, "I'll make no bones about this—it's a treasure map. I took it off a rascal in the Mexican War, this young lady's brother and I, and I think it originally came from the Bahamas. Intending no regional allusions to piracy, you understand. I mean us all to share and share alike."

Mr. Prindle was practically the only Conch we knew who thought the pirating background was funny. His father had skipped the tightrope betwixt piracy and wrecking, like most of them, and he took it in easy stride. He knew Mr. Skaggs, too, and admired him, and sounded like him sometimes, just as I said.

"Well," he said, gazing it over close, "there ain't any hargument over it; oil-skin, so they always done, and the Keys laid out as pretty as marbles. I'll 'elp you dig, and 'appy; I'd welcome a wacation from soil bustin'."

"Did you ever hear of a place called Teach's Cove?" said Uncle Jim. "It's mentioned here."

"Yes," said Mr. Prindle, growing excited. "I mind my hunkle telling me once—they scudded in under lee of land, and a ship throwed in sight—'ostile, and run them off. He called it Teach's Cove. Hit were before we took up here permanent."

"Can you find it?"

"I mind another time—there was a wreck near there; we was two days to her. I wasn't more'n a sprig."

"Where is it?"

We looked the map over, and Mr. Prindle slewed it this way and that, making the compass-rose at the top point true north. "Line of dots from Teach's Cove, land with an inlet running through highest ground, with five ironwood trees shaped in a—why, it's Lignum Vitey drain! And Lignum Vitey Key. I recollect it now."

"Anybody living there?"

"Hit's a low swale, that and Lower Matecumbe both. Once you've rounded up the fiddlers, and shooed off the birds, you've got hit alone. But it's mortal brushy."

Uncle Jim rubbed his hands together, with a high flush on his cheek. This was right in his line; he was satisfied, because there was action going on.

"Are you game? First thing tomorrow morning, counting on the weather."

"I'll lay outside in my schooner, and skiff ashore to take on 'ands. Hit makes mention of, let's see—'bar silver, julery settings and loose stones.' Why, I wouldn't never have to strike another lick!"

"Well, we won't count our chickens," said Uncle Jim,

"but we've got a good chance, a wonderful chance." He began to hum, then sang, "Oh, the rubies grow big as pineapples, on Lignum Vitey Key," and caught up Lauriette to dance. She turned scarlet, and said, breaking free, "What a schoolboy you are!"

"Yes," said Uncle Jim, looking rueful, "I am. It's been my curse, and cost me dear."

"There comes a time when we're supposed to grow up, or so I was told."

It was embarrassing, to have Uncle Jim rated by this snappish female, and right on top of another like it, as Dr. Snodgrass said. Of late weeks, Lauriette had fined down some; her face had just a faint sharpness to it. She was lovely and golden-blond, but she'd maybe been wrong about having enough to do here.

Nobody knew what to say, but looked at the floor rather than Uncle Jim. I'd seen him used so before. While a loose-jawed man might land in the cemetery, women could shame him by a look.

But for once he behaved very unexpected.

"I must make a note to grow up and earn your respect," he said, and putting his hands just under her breasts, bulging them up almost out of her blouse, he lifted her off of the floor and kissed her flush on the mouth. He did a good job of it, spraddling her out against him in a grasp that must have left marks on her ribs. Dr. Snodgrass said later it was probably the first time in Uncle Jim's life he ever acted toward a well brought-up girl as he might in a Bourbon Street crib, whatever that meant.

Anyhow, she slapped him, when he finally let her down, but there wasn't any sting in it. Then she burst into tears and ran out of the house. It was about what I figured. If Uncle Jim insisted on taking liberties with a sassy tyrant like that, he'd have to suffer the consequences.

"You see?" he said, rubbing his face. "Whatever I do, it's always wrong. It wouldn't make any difference."

"Begging your pardon," said Dr. Snodgrass, "but I suggest that your present methods were, if not perfectly suited to the occasion, then a trifle on the mild side. Speaking (*sans* modesty), as a one-time familiar of a variety of the opposite sex, with several imbedded posterior birdshot to prove it, nothing can be too, er, direct, or, as it were, vulgar, if you follow my meaning."

"I'll stick to farming," said Uncle Jim. "That icy directness freezes my marrow. And to come right out and tell you the truth, intelligent females always did rub me the wrong way. Women should be felt and not heard."

It was the only time I ever heard him make an uncourteous reference to them. But I didn't blame him in this case.

Not long after dawn the next day, Mr. Prindle's boat flapped to anchor in deep water out in front—our harbor was for the flatbottom sail-skiff; we still kept our own schooner around a drain on the Bay side—and in a minute we heard the steady working of oars in rowlocks; then he crunched his dinghy up on the beach.

Sailing to the channel between Lower and Upper Matecumbe, so as to get through to Lignum Vitey (which lay on the Bay side, within sight of the main chain) Mr. Prindle said there was a deep-water stretch about midway between the Matecumbes that, at high tide, ran as much as seventeen feet on around the right side of Lignum Vitey, between two banks, or flats. It was unusual, in this place of extreme shallows. He said we could lie off the Key and skiff in, or, at high tide, go clear on up and careen. He preferred to anchor in the deep water, because otherwise we'd have to wait till the next high tide and hand-kedge the schooner off.

He seemed as feverish as Uncle Jim, but Lauriette was pale and untalkative after her outburst of yesterday. It didn't bother me any. I'd taken a lot of her sauce on the trip down, and so had the Seminoles, and while she was a good and forceful person, she was too high-handed for any practical use. It was the way she was raised. If she lifted a finger, three or four people always sprang up to see what she wanted. Says I to myself, let her stew awhile.

Mr. Prindle was familiar with all the pirates in these parts, way back before he was born, and said if Teach, who they called Blackbeard, had hid treasure here, it was bound to be a considerable sum. But Mr. Prindle hoped it was part of Morgan's plunder; *his* takings, calculated in a newspaper, ran high: a million and a half from the sack of Panama, nearly a million each from Porto Bello and Puerto del Principe, and about half that from Maracaibo and Gibraltar, aside from what he took off ships. It all came out fine, too, because that monster, instead of being punished, got himself knighted by King Charles II, retired from murder, and was appointed Governor of Jamaica! But they do say he never got a chance to lift his bloody treasure, and of course that was good for us.

Tortuga, a little island off Santo Domingo, was the chief place where most of these fine-feathered rogues holed up for awhile; from it, they swooped down on the shipping that passed along the Bahama Channel to the West Indies and the Spanish Main, which was the northern coast of Spanish America. The real ones, that is, in the old days.

Well, the *Dry* Tortugas (which were named from being shaped like a turtle, and had a good harbor) became pretty popular, too; they were nothing but an extension of our Key chain. And then, Key Vaca had *its* day as a stopping place; that whole general area of the Caribbean swarmed with pirates.

It was curious to me that those scoundrels got their name of buccaneer from a process of meat-curing called "buccanning," which was cutting it in thin strips, then salting, smoking and drying it in the sun. The first boat-loads of rovers discovered the island of Hispaniola, or Santo Domingo, and found great numbers there of wild cattle, horses and swine. Well, vessels revictualling for the return voyage to Europe needed flesh, and the free-roaming gentlemen of fortune worked out a second profit in rounding up animals for buccanning. Usually, the animals were taken to Tortuga, a very wild and unclaimed spot, and one, of course, that lay near four-fifths of the Spanish-Indian trade.

Mr. Prindle could hold out for Morgan; as for me, Mr. Edward Teach would do. That old rip *was* a real one—face covered with a black bush "like a frightful meteor," as a historian said, and parts of it twisted into small tails, like a wig; wearing a sling over his shoulder with three brace of pistols; with lighted matches stuck under his hat during a fight, so that, according to a witness, "imagination cannot form an idea of a Fury from hell to look more frightful."

He picked up a sight of money, too, and accompanied it all to the tune of as many murders as he could manage. Everybody agreed on that; Mr. Edward Teach—Blackbeard—probably enjoyed killing his fellow creatures as much as anybody that ever lived. He got command of a privateering sloop, then overhauled one vessel after another. How such a demon of a human being could win a pretty young wife was a mystery to all, but he did, and when somebody asked him if that poor, ill-treated girl knew where his treasure was, he said, with some appropriate oaths, "No; nobody but the Devil and I know where it is, and the longest liver shall have all."

Well, it turned out to be the Devil, because the United States Government got mighty sick of this fellow, and set out to get him. You could hardly blame them. Of all the pirates anywhere, he was the champion for impudence and wickedness.

Why, he laid off the bar of Charleston Harbor for six days, blockading the port, stopping all incoming and outgoing vessels, plucking off this nabob and that to be a "prisoner of war," and having a merry old time, with his black flag bearing the white skull and crossbones fluttering right under the noses of the city.   But at last there came along a quiet, unferocious young Navy lieutenant named Maynard, commanding the *Pearl,* and chased the villian up Okracoke Inlet in North Carolina and made some modest preparations for a fight.

To give the old rapscallion credit, Teach stuck his black bush over the side, when he saw Maynard intended business where all others had quailed, and drained off a glass of grog, then wished him "luck in getting aboard."

Not to go on about it, they closed in for hand-to-hand fighting, pistol and cutlass, and Mr. Edward Teach Blackbeard died, carrying five bullets and twenty cutlass cuts, as he was trying to discharge an empty pistol. He was a rip-roarer, and no mistake.

Lieutenant Maynard finished the fight with his cutlass

broke off at the hilt; perfectly unemotional but aiming only to collect his lieutenant's pay (which would likely buy about a double handful of salt). He said the encounter had been "very interesting," and he was glad it was over. Even for the Navy, it had turned out to be an unusually stiff day's work.

Well, if we were after Blackbeard's treasure, I was glad, because it seemed to me *some*body should get some good out of a man so totally and joyously bad.

It was another warm day. The sun lay up there as white and big and flat as a disc of melted-hot silver. It was closer than it should be; there wasn't any way to get away from it.

We sailed into the main channel between the Matecumbes, with Mr. Prindle being wonderfully nimble about the boat, (like Mr. Skaggs), and worked it up off Lignum Vitey, then plopped down the anchor. We swung to the tide, and looked ashore, each wondering what it might bring.

It was a pretty island, not so low as Mr. Prindle said, and I wondered if he'd ever landed there. It rose up like a green potted plant with dry crookedy gray mangrove roots crawling round most of the edge; a big island, big enough to bury treasure on and not have somebody stumble over it right off.

"Well," said Mr. Prindle, startling us out of our reflections, "we've harrived. Yonder's a break in the mangrove —a little beach, like, or cove. We can land."

Though shining green and handsome, the place had something broody about it. Maybe it was all of those people that had to be killed, and ships sunk, before we were brought to this moment.

But here we were, and we skiffed ashore in two loads. The sand was coarse and mushy, with the tide just off it, and mullet were jumping around the bend, in a quiet pool. It was one of those days when they all jump; nobody knows why. You could fix your gaze on a spot and if you watched long enough, a slim, silvery shape would rise out of the water, slightly arched, ever so graceful, like a circus acrobat, and fall back in with a merry splash.

Mr. Prindle had brought a bush knife, and Zeb had the picks and shovels. The rest of us carried gunny sacks, but that seemed like stretching it pretty thin to me. There was such a thing as pushing your luck; we could easy have gone back for the treasure, if we found any, and left a man to guard.

Well, right off, we flushed a rattlesnake out of that undergrowth that must have measured six feet long. He slithered out like a streak and wriggled himself *into the water*. Don't let anybody tell you a rattlesnake won't swim. Or bite you when he's doing it. A man down to Key West, a stranger from the North, and a bonehead, swam out, drunk, to scoop one swimming offshore and was bit in the thumb. He'd made a brag how he could do it but he didn't look so pert when they hauled him in. And they had to shuffle to save his life, for he'd thrashed around and pumped the poison all through him.

That was the first setback we had, because Zeb threw down his tools and said, "I ain' fixin to go dig where they's rattling snakes. Snake take and have the treasure; he can put rings on he tail. You find me settin on boat when you git through. *If* you git through."

"Now look here," said Uncle Jim peevishly, swatting a mosquito on his neck, "don't choose this time to play granny. We've got riches almost in our hands—your hands, too—so pick up those spades. You don't see Miss Lauriette crying fraidy cat, do you?"

"You may," said Lauriette. "You just may. The whole expedition's preposterous. Blackbeard's treasure! It's nothing but a child's dream."

"Nobody claimed it was Blackbeard," said Uncle Jim. "The only reference to that fellow is the place-name, Teach's Cove. Personally, I think it was somebody long after—it could be any one of dozens."

Mr. Prindle soothed them over; he was one of those people who never actually take note that there's a dispute going on, but fix things up by ignoring it and shifting the subject slightly. He made several references to mosquitoes (which didn't bother him; his neck was too tough), and said he'd been meaning to carry half of the spades (and picked up two); then he recalled that a settler near

Tampa, digging a garden, had unearthed a wooden cask containing $26,000 in Spanish gold.

"They henjoyed it, as there was a 'eap of things they'd been pining to buy."

It was just that easy. I wondered if any combination of annoyances could get him out of sorts, and doubted it. He hadn't any meanness in him, or jealousy, or greed, or anything but good humor and enjoyment from everything around him. Cut him down to a stick of sugar cane a day and he'd find some reason to prove it was better than gorging.

We went on, studying the map in that bright hot sun. The oil-skin seemed to dance in Uncle Jim's hand.

"Teach's Cove was where we landed," he said. "It stands to reason—then there's the line of dots running south-southeast, according to the compass-rose. Hold on —what's this?"

He stooped down to examine a rock, lying free of trees, with a marking chipped on top.

Mr. Prindle practically did a jig of excitement.

"Hit's a symbol—a turtle, so, with 'ead pointing forward, right in line."

"What kind of symbol? What for?"

Mr. Prindle appeared embarrassed. "I heard it said pirates hemployed them—all manner of, to point and steer."

We cleaned the rock off, and the turtle's outline stood out as fresh as paint, so:

The head lay south-southeast, sure enough; even Lauriette looked stirred up; her eyes shone. It's an odd thing what easy gold will do to people, including her that had never thought about money her whole life long. It's natural as a squirrel after nuts.

"You don't *really* suppose—" she began, but Uncle Jim snapped, "Of course, I do. See here, Prindle, old fellow, how many of these symbols do you know?"

Mr. Prindle coughed and said, "Why, in a general way, and honely happroximate—all, unless they've inwented new ones in the last twenty year."

"Then the line of dots is rocks. Push on! Great Scott —push on! Give me that knife."

In about five minutes, hacking away, we came to a little clearing, from which a cloud of white birds flapped off, squalling a protest, and another big rock lay there with several small chipped-in drawings:

Mr. Prindle looked uneasy.

"Sombreros, five, strung out artistic-like."

"Well, what is it? How do you read it?"

"Five buried treasure, or five died, afterwards. Sometimes one way, sometimes t'other."

"Well, we can't bring them back to life, poor devils, and in any case, they're *all* dust now, so don't let's moon about it. Follow the line of those hats."

He laid into the bushes again, and the next rock showed up in a hundred yards, a slab with three wavy lines:

"Buried near a stream, or 'ave to cross a stream to approach."

We waded over a tidal inlet not long afterward, and the land rose up so that we could knock off hacking. It was still as death, except for the flapping and shrilly crying noises of big white birds—herons and such—and black ones on the order of cormorants. They rose clumsy and slow from tree branches, and made off as though they could scarcely stay in the air. I said to myself, I'll be just as happy to get out of here.

The next rock, almost covered by creepers, had what Mr. Prindle said was a gourd—

—and meant either water or that the treasure was buried near a spring.

"Why, it's as plain as daylight!" cried Uncle Jim, holding up his map again, " '—directly north of natural pot-hole well.' It's set down here in black and white; a baby could follow it. We're closing in!"

I have to admit we were all bubbling over by now, no matter how dismal lonely and mournful the spot. We were so worked up, Zeb dropped the shovels again, but not on purpose this time, and even Mr. Prindle tripped on a vine and took a header into some coral sumac, which he said never bothered him at all, except for some itching at night. He was practically gibbering.

The next rock, the last, had a sign like this—

—which indicated that the treasure was buried either in a tunnel or a mine shaft, Mr. Prindle said. It was curious, and cooled down our spirits some.

When we'd pushed a few hundred yards further, we saw water again through the trees, but we were near high ground still, and there, in another tidal inlet, we stumbled across the pot-hole well. It was a wide pool in coral and looked deep, and as the tide now had run out, Mr. Prindle stuck his finger in and tasted it. So did I; it was fresh but brackish.

"Come on! Come on!" said Uncle Jim. "North up the slope. We can drink water any time."

"Not hexactly," said Mr. Prindle in a peculiar tone, and I remembered the talk of terrible droughts when the cisterns went dry.

But we scrambled up the slope like mad people, now, being this close, and Uncle Jim, in front, all but fell in a built well that gaped open, set around with perfectly chiseled rocks, maybe eight feet across—as handsome a job of masonry as you'd find in the tallest city.

"What in hades—"

He pulled himself back off the ledge, and we stared down. It was deep—thirty feet or so—and had a spiral stairway of stepping-stone rocks that went down around the sides. I never saw a finer piece of building. But a mound of old marl lay heaped up beside it, and on one of the ledge rocks was a sign:

"Underneath, gold underneath, down there," said Mr. Prindle on his hands and knees, pointing to the empty hole.

"We aren't whipped yet," Uncle Jim cried. "Down, boys—it may be there still. It's two to one they missed it."

I scrambled to the bottom right after him, and nothing was seen but a heavy iron chest with round studs all over it. It must have weighed half a ton, and was beautiful. It had hardly any rust at all.

"Locked tight," he called up. "I can't budge her; the treasure's still here, lads. But where's the keyhole?"

"Hit's likely to 'ave a combination," Mr. Prindle called down. "Take and move all the top studs, ever which way. Hi've seen similar!"

He climbed down, and we shoved and sweated in that dank hole, but they refused to budge. Then Mr. Prindle got Zeb to throw down a spade and we knocked at them, hard, from every direction.

"You've done it!" Uncle Jim cried. "Pull her open, boys, and shove your arms into jewels up to your elbows!"

When the stud slid over a couple of inches, a little groove of a handle could be seen beneath, and we threw open the heavy lid.

It was cleaned out; empty except for a smashed pipe stem and a broken silver ring mounting without a stone in it, worn thin.

We stared in hungrily for several moments, then Uncle Jim straightened up and said, "Well, it was a close run. If we'd landed here a hundred years sooner, we'd be as rich as Croesus."

But he was really disappointed; I could tell by the mocky flicker in his eyes and the way his mouth turned down just slightly at the corners. He needed that money; we were reduced to almost nothing, and I knew he'd die before he'd write to Aunt Effie for more. Grassy barely made out in these after-war years as it was.

And Lauriette, when we came up, looked at him in a soft, anxious sort of way, nearly in tears, but it was too embarrassing to say much, so we didn't say anything. That's always best, anyhow.

Instead, we examined the well, and they agreed it was built by Caloosa Indians hundreds of years ago, for use when the pot-hole went dry or filled with sea water, and that Spanish pirates stumbled on it while roistering ashore. They'd filled it up, after burying the treasure, of course, so it must have been much deeper, also built high to avoid hurricane seas washing in.

And then, by golly, Zeb, down in the bottom at last, after he'd been convinced no snakes were there, dug around with the spade and found two gold coins and a silver one, tarnished black. We were excited all over again, but he never located another, though he dug for more than an hour.

"They dropped them," said Uncle Jim. "You can afford to be careless when you're carrying up a million."

We never found a skeleton, either, so Mr. Prindle said the sombreros meant that five men buried the treasure, and not that anybody got killed. I was glad of that. It was maybe the only good feature of the day.

We made out from week to week, awaiting the pineapple crop. I fished with Mr. Prindle, and turtled, and now and then sailed in his small boat across the flats, finding the little winding drains, to Madeira Bay, in the Everglades, to get Madeira wood for boat ribs. That tree had roots which grew in the shape of ribs, down in the ground, so a man building a skiff was spared the trouble of steaming lumber into shape.

Whiskers made the real boats on the Keys in these early years, but our neighbors built their own skiffs.

Uncle Jim learned to sail our schooner, and went to Key West once a week, and sometimes he came home drunk. It was disturbing; it bothered us all. And he scarcely paid any attention to Lauriette. He was worried about money, for maybe the first time in his life, and his worry was for us, not himself. So he made it worse by drinking in the Cuban saloons.

Nobody else minded our life. Helped by the Prindles, we had enough. We always had food. Often Mr. Prindle and I sold fish or turtles to Key West, so raised cash for needed things. And we had vegetables from the garden, and fish from the sea, and fine loaves from our outdoor oven—the best you ever tasted. Even cooking them was fun.

The oven was built of rocks plastered with mud, nearly five feet high, with a big door in it. You built a fire, of button-wood or something like, then drew out the fire and put the bread in.

Even with the heat, it was best to bake at midday, for this was a bad mosquito year, they said. Mosquitoes swarmed in during the early morning, and again at night.

Soon after dawn we got up and lit smudge pots to stand in the doorways, so we could open up for the day. There were no screens, you see; everybody slept under mosquito bars, and the windows must be kept open, else you'd stifle to death on a hot, windless night.

A lot of the older Conchs used "insect powder" and set cans of it outside the doors and sprinkled it in the sand roundabout. They smoked considerable, too, and that helped, particularly with the kind of tobacco they used, which Uncle Jim said was dangerous to leave around if you had pets. It not only sent mosquitoes hiking; it would shoo off gulls, if they flew within a mile or two, he said. But that was stretching things maybe.

From some of our fish and turtle money, we bought chickens and a sow at Key West, and Lauriette stuck her oar in, as usual, being tiresome positive for anybody so ignorant, and acquired a cow off a ship. She said a growing boy (me) needed milk, and she couldn't think of only one other way to get it, which wasn't "practical"—coarse as usual.

Everybody warned her off, saying cows never thrived in the middle Keys, but she knew best, and bulled on ahead.

And sure enough, a week after we got it home—and an annoysome lot of trouble, too—it browsed into some weeds that they called "hot vine"—with a sweetish, milky substance in it—and died on our hands. Ten dollars gone right there.

In town, Mr. Prindle said he'd heard they had a "genuine full-blooded Jew" there, that had opened a store. So we went down to see him, being naturally interested in a curiosity like that, though I wasn't altogether clear what he was. But he looked just like anybody else, and if you spoke to him, he answered back perfectly civil and lucid. And a man up the street, who'd got to know him, said he talked and acted entirely normal. It seems peculiar, but it was so.

Also, in Key West, they'd approached me from the sponge boats, felt my muscles, which were growing some (I was "about to turn into a man," Uncle Jim said) and offered me a bounty of twenty dollars to go sponging. They never could fetch enough hands, and were always slew-footing around town trying to bribe people with bounty money.

They found it hard to fill crews for those four-week sponging trips, you understand, because the expanding cigar factories took most of the labor. According to the spongers, it was foolhardy to go with the cigar people, because it was an up-and-down business, and sometimes you got laid off.

At those times, the spongers had a little song they sang, very derisive and spiteful:

> "Sponging money never done;
> Cigar makers on the bum."

Well, I wanted to voyage with them, and wondered if I'd be homesick, but Uncle Jim said I wasn't ready yet for that rough bunch; I'd best stay home and give more help to Lauriette instead.

She *did* work hard, in a style she'd never done before, and Dr. Snodgrass said she represented "a reaction from loveless over-nursing."

I went there one day, and she was down on her knees scrubbing a floor with a turbot skin, which was what everybody used for floors and greasy pots. I felt so ashamed for her, I took it away and did the work myself. Zeb and I helped bail out and lime her cistern, too, which you had to do every so often.

We made our own soap, made lye out of ashes, and managed as crafty as Robinson Crusoe. A great number of wooden casks floated in one day, from some unhappy ship in distress way out in the ocean, and the families towed them in from the shallows. These oak casks would serve to store water in, and tide over dry times; it isn't generally known that water sealed up like that sometimes stays sweet for years.

After our miserable luck in the wrecking business, it seemed curious that an authentic wreck should heave up one night directly off our shore. We heard a gun booming, and when we rushed to the windows saw rockets, and right after that, Mr. Prindle ran down our beach in his night-shirt.

Poor man, he was short-handed as a sailor, with all of those daughters, and so needed help to get shares.

All day the sea had run very high, with squall after squall, and through the glass you could see the great rollers going out there in the Stream. It blew hard toward shore, and a sailing vessel drifted in too close to the reef. We could see her lights, two or three miles out, and had to rush if we got her off in time.

We made it down to Mr. Prindle's cove in quick order, he and Uncle Jim and I, leaving the others behind. It rained a little on the way, and big wisps of sea-foam blew in your face now and then, so I was soaked by the time we sailed out.

We ran under bare spars almost, it was that gusty, and Mr. Prindle watched his canvas like a hawk, when we got it up briefly. Sails didn't come cheap in these parts. Down to our left, we saw other lights, now, and knew the Russells and Lowes and Pinders would be out to help.

"When we come to lay by, mind the Taverniers," shouted Mr. Prindle in Uncle Jim's ear. "They'll try to hog shares."

It was venturesome business, sailing in the dark toward those reefs, in a storm besides, and our centerboard scraped several times before we got clear of the channel, but everybody said Mr. Prindle was one of the few that could sail these waters at night, and he did it. We were out and headed away first, though there were two other Matecumbe boats astern, and behind them we could see the Taverniers coming. It was nip and tuck.

She lay heeled at the reef, a considerable vessel, a three-masted barkentine, with the two forward masts square-rigged and the mizzen fore-and-aft. I hung onto the rail, straining to make her out, and wondering if I'd see dead men floating in the water, wishing not but half hoping I would, too, for the excitement, the way you do.

They had lights rigged everywhere, and I saw men running this way and that. Somebody had tried to put a boat over, but the list was severe and it hung bow-down, with a davit broken. People most always act like fools when putting boats off a distressed vessel; Mr. Prindle said so later. They rarely do anything right, and things wind up in a snarl.

"Ahoy!" yelled Mr. Prindle through a galvanized iron trumpet. "Ahoy, bark! Do you request salvage?" He was skimming us right along the edge of the reef—I could tell where it was now by being out here before—and I held my breath. It was low tide, too, else the bark wouldn't have stuck, I judged.

We heard a moose's bellow come across the seventy or so yards that separated us. Then I saw the captain—a pompish fat man with side whiskers; he was hanging on to a stay.

"Be you masonic?"

"How's that?" cried Mr. Prindle, startled, but I heard him mutter a kind of curse aside, being the only one I ever heard him use.

"We ain't in mortal danger; I'd prefer a masonic wrecker."

"This wind's rising. You'll be reef-chewed in a 'our's time. Speak hup, man!"

The bark took a sudden shift just then, and you could hear a grinding sound, along with cries of alarm from several of her crew. The captain didn't appear so brash at this, but he made one last stab at it.

"Be they any masons hereabouts?"

I heard Mr. Prindle mutter "Dummed Connecticutter!" but out loud he yelled, "Nary a one—this hain't Noo York. Oncet again, do you request salvage afore these witnesses?"

There was a hasty conference aft in the bark, then the captain called, "I request salvage," but he didn't sound overjoyed. You could barely hear him above the wind.

By now, our neighbors had heaved up within shouting, and one called out, "Cephus Prindle's wrecking master; 'e's first on."

It was good news for us that they'd beat the Taverniers, because there were some hard cases still hung out there, not as settlers but off-and-on traders, and were, as Mr. Prindle said, "as crooked as the devil's claw."

But there wasn't any use for them to argue; they joined

in to help, two boatfuls, a schooner and a smack with a right smart of Cubans aboard, but Mr. Prindle directed everything.

We laid about on the opposite tack, running back, then came into the wind, out from the reef edge, and let go an anchor with a lot of line. Mr. Prindle tested its hold, then we got a dory over the side and he and Uncle Jim pulled to the wreck, over waves that lifted them high one second and dropped them out of sight the next. They left me in the bow with an axe, and said if the anchor started to drag, chop the line, hoist canvas, and shove in a hurry.

As to the bark, Mr. Prindle said they had "to sling an anchor to her stern," and they did it, after which the boats helping us added two more, then got other lines to her.

"The tide'll be turning any minute, boys," cried Mr. Prindle when he came back dripping over the rail. "I think we got 'er."

We took in our dory, and banged it up some forward, doing so, but it wouldn't make much difference, because this bark was a fat prize; there'd be salvage money enough for all.

It was a toss-up still whether the rising wind would beat the tide-turn, but it didn't, and within half an hour, with that barkentine's captain now in a fever to get off, and complaining about it through his trumpet, we were ready to heave. Mr. Prindle never listened to him, and one of the Russells told me afterward, if we'd heaved beforehand, the lines might have snapped and we'd lost her for good.

" 'Aul it!" yelled Mr. Prindle. " 'Eave! Tramp it round the capstan, and hoff she'll come."

I couldn't help but think it was a sorry time for him to mix up his "h's" that way, because I don't think the captain rightly got his directions, and of course the Cubans wouldn't understand him anyhow, so all in all it was on the order of a picnic involving the various kinds of animals in a zoo.

Even so, everybody *did* heave—they were crack sailors in these Keys—and we heard another grinding of her hull against the reef, only this time it was good, for we had her free and floating clear in a matter of minutes.

"How much water's making?" yelled Mr. Prindle.

"I'll report back," called the captain, but he added, as any Christian man might, "and thankee." He might be a stuffy pinch-soul Connecticutter, as Mr. Prindle claimed, but he wasn't a total jackass. Uncle Jim said those New Englanders rasped hard on a southern man, but they had a tendency to "wear like iron," or words like that.

"I calculate to rig a canvas sling and stay even with pumps," the captain cried out after an inspection of the bark, and after that he yelled, "But my rudder gear's smashed. We ain't got steerage."

"We'll take you in tow," cried Mr. Prindle, as cheerful as a porpoise. Everything the bark couldn't do added to the salvage, and we headed for Key West, laboring slow through the heavy seas, with a very long tow-rope to avoid collision. Dawn broke before we arrived, which was just as well, for the wind had remained a steady gale, and it would have been tricky to come in through darkness.

We loafed around town till the salvage court opened, along with our neighbors, but mostly everybody went into different coffee shops to figure out their bill. The way it worked was, the total sum allowed—and it looked like a backbreaker for that bark—got divided pretty even amongst the boats at the scene, depending some on their tonnage, but the wrecking master won an extra fee.

As between the boats, commonly half a boat share went to the owner and half was distributed around among the crew, but this was generally in cases of bigger vessels in the outright business of wrecking.

Still and all, the number of men working on a boat helped decide its share, and right there we had trouble in court. It was the same lunkheaded referee that had skinned Uncle Jim, so he scrunched down out of sight.

The Tavernier schooner belonged to a family there, a run-down bunch that had wrecked professional since they lived in the Bahamas, and when the captain got up to read off his offspring crew, he said, "—along with Cyrus, Jeremiah, Nebuchadnezzar, Stockings, and—"

"Hold on," said the referee sourly. "This Stockings,

now—it sounds unlikely, don't it?" To give him credit, he'd heard all this kind of thing before, and was sharp-eyed and suspicious.

The captain seemed confused, and started to drop it from his list, but Mr. Prindle sprang up and cried, "Objection! Stockings is a cat, Your 'Onor; and so's Jeremiah, whilst Nebuchadnezzar's a half-breed Spaniel dog. Them Taverniers is alluz writing in pet animals for crew; they're noted for it."

Well, there was a lot of bluster and noise, as the Tavernier captain tried to appear offended, and said, if one of his sons was listed as a dog, that throwed his mother in a mighty peculiar light, now didn't it? And he'd take it very kindly if nobody would insult her thataway again.

But Mr. Prindle stuck to his guns, with the aid of our Matecumbe neighbors, and Cyrus, Jeremiah, and Nebuchadnezzar were dropped. They'd been asleep at the time, under a porch, as Mr. Prindle pointed out, so it was sap-headed to include them.

In the end, a total fee of $7,500 was declared, for the bark was loaded with a valuable cargo of silk and wine and silverware, and we'd saved its skin; there was no argument about *that,* though the barkentine Captain grumbled some more and said a masonic wrecker could have done it better. He was more hipped on masons than any man I ever saw; his head was sort of turned with it.

Uncle Jim's and my share came to nearly $400 apiece, so here we were in funds again, and just in time, because the pineapple season was coming, and we had to throw up some flimsy-wood bunk-houses for the Behamy darkies that soon would be drifting over to work.

27

THIS BEGAN a busy period for us in that year, and one that I enjoy looking back on. The darkies came across in rickety old sloops, soft in their speech, not like an Englishman exactly, because many had settled in the Bahamas from French and Spanish islands farther south, and their talk had the curiousest kinds of accents. Morning, noon and night, they were always laughing.

If it hadn't been for our neighbors, we might never have harvested a pineapple; we were just that clumsy. But we pitched in and sweated ourselves silly, Dr. Snodgrass and Lauriette, too, and the Prindles and the Russells and the Lowes and the Pinders and those came in every day to see how we managed.

The darkies themselves put in the last licks on the bunks; with them were colored cooks to prepare their food out of doors, and when Mr. Prindle said the pineapples were "full enough," they started getting in the crop. The going rate was a dollar a day each for breaking, or picking, and fifty cents for weeding.

These darkies brought Nassau baskets that they toted perfectly level and unmoving on their heads, women as well, and some of the girls were so straight and proud, with a nice arch to their backs; high, strong hams sawing up and down, and chests thrust bouncy forward in the thin striped blouses, that it did you good to see them. They could heft a load, too, just like a man.

First off, they broke the slips—for the next crop, you know—getting maybe four or five slips from a single pine, and then started breaking the pines themselves, with darkies down on their knees throwing them out and singing a chant that had a nice jingly beat to it:

374

> "One she go
> Two she go
> T'ree she go—"

—and on like that to a dozen, when they cried, "Tally!"
And so kept a count of how many were picked.

One pineapple grew to a stalk, and sometimes the
Porto Rican variety weighed as much as eighteen pounds.
It was handsome fruit, sweet and juicy, but prickly, too,
before you sliced into it, and most pickers wore stiff canvas pants and one-finger canvas gloves up to the elbows.
But in spite of all that protection, you saw a lot of stick-
ings, with blood running down arms onto the fruit, and
the girls giggling about it. They were a happy-go-lucky
lot, and still are.

They heaped up the pines in a mound as high as a
house, keeping count, and one of our neighbors that had
by far the biggest crop said he'd have 60,000 dozen on
the "first breaking" this season. Now that the fruit was
ready, a big ship showed up and anchored a mile or so
offshore, waiting for the load. Others would come and lie
there for two or three weeks.

I don't mind saying that our spirits were high. We had
the smallest crop on the island, of course, and probably
the poorest quality, but Mr. Prindle reckoned we'd clear
more than a thousand dollars, and that would see us over
the hump of our hardships.

We buckled down, making those piles grow into mountains, and then, at noon one day, with two ships—steam-
ers, both—setting offshore and about ready now to start
loading, I saw a familiar-looking brown sail coming over
the reef, and ran to get the glass.

"It's Mr. Skaggs!" I shouted to the others, and they
knocked off eating lunch, which had been set up at a long
table beside the outdoor oven.

"Well, yes," said Lauriette, "I can't imagine there'd be
two such filthy, disgraceful vessels in any one part of the
world."

"You know something? It'll be fun to see him."

We went down to the water's edge and waved a red
undershirt of Zeb's, but we didn't have to, because the

next time I caught Mr. Skaggs in the glass, he was looking through a glass at *me*.

"Count on that old rooster to know what he's doing," said Uncle Jim. "He's made inquiries in Key West, and laid her right in our laps."

It was a deadly calm day, so he could drop anchor out there; and soon after, the sound of oars came over the water, even before we saw them row. For he was not alone; there seemed to be three people in the boat, two smaller than him, and as I studied them over, I thought, maybe—

"Why, it's Crazy Short Tail, the Seminoley boy, and a girl!"

Well, they pulled into our little harbor, and Mr. Skaggs hopped out in his usual monkey style, and the boy and girl followed.

"How sweet of you to come all this way to visit, Mr. Skaggs," said Lauriette, edging around to get upwind of him, because he *was* pretty rank, and had likely been below amidst all that fish stink.

"You better listen to him," said Mr. Skaggs. " 'E's got something to say, and there's precious little time for it."

Crazy Short Tail said, "Seminolies moving to high ground. Two days ago, three—"

"What do you mean?" asked Uncle Jim. I thought at first this was some kind of skylarking, but he could see they were mighty serious.

" 'Urricane!" said Mr. Skaggs, and it was the first time his face ever had a look of respect on it.

"Bosh!" said Lauriette. "Look at the day—it's brilliantly clear."

It was, too, but not quite. It was too still; there was a hush in the air, and "clear" didn't exactly describe it, for everything had a peculiar haze, though the sun was shining, right enough.

"Seminoles count the saw-grass pollen floating in the hair," said Mr. Skaggs. "A pecoolier calm aforehand makes it wisible for days in advance. My adwice is, bundle up. Git off these Keys; they're all backbone and no arse."

"Thank you, Mr. Skaggs," said Lauriette sweetly, "but

we *like* our backbone country, and I think we'll stick it
out. We've seen storms here before."

"Wait a minute," said Uncle Jim. Turning to Crazy
Short Tail, he said, "Do the Seminoley brothers feel that
it's a *big* storm?"

"Medicine men say worst Yuracan"—Lauriette said
later it was funny he used the old original Carib Indian
term—"in hundred years. Seminolies make big preparations."

"I think we'd better pay heed," said Uncle Jim briskly.
"Mr. Skaggs, we're indebted to you for this act of kindness. We'll alert our good neighbors, and make ready."

"*What?* And leave all our work, all this wonderful result of a year's planning and hoping and starving and
waiting?" cried Lauriette. "Not I. This is the first thing in
my life I've ever done on my own, and I'm proud of it.
You might even say I love it. You'll have to *carry* me off
the island."

"That's just what we'll do, honey," said Uncle Jim. In
the hurly-burly excitement, nobody noticed what he'd
called her. But I did.

The girl with them was Crazy's sister. I recognized her
now, but not so much. She'd filled out, and wasn't so
gangly any more. Her face wasn't so hideous, either, but
in its darkish-paley way looked thoughtful, practically
painless. She gazed at me steady out of her dark brown
eyes, and said, "You don't remember me, do you?"

"I'd forgotten your mother was white, and taught you
English."

"Yes, I'm almost as smart as a white person now."

Well, there you were—another of them. They were all
alike. But there wasn't any time to haggle it over, because
Uncle Jim set out at a dead run for the Prindles. It was
wasted energy; we met Mr. Prindle coming our way, and
he looked curious.

"I saw the boat. Is anything wrong?"

"Yes, there is," said Uncle Jim. "This boy and girl are
Seminole children, from the Big Cypress. Davey knew
them. The Mikasukis are moving to high ground, all
through the 'Glades."

"God in Heaven preserve us!" cried Mr. Prindle,

shaken up for the only time since we'd known him. Then he, too, turned to Crazy and asked the same old thing.

"Do Seminolies say *big* storm?"

"Yuracan, that will sweep everything before it on low ground."

You could see Mr. Prindle struggling with his conscience about his family, and his feeling for all those pineapples piled up on his homestead. Then his good sense got the upper hand, and he said, "Hall right, Capting,—we've got to go. And we'd better 'urry. Warn all the others. I'll go out to the ships."

"But see here, Prindle, have we got *time* to break out a boat and run three miles back and forth to the reef?"

"Have we, boy?"

Crazy shrugged, and spread out his hands.

Mr. Skaggs watched it all with a look of great satisfaction. He was scared of the hurricane, true enough, but he enjoyed seeing people tied up with troubles, too. Still and all, he'd sailed all this way to warn us. You never could tell what the old goat *would* do.

"Hi've been put out considerable, and ain't hanxious to lose my boat," he said. "Nor my neck, neither, not to put too small a price on *that*."

So, having added as disturbing a note as possible, he waited to see what came next.

"Son," said Uncle Jim to Crazy. "You're a trump; you really are, and so is your pretty sister. We shan't forget you."

"Seminolies don't wish payment," said Crazy, with a scornful look.

"I know you don't, but we can all use friendship, or so *I've* found. Prindle! Prindle!" but it was no good. He was already offshore in his skiff, headed for the ships. He was right, but how we cursed his Methodist conscience! He *had* to tell those skippers, no matter what came; it was part of his religion.

"Board up," said Uncle Jim to Lauriette. "Go back, Doctor and Zeb, and help her. Now board *up!* I mean *business!*" he said to Lauriette.

"This is my home. I will stay in it as long as it floats."

"Close her house up, the way Prindle showed us," said Uncle Jim. "I'll carry her aboard Skaggs' boat."

The next minutes were mixed up. I remember seeing the black smoke come from the ships' funnels, and then watching them head out toward the open ocean, to take their chances riding out the hurricane bow-on under power; and then I remember running from one to another of our neighbors' houses with Uncle Jim and Crazy.

I'll say this for those Conchs; they never argued, and they didn't waste a minute in undecision. They gave a good keen look at Crazy, heard his story of floating pollen and emigrating Seminoles, and promptly turned their backs on those valuable pineapples, that they'd harvested with so much care. Then they made ready to get out.

And I'll say this further: not one family gave the least indication of leaving behind a single Bahama darky. Anyhow, it would have been too cruel for anybody but a downright villain; as soon as the word went out, the lamentations and carrying on of those poor blacks was enough to curdle your blood. The Conch men counted up the boats, dividing them into eighteen-foot centerboard skiffs and schooners or smacks, and decided that the small boats would head across the flats to Madeira Bay, from which the people could find hummocks in the Everglades, with solid trees to hang to, and the big boats could sail for Cape Sable.

Where we went wrong was in thinking we had time. That is, time enough to board up houses and pack belongings on boats. We almost made it, but when Mr. Prindle came back, he fell off the coral wall and sprained his ankle so bad we carried him in the house for Dr. Snodgrass to truss it up.

Before it was through, one of our neighbors, a Russell or a Lowe, ran down our beach and said,

"You'd better 'urry—the weather's changing, fast."

I ran outside, and things were different. Instead of the milky haze, clouds now moved across the sky, and Mr. Prindle, from the doorway, said, "See how they do send, low, low, low," which was the Conch preliminary observation to a hurricane generally.

The sea had started to rise, and in a few minutes a rain

shower sprinkled down briefly. After that, the wind begun to blow.

"Boys, there's no time to cross the Bay," said a neighbor. "The Lord has seen fit to punish us for our greed."

It was true, I reckon, but tiresome. These Conchs couldn't get up and go to the privy without making some reference to the Lord. Still and all, if we hadn't thought of our belongings, we might have got off.

"Sink the boats, and batten down!" They carried that cry up and down the island, and one religious man sailed across the channel to Tavernier, to give the word there.

In the next few hours, all the boats on Matecumbe were taken around to deep-water holes in the Bay and sunk, and then, with Mr. Prindle showing how, we wrapped cables and ropes around our houses, tying them to trees and coral.

"Mr. Skaggs, and you youngsters, too—we're sorry about this," said Uncle Jim, taking time off for a second. "It's poor payment to get caught yourselves."

"I hexpected it," said Mr. Skaggs with satisfaction. "Hit were no more than I hexpected. A 'ouse kin fall on some folks, afore they'll take adwice."

"Mr. Skaggs, you're *not* as awful as you seem," said Lauriette. "In fact, you're a nice old man, in a revolting sort of way."

"We can 'old the nupturals afore the hurricane 'its," said Mr. Skaggs, "or right atter; I don't mind which."

She actually broke down and laughed, and gave him a kind of hug.

But things were moving in a hurry. The wind was rising, the sky was overcast, whitecaps whipped off the ocean out in front, and the rain squalls began slashing at us like buckshot—a dreadful burst one minute, and a total let-up the next. It was unsettling to the nerves. I noticed Dr. Snodgrass taking a pull of Spooju, and then Zeb on his knees in the corner, praying. He'd complained considerable before that, and said he knew water would get him sooner or later, and it was all Uncle Jim's fault for coaxing him into that rowboat back at Grassy. For once, Uncle Jim didn't answer back, but only stared at him concerned and uncomfortable.

All of us, Lauriette, too, were inside our house, with shutters nailed, extra food and water in, as Mr. Prindle advised, and candles set out in place of kerosene lamps, which might tumble over and blow up. There was nothing we could do for our chickens or our pig, poor things; Uncle Jim said they must take their chances, and he wished them luck. But he reinforced the bunk-houses the best way possible, with ropes and coral chunks all around the bottom.

We waited, edgy and over-eager to be easy and offhand. In an hour, the sky had darkened down, and when I crept out the back for a minute, the sea was slate-gray, and sand flung along that stung your eyes. I came back in, and when Uncle Jim saw me, he slammed and bolted the door with the first impatience he'd showed.

"And *stay* here!" he said.

Right after that commenced an overhead roaring noise that was ugly and continuous, like railroad freight cars rumbling past.

"Oh, Lordy, Lordy!" Zeb cried. "It's done come—the Day of Judgment! I knowed it; I knowed it all along."

There wasn't any chance to bawl him out, for Uncle Jim said, in an awed voice, "Great day in the morning! Did you feel that?"

We all did. The narrow land shook, and was still shaking. You could scarcely hear yourself think now for the roaring, and soon after, the first water came trickling under the door. We stared at it, frozen.

"Quick! Pile those tables up! Get up there, youngsters; you, too, Lauriette. Nip up; be spry, now. Miss *Farrow!*"

"There isn't room. Give it to the children."

"Yes, *ma'am!*" said Uncle Jim, and seizing her between the shoulders and rump, he *threw* her up, and almost threw her clear over. She said something down, but I couldn't tell what it was.

By now, it made no difference. I could hear the smash of water against our front wall; the house quivered and shook, and the water came on in.

"She's going! She's going!" Uncle Jim shouted. "Grab something wood—anything that floats, and hang on.

Hang *on,* do you understand? Never let go, no matter what happens!"

With a terrible smashing rush, the front wall caved in, just ripped away, and the sea hit us like a hammer-blow. That wave, they said later, must have been ninety feet high, and our topmost wind gusts here were reckoned by the Key West people at 250 miles an hour. What's more, the barometer there registered 26.31 inches, which was the lowest in all of the history of that place. The last thing I remembered clear was Dr. Snodgrass, bareheaded, his gorgeous white mane flowing, Lauriette's legs in one of his arms and the Indian girl's in the other, with his great medicine man's voice braying out a church hymn that I had no idea he knew. His head was lifted up as brave as a lion, and he was holding those two women above the rising water.

It was the last time I ever saw him alive.

When I came to, I was lodged in a crotch of our tough little guava tree, that had roots deep in the rock, and my head had a knot on it the size of an egg. I tried to shake off my dizziness, not yet recalling what happened, but I couldn't seem to get things sorted out.

Overhead, the sky was perfectly serene, but below, there was nothing but foundation where our house had been. And bits and pieces of furniture were strewn just everywhere, in trees, rocks, along the beach where the tide had sucked back after the giant wave—everywhere. None of our people were in sight any place you looked. And over across the fields not a single trace of that bunk-house showed; not a stick.

I started to climb down, then remembered a story of Mr. Prindle's: "And then there came a glistening calm." So this might be the eye of the storm, the hurricane center, and I concluded to hang on awhile. It was a very good thing. In forty minutes or so, the roaring started up again, and we had it all over. If anything, the second half was worse than the first, though it didn't do nearly so much damage, of course, because that had already been done.

I hung on, with water up to my shoe-soles and the guava tree bent double, and tried to dodge the flying things in the air—our black rocker from the beach, bed-boards, a mattress—a battleship broadside of sticks and utensils aimed right at me. Something struck me under the right arm, in my ribs, and I grunted and nearly slipped free. I could hear the limbs crack, but I hung on, and have no idea to this day how long I was in that tree. It went on through the night, I know that, and some time the following morning I climbed down, then sloshed through the rain and the debris to where our house had been. Nothing was left except the kettle where the craw-fish stayed. I was almost too stiff and sore to walk, but I wasn't hungry. I felt hollow, washed out, and wished I could find Uncle Jim.

The best thing, I decided, was to tramp across the island, but before I got there, I saw them coming with Lau-riette—Uncle Jim and Zeb and one of the Bahama hands —carrying her on a door. Her head was nothing but blood, the silky blond hair sticky with it, and Uncle Jim's face was slate-gray. I never noticed before how old he'd looked lately; there was some gray hair amongst the oth-ers, too.

"Davey, boy," he said in a tired-out voice. "Thank God."

"Where's Crazy Short Tail and his sister? I've got some broken ribs."

"The last I saw them, I *think* they were swept on out in the flats. There's a mangrove Key beyond; we'll search it when this is over."

"And Dr. Snodgrass?"

"No sign of him at all. Down with her, boys. The jos-tling's making her bleed, and she's trying to say some-thing."

They set the door on the ground, and we knelt over, watching her mouth move. "Dear Jim," she said.

Both Mr. and Mrs. Prindle lived by floating with furni-ture. They had their nine children clustered around them, but all except four were snatched away by waves during the night, and one of these, a pretty little girl two years old was dead in Mr. Prindle's arms when dawn came. We found both Crazy Short Tail and his sister alive but hurt

in trees in the mangrove that evening, and Mr. Skaggs
was nearby, neither damaged nor out of sorts. In fact, he
was in the best spirits I ever saw him have. Zeb had held
Crazy and the girl above water for six hours; then, when
they were torn away, he slapped Uncle Jim back to consciousness after a limb hit him. "Good old Zeb," Uncle
Jim said when he told it, smiling thinly. "Those gorilla
shoulders come in handy from time to time, especially for
a man who hates water." What he forgot to tell, of
course, was that he himself had swum Lauriette, more
dead than alive, to a tree first of all. Both he and Zeb
were bunged up some.

Among our neighbors—fifty-seven people in all
(counting all those children)—sixteen remained alive
when everything was over, and most of the Bahama darkies were drowned. Of the ones that survived, most said
they would settle in the Keys; they never wanted to go on
water again.

It makes my heart heavy to tell about Dr. Snodgrass,
who we found days later lying on the beach at Cape
Sable, just as Mr. Skaggs predicted, knowing the currents.
We raised the schooner and searched. "Poor physician,
poor quack and genius," said Uncle Jim, standing there
on the sand with the sun blazing out again, the water
sparkling blue and innocent, and the gulls making up for
lost time with their food. "In trying to save us, he forgot
to heal himself."

Zeb and Crazy put salves on Lauriette's injuries, and
tended her, with everybody anxious, but it was many a
day before she would be her old self again, and meanwhile she lay abed in a cabled rock "storm-house" of
Captain Lowe's. It was the only structure in Matecumbe
to resist the hurricane. Everybody that was left planned
to build one right away.

Now my story is nearly done, but not quite. Only a few
things are left to tell, and I'll be almighty glad when it's
over, for writing a book *can* get tedious (though simple if
you know how) and I'll be happy to take a breather.

Mr. Skaggs and the Indians stayed on awhile to help us

through the emergency; also, Millie and Captain Pereira came down in a week. We sat outside the makeshift hut we'd erected, and talked. But Uncle Jim was in such a slump that even his old friend from the war couldn't rouse him. He figured that everything was his fault, you see, and acted as if he hadn't anything left to fight with. Captain Pereira had letters, addressed to Dr. Snodgrass, from my Aunt Effie and Aunt Lou. Grassy was making a living. Several new babies had been born to the wives of field hands, and Clarissa's disposition seemed better. Maybe they would come to visit us, if the Ku Klux Klan trouble was over. It was good news; we'd be relieved to see them, and Zeb snuffled a little.

Then Millie went to visit Lauriette, and asked to be alone with her, and when she came out she was dabbing at her eyes with a kerchief, but looked happy, too. Women always appear to be in their most enjoyable humor when bawling, I've noticed. It tones up their system, because it makes everybody nearby miserable.

Then there came a day when they brought Lauriette home, and we walked out, helping her, and looked at our fields. Not even a brown patch was visible where our house-high pile of pineapples stood. Though a lot of the top-soil was gone with the wind and the water, enough remained for a crop. But all our money was spent, except for the loan that Captain Pereira forced on Uncle Jim before going back to Havana. And by George, he had to throw it down on the sand in a temper, Uncle Jim was just that stubborn.

"Well," said Laureitte, with a curious sideways look at Uncle Jim, who stood silently smoking a cigar, "I suppose the only sensible thing to do is leave. We're beaten."

Uncle Jim nodded, sad and morose; then he grinned and said, "Now you know better than that. Do? Why, we'll go to Key West and buy pine slips. We've hardly started. I'm used to this place. I hope to settle here."

"Oh, I *love* you," said Lauriette in a low voice. At first, I thought I'd misunderstood her. But I hadn't, because Uncle Jim said, "I was planning to get around to that soon."

There's only a little bit more, but it has to be put down.

We sailed to Key West, and Uncle Jim bought pineapple slips cheap, off some Cuba boats that had come across to bring help; people *can* be nice, no matter how awful they are at other times.

In the late morning, he went into a coffee shop for *un buchito*—the swallow of black, bitter brew (I declined with thanks)—and I walked down the shady street, sweet-smelling with the fruit trees and flowers, and the lacy-work balconies overhead, lots of them damaged, now, thinking back to our adventures—of the salt works, and Captain Pereira's courtship, and Uncle Jim's trial, then I noticed the man directly ahead of me.

He was dressed elegant, in a light-materialed, dove-colored suit and Panama hat, but he was thin to the point of outright frailness, and his skin was the color of parchment, as they say in books. I've never seen any myself, but it was yellow and kind of dried-up, like. He limped very bad, too, and walked with a cane.

Then I knew him in a flash, and after swallowing my heart three or four times, got flushed up and angry enough to be reckless, and so ran around in front and yelled:

"So you've found us, have you? Wait and see what good it does you! Your bullies are dead in the swamps, and your Indians lie ten foot deep in mud, exactly where you'll be when this is over!"

I realized it didn't make much sense, but I was spilling over with pent-up grievance, and meant to be heard.

"I suppose you recognized me by the limp?" He looked down at his leg.

"I'm *glad* I did it, and I'm glad what Uncle Jim's going to do—"

He said, "Hold on, confound it—" but I interrupted: "Uncle Jim! Uncle Jim!" and ran down the street toward the coffee house. A number of people pulled to one side, curious, and several men came to the doorway of their stores.

When I burst into the coffee house, Uncle Jim was

seated at a table with two acquaintances, and it was a pesky while before he got what I was yelling about.

Well, he'd mellowed up some since we left home, I reckon, but this was one score too many, so he scrambled up from that table, overturning it, and everybody there hot-footed it out behind him.

He walked up the street, with the coat open that he always wore in town, but he'd thrown away his cigar, I noticed, and the brown skin was stretched very tight around his mouth.

People were everywhere, looking on, and I heard a man say, "We'd better fetch the Sheriff," but nobody did it.

Uncle Jim stopped about ten paces in front of Rex Farrow, who stood there quiet, leaning on his cane.

Uncle Jim said, "We finally meet. I figured we would."

"I have something to say. Stop a minute—"

"Now you've got five seconds to draw a gun and start shooting," said Uncle Jim. "It's five more than you deserve, but you've got it."

"Don't draw. I can't outshoot you. I'm not even armed."

"That kind of speech once cost me a hole through the shoulder."

"For God's sake, Burnie. *Look* at me. I'm a dying man." He threw off his coat and showed he hadn't a gun. "Don't shoot; not yet."

Uncle Jim walked forward, confused a little, but not ready to give it up, either.

"That boy's back bears stripes that will never heal, you miserable coward. Now one of us isn't going to leave this island, ever. Call the turn. I haven't had a saber in my hand for five years, but I'll play your game. Speak up."

Somehow, he didn't sound too convincing, and I figured he was trying to keep his anger up, because this fellow *was* a pitiful-looking wreck. Still, he was full of trickery, and always had been.

"You can't make me fight you, Burnie," and when he said it, a number of people, looking at Uncle Jim, said, "For shame!" and "Cold-blooded murder!" They were friends of his, too. It halted him; he'd never done murder or anything else shameful in his life, and the fights he'd been in, the other fellow drew a gun first.

"What *do* you want? Why'd you come here?"

"Take me to my sister. I've got six months, maybe less. It isn't very long to make up for the sins of a lifetime."

We all stood, watching Uncle Jim's face. The people in that town knew him well enough by now, and nobody would have dared interfere for a mortgage on Havana. It wasn't safe, not in this humor.

Finally he sighed, and the rigidness went out of his shoulders. "Come on, then. You look as though a cup of coffee wouldn't hurt you. But God help you if you're lying."

"Nothing could hurt me," said Rex Fallow, and I think everybody believed him, because there was a general letting-down, and several men slapped each other on the back, and one or two stepped up to Uncle Jim and said, "We never figured you to gun down an unarmed man, Captain. We knowed you was too true-blue for *that*."

By chance, this was the ringleader of the bunch that once tried to lynch Uncle Jim, so he only smiled back, sort of thoughtful, and we went on down the street.

Now I've come to the last section of our adventures, and in a way it makes me sad to wind it up. Rex Farrow was as sick as he said, and we took him to Matecumbe on our schooner. I never thought he would survive the trip; his face hadn't any more color than a fish's belly toward the last, and we laid him on a bunk before we got there. He was practically delirious.

"Cheated," I heard him say when Uncle Jim put a blanket over him, and then, with a flicker of a smile, eyes wide open and seeing—"No excuse."

When we got there, and explained all, Lauriette put her hands to her face, and we helped him to a bed in her house, which the neighbors were helping build back, and Uncle Jim said Zeb should stay there with them.

But if Uncle Jim had any idea that this wretched man had a shot left in his locker, he was mistaken. The poor creature never got out of that bed again in this world, but only wasted away a little more each week.

The strange thing was, he stayed cheerful and happy, and he made Lauriette happy besides.

Belle Mead was run by an uncle, so the black cloud of deceit and bitterness was lifted from that place at last. Mr. Paxton Farrow was in a sanitarium in Louisiana, and the uncle had given this dying fellow an allowance to go where he pleased. The rest were welcome to live at home and be cared for. It wasn't very much allowance, but he turned it over to Lauriette, because we were dreadful poor. All we could do was wait, and while we did, life stirred again on Matecumbe. All the neighbors helped each other, and the crops began to grow.

I hated to see Uncle Jim in such poverty, because he'd always treated money with a kind of contempt, and curled up his lip at those who guarded it and respected and worshipped it.

So we worked hard to keep body and soul together, but I couldn't help feeling wistful that we hadn't found *some* of the treasure. Riches may not make you happy, but not having enough can make unhappiness almost certain, it seems to me.

We worked hard. Mr. Prindle was burdened down with crops, because six of his nine daughters were gone, and their chores fell on him and his wife. So Uncle Jim said I should provide them as well as us with food from the sea, and I went out every day the wind blew soft. I caught all manner of fine things.

I learned my way through the drains in the "back country," across the broad lakes between the flats, and learned dozens of Keys that lay between our chain and the mainland, off twenty miles there out of sight.

Mr. Prindle tried to teach them to me, but when you came right down to it, he couldn't; he knew them in his head, and they only came out as "a big square Key," "a little square Key," "a big round Key," or "a small round Key," and that didn't fill the bill, not if you wanted to get home again.

So I learned them myself, and sailed out in our eighteen-foot skiff, winding my way here and there, and often explored all day, and stayed over night once in a while, too.

At the ends of little Keys were usually holes crammed full of speckled trout; and redfish and tarpon lay piled like logs near the flats. If you threw a feathered hook at their nose, you were in for a tussle, I tell you. And if you tried to boat them when they were still green, you were apt to get knocked halfway to Cuba.

Snook, which I thought was the most beauiful eating fish of all, with a pretty black stripe midway along its sides—snook lay thick in a lake at the end of a creek entering the mainland. A person could have hauled them out with a net, and Mr. Prindle said somebody would, some day, but he didn't favor it.

I caught sharks with black remoras attached underneath to pilot them, caught bonefish on the near flats that ran like wild horses (but were no good to eat, and only fun to play with). Still and all, I was just a boy yet (though growing, as they said) and some days I loafed back there, exploring and poking around. You could find crocodiles—real crocodiles—slithering off the mainland banks on sunny days, but a person didn't want to get mixed up with them. And I knew where two eagle nests were, six feet square, like a box, and the gray-streaked sea eagles called ospreys shrilled about me in the boat when I moved up to *their* nests. But they never swooped down, and I was glad, for they were nervous and had sharp beaks.

On the other side, in the ocean, I anchored on the reef and caught all the bottom fish that I told about before, and if the day was blistering hot, I might slip overboard for a swim. Sharks and barracuda had never bothered anybody here, not so far. The water beckoned to you out there, clear like a spring, clear to the bottom.

Back home at Grassy I'd always been able to swim under the packet boats tied up at our town; we made a game out of it. Down here I could reach the reef rocks, then look at the scared, stripey fish. It was fun, but you couldn't stay down long in water that deep.

I saw something there on the bottom one day, on the order of an old spool coated-over, and brought it up, but it was too heavy to be water-soaked wood.

I took it home and showed it to Uncle Jim. For a second, I thought he might toss it back, in his absent way, with a sarcastic comment about swimming instead of fishing. But he straightened up and took it out in the sunlight. Then he got a hammer and chisel and chipped the crust off the outside.

"Where'd you pick this up? Could you find the spot again?"

I noticed with an odd twinge that he was fighting to keep from getting excited.

"I know where it was. I could find it. Why?"

"Unless I'm very much mistaken, and we'll just step over and ask Prindle"—he jammed on his hat—"this is a Spanish bosun's whistle. Next thing is to see if it means anything."

Well, it was, and next morning he went out with me, but it required all day to locate the exact spot, and even then I'm not sure I did, but we finally saw what looked like old iron cannon, jagged with sea-things, and I went down almost thirty feet to the bottom, I judged. It was deeper than the place before; it nearly busted my lungs.

"Well, what, Davey?" he said when I popped up. "What's down there?"

"I found a chunk of iron, all chewed up, and there's some rotted timbers. Nothing any account."

"Can you do it again, son? Don't do it if it hurts. We won't take any chances."

I said, "Let me get my breath. I can do it, all right, but only once more today."

Uncle Jim handed me a line. "Let's just haul up that iron bar for good luck. Tie it around, Davey boy, and we'll see what's what. When you've got your breath—don't hurry, now."

I slid down our anchor rope, hand over hand, head-first, and fixed on my other line; then I scooted up.

Sitting in the boat, as I gasped for air and dried off, Uncle Jim examined it. It was pretty good-sized, heavy, and coated bad like everything else, but he took our hammer and chisel again and made a deep dent in the middle. I was surprised; iron never mushed up like that. It rusted out eventually, but this stuff was soft, if you compared them.

When I looked up, Uncle Jim had removed his hat. He threw the bar down; it landed with a thunk in the bottom of the boat.

"I don't know. There's a kind of destiny in this. A little child shall lead them. It was touch and go, boy. I wasn't sure—none of us were sure we'd make it through this year."

"What is it?" I cried. "What are you talking about?"

"Your 'chunk of iron' happens to be bar silver; I'm almost positive about it. See the mark here at the end to show that the Church got it's share? I don't know what it's worth, but I suppose it's a considerable sum, after the oxidized layer's taken off. *Davey!* By God, you've *done* it!" He yelled "Whoopee!" and tossed his hat up about twenty feet in the air. It came down in the water and sunk. I was kind of sore; as poor as we were, hats didn't grow on trees. And I said so.

"Don't you understand, you idiot! You've *done* it. I'm not sure yet what lies down there—we'll go to Key West tomorrow and find out—but *this*"—and he held up the bar "represents the freedom of the city for *us*. We're over the hump, old fellow, and I don't mind saying it's taken a little scuffling."

Next day we sailed to Key West, and found that a Spanish fleet of twenty-one heavily loaded merchant ships, along with some galleons under Admiral Don Rodriguez, were wrecked by a hurricane off our reef in 1733. According to the records, the Admiral saved his own galleon, and some silver, but he burned a number of the other wrecks "to keep their cargoes from the Bahama pirates."

Same old story. Mr. Prindle, when we told him (with apologies) said there were "pro-Behamy 'istorians, and 'anti-Behamy," and this was evidently one of the anti kind.

Well, to sum it up, that big bar of silver fetched $2,500, but we never found another, and neither did the rest of the people that tried. They brought up all kinds of oddities—pistols, cups, several long strips of irregular silver, corroded worthless except as souvenirs, that were "pieces of eight," each small square with its stamp. Pieces of eight were stamped on a silver strip and then snipped off one at a time. Occasionally the cutting didn't come out quite right, then the left-over corner was called a "bit." That's where we got the word "two-bits."

I found a beautiful gold earring one morning, with a real emerald hanging down, on the order of a dew-drop, and Uncle Jim advised me to save it for a rainy day.

Then another storm came, not really bad, and shifted all the bottom wreckage that wasn't covered up by sand. We never found it again.

Maybe it was just as well. None of us wanted very much to be rich. We had a good life, the pineapples would soon be here again; everybody seemed happy.

One day Rex Farrow called me into his room and said, propping his head higher on a pillow, "Lad, I wanted to tell you, I really did want to tell you—" and then stopped. His eyes were still open, but the life had gone out of him. I'd never seen a person die like that before, and was scared.

We buried him in a cleared place with a cable around it, near our pineapple fields, where we'd put up a board for Dr. Snodgrass. It was pretty there, and high; you could see the water on both sides. All of us cried a little for Dr. Snodgrass, and wanted him back. Walking home, I saw Uncle Jim put his arm around Lauriette's shoulder, and she went all to pieces. She'd been under an awful strain; it hadn't occurred to me before. Women are such a nuisance you sometimes forget that they fight with nerve instead of muscles.

She hung on, and cried and cried. We drifted along, the Prindles, and Zeb with a Behamy girl that was sewing him a new pair of pants, he said, and me last.

"I should have got around to it before," I heard Uncle Jim say. "Even crying, you're the most beautiful girl they ever made. What I mean is—"

"Don't talk," she said, lifting up her face. "You're not very good at it. My knees turned to water when you walked into Belle Mead. I've never been the same since. I don't ever want to be again."

"I was about to say I love you," said Uncle Jim. "I'll get it out if it kills me."

I don't think it slowed him up any. When I rounded the grove of trees, he was holding up very well, and he had a man-sized job on his hands. Her knees seemed to have got their strength back all of a sudden.

Now I'm done, and it's sadful, as stated. But Uncle Jim tells me I can go visit Crazy Short Tail and his gangly sister that isn't so gangly any more, when the pineapple crop's in. And in the meantime, Mr. Prindle's oldest daughter, Samantha (the red-haired one), wants to learn how to sail. The funny part is, she knows how already.

It's hard. As I look ahead, I can see all manner of woman troubles coming. But Uncle Jim says I can solve them. "Davey, old scamp," he said, as careless and uncomplimentary as always, "You were fifty years older than me the day you were born."

I don't intend to worry. Almost any way it goes, the years ahead should be good ones for us here on Matecumbe.

ACKNOWLEDGMENTS

The author is first and foremost indebted to Margaret Green, of Islamorada (once Upper Matecumbe), Florida, and her husband, Cecil Green, the noted fishing guide and pool ace, whose close acquaintance with the Pioneer Bahamian, or "Conch," families of Matecumbe made researches into the early life there both pleasant and easy.

The Russell and Lowe families, first settlers, were especially helpful, and the octogenarian Mr. Preston Pinder recalled extraordinary details of his boyhood in the Keys.

I am also grateful to Earl Mohn, movie scenarist and feature writer for *The Sarasota News,* whose friendship with the Seminoles opened areas of inquiry that to this day remain difficult for both scholars and journalists.

At the University of Miami, Dr. Archibald McNeal, Mr. George Rosner, and Mrs. Madeline Riffey provided every cooperation in suggesting and unearthing elderly volumes pertinent to travel and living in Florida of the 1800's.

A few points should be noted. Mild license has been taken with time. For example, no serious storm disturbed the Keys in 1870, though there were hurricanes in other years of that era. During Reconstruction, Key West *did* have a negro Sheriff and a negro Magistrate; the first was liked and admired, the second was a scoundrel. There *was* a sixty-foot serpent, in the Cape Sable area; it was frequently seen and mentioned by, among others, Johnny Gomez, some of whose lively eccentricities have been carried forward in the Mr. Skaggs of *A Journey to Matecumbe*. Dr. Snodgrass's medical career, with particular emphasis on the glassless spectacles, was in part that of the late Ike Eagle, father of Ringling's Nate Eagle, whose life, also spirited and original, has been recorded by the author in the Profile department of *The New Yorker* magazine. The doctor's Chinese clinic was inspired by that of Mrs. Violet Blossom (Queen of the Pitch Women), whose routine has been set forth by Stewart H. Holbrook in his entertaining book *The Golden Age of Quackery,* and which was witnessed by the author in his youth.

Remnants of the wrecked Spanish fleet, described in the last chapters of the book, lie today in the coral off Upper Matecumbe and provide the livelihood, bit by salvaged bit, of Captain Art McKee, proprietor of McKee's Sunken Treasure, a popular exhibit of the region.

My wife, Judith Martin Taylor, who typed, copyread and proofread this book, continues in good mental health, and, more surprising, still likes to read.

R.L.T.

SELECTED BIBLIOGRAPHY

Adair, James. *History of American Indians*

A Guide to Key West. Compiled by workers of the Writers' Program of the Works Projects Administration in the State of Florida

American Medical Association. *Nostrums and Quackery*

American State Papers, Military Affairs

Andrews, Allen H. *A Yank Pioneer in Florida*

Audubon, John James. *Scenery and Character of Florida*

Bache, R. M. *Young Wrecker of the Florida Reef*

Ballantine, George. *Autobiography of an English Soldier in the United States*

Beard, James Melville. *Ku Klux Klan Sketches, Humorous and Didactic*

Beater, Jack. *Islands of the Florida Coast*

Bethell, John A. *History of Pinellas Peninsula*

Bickel, Karl A. *The Mangrove Coast*

Brevard, Caroline Mays. *A History of Florida*

Brinton, Daniel G. *The Florida Peninsula*

Brookfield, Charles M. & Griswold, Oliver. *They Called It Tropical*

Brown-Hazen, Mrs. Pauline. *Tampa Blue Book of Pioneers*

Bryant, William Cullen. *Letters of a Traveler*

Canova, Andrew P. *Life and Adventures in South Florida*

Cash, W .T. *The Story of Florida*

Chambers, Julius. *The Mississippi*

Clowes, Ernest Seabury. *Shipways to the Sea*

Coe, Charles H. *Red Patriots: The Story of the Seminole*

Cohn, David L. *The Good Old Days*

Collings, Francis A. *Our Harbors and Inland Waterways*

Collins, Henry H., Jr. *Birds of the Everglades*

Connor, Jeannette T., translator and editor. *Colonial Records of Spanish Florida*

Cook, James. *Remedies and Rackets*

Cramer, Zadoc. *The Navigator*

Cumings, Samuel. *The Western Pilot*

Cushing, Frank H. *Exploration of Ancient Key Dwellers Remains on the Gulf Coast of Florida*

Dau, Frederick W. *Florida Old and New*

Davis, T. Frederick. "The Beginning of Tampa," "Disston Land Purchase," *Florida History Quarterly*

Dayton, Frederick Erving. *Steamboat Days*

Devol, George H. *Forty Years a Gambler on the Mississippi.*

Dimock, A. W. *Florida Enchantments*

Dixon, Thomas. *The Black Hood*

Douglas, Marjory Stoneman. *The Everglades: River of Grass*
————. *Hurricane*

Dunbar, Seymour. *A History of Travel in America*

Engineers' Report to the Navigation and Hydraulic Company of the Mississippi Rapids

Fairbanks, George R. "Florida, Its History and Romance," "Moses Elias Levy Yulee," *Florida Historical Quarterly*

Florida Railroad Commission and Works Projects Administration. *The Railroads of Florida.*

Ford, Alice, editor. *The Bird Biographies of John James Audubon*

Francis, Philip. *Florida Fish and Fishing*

Gifford, John. *The Everglades*

Glazier, Willard. *Down the Great River*

Gould, Emerson W. *Fifty Years on the Mississippi*

Greene, Francis Vinton. *The Mississippi*

Grismer, Karl H. *Tampa, A History of the City of Tampa and the Tampa Bay Region of Florida*

Hall, Andrew. *The Ku Klux Klan in Southern Illinois*

Hall, F. Wyly. *Palms and Flowers of Florida*

————. *Be Careful in Florida*

Hanna, Alfred J. and Katherine A. *Florida's Golden Sands*

Hawks, Dr. J. M. *Florida Gazetteer*

Henshall, James A. *Camping and Cruising in Florida*

Holbrook, Stewart H. *The Golden Age of Quackery*

Hulbert, Archer Butler. *The Paths of Inland Commerce*

Jackson, General A. *Review of Battle of Horshoe and Facts re Killing of Sixteen Indians*

Kennedy, Stetson. *Palmetto Country*

The Key West Administration. *Key West*

Lester, John C. *Ku Klux Klan*

McDuffie, Lillie B. *Lures of the Manatee*

McNeal, Violet. *Four White Horses and a Brass Band*

Monnette, John W. *Progress of Navigation and Commerce on the Mississippi and Great Lakes*

Morrison, John H. *History of American Steam Navigation*

Muir, Helen. *Miami, USA*

Munro, Kirk. *Big Cypress*

Nordhoff, C. *Wrecking on the Florida East Coast*

National Police Gazette, editors of. *Life and Adventure of John A. Murrell*

Pearse, Eleanor H. D. *Florida's Vanishing Era*

Pettengill, George W., Jr. *The Story of the Florida Railroads*

Pierce, R. V., M.D. *The People's Common Sense Medical Adviser in Plain English; or Medicine Simplified*

Piethmann, Irving M. *The Unconquered Seminole Indians*

Poor's Manuals of Railroads

Preble, G. H. *A Chronological History of Steam Navigation*

Procter, Lucille. *Handbook of Florida Flowers*

Quick, Herbert and Edward. *Mississippi Steamboatin'*

Quick, Herbert. *American Inland Waterways*

Reid, Mayne. *Osceola*

Richardson, William T. *Historic Pulaski, Birthplace of the Ku Klux Klan*

Robertson, Rev. Frederick W. *Sermons Preached at Brighton*

Romine, Willam Bethel. *A Story of the Original Ku Klux Klan*

Rothert, Otto A. *The Outlaws of Cave-In-Rock*

Scudder, Dr. John M. *The Electric Practice of Medicine*
Seminole War & Miraculous Escape of Mrs. Mary Godfrey
Siekman, Lula. *Handbook of Florida Shells*
Simpson, C. *Out of Doors in Florida*
Smiley, Nora K., and White, Louis V. *Hurricane Road*
Sprunt, Alexander, Jr. *Florida Bird Life*
Stanton, Samuel W. *American Steam Vessels*
Swanton, John R. *The Indians of the Southeastern United States*
Tebeau, Charlton W. *The Story of the Chokoloskee Bay Country*
————. *Florida's Last Frontier: The History of Collier County*
————, editor. Articles from *Tequesta*, The Journal of the Histor-
    ical Association of Southern Florida
Tourgee, Albert W. *The Invisible Empire*
Townsend, Trench. *Wild Life in Florida*
Twain, Mark. *Life on the Mississippi*
Waldin, Walter. *Truck Farming in the Everglades*
Waters, Donald. *"Gypsy Waters" Cruises South*
Whitehead, Charles E. *Camp Fires of the Everglades, or Wild
    Sports in the South*
Willoughby, Hugh L. *Across the Everglades*
Wise, John S. *The End of an Era*

From *The Southern Folklore Quarterly:*
    Campbell, Marie. "Liquor Ballads from the Kentucky Moun-
        tains."
    Clark, J. D. "Similes from the Folk Speech of the South."
    Farr, T. J. "Middle Tennessee Folk Beliefs concerning Love
        and Marriage."
    Hauptmann, O. H. "Spanish Folklore from Tampa, Florida."
    Hudson, Arthur Palmer. "Some Curious Negro Names."
    Redfield, W. A. "A Collection of Middle Tennessee Riddles."
    Werner, Evelyn and Huss, Veronica. "The Conchs of Riviera,
        Florida."

Mohn, Earl, From *The Sarasota* (Fla.) *News.*
    "Travel in the Everglades: Then and Now."
    "Massacre at Indian Key."
    "The Seminole Indian War."
    "Draining the Everglades: A Problem."
    "The Feather Fight and the Death of Guy Bradley."
    "Menendez and His Indian Bride."
    "Ponce de Leon: How Florida Got Its Name."
    "Big Blow in the Keys, 1935."
    "Conquering Everglades: Feat of Builders."
    "The Hurricane Story."
    "Deaconess Bedell and the Glade Cross Mission."

Articles too numerous to mention from newspapers of early Florida towns and cities.

ROBERT LEWIS TAYLOR was born in southern Illinois and educated at Southern Illinois University and the University of Illinois (A.B.). Upon graduation he lived in Europe and in Polynesia; then, after a brief interlude as editor of a weekly newspaper, he became a reporter for the St. Louis *Post-Dispatch*. In 1940, he joined *The New Yorker* as a writer of profiles and other long pieces, and has since remained a member of the staff.

In addition to A JOURNEY TO MATECUMBE, Mr. Taylor is the author of the Pulitzer Prize-winning THE TRAVELS OF JAIMIE McPHEETERS and the bestselling novel TWO ROADS TO GUADALUPE. He has also written such widely acclaimed biographies as W. C. FIELDS: HIS FOLLIES AND FORTUNES; WINSTON CHURCHILL: AN INFORMAL STUDY OF GREATNESS; and VESSEL OF WRATH: THE LIFE AND TIMES OF CARRY NATION.